The Running Moon

The Running Moon

Brett Hayes

For Kila and Marilyn,
who believed in me when others did not.

Acknowledgments

For this story, I have to thank my wife, Kila. She was the inspiration for Piper's character, but above all I thank her for her patience while I was writing the story. I thank the good Lord every day for allowing me to have such an awesome person in my life. I definitely am *not* worthy.

My "gym rat" kids—Bryce (more football), Jared, Paden, and Jase Bode—who I forced to leave the gym long enough for me to bend their ears with my story.

I truly appreciate the hard work, dedication, and services that the citizens of the Choctaw and Chickasaw Nations perform for the people in our local communities. It is an honor and privilege to be a member of the Choctaw Tribe.

A tip of my hat to all my friends for their creative suggestions— Jon Dohrer, Dr. Woody Haigood, Rodney Davis, Jena Craven, Melissa and Calli Rogers, Jenny Fox, Ramona Fox, Trina and Taylor Williams, Mika Gerken, Sam McNiel, Shannon Hodges, Tim and Vicki Brown, Johnny "Flake" Altstatt, Vicki Droddy (my computer wiz friend), Ethan Cox and his gang, Denise Sanders, Karen Thomas, Kathy Mathews, Charlie Anderson, Jeremy Shipp, Sasha Hogstad, Dr. Mary Hitchcock, Dr. Stephoni Case, Sheryl Johnson, BG's Restaurant, Donut Shop, and countless others I know I have forgotten but will remember when this story goes to print.

My family—Rick and Marilyn Mackey, Art and Imogene Kinsey, brothers and sisters, and numerous in-laws—who I wouldn't trade for anything in this world.

A special shout-out to all my students who said, "Read us more."

My praise goes out to all the FCA (Fellowship of Christian Athletes) huddle groups and their sponsors, especially Coach John Capps, Drew Beard, and Coach Joe Patterson.

I would like to close by giving my personal Lord and Savior, Jesus Christ, praise and glory for everything in my life. Without him in my life, I have nothing.

Contents

Part Three: The Revelation

Part Four: The Resolution

Part One
The Run

Don't hide your face from me, or I will be like those going down to the Pit.

—Psalm 143:7b (NIV)

The Prey

A *lone.*
The sun was melting behind the black hills of Oklahoma as silhouettes of great pine trees protruded toward the orange sky. A shadow chased across the valley floor below as the sun was lost beneath the rushing darkness. A single star, the morning star, appeared on the malevolent horizon. A wishing star some have called it, but there were no wishes that night—only dreams.

From the wall of trees darted a shadowy figure across the valley floor with the flowing grace of a gazelle, with two legs feverishly pounding down the prairie grass. Long dark hair fell upon his shoulders with each stride. Naked feet and legs were stained with blood from deep scratches made by unseen briars and thickets. He wore a buckskin breechcloth of an ancient time when men were savages. His bronze figure glistened under the rising moon as sweat wept through the pores of his skin.

A small incline approached as he raced against the devil himself. Well-defined muscles rippled his skin as arms and legs pumped madly, fighting the gravity of what at first appeared to be a small hill but now had turned into a steep mountain.

The bronze man stopped to survey a possible escape route when from behind him morbid shrieks pierced the lonely night. He glanced back and listened as his pursuers simultaneously began to wail. They were quickly gaining ground. He stared up at the mountainside and then back across the empty valley floor.

He must go up. They were too close and too many. With a quick leap, he scrambled up the steep ridge, never second-guessing his decision.

The beasts of prey had come.

Halfway up the slope, he turned his head slightly toward the grunting sounds of the distant stalkers, daring not a long glance with his keen night-eyes, an ancestral trait handed down through countless generations of twilight hunters. The bronze man directed his attention back to the path he had carefully chosen.

His legs had become numb with pain. A burning fire was present in his chest; his lungs felt like they were going to explode through their protective rib cage. His superb physique was being worn down to an almost useless mass of flesh and bones by the relentless pursuit of the unseen beasts, but the prey ran tirelessly, refusing to yield to the beasts' defiant screams.

The lone bronze figure crested the ridge, finding a more flat terrain. The footing was steady on the plateau compared to the loose gravel at the base of the mountain. He skillfully weaved his way, often turning sideways to get through clusters of pine trees and black oaks, running almost blindly, as if he had traveled in this labyrinth before. Here, on the damp leaves and fallen trees, he left no mark of his passing, but his scent was rich in the air.

The hunters were hunting.

Dark figures ran effortlessly up the face of the mountain. Their four legs were driving hard into the ground, sending small avalanches of rocks down the ridge.

The beasts were near a frenzied climax from the thick smell of blood floating heavily on the thin air. Long streamers of milky saliva drooled from massive yellow fangs. Impassive red-rimmed eyes sat in shallow unblinking sockets.

In front of the darkness, the beasts had come. A ghoulish grin was concreted on each beast's face. They must be fed.

They moved in perfect unison, three rows of two, up the mountain face, shoulder to shoulder, never breaking stride, thoroughly trained in the art of the stalk.

Tonight was not the first time the stalkers had run a prey, nor would it be their last.

When the six predators reached the plateau, they broke rank. One in the lead, followed by two that were offset ten feet on each flank of the leader. The remaining three were at different locations at the rear that would be advantageous for the kill. The leader would attack first, when the prey could flee no more. Then, the others would carefully surround the victim for the final slaughter. This course of action prevented any kind of escape.

No living thing had ever escaped these vicious hunters.

The full moon was slowly creeping into the blacker-than-black sky, revealing the six beasts in their kill mode. The moonlight bared stalky-framed bodies with oversized boxed heads that were out of proportion to their bodies, which were mounted on short thick legs. Their fine fur was brown with traces of scattered black and white patches.

One stood out considerably among the six. He was bigger and stronger than the rest, the leader of the pack. His fur was jet-black, except for a small patch of white on his chest that was in the shape of an hourglass. He was the timekeeper, and time was running out for the bronze man of prey.

The bronze man had been running along a game trail on top of the ridge for a half mile. He could hear the constant howling of his pursuers. He veered right, leaving the easy running of the path, hoping to slow down his followers. The brush and briars were thick, ripping flesh from his legs with each stride. His body was riddled with multiple slashes and cuts, some deep enough for stitches. Fortunately, no main arteries had been ripped open, or the game would be over.

Pine trees had become a stilled audience to the game, never once voicing any favoritism, only softly whispering to each other upon the cool evening breeze.

An owl hooted from atop a pine tree as the prey zigzagged between the thick barked cottonwoods. The owl was an omen of ill fate, the bronze man thought. His people, the red people, believed *Ishkitini* (owl) to be a harbinger of death, who fulfilled three functions: It searched. It demanded. It disciplined.

The stalkers were closing ground with the timekeeper leading the way. He had the prey in sight. Usually a breed of his kind was cursed with poor eyesight, but in him was bred the night vision of a bobcat.

The kill was at hand. The quarry would die a slow painful death. They would gut the prey first, stringing out its insides and gnawing on the intestines and other organs that might come out, licking up the juices and blood that exploded from the victim's body. The prey's screams would only intensify their feeding frenzy. The timekeeper would then go to the dying prey, rip out the victim's heart before his very eyes, steal his soul as if he were the devil.

The bronze man had entered a small clearing on top of the ridge. His time was almost out; all his elusive tricks had failed.

He stopped.

At the far end of the clearing, some thirty yards away, was a huge gorge. He might try to scale down the sheer cliff, he thought, but there was not enough time. The beasts were upon him.

He turned, swiftly sizing up the tall pines surrounding the clearing. He could climb a tree to evade the stalker's fierce fangs, but the bronze man knew he would be gunned down by the beasts' master's rifles, like a treed coon.

The prey abruptly turned toward the gorge. He reached up and touched a small buckskin bag, a totem, hanging around his neck. The small bag was filled with various objects that were secret to all but himself. Every warrior kept a totem on his person, whom he believed when called upon would aid him against his enemies. Then he whispered something softly in his native tongue.

His muscles had become stiff and cramped from the brief rest as he took off running for the cliff 's edge, gaining momentum as blood began to circulate through his legs again. His legs had been drained completely of strength and now were working only on instinct and his will to survive. His heart was beating so fast and hard that his chest ached. He didn't know how much farther he could go at this pace.

Not far.

The timekeeper broke into the clearing on the plateau, pulling away from the others. His red eyes were a fiery blaze. His yellow fangs glowed through a virulent grin.

He licked his lips, longing for the salty, sweet taste of human flesh. It was only a matter of time—maybe minutes, perhaps seconds away. But the stocky predator, almost in complete shock, feeling cheated, came to an abrupt stop. Totally confused and bewildered, he just stood at the edge of the plateau.

Twenty feet from the cliff 's rocky face stood a cluster of pine trees, extending up from the gorge until they were almost even with the plateau.

The bronze man leaped into the darkness, falling endlessly through the night air. He clipped the first pine, but was unable to catch hold. Branches snapped under his weight as the ground rushed up to catch him. Black and green flashed around him until finally his hand hooked an unyielding limb. He held on. His nails dug deep into the bark. He tried to lift his other hand to pull himself up, but his arm would not respond. There was a deep pain in his shoulder.

Angry wails echoed in the canyon as the timekeeper barked orders to the beasts. The prey looked up into the glowing red eyes of the stalker standing in the pale moonlight.

The timekeeper seemingly smiled and then barked. A dark figure had come to stand beside him, and then retreated.

The owl screeched; first, it searched.

Instantly, the bronze man knew what was going to happen, but before he could move, the dark figure was falling toward him. The impact knocked him out of the tree. He hit the ground hard, clearing the air from his lungs. If not for the soft bed of pine needles, he surely would have broken his back.

He was not unconscious, but it was clear that he was not yet in any condition to get up. Instinct was commanding him to move, do something. *What had happened to the beast that hit me?* He must do something, but the pain in his shoulder had to be fixed first. He gritted his teeth and grabbed his left elbow, jerking it up quickly. *Snap!* The shoulder popped into its socket. The pain was still there, but bearable. He tried to lift himself, but he collapsed. He was weakened by loss of blood and dizzy from trying to move about too quickly.

The beast growled.

The bronze man grabbed a broken branch lying next to him on the ground and rolled over just in time to see the beast charging toward him.

Insanity was in the beast's red eyes as it leaped through the air.

The prey raised the splintered stick, piercing the heart of the beast as it came down.

Yelp! A deafening shriek escaped from the beast. Blood and drool splattered from its mouth.

He tossed the thing to the side as he tried to get up.

Still a little shaky on his feet, he walked to the wall and looked up. The same glowing red eyes glared down at him. The bronze man walked back to the dead stalker and placed both hands on its wounds. He covered his face with red blood and drew a black circle around his chin and put a black line down the bridge of his nose, using sap and dirt. The bronze man was now the *warrior.*

He returned to the cliff to find not one set of red eyes, but five. This time, the warrior was smiling. He grabbed the totem with one hand and raised the other, making a crossing motion, going up and down, sideways, and then a quick circle.

"*Chitokaka*, give me strength to defeat my enemies," the warrior growled and then spat.

The warrior turned and trotted off slowly.

The Hunters

I t was late evening now; the night was black except for the moonlight that shone through the boughs of the pine trees. Two figures appeared at the gorge's edge. It was Billy Ray and Jake Monger. Brothers, one was a psychotic with high intelligence, the other an idiot.

Billy Ray was twenty-two, two years older than Jake. They had the same father, Nate Monger, but different mothers. Billy Ray's mother died when he was born. Jake's mother was Mary Sue, who was Billy Ray's oldest sister. Therefore, that made Jake, Billy Ray's brother-nephew.

After Billy Ray's mother died, Nate Monger had his way with all his children, including the boys. Nate would come home drunk almost every night and do the deed to whomever he happened upon first. They wouldn't fight, because they were too afraid. Nate was a powerfully built man, standing six-four and a solid 260 pounds.

Mary Sue found a way out. Shortly after Jake was born, Mary Sue took her own life. The doctors labeled her death as a suicide due to postpartum depression. But in reality, she suffered from a far deeper mental depression.

The Monger children longed for the full moon because it was the only night their father didn't drink. The full moon meant it was time for the running of the prey, a tradition that had been in their family for two hundred years. Their daddy would tell them stories about how their great-great-great grandfather, Jules Monger, would breed slaves, and during each full moon, he would take the fastest and strongest slaves, and run them until they died. If a prey could outrun the dogs and survived until dawn, then the prey was set free. "No one had ever escaped the stalkers. But those slaves sure could run. They don't make them like that anymore," Nate would say. "Nowadays, after our kin was forced to move to this part of the country, all we have to run are white-trash bums and drunken Injuns. Remember that white hitchhiker we picked up, he didn't even make it a half mile. Boy howdy, how I dream of those days."

Tonight, Nate's dream might come true.

Billy Ray and Jake loved to stalk the prey. Especially Billy Ray, because he could take out his hatred of his father on someone else. Animal or human, he didn't care. Billy Ray felt passion to harm something—the more pain and suffering, the better. Tonight they had chosen the warrior.

"Can ya see anythin', Billy Ray?" Jake asked as he shined a flashlight down into the gorge.

"I can't see nothin', Jake. Hold the flashlight still!" Billy Ray exclaimed angrily.

"Do ya think that Injun jumped off the cliff?"

"I dunno. Let me have that flashlight!" Billy Ray roared, grabbing the flashlight from Jake. He swept the beam of light along the base of the cliff, stopping on a mass of matted fur and blood. "I see something."

"It's Mabel! He killed my Mabel!" Jake sobbed.

"Shudup!"

"He killed my dog!"

"If you don't shut your trap, Jake, you're goin' join her."

Jake backed away from Billy Ray, hanging his head and whimpering. "Sorry, Billy Ray."

Billy Ray looked at him with pitiless eyes, shaking his head in disgust. "Just like Daddy says. You're weak. You'd better stop that cryin' before I give you somethin' to cry 'bout. We have ten dogs better'n old Mabel. Daddy only used her to flush the prey. She's too stupid for anythin' else. Kinda' like you, Jake. Stupid. Daddy only lets you tag along, hopin' you might be a man someday. Fat chance."

Jake crossed his arms and lowered his head until his chin touched his chest. His left foot playfully kicked a pine cone, giving him the appearance of a pouting oversized kid, with lower lip puckered out, withdrawing further into a childlike state. Memories of a little boy and a puppy playing in back of the shed filled his mind. Jake's daddy always said that he and Mabel were two peas in a pod; they were both "dumb as dirt." Jake didn't think Mabel was dumb. He loved her. She was the only thing in this world that wasn't mean to him.

"Better call Daddy," Billy Ray announced, pulling a two-way radio from his backpack. "Daddy's goin' to be chapped, and it's all your fault, Jake."

Jake removed himself further from reality. He knelt down and started driving pine cones on a little road he had cleared with his hand, pretending they were match box cars. "*Varoom, varoom,*" was coming from his lips. *Crash!* Two pine cones collided together. "They're dead. All dead. Just like I want them to be."

Billy Ray turned and walked back toward the wall of pines, disgusted by the sight of his brother. He looked back sharply, almost in disbelief, seeing Jake crouched down with a stick, digging up wood ants, picking them off with his finger, and shoveling them into his mouth like a Neanderthal man feasting at an ant mound. Billy Ray turned away abruptly and stopped. He raised the radio to his mouth. "Night Runner. Night Runner, come in. This is Badger. You copy?"

He paused.

"Night Runner. You copy? We have a situation here," Billy Ray insisted as visions of the Gulf War entered his mind. Hatred was replacing the fear of his father. A hatred for society, the system. *How could they dishonorably discharge me from the Marines? A Section Eight of all things. I received two Purple Hearts for being wounded in battle. Two tours of combat duty. A hero. Who cares if I singlehandedly wiped out a village of women and children. They were the enemy. Intelligence reported they were supplying food to the Iraqi forces and Hussein's henchmen. So what, intelligence made a mistake about the village. What's the big deal? Collateral damage. Those people should have been somewhere else—not hanging with the bad guys.* In his sick, demented mind, he believed that they were all terrorists in the Middle East.

"Badger, come in. You copy?" a voice replied in the radio.

No response.

"Badger! Where the hell are you? This is Night Runner!" roared the voice.

Nate Monger's voice was so cold that Billy Ray could feel the chills run up his spine, returning him to a different game.

"Night Runner. This is Badger," Billy Ray muttered. His voice muffled with fear as he miked the radio. "We're on the north ridge, overlooking Cooper's Canyon. We have a situation here. One soldier is down. The remaining team is in hot pursuit. They appear to be heading toward the west end of Cooper's Canyon. What are your orders, sir? Copy."

"What happened?" Nate screamed. "Can't you and that idiot brother of yours do anything right? Sometimes I wonder who's the bigger idiot, you or Jake."

"Yes, sir," Billy Ray answered, his knuckles had turned white from gripping the radio too tightly.

"Who bit it?"

"Mabel, sir."

"Go figure. Dumb as dirt."

"Yes, sir."

"What's that imbecile brother of yours doing?"

He glanced over his shoulder. Jake was standing at the cliff's edge with his overalls pulled down to his ankles, urinating down into the gorge below. His bare butt cheeks glowed in the moonlight as he was singing, "London Bridge Is Falling Down." "Teddy Bear's standing lookout over Cooper's Canyon, sir," Billy Ray lied, not quite sure why he did it. "What are our orders, sir?"

"Follow the team. Do you have your night scope mounted on your sniper rifle?"

"Yes, sir. But I don't think we will need it. The team will …"

"Are you questioning my orders?" Nate shouted angrily.

"No, sir."

"Then shoot the bastard!" Nate roared. "If we have another situation like this one, you will spend one day in the sweat house, without food or water, for every member of the team that is killed. Do I make myself clear, Mr. Badger!"

"Yes, sir."

"We are already positioned on the west end of Cooper's Canyon. I can hear the team barking. They're coming up Lightning Creek. They're close to the prey; I can tell by Timer's bays. We have a little surprise waiting for the Injun. You're needed up here. *Now!*"

"Right away, sir. Badger out."

The radio fell silent as Billy Ray placed it in his backpack. Behind him, Jake had resumed playing with pine cones. He almost felt pity for Jake, that poor bastard child. Almost. His only concern was killing the man of prey. He longed for it. He had a propelling desire to kill that was driving him to the brink of insanity. The hunger must be fed. He picked up his rifle that was leaning against a tree and walked back to Jake.

"Time to go."

"Goody. I was getting bored. Can I take my cars with me?"

Billy Ray glared at him with irritable eyes, sending a chill up Jake's spine, causing the hairs on his arms to stand up straight. Jake dropped the pine cones and picked up his bag and toy gun. Nate wouldn't let him carry a real gun. He was afraid Jake might accidentally shoot someone or himself, not that it would be such a great loss.

Without further word, Billy Ray and Jake walked west along the edge of the gorge. One was thinking about toys, a warm bed, and a generous helping of hot food to appease his ravenous appetite; the other was thinking of a different hunger.

The owl screeched; second, it demanded.

First Blood

There was a slight chill in the night air as a heavy mist lifted from the damp ground. The warrior descended a path that stretched unevenly down the northern slope, winding through huge boulders and tall cottonwoods. He moved slowly along the path. The familiar buzzing of insects normally present in the quiet of the night was missing. The warrior stopped and listened intensely for some sound of life, but his keen ears could detect nothing. The deep silence was unsettling. The beasts should have been here by now, or at least he should be able to hear them, but nothing—only heavy silence. A trap. There must be a trap ahead. Something or someone was waiting for him, watching with patience and cunning, filled with vindictive hatred of him.

Pausing momentarily in a small clearing, the warrior gazed at the fullness of the night sky before entering the trees beyond. He walked cautiously, carefully picking his way along the winding path that now seemed to disappear beneath the towering trees and bushes beyond.

Just inside the wall of pines and oaks, the warrior busied himself with his own traps. He found a sharp piece of granite rock among the huge boulders and used it to cut vines and sharpen sticks. He set a series of foot snares along the path, and then he made a crude spear of hickory. He demanded and needed a knife. The damage he could do if only he possessed a knife.

The warrior crouched silently in the cover of the bushes along the path leading up toward the west end of Cooper's Canyon. He needed rest. If they wanted him, they must come and get him.

The hunted had become the hunter.

Dewey Monger trudged clumsily down the familiar path, his light pack slung over his shoulder. He was a young man, twenty-three, with grizzled brown hair and shaggy beard. Though he was stocky built, he had the agility of a newborn puppy.

Uneasiness had crept over him; the only sound in the black forest was his heavy boots snapping twigs and crunching leaves, like a giant pine falling to the ax of a lumberjack. No matter how carefully he tried to step, the noise was deafening. Nate had ordered him not to use his flashlight, and he always obeyed his daddy.

He hesitantly entered the small clearing, raising the point of his rifle, cautious of the wall of trees beyond. The full moon clearly illuminated the landscape, but it was unable to penetrate the thick boughs of trees. Slowly, he inched his way toward the underbrush. One hand came up nervously to scratch his beard. Dewey was not one easily taken scared, except with his daddy. But something wasn't right here. He'd lived in the woods all his life, sometimes spending several days by himself, sleeping in a bed of leaves or in a cave. He was the loner of the family. He preferred it that way.

But now, Dewey wished that he wasn't alone.

He wasn't.

Dewey knew that someone was waiting.

Maybe one of his brothers. Yes, that was it. Billy Ray or Tyrel was coming to meet him to show off the prey's scalp. The prey was surely dead by now. His brothers got all the fun. Dewey's fear was replaced with a ravenous hunger for the kill.

He quickened his pace, lowering his gun until it pointed at the ground, all caution forgotten. The end of the clearing was only a few feet away. He wasn't going to be left out of the killing this time. He received his wish.

Unfortunately, he was on the receiving end.

Dewey's first step into the tree line was fatal. The snare collapsed around his boot, jerking his foot into the air. He was suspended upside down, three feet above the ground, spinning out of control. It took a few seconds for him to figure out what had happened. The spinning stopped. His head cleared. Dewey eyed the warrior standing before him. Then, he suddenly struggled to free his foot, as fear and hate overwhelmed him.

The warrior took one step forward.

The vine broke.

Dewey hit the ground and rolled. In one quick motion he removed a nine-inch bowie knife from its sheath. He tossed the knife back and forth, left hand to right, rolling it with his fingers, lunging the blade forward at the prey, then retreating.

The warrior recoiled with Dewey's awkward thrusts, watching and waiting patiently for his opponent to make a mistake.

Dewey smiled boldly. "It looks like the boys didn't get all the fun after all. There's goin' to be a scalping party tonight, and you're the *head* guest, Injun. Make this easy on yourself, and I promise you a quick death."

He stood a head taller and a foot wider, but he was no match for the quickness of the prey. He lunged clumsily forward. The warrior side stepped, catching hold of the big man's elbow and wrist, causing the knife to turn in.

"*Eeeaaaccckkk!*" Dewey screamed.

He fell dead, hitting the ground with a dull thud. The knife buried deep in his chest.

The warrior removed the knife, along with the top of Dewey's scalp, then spat, cursing the corpse. He raised the scalp high into the air, giving praise to the Great Spirit, *Shilup Chitoh Osh*, for his bravery and skill.

A howling shriek pierced the still night. The warrior turned abruptly toward the sound. The beasts were coming, but this time, there were more.

Nate and Tyrel Monger lay in ambush at the west end of Cooper's Canyon. It was only a matter of time.

Cooper's was a boxed canyon with only one way in and one way out: the west end. The walls were sheer, so sharply inclined as to be almost perpendicular to the floor below. The surface walls were smooth and lustrous as if polished under the moonlit night. They offered little or no place for a climber to catch hold. Even the most expert climber might find these ridges too challenging. An attempt to scale the wall would surely mean an instant death for any normal human, but the prey was not human. He was the warrior—a breed apart.

Nate Monger was slowly realizing that the game was changing hands. They should have killed the Indian hours ago. The moon was disappearing behind the dark hills. Daylight was only a few hours away. He was experiencing something that he had never felt before: panic.

"Tyrel. Call Jim Bob at the pens and tell him to release all the dogs."

"Yes, sir," Tyrel whispered in a whiny, high-pitched voice.

Tyrel was different from his brothers. He was the oldest, but also the smallest. He was one of the biggest kids in his class until the seventh grade, when he completely stopped growing. Now, he stood about five-three with a 120-pound wiry framed body. Even though his stature was small, his much larger brothers would leave him well enough alone. He had the temperament and reflexes of a mountain lion.

Tyrel almost killed Jim Bob in a fist fight over a can of beer. Jim Bob suffered a broken nose, cracked cheek bone, and three busted ribs. Tyrel had passed the threshold of sanity, entering into the dark bowels of hate and destruction hidden deep in a sick mind. If not for Billy Ray and Skeeter pulling Tyrel off of him, Jim Bob would have died. Tyrel had the respect of his brothers.

Tyrel picked up a two-way radio and crawled off into the underbrush.

"Kitten. You copy," Tyrel smiled, as he released the button on the radio. "Kitten, this is Coyote. Come in."

"I thought I told you to never call me that again," Jim Bob's voice blared from the radio. "My name is *Bobcat*!"

"A little testy this morning, are we. My cute little kitten."

"Shudup! Or I will …"

"Or you'll what?" Tyrel demanded.

The radio was silent.

"Or you'll what?" he repeated.

"Nothing. Did ya'll get the Injun?" Jim Bob asked in a subdued tone.

"Now, that's much better," Tyrel replied, spinning around to look at his father, who had a pair of infrared binoculars aimed at a narrow path cutting through the middle of Cooper's Canyon. "Negative, we didn't get the Injun. Now, shut your face and listen carefully. Night Runner wants the floodgates opened."

"What?"

"Repeat. Night Runner wants the floodgates opened."

"All of 'em?"

"Is that not what I said, you moron!" hissed Tyrel. He didn't want his daddy to hear him, or all hell would have to be paid. "Listen to me. I don't have time for anymore of this crap. We're set up at the west end of Cooper's Canyon. You and Jackrabbit bring the reinforcements to the southeast ridge at Trosper's Point. It's only thirty feet down. Use the winch to lower the cages. Night Runner wants this done *now*. Condition: code red. Copy?"

"Copy, Coyote. Me and Jackrabbit are on our way."

"Don't screw up, or Night Runner will hang us by our balls. Starting with yours."

"Ten-four. Troops are already loaded. Give us twenty minutes."

"You have fifteen. Out."

He quietly crawled back to the bulky stump where Nate was crouched behind, careful not to make a sound. The dead silence of the woods was unsettling to Tyrel. Where were the chirping and buzzing insects? The mosquitoes had even vanished. He had staked out several ambushes through the years, and the forest sounds were always there. He wanted to express his concern to his father, but he was afraid of what Nate would do. Probably slap him and call him a coward.

"Orders delivered, sir," Tyrel said sounding slightly unsure.

"How long?" Nate asked, never lowering his binoculars.

"Fifteen minutes."

"It better not be a second longer."

Tyrel heard an uneasiness in his father's voice. He understood Nate the best. Maybe that's the reason his daddy always picked him to be by his side. He had never seen this side of his father. It unnerved him. *Maybe Daddy was not invincible after all.*

The thought was quickly replaced when he remembered his daddy killing a prey, not more than two months ago with his bare hands, snapping that fat boy's neck like it was a toothpick. *Daddy isn't afraid of nothing. Fear breeds weak men, and weak men deserve to die, Daddy always said. Yes, sir. Daddy raised us to be proud men and did a 'elluva job.*

Tyrel positioned himself next to Nate, feeling a little more self-assured about the situation. But just a little.

Jim Bob and Skeeter Monger, identical twins, were driving a two-ton flatbed Ford, heading east on a seldom-used dirt road. The grass had grown, making the road hard to see. The truck was carrying four stuffed, boxed crates made of plywood and rebar. Several one-inch holes were drilled into the top. A small window was cut out of what appeared to be a door. Low growls and snarls sang out from the boxes. The creatures knew what was forthcoming. And they were hungry.

Jim Bob knew that if they didn't get the boxes down into the canyon real soon, the dogs were going to attack each other. Jim Bob and Skeeter had spent two days in the sweat box when two dogs under their care hooked up and killed each other. The battle lasted for fifteen minutes. A vicious and bloody war. Jim Bob got his arm broke when he tried to pull them apart. In the end, a big brown pit bull had bled to death while its jaws were locked solid around the throat of a smaller brindled-colored pit bull. Skeeter tried to pry its jaws apart with a crowbar but couldn't budge them. The jaws were locked in a death grip; when that happened, nothing short of dynamite could break the hold. Jim Bob had to throw the dogs, still locked together, into the pit.

The pit was a natural cavern that appeared to be bottomless. Clovis Monger, in 1925, climbed down into the cavern but was never seen again. The Monger boys referred to the pit as the Devil's Throat. After the beasts had their feast of a prey, the remains were gathered and dumped into the Devil's Throat, never to be found.

The twins were afraid of the pit. If it was their turn to dispose of the remains—"garbage duty" was what their daddy called it— they would take care of business and bug out as fast as they could. The place gave them the willies. Tonight, their number had come up. It was the twins' turn to dump the body. And right now was not soon enough.

The flatbed Ford arrived at Trosper's Point. The boxes were rocking back and forth, as frantic howling escaped from within. The stalk was upon them. They wanted it. They needed it.

The beasts must be fed.

Jim Bob backed the truck to the gorge's edge. Skeeter jumped out and quickly hooked up the gin poles on the truck. Jim Bob disconnected the one-inch winch cable from the front of the flatbed and threaded it through the gin poles' pulley. Skeeter grabbed the hook on the end of the cable and fastened it to a special harness that was built into the carry boxes. Jim Bob had gone to the winch's control box. Skeeter steadied the cable as Jim Bob pushed the buttons. Each had an operation to complete, and they performed it with fluid precision and speed. They were the perfect team.

Jim Bob and Skeeter were inseparable. A person never saw one without the other. They were tall like their brothers, excluding Tyrel, but the stocky physiques were replaced by chunky bodies pushing the threshold of being obese. If not for the fact that Tyrel tried to rearrange Jim Bob's face, offsetting his nose a good half inch, they would be impossible to distinguish.

They were the tinkers of the family. Always building and tearing down machines, then rebuilding them again. Sometimes tearing one apart and rebuilding it just for the fun and gratification of satisfying a desire to be in control of at least one element of their life. There was no machine the twins couldn't fix and make work.

Right now, they were only concerned with the job on hand. So far, not one hang-up. Three boxes had been lowered to the canyon floor. One left.

"Skeet. You go down with the last one and open the gates," Jim Bob suggested as he pushed a green button that signaled the winch to reel in the excess cable, lifting the box into the air.

Skeeter nodded and stepped on the box.

"How much time we have left?"

"Three minutes."

"Hot dog we're good!" Jim Bob bellowed, pushing a red button that notified the winch to lower the crate into the canyon. "We even have time to suck down a few brewskies."

But the celebration was short lived. In the dead of night, the twins heard something that made their blood run cold. "*Eeeaaaccckkk!*"

Jim Bob released his finger from the red button. The sudden stop caused Skeeter to lose his balance. The crate tipped slightly. Skeeter grabbed for the main cable but missed. He was falling over the edge, when somehow his arm hooked around the harness cable. "Get me *down!*"

The beasts were crazed.

Jim Bob quickly lowered the last crate, allowing Skeeter's feet to touch the ground.

Skeeter hurriedly pulled the pins on each gate. When the last pin was removed, he was nearly trampled to death by a pack of deranged killers, driven by the extreme excitement of the hunt.

The beasts shot out of the crates like a bullet exploding from a gun. They were quickly lost in the darkness of the forest. Only their morbid screams could be heard bellowing in the night.

Skeeter picked himself off the ground, cursing as he dusted himself off. He had two big paw prints on his shirt, and one on his forehead. He was undoubtedly having a bad day.

"Skeet? You arright?" Jim Bob yelled down, trying not to laugh and cry at the same time.

"Yeah. I'm fine."

"Who was that screamin'?" Jim Bob asked, not sure if he wanted to know the answer.

"It sounded like Dewey, but I'm not sure. We'd better get over to the west end." Skeeter fixed a loop in the cable and set his foot in it. "Push the button and get me out of here."

Jim Bob pushed the green button. The winch reeled in the cable. It was moving too slow to please him. He was overwhelmed with fear and anxiety. His fingers trembled. Even though only a few seconds had gone by, it seemed like hours. "Could this thing move any slower?"

Skeeter's head crested the cliff's edge.

Jim Bob released the button when he saw that Skeeter was clear of the cliff. Seeing his brother was safe gave him a rush of comfort, but fear of the unknown had absorbed his mind. He grabbed the cable with trembling hands, finally hooking it through a hole in the rear bumper after three tries. He looked up at Skeeter. "What do you think happened?" his voice consumed in fear.

"I dunno!" Skeeter shouted. "But it's bad. Real bad. We've got to get over to Daddy. He needs us."

They jumped into the truck's cab. Jim Bob cranked it. When the engine roared, he popped the clutch and floored the accelerator. They disappeared into the dark woods.

Warrior's Vision

The moon had vanished, leaving only the stars to freckle the night sky. The early light of dawn would be there within the hour. Billy Ray and Jake had positioned themselves on the northern ridge, overlooking Cooper's Canyon. The entire canyon lay stretched out before them. If Billy Ray got the drop on the warrior, he was good as dead.

Billy Ray sat silently adjusting his scope for a five-hundred-yard shot. In Iraq, he had sniped several Iraqi assassins; one of Hussein's top henchmen was a nine-hundred-yard shot. He never missed. All heart shots. *The swiftest way to a man's soul is his heart.* He shouldered the 30-06 rifle, using the infrared scope to police the canyon. Nothing. Not even the dogs.

Jake was lying down on his belly. He had his toy gun aimed toward the woody canyon, squeezing off several rounds of imaginary bullets, killing the enemy with every blast. "Bang! Bang! Bang!"

Billy Ray reached over and slapped Jake's face, knocking his camouflaged hat to the ground. "Shudup! I can't concentrate!"

Jake crawled away sobbing, leaving his hat on the ground where it had fallen. Several feet away, he stopped under a bushy evergreen and removed his backpack. He unzipped the pack, spilling toys, balls, pine cones, and acorns on to the ground. He picked up a GI Joe doll and removed its clothing. After taking a small folding knife from his pocket he stabbed it over and over. "Die, dirtbag, die," he whispered, as he ripped the doll to shreds.

Billy Ray could hear the commotion behind him, but dared not a look. "That poor fool," he mumbled, feeling a little guilty for hitting his brother. But whatever guilt he might have felt was completely erased when his ears caught the sweet sounds of Timer's voice, singing the song of hot pursuit.

Apparently Jake had heard Timer's howling because he had crawled and settled next to Billy Ray to watch the show.

The blood in Billy Ray's veins was boiling. His adrenaline was pumping. His whole body went rigid as his lust for the kill approached an exploding climax.

He was combing the canyon with his scope and hadn't noticed Jake's return. His concern was the prey. *Where is that freakin' Injun?*

Movement. Something moved toward the east. Billy Ray swung the rifle to his left. There it was. The movement was a pack of stalkers running rampant toward the west. *Daddy had opened the gates*, he thought. But where's Timer? He swung the rifle to the right, that time. "There he is, coming in the mouth of the canyon. It's all over but the cryin'," Billy Ray hooted.

"Look, Billy Ray. I'm not crying anymore. See, I have dry eyes."

But Billy Ray never heard him. He was lost in the ecstasy of the hunt.

The beasts were coming from the east and west. The warrior could hear their long, eardrum-piercing cries getting close. Too close. The north was out of the question; he had just come from there. He headed south.

Pine trees were replaced by oaks and cottonwoods as he traveled down toward the center of the canyon. The underbrush was littered with plum thickets and briars. The warrior shied away from the thickets; he couldn't afford to lose any more blood.

He stopped at a creek and packed mud on the wounds that were bleeding. Some of his strength had returned, but he was still very weak. As he dressed the wounds, a vision appeared on the calm pool of water before him.

He saw a beautiful young woman lying in a bed. The people around her were crying. Her skin was drawn tightly over her high cheek bones. A small child with long dark hair was holding her hand. The child was a boy, perhaps eleven or twelve. His gray eyes were pools of tears, but none fell. A large eagle flew down and picked the boy up by his shoulders. The boy's face was stolid as they flew off together. The vision was blurry, fading in and out. The warrior thought that he knew these people but wasn't sure. The picture was becoming clear again when from the sky, a single leaf hit the water. When the ripples had cleared the vision was gone. Nothing. Only clear blue water.

The warrior looked up.

An owl was perched on the bough of a tree, staring down with prodigious eyes. Then it pumped its wings and lifted off the branch like a hushed whisper.

He watched it disappear into the night. The fortitude to survive had become more than mere instinct. It was now an overwhelming desire to protect his people from something very powerful and very evil. He must not fail. He must escape.

He raced through the woods with the agility and speed of a deer. All his wounds and pains were forgotten. He was on a quest. The quest for the survival of the people he loved.

The night was streaked with orange and yellow as dawn broke the eastern sky. Friendly stars faded with the morning. The light fog had become a soupy mix of dew and mist. The forest was totally absent of any sounds of chirping birds and insects.

Rhythmic grunts disrupted the silence.

The beasts were drawing near.

Timer had caught the prey's scent first and broke rank, leaving the others behind. No living thing had ever escaped him, and the warrior was not going to be the first. He stormed through the woods, like a crazed rabid beast, knocking down small trees and tearing through patches of briars. Like the warrior, Timer's body was riddled with deep cuts and slashes. But only death would stop him.

The beasts were bred to stalk, kill, and feed. They would die before giving up the stalking of a prey. And Timer was the best. He was the bloodline of generations past, present, and future. He was the timekeeper.

Timer followed the warrior's scent. It was strong. Very strong. He could almost taste the prey's flesh, floating on the misty air. He charged forward with a vengeance.

The southern edge of the canyon was rapidly approaching as two groups of predators were converging upon the prey. One from the west, the other from the east, and Timer in the middle. No way up. No way out. The warrior was trapped.

"Tyrel! Get your brothers on the com and find out *what the hell's goin' on!*" Nate screamed.

"Yes, sir," Tyrel snapped as he unclipped the radio from his belt. "Bobcat! Jackrabbit! You copy!"

"You got us, Coyote," Jim Bob answered.

"What's your ten-twenty?"

"We're headin' west on Whiskey Road, 'bout a half a click from the mouth of Cooper's Canyon."

"What's your situation?"

"Floodgates open. Troops movin' west."

"Any sign of the prey?"

"Negative."

"Set up post at canyon's mouth. Keep your eyes open and mouth shut. Condition: code red. You copy."

"Ten-four. Coyote ... we heard something earlier ... but Night Runner ordered complete radio silence."

"What is it? The sun will be up in twenty minutes. Spit it out!"

"It's Mountain Man ... we think we heard him scream."

"You think!"

"I mean ..." Jim Bob paused and then cried out, "Tyrel, it was Dewey. We heard him scream."

"Have you seen him?"

"Negative."

"Set up post. I'll worry about Mountain Man. Out." Tyrel reached up and turned a knob on top of the radio, switching it to a different frequency. "Mountain Man. You copy."

Silence.

"Mountain Man, come in!"

Nothing.

"Mountain Man, if you can hear me, click your mike."

A still deeper silence.

Nate had been listening and charged over to Tyrel, snatching the radio from his hand. "Mountain Man. Where are you?"

Pause.

No response.

"Dewey. Dewey, come in," Nate pleaded, fear was replacing his anger. Nate turned the knob, changing frequency again. "Badger, come in."

"Yes, sir," Billy Ray answered.

"Where are you?"

"North ridge overlooking Cooper's."

"What's the situation?"

"Helluva show."

"Cut the crap, and tell me what's going on!"

"Prey is penned in along the south wall. Soon as I get a bead on him, the sucker is mine."

"Finally, some competence. Good job, Badger. Have you seen Mountain Man?"

"Negative, sir."

"Keep me posted. And drop that turkey."

"Affirmative, sir. Out."

The black sky had faded to a light yellowish blue as the sun crept slowly upward. The warrior was standing at the base of a sheer cliff. He heard the predators' hideous cries in both the east and west. Climbing the wall would mean instant death if he were to fall. He stepped toward the north, the way he had just come, but stopped abruptly.

From out of the trees had come the beast, Timer. The two opponents squared off and stared. The warrior crouched slightly with Dewey's knife in his hand. Timer grinned his yellow fangs.

Time was momentarily suspended. Each remained perfectly still, sizing up the other, looking for any weakness or flaw in the other's defense they could attack.

Timer raced forward. After three quick bounds, he leaped into the air. The warrior sidestepped, bringing the knife straight up. Missed. The beast quickly turned, causing the prey to lose balance. The warrior fell, dropping the knife. Timer pounced upon him, all 120 pounds, but to the warrior, it felt more like two hundred. The wind rushed from the warrior's lungs, but he somehow managed to get his hands up in time to catch the beast's head before the mighty jaws locked around his throat. Claws were ripping new flesh from the prey's chest as Timer fought madly to free himself. The warrior brought his knee up hard into the side of the beast, sending it rolling away. He turned and grabbed the knife. Timer charged again. The warrior lunged forward.

Yelp!

The knife lodged deep in Timer's side. He staggered away, biting furiously at the knife's handle, trying unsuccessfully to dislodge it. He took three steps, and then collapsed.

The warrior stood up and limped over to the beast. He pulled out the knife, wiping the blood clean on Timer's fur. "*Na-lusa-chi-to*, soul eater, you will not feast today," the warrior stated through gritted teeth. Then he spat.

There was not enough time to go back north. He heard the beasts barking throughout the canyon. The only chance for escape was up. He limped slightly to the cliff 's face. The wall was straight up, maybe forty feet.

The vision was weighing heavily upon the warrior's mind.

He placed the knife in his mouth and began to scale the wall. The first twenty feet were easy. The warrior had little trouble finding places to hold and climb. But the next twenty feet were like polished marble. The howling was closer. There was no turning back. He used his fingertips, toes, nails—whatever it took—to get him to the top. Ten feet was all that lay between him and freedom. He must not fail.

The beasts had reached the wall. Snarls and growls sang up to the warrior. Then silence. He dared not a look. They were going to try to cut him off. Five feet to the top. Every muscle in his body burned with fire. Four. Three. Two feet left. How long had he been on the wall? Fifteen. Twenty minutes. He didn't know. The sun was low in the sky. One foot. Almost there. He saw clumps of grass hanging over the edge. He reached for the top. The rock he grabbed broke free, falling to the floor below. He quickly grabbed another, this time it held fast. Slowly he pulled himself up onto the plateau.

He laid there for a few seconds, trying to let his muscles unwind from the strenuous climb. He had to get moving. Where were the beasts? There would be hunters. He sluggishly lifted himself to his feet. His head was spinning.

The warrior looked down into the gorge. No beasts. He blinked. No Timer. He blinked again, this time rubbing his eyes. Still no Timer.

Something bad was about to happen, the warrior could sense it. He looked out over the canyon. A flash ignited from the ridge beyond. Then *boom*!

Fallen Warrior

The fog had burned off with the rising sun. Billy Ray and Jake were crouched in silence behind a fallen tree, two hundred yards up the northern ridge. Billy Ray straddled his rifle across the log, pressing his cheek against the stock as he stared through the scope. His face was placid blank. Billy Ray was in the zone.

"What'cha lookin' at, Billy Ray?"

He squinted, ignoring Jake's question. He raised his hand to adjust a knob on the scope. A blurry figure was zooming in and out of focus. When the picture cleared, the cross hairs were resting across the prey's back as he reached for the cliff 's crest. "Hot dog! The Injun's part monkey," Billy Ray exclaimed through a cold grin. "You're all mine, Mr. Injun." He fingered the trigger with an icy calmness, gently squeezing.

Jake had been sitting in an idled state of mind, curiously watching his older brother, when the realization of the situation materialized in his feeble mind. He reached out and squeezed Billy Ray's arm, almost causing the gun to fire. "Stop, Billy Ray! Daddy says, 'If a runner can make it through the night, and the sun comes up, then they're free to go.' I heard him say that. Look, the sun's up," Jake pleaded in a childlike voice. "You can't shoot him, Billy Ray. The sun's up. He won!"

In a powerful sweeping motion Billy Ray backhanded Jake, catching him squarely on the mouth. Jake went flying back. The blow knocked out one tooth and chipped another. His upper and lower lips were split wide open, bleeding profusely. Jake curled into a ball and cupped his hands over his face. A bubbly sob and blood leaked through his fingers.

"Fool!"

Wasting no time, Billy Ray snapped his rifle into position and took aim. The cross hairs centered on the prey's chest, who now stood at the cliff's edge. "You haven't won jack, Red Man." His finger mechanically tightened against the trigger. "It's a good day to die."

He inhaled deeply. Squeezed.

Kaboom! The rifle thundered, echoing throughout the canyon.

"Bingo!"

The warrior spun around, clutching his chest. He felt like he had been hit by a sledgehammer. Blood was gushing from his chest. In one quick motion, he ripped the totem from his neck. Lifting both hands into the air, he chanted a song in his native tongue, asking *Shilup Chitoh Osh*, the Great Spirit, to give him power. He staggered to the cliff's edge, momentarily stopping.

The warrior released a final battle cry and fell over the edge.

"Definitely a good day to die," Billy Ray announced triumphantly. He glanced over at his brother.

Jake had pulled a handkerchief from his pocket and held it over his mouth. The fingers on his free hand were raking through the grass, trying to locate his missing tooth.

Billy Ray glared hard at Jake but refused to let him spoil his moment of victory. He turned and picked up the radio that was laying on top of his pack. "Night Runner. This is Badger. You copy."

"I copy, Badger. We saw the shot. Very impressive. Tonight, we celebrate. And you will be highly rewarded," Nate said approvingly; that was about as close as he could come to praising his children.

"Thank you, sir. Have you heard from Mountain Man?"

"Negative. You and Teddy Bear take Logan's Pass into the canyon. Check the main trail. He last reported from that location. Me and the boys will meet you at the downed prey."

"Very good, sir. What about honors, sir?"

"Don't worry, Badger. The honors are yours. You've earned them."

"Thank you, sir. We're on our way."

"And, Badger, you'd better hurry, boy. The dogs are up on the south ridge. It won't take 'em long to figure out what has happened. And they'll be comin' back. They gotta be fed. When they commence to feedin', there ain't no stoppin' 'em."

"Yes, sir. We'll hurry. Out."

The radio fell silent.

Billy Ray slung the rifle over his shoulder and picked up his pack. "Jake, get your stuff. It's time to bug out."

Still on his knees, Jake raised his hand into the air, holding a small, rectangular object between his thumb and index finger. It was yellow with black cavities. "Look, Billy Ray. I found it. Do ya think the tooth fairy will bring me a nickel tonight?" He smiled, exposing a huge gap between his front teeth. The bleeding from his lips had almost stopped. He replaced the bloody rag to his mouth.

"Sure," Billy Ray said, feeling pity again for his feebleminded brother. Pity was a feeling he absolutely hated. It was a weakness. He wanted to shoot the poor retard, putting him out of his misery. He could make it look like an accident. Nobody would question him. Man, nobody would even care. He would be doing everybody a favor. But Jake was his brother; his blood kin. No matter how big an idiot Jake was, he will always be his brother. Billy Ray would have to look out for him.

"Goody," Jake beamed, as he carefully put the tooth in a small pocket of his pack. He pulled the zipper close and picked up his bag. "I'm ready."

"Let's go. We'll have to double-time."

They jogged off toward the west.

It was midmorning. The sun had climbed high into the cloudless sky. The coolness of the night had been replaced by a sultry heat, even at this early hour. The temperature would have no problem reaching the century mark today.

Nate, Tyrel, and the twins had been standing over the prey's broken body for ten minutes. Tyrel removed his hat and wiped the sweat from his forehead with the sleeve of his shirt. He looked up at the sun before replacing his hat. "What's takin' so long? They should've been here by now," he said impatiently, mixed with a touch of jealousy.

"Shudup your whining, Ty. They'll be along shortly. Billy Ray's not goin' miss a chance at doin' the honors. When's the last time you had the honors?"

Tyrel turned angrily away. He wasn't going to play these word games with his father. He could have killed the prey. But, no, his daddy wanted him close by. He was a better runner than Billy Ray, and everyone knew it. Everyone except Nate.

"Huh, Ty. When was the last time?" Nate asked sarcastically.

"I dunno."

"Sure ya do. Come on. Tell me. When was it? One? Two? Three runs ago?"

"I can't remember."

"Come on. You know."

"F-fo … I dunno."

"Try again," Nate taunted.

"Six." He paused a moment, the blood rushed to his head. "Maybe seven or eight. I dunno."

"You can say that again, Ty. You don't know jack. Why don't you try ten."

Tyrel was about to blurt out something that he would later regret when, from the tree line, appeared Billy Ray and Jake.

Jake was bouncing playfully along, swatting at a yellow butterfly that busied itself on a wildseed flower.

Moving as if he were treading on eggshells, Billy Ray held his head low, troubled by the news that he was about to give Nate. Tears had left salty streams on his camouflaged face. His body trembled with each step. He could feel his daddy's icy blue eyes staring through him. He wanted to look up, but his chin was locked down with an invisible chain. Weak. Just like his daddy said. They're all weak.

He was only a few feet away when the chain was broken by Nate's boisterous voice. "Did you find Dewey?"

Billy Ray hesitated, then spoke. "Yes, sir … Dewey's dead. The Injun got him with his own knife."

A dozen seconds of silence had gone by. Nate was temporarily possessed by a terrifying cold rage. The color rushed from his face. His knuckles were white from tightly clenched fists. "Jim

Bob. You and Skeeter got "garbage duty" this run, go get Dewey and take him to the pit," he ordered without emotion.

"But—" Jim Bob sniffed.

"*Now!*"

"Yes, sir."

He pointed down toward the warrior. "Then come and get what's left of this piece of trash," Nate charged, as he walked over and kicked the lifeless body.

The twins nodded simultaneously and then ran to the flatbed truck and got in. Jim Bob started the engine and drove away.

Within the hour, they had disposed of Dewey's body, dumping it reluctantly into the pit.

Later, Jim Bob and Skeeter returned to the base of the southern wall of Cooper's Canyon, where the warrior had fallen, but the warrior's body was nowhere to be found. They quickly scanned the immediate surroundings. Nothing. After a brief discussion, they determined that the dogs must have scattered the prey's remains across the countryside.

"It will take all afternoon and long into the night to find even some of the body. We'll miss the celebration. What Daddy doesn't know won't hurt him," Jim Bob fumed.

Or will it?

After the twins had left the first time, the hunters had gathered around the fallen warrior along the cliff 's base. They didn't notice the empty totem bag lying nearby, for their attention was directed toward the warrior. There was something vague and disturbing about the fallen prey's presence.

Despite Nate's obvious relief that the game was over, an uneasiness had crept over him. Perhaps the loss of his son had affected him. Perhaps not. He felt like someone or something was watching him. He nervously looked around, seeing only dark shadows of thick underbrush. He quickly turned back, shaking his head, as if disgusted with himself. *I'm not weak; my children are weak. Dewey was a fool for letting himself get killed*, he thought. He pulled out his knife and handed it to Billy Ray. "Be done with it, before I give the honors to someone else."

He snatched the hilt of the knife and knelt down, grabbing a handful of the warrior's hair with his free hand. "This is for Dewey." In a swift sweeping motion, Billy Ray removed the top of the prey's scalp. He stood up and kicked the warrior's lifeless body, raising the black bonnet into the air. "Dewey has been avenged!"

The small group howled halfheartedly.

Except Jake. He was grossly attentive to the warrior's bare feet. "Look, Billy Ray. He only has three toes on each foot."

The band of hunters relaxed their celebration and looked down.

"The Injun was a freak," Billy Ray proclaimed.

"Some kind of deformed mutant," Tyrel agreed.

"No wonder he could run so fast. He's part wolf," Billy Ray joked halfheartedly.

The feeling of someone watching had returned. This time, they all felt it.

"Let's go home. We have some celebrating to do," Nate declared. He wanted to rid himself of this place. They all did.

They quickly picked up their packs and left, leaving the dead warrior *alone* to face the onslaught of the beasts.

Or was he *alone?*

In their hurried retreat, the hunters failed to see the strange three-tipped paw prints in the soft dirt that led away from the warrior, heading toward the black shadows of the underbrush, where a pair of glowing eyes, patiently watched.

The owl screeched; third, it disciplined.

Part Two
The Return

My life has led me down the road that's so uncertain
Now I am left alone and I am broken
Trying to find my way
Trying to find the faith that's gone

—Third Day

Bryson Keahbone's Homecoming

T wenty years later.
    Bryson Keahbone was driving south on Highway 63.The rag top was off his Jeep. Long dark hair danced with the rushing wind. A short growth of beard shadowed a well-sculptured face. He hadn't shaved since he started this trip five days ago. Everything that he owned was packed in his Jeep: four boxes of books and papers, a duffle bag of clothes, and a sleeping bag.

He removed a map from the glove compartment. Tired of fighting the wind, he pulled onto the shoulder to study the map. Satisfied with his findings, he continued on.

He glanced down at his watch. He didn't have much time and would have to hurry. He didn't like to be hurried. The appointment would have to wait. There was something that must be taken care of first.

The deep green of summer littered the scenery surrounding the highway as it twisted through the northern edge of the Kiamichi Mountains. The mountains blanketed with towering pines, oaks, and hickories. Bryson marveled over the beauty of the picturesque view. A feeling of cool tranquility replaced the heated anxiety of being hurried. It was a feeling that he had not experienced since he was a small boy.

He remembered climbing these hills, tracking deer, chasing rabbits, watching the brown bears lumbering out of their caves in the spring to sun themselves on the rocks, and catching trout with their paws in the cold running streams that fed into the Kiamichi River. He longed for the inner peace his native home had brought.

Bryson thought that he had finally found the escape he had been searching for the past two years. But could these hills be just another lost hope of a tragic past ending in yet another disappointment. He did not know. But he would try—his sanity depended on it. He was tired of running—running a race he could not win. Racing against the past.

The highway had taken on a steep descent. Bryson eased off the accelerator. A mileage sign appeared on the side of the road reading: Talihina, 10 miles. He pulled a wrinkled letter from his shirt pocket. He had it memorized from countless readings, but opened and read it anyway:

My dearest Bryson,

It was so wonderful to hear from you after these past two years. When I read your request in the letter you had written to me, I was absolutely flabbergasted. Then come to find out that Dr. Brown had known all along about your plan and did not tell me. I could have killed him. I know, Timothy told me that you made him promise not to tell. Anyway, I'm babbling here. I say this without reservation—I have agreed wholeheartedly to all your terms. I will have all the papers drawn up and ready for you to sign. Bryson, I wouldn't do this for anyone, but for you I am willing to make an exception. Call Timothy or me, and let us know when you will be here. I look forward to seeing you again.

With love,
V. Buchanan

PS. Here are the directions in case you have forgotten how to get there: Turn south on County Line Road—about two miles west of town. Go six miles to where the road ends. Turn right on a dirt road, then left—follow the dirt road until it ends. You're there!

He closed the letter and placed it back in his shirt pocket. The surrounding forest was densely packed with trees and underbrush. The road would be hard to see. He decelerated. There it was on a little green sign: Leflore County Road. He slammed on his brakes. The Jeep skidded past the road. He reversed and then proceeded down the road.

He followed the directions in the letter from memory. The first mile was black top, but after that, nothing but dirt and gravel. The road was dusty and rugged, having the appearance of little or no travel. Branches of pines and oak were hanging low over the road, occasionally hitting the windshield. Travel was slow. The Jeep crept up the hill for what he felt an eternity. He checked his watch. His visit would have to be short.

Finally!

Bryson crested the hill in his Jeep, but the trees were too thick to see what lay ahead. He was overcome with doubt. Maybe he had made a wrong turn. He hoped not. There was no place to turn around on the narrow road. The only way out was straight ahead.

The descent into the valley was even slower than the climb. The road was cut with deep ruts from the runoff of spring rains. Bryson got out of the Jeep and locked in the hubs on the front differential. If he high-centered in a rut, he trusted that the four-wheel drive would get him out, but the size of the ruts vacillated his trust.

So far, no problems.

But doubt was again entering his mind. Maybe he should have gone to his appointment first.

No!

He must find the valley. He had come a long way for this moment, a moment that had been put off for far too long. If he had to travel all day and into the night, he would do so.

In his mind, Bryson was retracing the route he had taken, thinking that maybe he had made a wrong turn. But then, all his doubts were released when, from the tunnel of trees, he escaped into a brilliant green valley filled with yellow and white clouds of wildflowers. He stopped and stood up on his seat. The view was breathtaking. The valley was surrounded by blue-tinged mountains. In the far corner of the meadow was a small log cabin nestled in with lofty pine trees.

"Home," Bryson sighed as he plopped back down into the seat and drove on.

The road had come to an abrupt stop at a rusty gate, which was locked with a chain and padlock. He judged from the corrosion on the lock and chain that no one had been there for years.

Although he would have to walk the rest of the way, he didn't care. His legs were cramped from the long drive and were in serious need of movement.

Bryson got out and climbed the gate. Excitement was building inside him. The log cabin was less than a quarter mile down a road overgrown by timeless age. He could no longer control these inner desires. He started to jog. As he was drawing near the cabin, he increased speed with each stride until now he was at a dead run. Something was pulling him. His heart was racing. His lungs were burning. He could not slow down. Almost there. Fifty yards away. Thirty. Twenty. At ten yards, he stopped. Trying to catch his breath, he bent over and put his hands on his knees, and then he stood up, locking his fingers over his head. He was breathing very hard through his mouth. His right side had a stabbing pain; he couldn't believe how out-of-shape he had become. When he got settled in, he would quickly take care of that, he thought.

He dropped his hands and looked at the log cabin. It wasn't at all how he remembered. When he was forced unwillingly to leave twenty years ago, everything was in perfect order. Now, the two front windows were broken out, the big wooden door was gone, half the front porch had collapsed, boards were missing from the floor, and some of the mortar had crumbled between the logs and lay on the ground. Also missing was a section of wooden shingles. The place was an absolute wreck.

He smiled warmly. "I would say the place needs a little fixing up."

Bryson started for the porch. In midstep he abruptly stopped. Uneasiness had crept over him. He glanced to his left. About fifty feet away was a huge oak tree with its proud boughs soaring high into the clear blue sky.

He hesitated, not sure of what direction he wanted to take. Bryson wanted nothing more than to gain possession of his soul and preserve an inward peace. He looked at the cabin, then back at the tree. An almost unyielding duty to visit the tree was pulling in part at his soul. But another part of his soul was reluctant to go. Was that not the purpose for his coming home—to find peace within himself ? The enigma of the mighty oak patiently waited.

Seconds seemed like hours. He had no idea how long he had stood mesmerized when he finally succumbed to the calling of the tree.

He stepped slowly toward the oak. A rabbit bounced away unnoticed as Bryson waded through the waist-high grass. An intimate serenity rushed through him, paralyzing the inner conflict that had been so much a part of his life. As he approached, he saw a large heart on the massive trunk of the tree. It had been carved with a knife. Although splintered bark had partially grown back over the deep scars, the figure remained virtually unaltered.

Only a foot away, he stopped.

Warm memories began to flood his mind as he examined two sets of initials located inside the heart. Bryson slowly raised his hand and touched the rough grooves that were cut so long ago. His mind drifted back as childhood memories charged ahead.

"Momma! Momma!" a young boy shouted as he raced across the yard like a rock launching from a slingshot. He jumped on to the porch, never breaking stride, pausing briefly to open the screen door. Then he dashed into the log cabin screaming, "Mom, come see this!"

He stopped in the living room and anxiously looked around. He was breathing heavily, hardly able to control his excitement. "Mom! Where are you?"

"In here," a gentle voice said through a doorway.

He hurried toward the voice, passing through the doorway into the kitchen. Mounds of pickled okra, tomatoes, green beans, and apples were scattered around the room. It looked like a corner vegetable stand with vegetables and fruits lying on the table, cabinet, and floor. Some were even loaded in a red Radio Flyer wagon.

A young woman in her early thirties was standing next to a cast iron stove. She was wearing a light-blue cotton dress with a white apron pulled tightly around her waist. Her long auburn hair was put up in a bun and held neatly by a single barrette, exposing a beautifully defined face. Weathered lines of age had not formed around her eyes, which sometimes happen when a young woman takes on the responsibilities of a family and farm as she had done. Her happiness was the key to her ageless beauty. She had told herself many times that she was the most blessed woman alive for having a loving husband and wonderful child, and she thanked God for them every day.

On the stove, a small flame flickered under a two-gallon cooking pot. It was full of boiling water and empty Mason jars. She was preparing preserves of vegetables and fruit from the summer harvest enough, she hoped, to last through winter. She sat down her wooden spoon and grabbed her apron to dry her hands. She leaned over and kissed the small boy, now standing next to her, on the forehead.

He quickly rubbed his hand across his forehead, trying to erase the kiss. "Gosh, Mom. I could have been out in the yard dying."

"Just one second, young man. We are not to use the word *gosh* in this house or anytime. It's an alteration of God. You understand me?" she firmly stated.

"Yes, ma'am. But, Mom, I could have been out in the yard bleeding to death because a bear had come out of the woods and chewed my arm off while you're in here cooking jars. We can't even eat jars."

"I boil the jars to purify them so bacteria and other yucky things won't get into the food and make you sick. As for your screams, I'm your mother. I know the difference between a hurt scream and a come-and-look-Mom-I-have-another-cat-in-my-snare scream." She smiled.

"Mom. Will you please come outside? I have something to show you," he pleaded impatiently.

She looked down into his deep-blue eyes. *How can I say no to those eyes*, she thought. *You look just like your father with your dark skin, long dark hair, high cheek bones, and slightly hooked nose. But your eyes, those crystal blue eyes, you got from me.*

The boy was restless, fidgeting back and forth.

She untied her apron and placed it over the tomatoes that lay on the kitchen table.

The boy grabbed her hand and dragged her toward the front door. "Come on, Momma!" he roared with excitement.

"You didn't snare old Tom again? Or maybe one of my chickens?"

"No! Come on, and I'll show you."

As they stepped onto the porch, the boy broke free and rushed toward the big oak tree.

"Hurry! It's over here!"

She picked up the front of her skirt and trotted along behind the boy. She couldn't keep up with him, as he was quick as a jackrabbit.

When the boy arrived at the tree, he stopped and walked around to the far side. He glared back excitably at his mother, who was only halfway across the yard. "Hurry up!"

A growing curiosity was building inside her. She wondered what could have possibly made her son so vivacious. Then again, was he not the same high-spirited little boy who three days ago was screaming at the top of his lungs when a skunk sprayed him?

"I was just trying to pet it, Momma, and it pooped on me," he had told his mother. He didn't much care for the two-hour bath in tomato juice, but he learned a valuable lesson that day.

But somehow, this time it was different; she could sense it.

The young woman stopped jogging fifteen feet short of the tree and walked the rest of the way. She placed her hands on her hips, trying to catch her breath. The shade of the oak offered some relief from the blistering heat of the hot summer sun. But not much.

"Look, Momma. It's right here. Come on this side and you'll see it," the small boy exclaimed, pointing at the hidden side of the oak tree.

"What is it that has you in such an uproar?" she asked, peering carefully around the edge of the tree as if she was expecting a snake to strike out at her. She was suddenly overwhelmed with joy and amazement—the amazement she felt when she gazed upon the symbol carved deep into the tree and the joy that nothing jumped out at her. Her eyes swelled with tears.

A huge heart, two feet wide and a foot and a half tall, had been carefully engraved into the trunk of the big oak. Located in the upper left corner of the heart was a small animal figure with three long grooves notched under it. The figure had been delicately sculptured; well-defined lines were present in the long tail, body, and four legs, giving it the appearance of having a heavy fur coat. But the head was different—it almost appeared human.

"Mom, is this cool or what?"

"Yes. It's lovely," she replied, lifting the front of her long skirt to wipe away the falling tears.

"Dad must have carved this heart sometime this morning," he said after bending down to pick up some wood shavings. "See. These wood chips are still damp. That means this was done a short time ago. Maybe two hours. Dad taught me how to read signs like these when we were tracking the beaver," he announced proudly.

"You sure are a fine student." She smiled, positioning herself next to her son, running her fingers like a comb through his long curly locks of hair. "But are you sure your father carved these figures this morning? Remember he is performing a ceremonial dance at the Red Earth Celebration in Oklahoma City."

"I know, Mom. But this was carved this morning. I can tell."

"Okay, okay," she gave in, her heart swelling with pride.

"What do you think it is?" the boy asked, pointing at the engraved figure.

"I'm not sure. What do you think it might be?" she asked, allowing the boy to use his prior knowledge and imagination. In truth, she wasn't sure. She had seen that symbol only once before. A long time ago at the burial of her husband's father.

It was the custom of her husband's tribe, the Choctaw Indians, to offer gifts to the dead warriors for them to use on their journey across the Spirit Road, or Milky Way, to the happy hunting ground of the Sky Country. Her father-in-law's casket contained a bow, a quiver with several arrows, a hunting knife, food, and water. Her husband was the last to give a gift. It was a round block of wood about the size of a small saucer plate, and on it was carved the same animal-like figure with three grooves underneath. He placed it carefully in a totem bag before fastening it around his father's neck. She dared not to ask what the wood piece meant, for it would be an insult to speak during the funeral. Afterward, her husband must have noticed her puzzled look and told her that his gift was to protect his father as he journeyed through the ghost land, the region of condemned souls, when he tries to reach the Spirit Road. He never spoke of it again.

"It looks like a wolf with a man's head," the small boy explained when something shiny in the grass caught his eye. "Momma! Look!" He reached down and picked up a nine-inch bowie knife. "This must be the knife that Dad used. But it's not Dad's knife. I don't know whose it is. Look, it has the initials DM scratched in the handle."

DM.

The woman suddenly felt very faint and staggered back a few steps to catch her balance. *DM.* The world was spinning around her. *DM.* Something was wrong with this picture. She couldn't explain it. Then as if hammered by a fast-moving freight train, she recognized the knife—it was Dewey Monger's. He always carried it in a sheath on his hip. Something was wrong. Terribly wrong.

The boy had been watching his mother. He dropped the knife and ran to her, burying his face in her blouse. He pulled away slightly, lifting his eyes to look at her. He was afraid, not for himself, but for his mother. Her face had turned pale and pasty. Tears were running down his cheeks. His voice cracked when he spoke, "Mom? Are you all right?"

He paused briefly, waiting for her to answer. But there was no response. Only a dark-hued silence.

He swallowed hard, trying to fight back the tears. "Mom?" the boy whispered, again pausing for an answer, but received none. "I had a dream about Dad last night. At least, I think it was a dream. I had forgotten about it until now. Dad came into my bedroom while I was sleeping and woke me up. He had this wolf skin pulled over his head and back. I was scared at first, but when Dad reached up and touched me, I wasn't afraid anymore. Dad said, 'My son, as like as not, you will fly away with the great eagle to a place where the water meets the sky. When my time is time upon the final scene, you must come find me beneath the Moon When Wolves Cry. You will know what to do.' Then Dad turned and left. But I d-d-don't know w-w-what it m-m-means." The boy hesitated, trying to control the twitch in his lip, and then murmured, "Mom? Dad's not coming home, is he?"

Upon hearing her son's final words, the young woman was crushed with emotions and collapsed to the ground. She died in her bed one week later from what some say there is no cure—a broken heart. Some people are survivors, some are not.

The Apology

Not a day had passed that Bryson did not dream of his father and the words that were spoken.

His hand trembled slightly as he removed his fingers from the grooves cut in the mighty oak. Tears formed clear pools in his eyes, but none fell. He slowly backed away from the tree. After five or six steps, he abruptly stopped, almost tripping over a small square stone partially covered by grass. This was it. This was the moment to put twenty years of bitter grief behind him forever. *No more running.* But he was disheartened by uncertainty. In his mind, he wanted to leave, to avoid this situation altogether, but his heart screamed no.

He could no longer hold back the tears. They streamed down his face like floodwaters cresting a dike. Bryson had not shed a tear since that fateful day with his mother when he found the carving in the tree. All those years were now pouring out of him.

He knelt to the ground and removed the grass from the face of the stone. There was a name and dates engraved roughly in the stone:

Katherine Abigail Keahbone
Born June 6, 1961
Died Aug. 14, 1994

Bryson raised his hand to wipe away the last of his tears. He gazed blindly at the stone, never seeing the two-foot bare oval spot located on the grave. He closed his eyes and breathed in deeply, holding it briefly. His breath released into an explosive sigh. "Hello, Mom," he finally spoke in a soft, controlled voice. "I really don't know where to begin." He paused and looked up at the big oak as if searching the boughs for the right words to say. "Please forgive me. I have been such a fool for all these years … I hated you, Mom, for leaving me. I needed you after Dad disappeared."

"*Coo-oo-oo, coo-oo-oo!*" The soft, sad sound floated down from above.

Bryson looked up.

A single dove perched on a low-hanging branch of the oak. It was a mourning dove. The dove watched him with a placid interest. Bryson thought that he saw sadness in the small bird's eyes. A sadness he was very familiar with. A story his mother had told him long ago suddenly entered his mind.

Swoosh!

Bang!

The young boy quickly reloaded his slingshot.

Swoosh!

Bing!

"Direct hit!" the boy exclaimed when the rock ricocheted off the empty can.

He removed another stone from his pocket and reloaded the slingshot. He pulled the rubber bands tight, pinching the leather pad that held the stone with his thumb and index finger. He carefully spied the yard and positioned the slingshot for a quick shot. He had grown tired of shooting cans and tree stumps. He wanted some real action—a live target.

There!

On the fence line, two doves had landed. Only twenty feet away. An easy shot. He cocked. His arms were steady. He aimed at the smaller bird on the right. He was about to release the stone when a young woman's voice broke his concentration, causing him to pull his arm slightly upward as he released, sending the stone over the head of the target.

"Bryson?"

The doves elevated quickly in flight at the disturbance and disappeared over the tree line.

"Rats! Momma, you made me miss."

"What were you shooting?"

"Some stupid old birds."

"Do you know what kind of birds they were?"

"They would have been dead birds if you hadn't scared them off," he protested.

The woman raised her eyebrows, giving the boy a look that would freeze water at the earth's core. He knew this *look*. He had reached the outer limits where he knew not to push his mother any further or he would be in serious trouble.

"I'm sorry, Momma, for being hateful to you. But they were just st-t—" He thought the matter over before he continued. "What kind of birds did you say they were?"

"They are called mourning doves," the woman answered.

"Mourning dove," the boy repeated. "Why are they called that?"

"Mourning doves are very special creatures. They are creatures of love, peace, and hope. The two doves you were about to shoot are bonded for life."

"What do you mean 'bonded for life'?" the boy interrupted.

"When two doves meet and choose to stay together, they form a special bond that will not be broken until one of them dies. When tragedy occurs and one dies, then the other will mourn the loss of their partner until their own death comes about. That is why they are called mourning dove. Sometimes, if you listen very carefully, late in the evening you can hear a lonely dove singing its sweet but sad song to its lost mate. It's very beautiful. If you would have killed one dove, then the other would be destined to live forever alone. Your father and I have this special bond …"

"*Coo-o-o, ah-coo-o-o-ooo-o-o-ooo!*" With whistling wings, the dove lifted gracefully from the tree branch and flew toward the tree-bordered field.

Bryson watched the dove until it was out of sight and then looked back at the stone. "Momma, I know the special bond that you and dad had together. I know the pain and loneliness that you must have felt when Dad did not return. I know the sorrow that breaks a heart."

He had that drowning feeling again as tears filled his eyes. He suddenly felt a flash of anger.

No!

There will be no more tears, Bryson silently vowed to himself. He tightly clenched his fists until the color rushed from his hands.

No more tears!

Slowly he relaxed his hands. Bryson felt as if a great burden was being lifted from his shoulders. A strange feeling of warmth and assurance was passing over him, covering him in a blanket of courage. The courage to live again.

"I have not spoken her name since her death two years ago. Her name was Rebekah. You would have loved her, Mom. Rebekah was an angel sent from heaven. She was beautiful, smart, witty, my best friend … she was my whole world. But now she's gone." His tone was steady and staunch. "Sometimes … when I get up in the morning, I have to remind myself to breathe. It takes every bit of strength I have to live from day to day. I cannot live like this anymore. *I refuse!* Something has pulled me back here. At first I thought it was to talk to you, Mom, but it's much more. My destiny lies here in these hills. I will find my *raison d 'etre*—my reason to be."

Bryson stood up and brushed the grass from his pants. He glanced down at his watch: one o'clock. "Oh, boy. I'm going to be late. Mom, I love you. I will be back later today."

He turned and started to walk away but abruptly stopped and glanced over his shoulder. "Mom," his voice laden with determination, "I'm back. And this time, nobody is going to make me leave. The truth about Dad is lost in these hills. There will be no peace until the truth is found."

Bryson turned and sprinted back to his Jeep. He arrived at the rusted iron gate. In a quick, catlike motion, he leaped on and over the gate without breaking stride. In the blink of an eye, he was seated in the Jeep, cranking the motor. When the engine roared, Bryson popped the clutch and raced down the dirt road. He had an appointment to keep.

Meet Principal Hitchcock

Entering Talihina City Limits, the green and white sign read as Bryson passed by in his Jeep.

Talihina was a typical southeastern Oklahoma small town. It was located in a valley hemmed in by blue-tinged mountains. Highway 63 turned into Main Street, running through the center of town. Main Street contained a bank, a few restaurants, three convenience stores, an arcade and video store with posters of recent movie releases hanging in the windows, an indoor flea market, a feed and fertilizer store, a funeral home, a host of furniture and antique shops, two hotels, and a small red bricked building that served as the town hall, courthouse, police and fire department, jailhouse, and community services all rolled up in one.

"What is this—*No McDonalds?* Man! You talk about personal sacrifice," Bryson said sarcastically as he headed down Main Street. He noticed that the bank was complete with a drive- through window, ATM machine, and a working digital clock that displayed time and temperature. *This place is not as backward as I first believed*, Bryson thought again with a touch of mordacity. But in reality, he loved the place. This was his new home away from the life-in-the-fast-lane living the big city had to offer. He didn't miss the big city. Not one bit. A phenomenal excitement was building inside him, like a boy might feel if he was attending the Ringling Brothers Circus for the first time. He felt as if he had at last found a place where he could finally be happy. But these feelings may be short-lived.

Bryson glanced up at the clock as he drove by. A few bulbs were burned out, but it was still readable. The big clock clicked to 1:30. Then after a few seconds the clock clicked again, changing to the temperature. It was 76 degrees, unusually cool for mid-August. When the clock clicked again it was 1:31.

Bryson was late. Very late. His appointment was at one. He usually prided himself on being punctual. But this time, he had followed his heart and the pressing matter of putting a piece of his past to rest.

Talihina was bigger than he remembered. Main Street was littered with people, who busied themselves here and there, frequenting the local stores, not necessarily to buy anything, but just to poke their heads inside to say "Hello" or "How ya doin'?" or "Anythin' new been happenin'?" (Small town gossip—very popular stuff.)

Several people waved. Some were walking; others were driving cars.

Bryson waved back, marveling at the townspeople's hospitality. He hadn't received this kind of cordial treatment since he visited the Gaelic village, Ulsterael, located in the lowlands of southern Ireland over a year ago. Bryson had made many life-long friends in his one-month stay at the village. Many of the villagers begged him to remain, but Bryson had to bid them a sad farewell. He could not stay. His destiny was calling him away. He didn't know where his fated path would lead him, but when he reached its end, he would know.

The longer Bryson remained in Talihina, the more he believed that this was his destined place to be. And right now, his destined place to be was at his appointment.

He needed directions. He spotted an old lady sitting alone on a bench in front of Carla's Country Kitchen and decided to pull over and ask for directions. Bryson parked the Jeep by the curb and climbed out. "Howdy," he announced as he walked toward her.

"Howdy back." Her voice was stern and pleasant.

"How are you doing today?" Bryson asked as he entered into the shade of the awning. The woman was younger than he first thought. Perhaps fifty-five years old. Although deep lines of a hard life were profoundly cut into her tanned, leathery skin, her crystal blue eyes were clear and alert. Her rusty-colored hair was heavily streaked with gray, falling in lots of ratty curls onto her shoulders. She was wearing a matching denim shirt and skirt. Judging from the ground-in dirt, her clothes looked as if they had not been washed in a while.

"Not bad," she quickly answered, "if you consider that my knee joints haven't quit aching since the cold front came through Sunday past. My corns swelled up like ripe tomatoes. It takes better'n all mornin' before I can straighten out my back. My gums have drawn up where my teeth don't fit no more. I haven't eaten a decent meal in three days. Other than that, I feel fine."

"I'm sorry you don't feel well," Bryson commented and then debated whether to ask her for directions.

"Oh, fiddle-fuss! I wouldn't know how to act if I didn't have all this pain to live with. Now what ya want with me? I know ya didn't stop out of the kindness of your heart to see how I'm a doin'."

Bryson smiled. He liked this woman, she had character. "I'm looking for the school. I'm going to be teaching there this school year. Can you tell me how to get there from here?"

She gazed at him for a short period of time, sizing him up. Then she leaned over and reached into one of her bags sitting on the ground and retrieved a can of W. E. Garrett Sweet Scottish Snuff. She pulled her teeth out and stuffed her upper lip with a big pinch of powdery snuff. "You don't look like no teacher that I've ever saw."

"If I don't get to the school in the next few minutes, I may not be teaching anywhere," he replied, trying very hard not to lose his patience.

"You young'uns are all alike. Can't go nowhere without rushin' around like a chicken with its head cut off. Arright, keep your pants on." She must have seen his patience was wearing thin. "I'm just funnin' ya." She pointed toward the east. "Go east three blocks to Second Street. Turn north. Go up to Hellen Street, and you'll find the school."

"Thank you kindly, miss." He winked at her and then turned abruptly and left.

"Don't mention it. Come back an' see me anytime. An' remember life ain't that short where ya have to scurry 'bout like some hunted rabbit," she called out after him as he climbed into his Jeep.

"What's your name?" he hollered back to her.

"Abbey. My friends call me Ms. Abbey. What's your name?"

"Bryson Keahbone."

"Glad to know ya, Mr. Bryson Keahbone."

"The pleasure was all mine, Ms. Abbey." He gave a quick wave and drove off down the road, leaving her sitting there rubbing her chin, searching the archives of her mind, trying to recollect where she had heard that name before.

Bryson arrived at Talihina High School five minutes later. The parking lot was full of parked cars except for one empty slot next to the front door. *What luck*, Bryson thought as he whipped the Jeep into the parking space. He glanced into the rearview mirror. "Definitely having a bad hair day." He raked his fingers through his long dark hair. No help. "It's going to have to do," he murmured, as he climbed out of the side door on the Jeep.

Bryson headed for the front door of the high school. He blindly passed a twelve-by-twelve sign standing directly in front of the parking space he had used. The sign proclaimed in big block letters:

Reserved Parking
Principal Hitchcock

But Bryson never saw it. His thoughts were only attentive to what lay ahead for him in the building.

Bryson quickened his pace. He stepped through the plate-glass door. He was twelve years old the last time he had been in the elementary building. He didn't have much memory about the school except for the location of the principal's office. He was constantly sent to the office for boyish mischief. He often wondered if he spent more time in the office or the classroom. Hiding the cat in Principal Brown's desk right before he was evaluated by the superintendent was a *classic*. *I was a teacher's living nightmare*, Bryson mused.

It was a short walk to the office. Bryson felt a little tightness in his stomach as he passed through the doorway.

A young woman in her early twenties sat behind the only desk in the room. She was an attractive woman. Her hair fell around her heart-shaped face in long strawberry-blonde curls, which conflicted with her dark eyes and dark brows. Could be hair color, but Bryson didn't think so. Her slim figure was covered by a light blue dress shrouded in little yellow flowers. She smiled warmly and inquired, "May I help you?"

"Yes. My name is Bryson Keahbone. I have an appointment with Principal Hitchcock."

She glanced at her watch. "The appointment was at one. It's now one forty-five. Principal Hitchcock assumed that you weren't coming and went to lunch. Have a seat. It will be a few minutes."

"Thank you," he said as he sat down in a chair in front of the secretary's desk. "I'm really sorry. I was detained on other business."

"I understand. But Principal Hitchcock doesn't. If you have an appointment at one o'clock, death better be your only excuse for being late." Again she smiled. "Pardon my manners. My name is Jody Bretz."

"It's nice to meet you," Bryson greeted as he stood up and shook her hand.

"So you're our new freshman English teacher?"

"Yes … well, I hope."

"Don't worry. Principal Hitchcock is not a bad person to work for. You'll get a second chance. But never a third. So don't push your luck."

"Believe me, I won't."

The room fell silent. Jody went back to doing paperwork on her desk. Bryson looked around at the walls. They were pretty bare except for a clock and a painting of an Indian leaning over his horse's neck as he shot arrows at stampeding buffaloes. *The room needs a few more pieces of Native American artwork to liven this place up*, Bryson thought.

He glanced at the clock—2:00. It felt later, like he had been sitting there for hours. Finally, Bryson broke the silence. "What kind of person is Principal Hitchcock?"

"Well," the secretary began but was interrupted.

"Jody!" a woman wearing a red dress screamed as she came charging through the doorway. "Find the idiot who is driving the black Jeep parked outside and have him or her come to the office immediately!"

"He's already here," Bryson revealed as he stood up. "I am that idiot."

The woman turned toward Bryson. *She's beautiful*, he thought. Her long, almost black hair was pulled back in a barrette, exposing a flawless face. Her skin was fair and milky against her dark hair. Her icy blue eyes made it very hard for him to maintain eye contact. She reminded him of someone from his past. But Bryson received a reality check when the woman in red spoke again.

"Who are you?" she bluntly asked, trying very hard to control her temper.

"Bryson Keahbone."

"The same Bryson Keahbone that should have been here over an hour ago."

"Yes. Who are you?"

"I'm Principal Hitchcock." She noticed the surprised look on Bryson's face. Hitchcock knew that look. Many times in the past people have raised a brow in awe of her accomplishments. Possibly because of her young age—thirty-three years—or even more so the fact she is female in a male-dominated world. "Let's go into my office. Jody, please hold all my calls." She motioned with her hand for him to enter a room behind Jody's desk. "Have a seat in here. I will join you in a minute."

Bryson looked over at Jody as he walked into Hitchcock's office.

"Good luck," she whispered.

"Thanks," he said under his breath.

He entered and sat in a hard plastic chair in front of a huge desk. He wondered what would happen if he sat in her big, brand-new, black leather, swivel chair behind her desk and started writing obscenities on her computer, like "For a life full of agony and despair dial 555-PAIN and ask for Hitchcock." *I would be batting two-for-two with Ms. Hitchcock today*, he thought mischievously. He turned his attention to the room around him. Her office was plain and dull. Not a single picture on the wall. No wonder the woman is so uptight. *She needs a little color and variety in her life*, he thought. He shifted his position in his seat to look at the back wall. He was impressed. Principal Piper Hitchcock was a career woman, a strictly-do-it-by-the-book professional who had dedicated her life to her work. Located on the wall were several awards and degrees: bachelors degree of arts in elementary education, masters in education, magna cum laude awards from Southeastern and Oklahoma University, Principal of the Year Award for district and state, president of CCOSA (Cooperative Council of Oklahoma School Administrators), and several accommodations from different associations. "Probably never had a social life," Bryson murmured just as Hitchcock came in carrying a yellow folder.

"Excuse me," she said.

"I was just admiring your achievements."

"Mmm-hmm" She smirked as she walked behind her desk and sat down, placing the folder in front of her. She opened it and flipped through the papers, occasionally stopping to study one of interest.

Bryson wished that she would hurry this process along. He felt very uncomfortable and was anxious to leave. He doubted that he would ever be able to work for this woman, who probably lives and dies by the strong arm of authoritarian rule.

"You teach reading and literature, Mr. Keahbone," she stated as fact rather than a question as she looked up from the papers.

"Yes," sounded the toneless reply.

"Then can you explain to me how someone who teaches reading cannot read a large sign with the words: Reserved Parking—Principal Hitchcock."

They stared at each other. Hitchcock studied Bryson, wondering how far she could push him. Not very far. Bryson's patience was wearing thin. His body stiffened. Then he relaxed. "I apologize. I failed to notice the sign when I arrived."

"Apology accepted." Her voice sung triumphantly. "Now. Let's get on with this interview," she continued as their eyes remained locked. "You taught English for three years at Thomas Jefferson High School in Eugene, Oregon, out on the West Coast."

Bryson nodded.

"Then you dropped out of teaching for the past two years. Would you care to reflect on why you did not teach?"

"No, I would not. I took a personal leave of absence, and I wish to leave it at that."

Hitchcock stood up and leaned on her desk toward Bryson. "Look here, Mr. Keahbone, if you are going to work for me, then I must know what kind of person I've employed. I am responsible for the livelihood of each and every student enrolled at this school. For the children's sake, I have to make sure you're not one of those warped individuals who has filtered through the cracks in our educational system."

"All due respect, Ms. Hitchcock. I'm not one of those warped individuals you are talking about," Bryson said defensively. "I pride myself on my work as an educator and care very deeply for the welfare of my students. As for my past, it does not reflect or influence my ability to teach. I keep my private life separate from my teaching life." He paused. "It was my understanding from Dr. Brown that I had already been hired and that this interview was set up as a *friendly* get together so you and I could get acquainted. *Not* some attack on my character."

Bryson's eyebrows arched.

Hitchcock glanced down at her desk, breaking eye contact. A small victory for Bryson. But the victory was short-lived. She looked up quickly.

"Let me make one thing clear. I was most unhappy when Dr. Brown went behind my back and hired you. Although Tim and I are very good friends and I hold his judgment in high regard, he should not have hired you before I had a chance to interview you first," she said defiantly.

"You mean interrogate," he corrected.

"I reserve the right to ask any questions I deem appropriate during this interview. If I feel your personal life will affect your teaching abilities, then I need to know the circumstances that may produce any unwanted situations. Mr. Keahbone, I am going to be frank with you. You come in here wearing a worn out pair of holey blue jeans and a faded cotton T-shirt. You look like you haven't shaved in a week or bathed for that matter. If Dr. Brown wasn't my boss, I would never hire you. Not today, not tomorrow, *never*! I think you have an attitude problem. You look as professional as …"

Bryson's patience gave out. He stood up abruptly, coming nose to nose with her. "Look here, Hitchcock. I don't know who yanked your chain this afternoon, but you're not going to take it out on me. I'm not real sure I can even work for a tyrant like you. I'm not in education for the money. Look, lady, I would work for free. I love working with kids. I love my job. Working with children has become my life. If you don't want me working for you, then tell me *right now*, and I will walk."

They glared into each other's eyes. Neither was willing to budge an inch.

The tension was so thick in the air it could have been sliced with a knife.

Then the knife walked into the room.

Dr. "Hoot" Brown

T he door swung open.

"Hello," a cheerful voice said, cutting through the heavy tension between Bryson and Hitchcock. "I hope I'm not interrupting anything."

There was a brief silence before Piper Hitchcock finally said, "No. Not at all. Come on in, Dr. Brown. We are just finishing up." Dr. Timothy "Hoot" Brown was the superintendent for Talihina Independent School District. He got his nickname "Hoot" playing ironman football in college. Every time he carried the football on offense or made a tackle on defense, he hooted like an owl. His black, pin-stripped suit covered a very athletically built frame. He was still in fantastic shape for a man of fifty-three years. He loved to exercise. Running was his favorite hobby when he had time. His job carried a lot of responsibilities and kept him very busy. He blamed his salt-and-pepper-hair on these responsibilities. "I earned every gray hair I have," he would hoot with a smile.

"Bryson, my boy! It's great to see you." Dr. Brown walked over and shook hands vigorously and then grabbed Bryson in a bear hug.

"It's good to see you again, Dr. Brown."

"Call me, Hoot. This is an informal meeting. There will be no formalities here," Dr. Brown said as he broke the handshake to playfully punch Bryson in the stomach. "I trust Piper is taking good are of you."

"Yes … she has been showing me the ropes," Bryson said, but what he really wanted to say was that it was more like a hangman's noose.

"Great! If Piper doesn't object, then I will welcome you to our team."

Hitchcock had remained silent through the whole exchange between the two men. Bryson looked over at her, waiting for her approval or disapproval. There was a long pause; then she extended her hand. *I am totally going to regret this.* "Welcome aboard." Her words were cold.

Bryson hesitated before he extended his hand. He was certain that when their fingers met, he would be turned instantly to stone by her icy touch. But to his surprise, when their hands met, Bryson felt a strange warmth come over him, like he had been outdoors shoveling snow for a very long time and then came inside the house to thaw by the fire. Piper must have felt it too because she quickly pulled her hand away.

"Thank you, Hoot … Ms. Hitchcock," Bryson said.

Principal Hitchcock stepped out from behind her desk and walked toward Bryson. "School begins at eight thirty for the students. I require my staff to be here by eight o'clock sharp. Not 8:01. Is that clear?" she asked sharply.

"Crystal," Bryson snapped vehemently. Whatever spark that flared up a second ago was quickly extinguished.

"This is Friday. School begins on Monday. I would like for you to report to my office at seven o'clock on Monday morning so we can discuss the curriculum from which you will be teaching this school year. This should have been taken care of *today*. I run a tight ship here, Mr. Keahbone. There are rules to be followed. And they will be followed," Principal Hitchcock barked, sounding like a Marine drill sergeant.

"Yes, ma'am," Bryson acknowledged, clicking his heels together, but Hitchcock had turned toward the entry way, failing to notice his invective behavior.

"Ms. Bretz," Hitchcock called through the doorway.

The secretary walked in the room. "Yes?"

"Do you have Mr. Keahbone's paperwork and teacher's manual ready?"

"Yes, I do. Everything is sitting on my desk."

"Thank you, Ms. Bretz. Mr. Keahbone will be out directly to pick it up. I need you to show him which papers to sign while he's here and which ones he can take home and fill out. That will be all."

Ms. Bretz turned and disappeared from view.

Hitchcock looked over at Dr. Brown. "I'm finished here unless you have something else to add."

"No. I think you have covered everything, Piper," Dr. Brown said; then he directed his attention toward Bryson, putting his arm around his shoulder as they walked toward the door. "Are you still coming over to Vick's house for supper tonight?"

"Look forward to it." Bryson smiled.

"Great. I will see you around seven thirty. Do you have directions?"

"Yes, I do. I'll see you tonight, Hoot. Nice to meet you, Principal Hitchcock," Bryson said begrudgingly over Hoot's shoulder.

Hitchcock nodded slightly, barely lifting her face from a folder she had picked up and opened from her desk.

The two men shook hands. Bryson debated with himself whether to shake Hitchcock's hand. *Not today*, he quickly decided. He exited the room, signed the required forms, and then left the building.

Hitchcock lowered the folder and followed Bryson, closing the door rapidly behind him. She paused by the door for a few seconds, gathering her thoughts. Her hand rested limply on the handle. Then she turned abruptly, exploding like a lit pack of Black Cat firecrackers. "Hoot! How could you do this to me? You hire this man who looks like he just graduated the head of his class from the school of Charles-Manson-want-to-be. He comes in here with this major attitude problem. He wouldn't answer my questions. All I wanted to know was some background history— namely what he had been doing for the past two years, but he refused to tell me. He's a presumptuous male, who is going to be one big pain in the—"

"Now, now." Hoot grinned, reaching over and patting Hitchcock's arm in a patronizing manner. "If I know you as well as I think I know you, I would say that you kind of like the guy."

"Ohh … bull!" Hitchcock blasted, giving Hoot the meanest look she could muster.

"Quit with your dirty looks. You know they don't work on me," Hoot smirked shrewdly as he continued in a manipulative manner. "You are kind of stuck on him, aren't you?"

"I totally despised the man."

"Piper, I haven't seen you so worked up over a fellow since—"

"*Do not say that name!*" Hitchcock interrupted. "My past will remain in the past."

"Let me see if I have this figured out," Hoot began, raising his hand to rub his chin as he looked up in contemplation. "It is all right for you to bury something from your past, but not Bryson."

"That's different."

"How?" Hoot asked.

"Well … it is … kind of … all right. I see your point. I never could win an argument against you," she grumbled sullenly. Then she playfully wadded up a piece of paper and threw it at Hoot. It bounced off his forehead. "I hate you sometimes."

Hoot crossed his eyes, giving the impression that he had just been knocked cuckoo.

They both laughed until tears rolled down their faces.

Then quick as a light switch being flipped, Hitchcock was back to business. She quickly grabbed a tissue from the top of her desk, dabbing it under her eyes. After she discarded the tissue into the waste basket, she spoke resolutely, "Hoot, you know how I feel about my job and the people I work with. I demand the very best from everyone here. I have learned that high expectation leads to greater achievement. It's very important for me to develop a personality profile on each member of my staff. Will you at least tell me something about Mr. Keahbone?" she asked, sounding more like a plea than a question.

"Bryson Keahbone is a good man. He's good people," Hoot declared, pausing a few seconds before he began again. "Against my better judgment I shouldn't do this, but I know if I don't, you will badger Bryson until he leaves, and I wouldn't like that one bit. He is a personal friend of mine and a flat-out good teacher."

Hitchcock recoiled. She had never heard Dr. Brown speak so forceful about anything before. It caught her off guard.

"Piper, I have the utmost respect for you and the job you're doing here. I would never be able to find anyone who could fill your shoes in a million years. I understand your concerns, therefore, I am going to tell you a little of what I know about Mr. Bryson Keahbone. But only on one condition."

"What would that be?" she mumbled, still feeling a little unhinged. She had never seen this side of Hoot and was quite certain she did not like it.

"You must promise me on our friendship that you will never repeat what I am about to tell you … to Bryson or anyone. Not one word," Hoot instructed. His face was stolid, looking like the cold bust of an unsung hero.

"I promise. What you tell me will not leave this room," she said, her voice sounding more confident and controlled.

"I hope so," he said impassively, and then Hoot gestured with his hand. "Have a seat." She walked around her desk and sat down. Hoot remained standing. He felt more comfortable talking when he could move about.

Hoot licked his lips, hoping to ease the dryness in his mouth. It helped a little. But it wasn't the dryness that caused him to hesitate; it was doubt. Bryson was the most private individual he knew. *Am I doing the right thing?* Hoot asked himself. *I hope to God*, he answered silently. "I will start from the beginning," he proceeded, still sounding a little insecure about his decision to strip away Bryson's individuality, exposing his nakedness to a stranger.

"Do you remember the Old Kinsey Place?"

"Yes. It's only a few miles down from me at the end of Whiskey Road. The kids say it's haunted," Hitchcock replied.

"That's the one. Well, twenty years ago, it was the Keahbone Farm where Bryson was born. Vick and I went to school with Bryson's mother, Kate. Bryson's father was Joseph Keahbone, a half-breed Choctaw Indian, who preferred to be called by his Choctaw name, Tuchina Iyishke, which means Three-toes. Although Three-toes was a half-breed, he was a well-respected shaman of the Choctaws. Usually the shaman was a position reserved for full bloods. I was very close to Kate, but I didn't know her husband that well—he pretty much kept to himself. Don't misunderstand me—he was very friendly, but he never said a lot. His attention always seemed far away. I would ask him a question, thinking he wasn't listening, but to my surprise he always gave an appropriate response as if he had been following the conversation the whole time. Three-toes simply never spoke unless spoken to first. Bryson is a lot like his father. They were a very happy family until one day, something happened to Bryson's parents," Hoot said as he tensely paced back and forth in front of Hitchcock's desk, seemingly wearing a path upon the white tile floor. "Three-toes turned up missing. He had supposedly gone to Oklahoma City to perform a ceremonial dance at Red Earth Festival. His truck was found by County Line Road, but he was nowhere to be found. Kate was utterly convinced that something had happened to him. But when some of us began poking our noses into places they didn't belong, the sheriff quickly ordered us to back off and rudely reminded us that he had the situation under control."

Hoot walked over to the window and stopped. He looked out blindly. A single tear raced down his face. "Kate lost the will to live. Her body just simply shut down. The coroner called it death by natural causes, but we all knew that she died from a broken heart."

A brief blanket of silence fell over the room.

"Was Three-toes ever found?" Hitchcock wondered.

"No. Not conclusively anyway. There was not one clue of his whereabouts. Nada. To be perfectly honest with you, I don't think the sheriff 's office put forth any measurable effort in locating Bryson's father. They wrote him off as a drunken Indian who went AWOL. They found a mutilated body down in the willows by the railroad tracks. The head had been crushed, and the feet were chopped off and missing. Could have been the train. I don't know. The turkey buzzards and other scavengers had stripped the body beyond recognition. The sheriff proclaimed it to be Three-toes anyway and closed the case. We all knew well enough that was probably not what happened. Three-toes loved his family, especially Bryson. He would not have done anything to jeopardize his life unless it was to protect his family. I called the state bureau of investigation. They assured me they would check into the matter. If they followed up on the case, I never knew about it."

"What happened to Bryson?"

"They buried Kate on the Keahbone Farm beneath her favorite tree. A huge oak, I believe. The tree had a large heart carved in it. The most peculiar sight I had ever seen. There was this figure carved in the shape of a dog but it had a human head," Hoot described excitedly, like he was seeing it again on the big hickory tree standing next to the office window. "After the funeral, Bryson was flown to New Port, Oregon, to live with Kate's sister, Imogene. He would send Vicki and me a letter every once in a while. We would write back. Then the letters quit coming. We eventually lost track of him for a few years. It turned out that Bryson had found something that he really loved to do—*run*."

Hoot moved away from the window and began to pace again. The thought of running revved up his body motor. "You know how big a running fanatic I am. I subscribe to every running magazine and newsletters in print. On the cover of one of my magazines was a picture of this kid. It was Bryson. He was a child prodigy of the running world. He broke every long distance record in the United States and three World Records by the time he was twenty years old. He almost quit running when he failed to make the Olympic team the first time he tried. He was closing down on the twenty-mile line during the Olympic Marathon Trials when he suffered a freak injury."

Hoot paused to catch his breath as if he had been the one actually running the marathon. Then he continued, "He was a good mile ahead of the second place runner and decided to coast home. Big mistake. The instant he backed off—*rip*—a torn hamstring. The race was over. Bryson finished with a broken heart."

"Did he quit?"

"No. Not this time. Bryson bounced back like the real champion he is. He trained hard for the next four years. Broke a half dozen more records, most his own. Got married—"

"Got what?"

"Got married," he repeated. "Her name was Rebekah. She was a very beautiful woman. You remind me a lot of her."

"Was?" Hitchcock asked, glancing down at Bryson's application on her desk. "I see here on his application that he didn't mark any box—single, married, or divorced. Is he divorced? Is that what he wants to bury?" she questioned, arching a single brow.

"No. This is the part where my heart is laden with sorrow." Hoot paused, thinking he might have to clear another tear from his eye. "Bryson was on top of the world. He had everything: more money than he could ever spend from endorsements, a nice large home in the mountains of Oregon, an awesome wife, a new baby on the way—"

"A baby?" Hitchcock interrupted.

"Yes. Rebekah was eight months pregnant when the accident occurred."

"What accident?"

The Accident

"*It's a new world record!*" blared a voice from a huge speaker connected to the top of a tall wooden pole as Bryson crossed the finish line. "Bryson Keahbone has won the Olympic Marathon Trials!"

Hundreds of people swarmed the finish line, like ants on an unguarded picnic lunch. Everyone was trying to get to Bryson to congratulate him on his victory.

But at that moment, Bryson's only concerns were catching his breath and finding his wife. He doubled over, placing his hands on his knees. His arms and legs felt like rubber bands. People he didn't know were patting him on the back and shaking his hand. He straightened up and looked steadily about, gazing blindly past the people around him, searching the crowd for his wife. He hoped that she saw the finish; the race would not mean a thing to him if she wasn't there to celebrate in the victory. He would not have been there if not for her support when he wanted to quit. *She is my purpose in life—my* raison d'etre, he thought.

Then two big linebacker-looking fellows lifted Bryson to their shoulders. Bryson raised one arm and pointed his index finger into the air.

The crowd cheered, "Keee-bone! Keee-bone!"

Someone grabbed his leg. It was Hoot. "You did it! You finally did it!" He hollered up to Bryson. "We are so very proud of you." Then he joined in with the rest of the crowd.

"Keee-bone! Keee-bone!"

The two men paraded Bryson through the crowd. Bryson smiled and waved. Tears of joy began to stream down his face. This was his day. The day Bryson had worked so hard for. All the sacrifices Rebekah and he had made were now being repaid in full. This was the happiest and most self-fulfilling day of Bryson's life. Or was it?

"Hoot!" Bryson yelled. "Where's Becky?"

Hoot said something, but Bryson couldn't hear him. The words were lost in the crowd noise. He leaned over and asked the men to let him down. When he reached the ground, Bryson waded through the mass of people trying earnestly to reach Dr. Brown.

"Hoot. Have you seen Becky?"

"No," Hoot replied, glancing around. "I'm sure she's around here somewhere."

Bryson tiptoed, craning his neck to see over the crowd, offering thank yous to well-wishers between glances. He looked right, left, front, back, but she was nowhere to be found. Becky should have been here by now, or at least close enough for him to see her, he thought as he climbed a park bench for a better look. Nothing. *Where is she?* He began to feel a little panicky. He had asked her if it was wise for her to come to the race. She was so close to her due date. The race was televised; she could watch it at home. But Becky insisted she be there. She had never missed a race, and this one was definitely too important to start.

Bryson and Becky lived less than an hour's drive from the race course. Bryson had ridden with Hoot because he had to be at the race four hours early for check-in procedures and prerace warm-up. Becky insisted, against Bryson's wishes, that she drive down later for the finish. He argued briefly, but in the end, he reluctantly agreed.

But Becky never arrived.

"Excuse me, Mr. Keahbone?" The voice was deep and firm.

Bryson turned toward the voice. A stocky-framed black man in a blue-gray uniform stood before him.

"Mr. Keahbone. I'm Officer Johnson. I need you to come with me, please. There has been an accident."

"What has happened?" Bryson suddenly felt very weak. "Where's Becky?"

But the officer only responded, "We'll talk in the car. Now, please. We must go."

"May Dr. Brown come along?"

The policeman nodded.

They walked briskly to the squad car. Officer Johnson gestured Bryson toward the front seat. Hoot crawled in the back. He started the car and took off.

"What happened?" Bryson asked impatiently.

"Your wife has been in an accident. An eyewitness said a large black dog or wolf ran out in front of your wife's SUV. She swerved to miss the animal and lost control of her car, striking a pine tree head on. I am really sorry."

"Where is she?" Bryson was frantic. "Is she okay?"

"Calm down, Mr. Keahbone."

"You calm down! Where is my wife!" he shouted, punching the dash.

Hoot reached over the seat and grabbed Bryson firmly on the shoulder. "Bryson," his voice was calm and soothing.

Bryson relaxed a little, drawing in a deep breath. "I'm sorry," he whispered.

"I fully understand. If it were my wife, I would be doing the same thing. Your wife was rushed by ambulance to Memorial Hospital in Eugene. She has been injured. How badly? I do not know. My orders are to bring you to the hospital."

"Thank you, Officer," Hoot said, still holding on to Bryson's shoulder.

Bryson buried his face into his hands. *This is not happening. This is not real.* He kept repeating in his mind.

The squad car arrived twenty minutes later at Memorial Hospital's Emergency Room. Bryson bolted from the car, leaving the door rocking back and forth on its hinges. Once inside, he charged up to the first nurse he saw, demanding the whereabouts of his wife. It so happened that she was the nurse who checked Becky in and notified the police where to contact Bryson. She was most helpful, not only with information, but she had a good way with people. The nurse calmed Bryson down. Afterward, she explained everything that had happened up to that point.

"Right now," the nurse said to Bryson, "your wife and baby are in surgery. She has suffered a lot of internal injuries. When the doctors have completed the operation, they will come talk to you. But until then, try to get some rest. It may be a long haul."

Bryson sat glassy-eyed on the sofa, as deaf ears captured the nurse's fuzzy words.

"Thank you," Hoot said as he sat down and put his arm around Bryson, pulling him close. "I love you as a son … everything is going to be fine … you'll see … it's in God's hands now." Tears flowed uncontrollably down his face, drowning out the last of his words. Both men bowed their heads and prayed without ceasing.

Time appeared to stand still. Minutes seemed like hours, hours like days.

Conversation was light between the two men. Bryson leapt to his feet every time a person wearing a white coat walked by, but each time met with utter disappointment. His heart ached. A paralyzing coldness blanketed his entire body, like embalming fluid was being injected into his veins. He had known these same feelings a long time ago. He thought that he had buried them forever in his past. But now he was reliving that moment in his mother's bedroom when he held her frail, dry hand as she lay dying on her bed. *No! This time the result will not be the same. God will not allow it*, he thought dubiously, trying hard to convince himself.

Seven hours had passed when two surgeons finally walked into the waiting room. Bryson was instantly to his feet. Hoot was a little slower to stand; he knew by the solemn look on their faces that they were bearers of bad news.

"Mr. Keahbone?" the shorter one said, pulling a plastic cap from his head.

"Is Becky all right? When can I see her?"

The doctor paused. He hated this part of his job. "I'm sorry. We did all we could to save them both. The injuries were just too extensive …"

"*No!*" Bryson cried. "*No! No! I want to talk to Becky. Where is she? We have plans to make. She can't go anywhere! We're going to London for the Olympics. We have to pack. We're … going … to … "* Bryson's knees gave out as his arms collapsed around Hoot's neck. "*No! No, Hoot! Don't let her go!*"

"Oh … my … Bryson …" Hoot sobbed, locking his arms around his friend.

"*No! This is not Happening!*" Bryson jerked away from Hoot and staggered down the hall. After several wobbly steps, he stopped and fell to his knees. He lowered his head until his chin touched his chest. His body felt numb and limp. Then quick as an electrical shock running through his body, he doubled his hands into fists and raised them straight toward the ceiling.

"Why? Why has this happened to me? God, why did you let this happen? How could you … I blame you!" Then in a swift motion, Bryson was on his feet, running full speed down the narrow hall, darting around medicine carts, people, and other hospital items. At the end of the hall, he disappeared down a fire escape.

Three days later, there was a double funeral for Rebekah and the unborn child. Bryson was silent and tearless through the entire service. After the burial, he walked up to Hoot and Vicki. "Thank you for everything that you have done for me. I could not have handled it without you." They hugged. Vicki had black smears beneath her eyes, where tears and mascara had been mixed together with a handkerchief. "I'm leaving for France late this afternoon. I must get away from the media and reporters. I need some time to myself. In Europe, I will not be bothered. I will keep in touch. Good-bye, my friends."

Bryson turned to leave.

Hoot reached out and gently touched Bryson's arm. "What about the Olympics?"

Bryson raised his hand slightly, looking directly into Hoot's bloodshot eyes. Then he looked down and shook his head disappointedly. "I cannot," Bryson sighed. He abruptly turned and escaped the cemetery.

"Bryson walked away from the running world completely. He simply walked away. The Olympic committee offered to work with him. But he wouldn't talk to them. He wasn't talking to anyone. Not me. Not Vicki. No one. This was his way of dealing with the tragic deaths of his wife and baby." Hoot sighed. "This occurred over two years ago."

There was a long silence. Hoot pulled two tissues from a box on top of Hitchcock's desk, handing one to her. He sat down and looked blindly out the window, then gazed teary-eyed at Hitchcock.

"What has Mr. Keahbone been doing for the last two years?" she asked curiously.

"He has been traveling all over Europe, mainly by foot. Vick and I would receive a letter every couple of months, telling us that he was doing fine. He sent one from Ireland, Italy, Spain, and Russia, just to name a few. He would stay a month or two in one place and then move on. His longest stay was in France. Over six months. He wrote us that he liked the company and decided to stay a while."

"Who did he stay with? How did he live?" she asked.

"He made many friends in the running world. Some of them took care of him, but he mostly lived on his own. He is a survivor."

"But why did he go to Europe?"

"To escape his past. To find the will to live again. The Europeans did not pry into the things that Bryson wanted to let go. Even the notorious paparazzi let him be. Everything here in the US was a constant reminder of his once happy life. Then one day, Vick received a letter from Bryson, telling us he was ready to come home. He bought and paid in full the Old Kinsey Place. Vicki took care of the paperwork. And you know the rest of the story," Hoot finished, feeling disgruntled for revealing more about Bryson's past than he should have.

"An interesting story," Hitchcock replied, some of the coldness had returned to her voice.

Hoot sensed it too. "Maybe next time, before you begin to snoop into somebody's past, you might take a long, hard look at your own," he attacked.

"If Mr. Keahbone does his job, that will be all the past I need to observe," she counterattacked.

Hoot stood up abruptly. "I'm not believing this. Have you not heard a word I said? Did we not cry together a few minutes ago? Has your own past left you so hard and coldhearted that you have no more feelings?"

"I keep my personal feelings and my professional life separate. You hired me to do a job, Dr. Brown. I am going to perform my job to the best of my capabilities. My past or personal feelings will in no way influence the way I conduct myself while I'm employed here," she proclaimed.

"Ms. Hitchcock, I pity you. You're in for a long and lonely life," Hoot declared. He turned and stormed toward the door, leaving it swinging noiselessly on its hinges as he passed through.

Dinner at Vick's

The evening shadows rapidly approached, chasing away the bright colors of day. There was about an hour of daylight left, but in the valley, it would seem a lot less. Already the dense underbrush along the tree line had faded to a greenish black.

Clang. Clang. Clang.

The cattle guard rattled as Bryson's Jeep rolled across. Vick's house was located about two miles up the road from here at the northwest end of Buffalo Valley.

Vick Buchanan owned over half of the valley. She inherited some of it, but mainly acquired most of her land (not just in Buffalo Valley but all over Leflore County) through calculated business deals. She could play the market, dealing the stocks like they were a deck of cards. Only one family in Leflore County owned as much or more land than her—the Mongers. On more than one occasion had she and the Mongers butted heads over a strip of land. The bitterest battle was when Vick bought the Old Kinsey Place out from under Nate Monger, then she turned around and sold it to Bryson. Nate swore revenge, and a day of resolution shall he see.

She was a shrewd business woman; she takes no prisoners, which was probably why she had never married even though Hoot had been pestering Vick off and on for over twenty years for matrimony. "I don't want to ruin a good friendship," Vick replied when the subject did come up.

Dusty chasers danced up from the Jeep's tires as Bryson drove down the winding gravel road. He didn't know the circumstances of how Vick had obtained his family's old place or even why she and Hoot had never married. That was their personal business. All he cared was that he was home, and nobody was going to make him leave.

Something suddenly caught the corner of Bryson's eye. He slowed the Jeep to a crawl. A twelve-point buck and doe stood poised in the nearby meadow. The buck stood guard like a mighty centurion as the doe dropped her head to browse the prairie grass for twigs and sprouts.

The Jeep slowly rolled to a stop after Bryson had thoughtlessly put the gear in neutral. He sat and marveled at the simplicity of nature. A warm feeling came over him, replacing the coldness of being alone. For the past two years, he had felt nothing but this bitter, lonely coldness inside.

Until today.

What is changing me inside, he thought? *Is it the tranquility of this place? The reconciliation with my mother? Maybe the companionship of close friends? Or could it be that this principal woman has sparked a long dead flame? She does possess that same air of assurance that I remember in Becky.*

No!

I'm not ready!

The doe darted off quickly as if she had heard his thoughts. Maybe he voiced his thoughts out loud—he wasn't sure. The buck abruptly turned and squared himself toward Bryson, raking his front hoof like an enraged bull who was about to charge. Bryson stepped out of the Jeep and walked three steps toward the buck and stopped. They remained motionless for several moments in time.

Bryson felt a presence, lurking above in the ever-growing shadows of the tree border, watching and waiting patiently. *But waiting for what?* He didn't know. The presence was not necessarily evil, but it was not a pure one either. He couldn't explain how he knew; he just did. He was trying to rationalize everything that had happened up to this point when, from the ridge above, he heard.

Awoooooooo!

Bryson looked up abruptly and saw on the ridge a dark, almost black, silhouette against the dusky sky. It was a large dog, or maybe a wolf. He wasn't sure. The figure disappeared as quickly as it had appeared. He lowered his gaze, turning his attention back to the deer. The mighty buck snorted and bounced away hurriedly, waving its white tail in a gesture of surrender.

He climbed back in his Jeep and sat a moment in bewilderment. *What just happened here?* Bryson had no answer. After an animated sanity self-check, he smiled and shook his head. "What a day. First, I meet Lady Hitler. Then, Bambi the killer deer. And now, Wolf-Dog, king of beast. Dare I journey on?" Before his mind could comprise an answer, Bryson slammed the shifter into first, popped the clutch, and headed down the road.

Darkness was rushing to cover the valley, like a blanket of dirt being shoveled on a grave. Bryson saw two windows hemmed in by the boughs of magnolias. The windows were glowing like the eyes of a dragon waiting to devour its prey when the road ended at its lair where the prey could flee no more.

The road winded around a small grove of black oaks before ending in front of a large two-story, white-framed house. The two windows that looked like dragon's eyes were the dining room windows. Bryson grinned when he saw Vick through these windows placing empty plates on a table. *She hasn't changed a bit.* His stomach growled loudly. *When was my last meal?* He couldn't remember. *McDonald's in McAlester? No. Herbie's Fast Foods at the Total convenience store? No. Who cares? What really matters is why I am sitting outside arguing with myself, when inside, there is a large table covered with food.*

Bryson started to swing his leg out the side of the Jeep but abruptly stopped. He turned and looked back across the field. The sun had almost melted from the sky. The trees were fast becoming dark shadows. There was an apprehensive feeling in the pit of Bryson's stomach. Something was watching him. Pulling him. He didn't know what it meant or what had drawn him back to this place. But he was sure that someday he would find the truth. Really soon, he hoped. His father's words drifted through Bryson's mind. "When my time is time upon the final scene, you must come find me beneath the Moon When Wolves Cry."

What does it mean? he asked himself for the zillionth time, and still, *nada.* He glanced up toward the sky and saw the soft silvery glow of the moon climbing from behind the ridge. *Where is beneath the Moon When—*

"Bryson!" Vick interrupted as she bolted through the doorway, slamming the screen door into Hoot, who closely followed, leaving a perfect imprint on the tip of his nose.

"Victoria," Hoot moaned as he rubbed his nose.

"Sorry," she replied, never looking back. She scrambled down the steps, recklessly hitting each one. The thought of leaping off the porch and simply bypassing all the steps had occurred to her, but she was no spring chicken anymore although she was in excellent shape for her fifty-four years. Silver streaks were overrunning her long blonde hair, which was put up neatly in a bun. Her eyes were alert and crystal blue, like two clear pools of spring water. Her smile was fresh, and her face beamed with happiness. She loved Bryson. He was the son she never had. At last, he had come home. "Bryson. You're home. I can't believe it. You're really here."

She embraced him tight around the neck. Bryson playfully stuck out his tongue as if he was being choked. "It's good to be home … I think."

Hoot grinned but remained on the porch out of harm's way, still rubbing his nose tip with his index finger.

Vick released her death grip as Bryson crawled out of the Jeep. Tears raced down her face like two roaring rivers. "Oh … I told myself I wasn't going to cry. Now look at me. And look at you with your long, shaggy hair and beard. You're beautiful. I've missed you. I was … so … worried … about … you," she sniffed; the last word was muffled as she buried her face into his shirt.

"Enough of this. You're going to make me cry," Bryson said, fighting back his own Nile of tears.

Hoot walked up and embraced the two. "Welcome home."

They remained in a huddle for a minute or two, and then Vick ordered them both inside before the roast burned in the oven.

Piper Hitchcock was traveling west on the winding section of Highway 63 as it cut through the lower slopes of the Kiamichi Mountains. It was late evening. The sun was disappearing quickly behind the dark hills. The tree borders were casting black shadows. But she hadn't noticed any of this. She was driving about ten miles per hour under the speed limit, trying to soak in all the events of the day.

Her thoughts were rushing through her mind like a band of NASCARs racing for the finish line of the Daytona 500.

First, Hoot Brown goes behind my back and hires a teacher.

Her speed had unconsciously increased to where she was going the speed limit and accelerating.

Second, this teacher-person is forty-five minutes late and then decides to park in my parking place when a sign is visibly posted of whose spot it belongs to. Really! Who does he think he is!

Her speed continued to increase rapidly. Fifty-five. Sixty.

Third, this person is dressed like a bum with long shaggy hair and scruffy beard.

Her knuckles were white on the steering wheel. Sixty-five.

Fourth, this person-man is an arrogant, pretentious, male-pompous jerk.

Seventy. Seventy-five.

She was totally consumed by the thought of Bryson Keahbone.

Fifth, this man. This man-animal. This animal. There is no other name for this—

Screech!

She slammed on her brakes. A large dog suddenly jumped in front of Piper's car. Her reflexes were ordering her to swerve, but her common sense took control and said no. She quickly rationalized that even a slight swerve at this speed would cause her to lose control of the car, crashing it into the trees and thick underbrush.

Piper gripped the steering wheel tight, bracing herself for the impact that she was sure to come but didn't.

The black dog's eyes glowed to a sinister red, not like the normal caught-in-the-headlight yellow glow. Then vanished. No collision. No bump in the road. No sickening dull thud.

Nothing.

The car skidded to a complete stop. She glanced in the rearview mirror.

Nothing.

She turned her body around 180 degrees, surveying the area outside her Ford Explorer's windows.

Nada.

She began to open her door but stopped. *It was just some stupid dog that was definitely having a better day than me*, she thought. *It must have jumped out of the way at the very last possible chance. But those red eyes.* They reminded her how sometimes a photograph taken by a flash camera will make the person in the picture have red demon eyes. *But not as evil as the dog's.*

A feeling of uneasiness suddenly fell over Piper, causing her to abruptly pull her hand away from the door handle. *Maybe some other night*, she thought as she put the car in gear and sped away.

From the deep shadows along side the highway a pair of red glowing eyes watched with a malevolent abomination of anyone who dared to cross its path.

Bryson and Hoot entered the study.

Vick busied herself in the kitchen preparing dinner for four. Not three. Four. She had placed four settings at the dinner table, unbeknownst to Bryson. She decided to let Bryson in on the "little secret" later. *It was going to be a great surprise.*

A humungous surprise.

The salad and vegetables were ready to eat, but the roast lacked about ten minutes of cooking. *Good*, Vick thought. *I can visit a little while before dinner. Maybe Bryson will tell a story about an adventure he had when he was living in Europe.* At this last thought, she hurried into the study, hoping she had not missed anything.

"You haven't begun any storytelling without me, have you?"

"No. We were talking about what Bryson saw and heard on his way up the valley," Hoot answered. "What happened?"

"I was asking Hoot if he had ever seen or heard any wolves around here recently. I believe I saw one along the crest of the east ridge."

"I haven't seen a wolf around these parts for twenty years," Vick replied.

"That's what I said too," Hoot agreed. "But I have seen on several occasions a pack of wild dogs roaming the countryside. We usually saw them at dusk or shortly after dark. And never two days in a row. It might be several weeks between sightings."

Hoot stopped and thought for a second. *Was there not a full moon each time he saw the dogs, or was he imagining a full moon? Probably not, but it wouldn't hurt to have a few silver bullets around*, he mused to himself.

"We have complained continuously to the sheriff 's office and even threatened to bring in outside help. You can bet if I see hide or hair of those animals, I am going to shoot them with my Remington 270. I told the same thing to the sheriff, but he blew up at the idea," Hoot said.

Vick rolled her eyes. "You know why? It's because he doesn't want anybody coming in and doing his job for him."

"Can't say that I blame him," Hoot stated as Vick's face turned beet red from the comment. Hoot noticed but continued anyway. "Anyhow, it must have motivated the sheriff to do something because I haven't seen any wild dogs for a very long time now."

"Who's sheriff ?" Bryson asked.

"Some weasel named Monger. Tyrel Monger," Vick answered exasperatedly.

"Look, Vick," Hoot declared. "I don't like Sheriff Monger anymore than you do, but he does a good job most of the time. He has cleaned the drugs out of our schools and community. When is the last time you can remember seeing any dealers or vagabonds hanging around town? You think maybe you're letting your personal feelings—"

"*No, I'm not!*" Vick fumed, almost in tears of anger.

Bryson opened his mouth to ask about the Mongers but quickly changed his mind. Flashes of his past were flying through his mind like fireworks. *Why has this name suddenly lay upon my tongue leaving a bitter taste?* As quickly as they appeared, the memory flashes were gone.

Hoot stood up and walked over to Vick, placing a firm hand on her shoulder. "Sorry," he said in a gentle voice.

"Oh, Hoot. It's okay. I'm the one who's sorry. I never get this emotional about anything. It's just … this is such a happy day for me. I want everything to be perfect." Vick looked over at Bryson. "Will you please tell us at least one story before dinner?"

Bryson started to object, feeling the effects of a very long and hectic day, along with the name Monger now weighing heavily on his mind.

"Please."

"Sure," Bryson said, caving in. He paused, searching his memory for an interesting tale. He smiled. "Have you ever heard of an Irish shotgun wedding?"

Shotgun Wedding—Irish Fashion

"What in the world is an Irish shotgun wedding?" Hoot asked.

"It's like when you go visit the farmer, and he catches you talking innocently to his daughter but without a chaperone. Out comes the shotgun, 'We're goin' have ourselves a weddin', boyz,'" Bryson explained, making his voice sound like a true country yokel, then changing to an Irish dialect. "Only this time, Irish fashion."

"All right, Mr. Jim Carrey. You have our attention. Now begin this story before dinner burns in the oven," Vick pleaded impatiently.

Bryson motioned with his hand for Vick to sit on the couch, but she waved him off. "Are you sure? You know how I ramble during my storytelling."

"Begin already, you're rambling now," she demanded, leaning against the back of the chair in which Hoot was sitting.

"The last eight weeks of my journey in Europe were spent in Northern Ireland. I must have been away from most of the violence usually associated with this beautiful island, because the Protestant and Catholic I saw were working and living in harmony. I stayed with my good Catholic friend, Paden O'Bryar, the 1,500-meter world champion. He lives in a very small village thirty miles southeast of Londonderry. It was like living back in the eighteenth century."

Bryson's mind drifted back to that small village and his last fate-filled day where he was to attend an Irish wedding as a very special guest—the *groom.*

Many small stone cottages with thatched roofs speckled the rolling green hills. The roads were dirt mixed with a little bit of limestone. There weren't any motor vehicles to be seen in this village. The only forms of transportation were either horseback, horse-drawn, foot, or an occasional bicycle. Only the main highways were paved, which the nearest one was over ten miles away. The terrain was extremely rough and rugged, but Bryson loved it. And the people who lived there were the most hospitable people Bryson had ever met. The only drawback was that each morning began with these gloomy soft showers. At least every morning until his very last in Ireland.

It was a beautiful spring day. The sun was shining brightly, like someone had opened a giant window in the sky. Paden was off racing in Paris. Bryson woke up early that morning feeling like something out of the ordinary was going to happen to him. Boy, was that ever an understatement.

The bees were buzzing. The birds were singing. Bryson had this compelling urge to run. He hadn't jogged any miles in over four weeks. He was getting a little restless to run again. In the middle of his run, he was approaching an old stone bridge, when he heard a woman screaming. He stopped but couldn't tell where the screams were coming from. He thought maybe the river, but wasn't sure. So he ran up to the bridge and stopped on it. The woman screamed again, but this time her scream sounded muffled and gargled, like water dancing on her vocal cords. He went to the bridge's edge and looked down and saw a woman waving her arms frantically above her head, as she bounced up and down in the water like a fishing bobber.

Bryson dove in and swam to her. He noticed right away that her foot was pinned beneath some big rocks, and that the current was moving swiftly, keeping her off balance to where she couldn't get enough leverage to free herself. He quickly freed her foot and dragged her to the safety of the shore. She wasn't breathing, so he performed CPR on her. After a minute of CPR, she finally spewed up a gallon of water and began breathing again. She opened her eyes and smiled. She thanked Bryson, and proceeded to explain how fate had brought them together, and how they were now *soul-matched*.

"Soul-matched? I'm sorry, but I'm not following you," wondered Bryson.

"*Soul-matched*. It means that my life will forever belong to you. It's an Irish custom," explained the young woman, as her sea-green eyes glowed beneath her fiery red hair.

Bryson stepped back, trying to gain his composure after being totally caught off guard. Then he smiled warmly, thinking maybe he didn't hear her correctly. "I'm sorry. What did you say? My ears must be full of water."

But before she could answer, a small group of people had gathered tightly around them. Then, Bryson's blood ran cold when a huge bearded man broke through the crowd demanding, "Where's me daughter?"

A small woman from the crowd gave the bearded man a detailed account of everything as it had occurred. Apparently she has seen the entire event from her back window. The bearded man came up to Bryson and put a big, hairy hand on his shoulder. In a voice like thunder, he told Bryson that his daughter was his to marry and that he would begin making wedding arrangements immediately. The crowd cheered. The redhead grabbed Bryson around the neck and kissed his cheek.

Everything was moving way too fast. Bryson told the bearded man that he was flattered about the offer and that his daughter was very lovely, but he couldn't marry her. Big mistake. The bloodshot look in the bearded man's bulking eyes told Bryson he was going to tear him from limb to limb. If not for the crowd intervening, he would have done so. Bryson explained to the bearded man that his soul was already matched, and there could never be another.

The crazed look in the bearded man's eyes had eased a little. Only a little. Then the crowd began chanting, "Three questions, three questions." The bearded man waved his big, hairy hands in the air. A deafening hush fell over the crowd. Then he turned toward Bryson and said, "Yank, if you can answer correctly three questions of my choosing, I will release you from your covenant engagement with me daughter."

"Yes, yes, sure," said Bryson, knowing that he probably couldn't answer one, let alone three. But what choice did he have except to try?

The bearded lifted one finger and asked, "What is the first thing I think of in the morning when I wake up?"

Bryson thought for a moment, and then answered, "What will I eat?"

"Correct," bellowed the bearded man with a heavy Irish dialect.

The bearded man held up two fingers. "How many wheelbarrow loads of sand does it take to line the entire seacoast of Ireland?"

Again Bryson thought for a moment, and then answered, "One, if the wheelbarrow is big enough."

"The luck of the Irish be with you today, Yank. But the third question nobody knows the answer but God Almighty and meself," declared the bearded man, holding up three fingers, indicating the third and final question. "How much am I worth?"

Again Bryson thought for a long moment before answering. The crowd was closing in around them until there was barely room to move. People began to congratulate the bearded man with pats on the back and handshakes. He was straightening his shoulders and blowing out his chest with pride of his victory that he knew was sure to come.

Finally, Bryson answered the question, "Twenty-nine pieces of silver."

The smile on the bearded man's face faded to a stern grin, as he slowly lowered his hands that were up in celebration of his victory.

"How do you come up with this fair amount?"

"Well, Jesus Christ was sold for thirty pieces of silver, and you can't be worth as much as Him."

"Well done, lad. You are free of your obligation to me daughter," stated the bearded man, as he extended his hand.

Bryson and the bearded man shook hands and parted ways.

Vick and Hoot sat motionless for a long minute, letting the tale soak into their minds. "Did this story really take place?" she asked jokingly, careful not to insult Bryson by insinuating he was lying.

Bryson's face turned to stone, remaining totally void of any emotion.

Vick began to apologize for asking but abruptly stopped.

Bryson grinned mischievously. "Hook, line, and sinker."

"Bryson Jonah Keahbone!" Vick roared, throwing her apron at the deceiver. "I'm going to kill you."

Bryson ducked and rolled off the couch as the flying apron hit Hoot square in the face. They laughed until their sides ached and tears rolled down their faces. Hoot pulled a handkerchief from his back pocket, offering it to Vick. She grabbed it and blew her nose. After a minute or two, the laughter had died down and they were able to talk again.

"Believe it or not, the story is true up to the point of 'soul matching.' The rest is Irish folklore. I did save a young woman from drowning. It happened just as I described except for the ending, which you must admit was pretty good."

They agreed amiably.

"Was she really beautiful?" Vick inquired.

"Yes. Very," Bryson replied.

"Did you ask her out?"

"No. She was engaged to a farmer."

"Have you been seeing anybody recently?" Vick asked, deciding to pry a little deeper while the atmosphere was light.

"No," Bryson answered, not really minding the questions at first, because he was going to have to answer them sooner or later. Right now, sooner was tolerable. "I haven't been on a date since the …"

"Do you think you'll ever date again?

"No. I don't know. Probably … probably not. Maybe when I'm ready," Bryson muttered, finding himself feeling exasperated with all these questions.

Hoot rose gingerly from his chair and began to walk behind the place where Bryson was sitting. He stopped momentarily at the fireplace, fidgeting with some objects on the mantel so not to attract attention to himself. He knew where Vick was heading with this line of questioning. He was sure this was not a good idea. He was working his way behind Bryson to gain her attention without him knowing it. Hoot was upset with himself for putting off telling Vick what had happened at school today.

"We have many beautiful women in our community," Vick stated.

Hoot had positioned himself directly behind Bryson and was waving his hands wildly and then pressed his right index finger to his lips in a jest for her to stop this line of talk.

"Hoot! What are you doing back there, swatting flies?"

Hoot stopped waving his arms just as Bryson turned around. "Yes ... there was ... this man-eating-dragon-moth thing, and I thought it was going to attack Bryson, so I'm trying to capture it."

"So where is it, Sir Hoot of the Square Table?"

"Where's what?"

"The man-eating-dragon-moth thing," Vick declared with raised eyebrows.

"Oh ... it must have escaped in all the excitement," Hoot said, returning to his chair, feeling the heated glare of Vick following his every step.

What has gotten into Hoot tonight? she asked herself and then answered it like she always did. *Hoot is Hoot. He is everybody's friend and nobody's enemy. You've got to love him because you're not going to change him.*

"As I was saying," she continued, still a little irked with Hoot. "We have many beautiful single women living in our community. There is one in particular I would like you to meet. I'm not saying for you to go out on a date immediately or anything like that, but I wish you would meet her. She's witty, intelligent, hardworking, and caring. You may have met her today, but I don't think so because Hoot would have told me," she decided, looking at Hoot, who had his head bowed down as if he was in prayer.

"I'm just n—" Bryson began.

"I know these past two years have been very rough on you," she interrupted. "Time is the best healer. But having someone to share the pain will sometimes help ease the pain. I'm not talking about simple friendship here, but something a lot deeper. You need someone who can be a friend, a companion, and perhaps a lover rolled up in a single package. I hope you don't mind, but I asked a friend to come over tonight. I know without a doubt you are going to like her. Her name is …"

Piper's Song

Piper Hitchcock did not notice the sign—Buffalo Valley, 5 miles—as she drove past it. Or how the full moon illuminated the countryside. Although the incident with the black dog with red glowing eyes had occurred only a few miles back (about the same time Bryson had begun his Irish tale), she had already put it out of her mind. Even the events that happened at school today were slowly becoming just another memory.

Piper prided herself on always being in *control.* When the black dog suddenly appeared in front of her car, she quickly gained control of the situation, acted upon it, and put it behind her. This was how she handled everything in her life—deal with it her way, then leave it in the past. She never dwelled on the past, so she would tell herself.

An image of Bryson emerged in her mind. She squeezed her eyes tight together, concentrating hard to make the image go away. *No! I don't want to think about him anymore.* She opened her eyes. The image was gone. She breathed a sigh of relief. She was in control. For now.

She reached down and turned the radio on, hoping it would keep her mind off—she didn't want to think about it but couldn't help it—*him.* She pushed the scan button on the radio. The first station scanned was a talk show. *Not in the mood.* She let the scan continue. The next two stations were country music; she passed them by too. She generally loved country music. *But tonight it would be too depressing*, she thought.

Piper was in the mood for—*yes, this is more like it.* She pushed the scan button to stop scanning. *A little southern rock and roll, but not too old, and none of that new wave stuff either.* She began singing along with Kings of Leon. "You know I can use somebody. Someone like you. Somebody. I've been running around, I was looking down and all I see …" The song faded out. There remained a few seconds of dead air on the radio.

Another song faded in. Piper recognized it immediately. It was a song from a different era that had once meant a lot to her. A song from a buried past. She lifted her hand toward the radio to change the station but stopped halfway when the soft melody of REO Speedwagon's "Keep on Loving You" sang out from the speakers. *It's just a song. A stupid song. It doesn't mean anything. I'm in control here. I'm in …* But as the song continued to play, her defensive barrier of control began to cave in.

Piper's thoughts drifted back to her college days when she was a young, self-determined, naïve freshman at Oklahoma University. She had finally gained control of her life and the path she would choose to live. But she never dreamed that her chosen path would be aboard the fast-moving roller coaster of life.

Piper had been playing softball in a coed league with the love of her life, or so she thought. His name was Darin. He was a law student who, in two weeks, was going to graduate. Third in his class. Afterward, he was going to work in his father's law firm.

It was a little after midnight. The parking lot at the university softball complex was empty except for Darin's red Corvette convertible. The top was down. They had been sitting in his car for an hour, talking about the future and listening to the radio. Piper wanted a commitment. Darin wanted loose reins on their relationship. She loved Darin with all her heart but refused to sleep with him until she was sure that he was the one she was going to spend the rest of her life with.

The conversation had died out between the two. Piper leaned back and looked up at the stars. She started to ask Darin to take her to the dorms when from the radio the deejay announced, "We have a special dedication for two love birds out there in fantasy land. Hey, Piper. Darin says, 'I am going to keep on loving you.' Piper, I think you have a real keeper here. You better not throw him back. Here's REO."

You should have seen by the look in my eyes, baby.

Tears filled Piper's eyes. "I love you, Darin." He smiled and hugged her over the console. She started to ask him how he managed to contact the radio station without her knowing it. But instead she asked, "Do you still have the blanket in the trunk?"

He nodded hesitantly, making sure he heard her right.

She opened her door. "Coming?"

Darin jerked the keys from the ignition; he wasn't waiting around to be asked twice. The car door was locked but instead of unlocking it, he climbed out and fell onto the ground. He half crawled and half walked back to the trunk. At the trunk, he fumbled through his keys to find the right one. After three tries, he heard the sweet sound—*click!* He whispered a short prayer, "Please still be in here." He opened the trunk lid—*Yes!*

Piper watched patiently, laughing silently at the act of the Three Stooges minus two.

Darin retrieved the blanket and followed Piper until she stopped beneath a large elm tree. Neither spoke a word. She took the blanket, spreading it out evenly upon the ground. They embraced hard and made passionate love into the early hours of morning. And in the first round, she conceived.

Thirty days later she broke the news to Darin. *A great graduation present.* To her surprise, he was elated. On the other hand, his parents were appalled by the news. Against their wishes, Darin and Piper planned to marry the following month. His parents accused her of being a gold digger and trapping Darin in their relationship by allowing herself to get pregnant. They swore never to acknowledge her and the unborn baby as family. His father stooped so low as to threaten to fire Darin if he went through with the wedding.

In spite of the numerous threats, they were married. Needless to say, Darin kept his job but had to pay for the wedding himself. The wedding was small. Most of the people who attended were close friends and Darin's family—except his mom and dad. Piper was adopted and had no real family to speak of. Her adopted parents were killed when she was young. She spent most of her teen years under foster supervision, bouncing from one foster home to another. She dreamed of the day when she would turn eighteen years old because she would be sole controller of her life. On the day before her eighteenth birthday, her dream came true. All the hard work and dedication during high school had finally paid off. She received a letter from Oklahoma University granting her a full academic scholarship.

After the wedding, Darin and Piper moved into a nice three-bedroom apartment. They didn't get a lot of visitors, and his parents refused to come over. Piper's relationship with her in-laws remained like the four winds. Some days were calm, but most days were like a typhoon.

Darin's father didn't talk about Piper and the marriage to his son. He dealt with it in other ways. He would send Darin away on a lot of needless business trips when the work could have been handled over the phone or fax machine. At first, Piper didn't mind; she liked the solitude. She kept herself busy preparing the baby's room by hanging wallpaper and shelves and painting doors and furniture. But she was becoming lonely. This was a job they should have shared together. It didn't seem to mean as much to her without Darin here to share in the experience. She greatly missed her husband.

At first, the business trips lasted two days. Now they have stretched from five to seven days. She refused to complain because she knew his work was important to him. She continued her studies at the university, burying herself in school work to help keep her mind off her loneliness.

Piper's due date was less than a week away, and her doctor was confident that she would go into labor long before that date arrived. She broke down and pleaded with Darin to postpone his trip until after the baby was born. He assured her that this particular trip was most essential to their future and guaranteed his immediate return if she was to go into labor. She gave in reluctantly.

The very night he left on his trip, she went into labor. Piper threw her bags on the passenger seat and drove herself to the hospital. She pulled up to the emergency room door and lay on the Corvette's horn. Two orderlies rushed outside to investigate. She waved them over to the car and informed them that she was very pregnant, stuck, and her water had just broken. After three minutes of careful pulling and tugging, they freed her.

Piper's labor was seventeen hours of pure hell. It was the most painful and lonely experience of her life. *If Darin is here, it would not have been as bad*, she thought. A nurse had contacted Darin at a number he had left at his office for emergencies. He told the nurse he was on his way home and would be there shortly.

He never showed up.

The baby was born the next day, early in the afternoon. It was an eight-pound, eleven-ounce boy. *He is the most beautiful thing in the world*, she thought, momentarily forgetting the terrible loneliness of not sharing the experience with the baby's father.

Late in the evening while the baby was in the nursery, Piper tried to call the same phone number the nurse had used earlier. But there was no answer. *Where can he be?* Postpartum depression was setting in. She felt like someone had set a two-hundred- pound weight on her chest. Her heart ached. She was short of breath. Her hormones were helter-skelter. She was slowly losing control and hated it. She needed desperately to rid herself of this prison cell.

The door to Piper's room opened slightly. She leaned forward smiling and then fell back in utter disappointment when she saw the doctor walk in. "Have you heard from my husband?"

The doctor shook his head. "He was probably delayed at the airport with all the new security regulations that have been imposed."

"When can I leave to go home?"

The doctor raised his brows. "As soon as we check you and the baby over. But what's your hurry?"

She shrugged her shoulders and looked away, fighting back the urge to bust out bawling.

"Is everything okay?" he asked sympathetically. "Would you like someone to talk to?"

"No. Everything's fine," she lied.

"I will be back in the morning. If everything checks out good, I will release you and the baby. We'll have you out of here by noon. But I wish you would consider staying another night."

"We'll see. Thank you, Doctor."

"Have the nurse page me if you need anything."

"I will."

The doctor walked to the door and turned around. "You did well today, young lady. See you in the morning."

"Thanks."

A nurse brought the baby in for feeding as the doctor departed. Piper relinquished a broad grin, letting go her blues for the moment, as she gazed for a minute or two at her new bundle of joy. The baby opened and closed his mouth repeatedly. "Oh, I'm sorry. You must be starving to death." Piper began to nurse her precious baby. The soreness quickly eased. She sighed in relief. *How could he not be here?* That was the question she wished she knew the answer to. Or did she?

The next morning the doctor signed the order to release Piper and her baby. She was still very weak and tired, but she didn't want to stay alone in this prison cell any longer than she had to. Darin hadn't called or showed up at the hospital. She called his emergency number again. Same results. Nothing. She was beginning to get worried. She wanted to call his parents. *Is it worth the heartache of being verbally slammed again?* She agonized over the dilemma. *Death would not be this painful.* She knew what she must do, but she would wait until she arrived home before she made the call.

Piper and the baby left the hospital shortly before noon. She made arrangements to pick up Darin's car in a few days. A nurse offered to give them a ride home, but Piper refused politely. Ten minutes later, a taxi arrived at the Emergency Room entrance doors. The driver loaded her bags in the trunk and drove them to their apartment.

During the ride, horrible thoughts were running through her mind. *What has happened to him? Why hasn't he called?* Her imagination began to run wild. *Darin's plane was hijacked, or worse—a plane crash! He was carjacked at the airport and left for dead at the terminal parking lot. A band of terrorists has kidnapped him. He flipped his company car in a ditch, where he's laying upside down and gasoline is gushing out all over the place. An angry client thought his fee was too high and decided to pay him with lead.* She ran through her mind every possible scenario that could have happened to Darin.

Except one.

The taxi driver carried Piper's bags to the front door. She handed him a twenty and told him to keep the change. He turned and stepped down, leaving her alone on the small porch. The loneliness she had grown to know so well was returning. *Where is he?* She glanced down at the sleeping baby boy, who seemed to radiate from beneath the soft blanket. She smiled warmly as tears slipped down her face. *I'm not alone. As long as I have you, I will never need anybody for all eternity.*

She pulled her keys from her purse and unlocked the door. The cool air from the air conditioner felt refreshing on her face as she walked in. She went straight to the answering machine. No messages. A sound from the back bedroom caught her attention. She walked cautiously toward the half-opened door. She used her free hand to push the door open. Stuck. A piece of clothing was pinned beneath the back edge of the door. She heard the sound again. It was giggling coming from the room. She kicked the door hard with her foot, causing it to fly open. The door handle smashed through the drywall.

Piper swayed on wobbly knees as she stood mesmerized in the doorway. Her heart fell from her chest. At first she wanted to cry. Then she became really angry. She had never felt so much hatred for any living thing as she did right then. If she would have had a gun in her purse or apartment, there would have been two less backdoor lovers.

Darin and his secretary had been playing sheet tag in the raw. They, in one swift motion, pulled the sheets up to their chins and sat goggle-eyed.

Piper tried to speak, but the words were locked to her tongue.

"Hi … uh … honey … what are … uh … you doing … home from the … uh … hospital … already?" Darin asked, cowering beneath the sheets, trying to escape the hate-filled eyes of his wife.

" I 'VE C OME T O GE T WHAT 'S MI NE, Y O U CHEATING BASTARD!" She walked to the side of the bed he was sitting. She moved the baby to her left side and cocked her right arm.

She released the trigger, hitting him as hard as she could muster on the chin. The impact knocked his head into his girlfriend's mouth, breaking her $4,000 bridge work he had bought.

Piper abruptly turned and ran out of the apartment. She decided right now wasn't a good time to get her belongings.

She didn't know where she would go. She just knew she had to leave fast.

"I just want to keep on loving you."

The song faded. Piper clicked the radio off and shook her head. *Why do people say things they don't mean? Why can't people be on the up-and-up? Why lie and hurt people? Why?*

Buffalo Valley—next right. She braked lightly and turned north. About two miles later she made another right and crossed a cattle guard. The same cattle guard Bryson had passed over twenty minutes earlier.

Her mind was still on Darin. Tonight was the first time in months she had thought about him. *Do I regret leaving Darin fourteen years ago? Yes and no. I regret that my son has no father figure in his life, but if his father is going to be a lying, cheating, sorry son-of—STOP. Stop thinking about it. You're going to give yourself a migraine. He is part of a buried past that will remain buried.* Piper took a deep breath and counted to ten. Better. Much better. *I am in control.* The pressure was easing.

Piper saw the soft lights of Vick's house as she approached. She couldn't wait to see them. They were truly good friends. She felt deplorable for her actions toward Hoot earlier at school. *Hoot means well. That's why Vick called me over tonight. Hoot told her everything that had happened today and wants to patch things up between us,* she rationalized in her mind. She grinned, feeling pleased with her brilliant deductions.

But these brilliant deductions were short-lived.

As Piper passed the last grove of trees, her mouth dropped open in shock. She couldn't believe it. She closed her mouth. Maybe she was mistaken. *No—there it is.* Plain as the beauty mark on her lip. *His Jeep. Mr. Miami-Vice-Wannabe. He's probably in there right now wearing a white sports jacket and sipping Margaritas.*

What is he doing here?

Piper stopped the vehicle. She gasped. "Oh no." She raised her hand to cover her eyes. "Hoot invited him for dinner. I totally forgot. I'm such an idiot."

She paused for a moment, thinking about her next move. *Okay, I'm in control here. What am I going to do? No, I can't do that. They probably saw my headlights when I arrived. I have to go in. I have to face this. NOW.* She parked the Explorer on the other side of the driveway as far away from Bryson's Jeep as she could get.

Piper reached up and turned the rearview mirror toward her. She ran her fingers through her hair. Her palms were clammy. She unconsciously wiped them on her pants. *I am going to go in there and be on my best behavior. I will be polite—regardless. I'm in control. What happened today is water under the bridge. For the sake of my friendship with Hoot and Vick, there will not be a scene. I'm in control.*

The car door shut noiselessly behind her. Piper walked slowly up the sidewalk. She stopped when she heard a ruffling noise in the hedge next to the porch. The noise got louder as the bush began to shake. She leaned forward for a better look, and suddenly a cat leaped from the hedge chasing a sparrow that had been nesting in the bush. Piper jumped back and let out a small scream. Embarrassed, she looked toward the porch to see if anyone was watching. No one there. *Good!* Through the window she saw Hoot waving his arms wildly over his head. At first, she thought he was waving at her, but then saw that his back was facing her. *Must be telling another one of his tall tales*, she thought. *I must admit they are usually very entertaining.* She climbed the steps at a pace a turtle could beat. She peeked in the window. Hoot had returned to his favorite chair. Vick was beside him. *Where is Mr. Bryson Keahbone?* She cringed a little at the thought of his name. She began to turn around to leave when a powerful voice inside her screamed. *No! You are not going to leave because of this man. You are in control!*

Piper walked hastily across the porch to the front door. She stopped to ring the bell. *I haven't rung this doorbell since I've known Hoot and Vick, and I'm not going to start now.* She turned the knob and swiftly pushed the door open. She was totally caught off guard when Vick seemingly announced, "Piper Hitchcock."

Piper froze in the doorway.

Bryson turned his head toward the door and abruptly stood up.

For five or six seconds, time ceased to exist as they awkwardly stared at each other. Bryson broke the trance and turned toward Vick. "I'm just not ready." He walked to the front door and stopped. Piper stepped aside. He half-glanced at her and then looked at Vick. "And I don't know if I will ever be ready." He exited through the doorway, walking briskly down the porch, leaping over the railing at the end.

Hoot and Vick promptly stepped out on to the porch, but it was too late. Bryson had already backed out and was heading down the gravel road. "What have I done? I was only trying to help, Hoot," Vick sobbed.

"I know you were. But it's going to take time. You must let Bryson work it out in his time. Whatever is meant to be will be. You cannot force it to happen. It will simply happen."

Vick turned toward the doorway where Piper now stood. "I'm truly sorry. I hope I didn't embarrass you." They walked to each other and embraced.

"It's okay, Vick. Believe me there was no harm done. Besides, you know me. I'm as hard as a rock," Piper said. But deep down she wasn't convinced.

As the women embraced again, Hoot watched Bryson's Jeep disappear around the grove of trees.

Bryson drove about a mile down the valley road before stopping in a patch of moonlight. He turned the lights off and killed the motor. He sat for a while, debating with himself whether to go back to Vick's or go home. *I know that Vick is only trying to help. But why, of all people, did it have to be her? This is my first*

day back. I was hoping to spend it with only my close friends. I'm not ready. Bryson tightly closed his eyes, leaning his head back gently until it came to rest on the seat. Visions of Becky, his mother, and father suddenly appeared in his mind. And then disappeared as fast. But his father's words remained: *When time is time upon the final scene, you must come find me beneath the Moon When Wolves Cry.*

Bryson gazed into the freckled darkness. Above in the purple night, a full moon illuminated the land below. *What moon in the sky is this that hangs before me?*

Running Moon

The bright yellow moon was still low in the sky, casting long shadows upon the land. A huge figure walked briskly toward a small wooden shed. A weak light broke through cracks of the planks of wood. Whimpering drifted through the cracks as well. The door creaked slowly open. A mountainous man filled the doorway. A rush of wind from the opened door caused the drop light to sway back and forth briefly exposing the hardened face of Nate Monger. A long, narrow scar streamed down from above his left brow over a cloudy eye coming to rest upon his chin. He stood silently with a large leather-bound book tucked under his arm in his left hand.

The whimpering had turned to soft sobbing. "Why am I he-e-re? Why are you doing this to … to me?" A young man in his twenties was curled up in a ball like an unborn embryo crying uncontrollably. His hands were bound in front with zip ties. His clothes were torn and mud-caked. His feet were white and bare. He sat up a little but remained in the fetal position. "What are you going to do with me?"

"You have been chosen," Nate declared as he stepped into the shed bending over slightly so not to hit his head. The light continued to sway. Nate's face faded, coming in and out of focus. A demented grin formed on his face.

"Chosen for what?" the young man cried as yellow stuff streamed down his legs. "I want to go home, mister. I promise I won't tell nobody nothing. Please, just let me go. Please!"

"You will have an opportunity to earn your freedom. No strings attached."

"How?"

"You have been chosen to participate in the Running Moon. A chance for immortality. A chance to do what no other has ever done before," Nate declared, grimacing a little when the thought of the bronze man entered his mind. Even after twenty years, the thought of the bronze man still haunted his existence and turned his stomach into knots. He started to become angry when Dewey Monger's agonizing face of horror entered his mind. *May that Injun's soul rot in hell.*

"I … don't understand," the man moaned.

"The rules are simple. You will be taken to a starting point and then released. You will be given an eleven-minute and six-second head start. You will be hunted. If you are not captured by daybreak, then you are released—freed to go about your business—no questions asked," Nate informed.

"Why me? I haven't done anything to you."

"Why not you? You're a vagabond. Road trash. Probably a drug dealer."

"No, mister. Please! I'm on my way home from college in Durant. My car broke down in McAlester, and I was hitchhiking home. I live in Heavener. The sheriff picked me up. I wasn't doing anything wrong. My parents are on a cruise, and there wasn't anybody to come get me. Please, mister. I promise I won't tell a soul. I swear," the young man pleaded.

Nate's face was expressionless, and then his lips turned up into a wicked grin. "You have been chosen. Time is time upon this scene. The Running Moon is climbing into the sky."

He held out the book that was under his arm. Nate opened the book to a ragged-edge page marked by a black ribbon three-fourths of the way through. There were several names on the milky page all written in red. "You must sign the *Book of the Running Moon*."

"No!"

"Wrong answer," Nate replied as he pulled his nine millimeter Barrett from a hip holster and shot off the top half of the man's left ear. Blood shot out through the man's fingers as he covered the remaining part of his ear.

The young man fell to ground screaming. "I'll sign! I'll sign! Please don't shoot again!"

Nate removed a knife from its sheath and made a small cut on the inside right palm of the young man. The blood dripped freely into a small tin cup that Nate held beneath. He cut the zip ties and then pulled a fountain pen from his shirt pocket and handed it to the young man.

His hand was shaking uncontrollably. "I don't know if I can …"

"Sign," Nate ordered as he grabbed the young man's hand, placing the pen between his fingers and then dipping the pen into the tin can of blood. The forked end of the fountain pen soaked up a small portion of the blood. He opened the old book and pointed to the place that needed to be signed.

The young man signed with a trembling hand. Ethan was barely legible.

Nate smiled. He took the pen and placed it back in his pocket. He blew on the signature to dry it and then gently closed the book, caressing the book's side like it was an infant.

"Young Ethan. Time is time upon this final scene," Nate stated as he pulled Ethan to his feet, dragging him through the door of the shed.

"*No!*" Ethan screamed as he broke free from Nate's grip. He darted down a dirt road. He had barely made it a hundred yards when a car was coming toward him with flashing lights on top. "Thank God! Thank God!" He sprinted toward the police car and fell panting on the hood. "Help me! Please help me! There's a psychopath trying to kill me!"

The police officer opened the door quickly and jumped out of the car. His face was hidden beneath the shadow of his hat.

"Arrest him, Officer! He's over there!" Ethan pointed down the empty dirt road.

"Over where?" the policeman asked as he looked down the dirt road. Then he turned slowly toward Ethan. "Well ... we might just have a problem here. You see that psychopath happens to be my daddy." Tyrel Monger smiled as he removed his hat.

Ethan recognized Tyrel immediately as the sheriff who picked him up on the highway. He had begun to cry again as he collapsed to the ground. Tyrel grabbed him under his armpits and dragged him to the police car. Nate walked up as Tyrel opened the trunk. Without speaking a word, Nate grabbed his feet as Tyrel held on to the armpits and in a single, swift motion they heaved him into the trunk and shut the lid.

"You have three minutes to get him to the starting line. I will see you in the field. You will be with me at Trosper's Point," Nate ordered.

Tyrel started to say something he might regret later but changed his mind. "Yes, sir. I will be there. Always."

"You better," Nate boomed, as he turned and walked away.

Tyrel swore under his breath as he got in his squad car and drove toward the starting location of the Running Moon.

The starting line was located on the top of a high hill. It was marked with two metal poles with a sized-down flare mounted on each. The flares were trimmed down to burn exactly eleven minutes and six seconds. The prey was standing weak-kneed between the poles, wobbling back and forth. He was blowing snot bubbles with each whimper. He couldn't keep his eyes off a green tarp that appeared to cover several crates. There were strange sounds and movement coming from beneath the tarp.

"You'll be introduced soon enough," Tyrel informed as he pulled a BIC lighter from his shirt pocket and held the flame against the first flare. "When the flares burn out you will become well acquainted with my friends."

Tyrel removed the tarp revealing six crazed beasts, ripping and biting the iron gates. The crates were rocking almost to the point of tipping over.

One black beast did not move. Only grinned.

Ethan was held mesmerized by the glowing red eyes of the jet-black beast. He noticed an hourglass shape on the beast's chest.

Timer.

"The clock is ticking. You are wasting time."

Ethan broke the trance and staggered past the starting line. He glanced back over his shoulder at Timer, who was still grinning, and then he stumbled down the hill in a sort of half-trot.

"Patience, my children. It is almost time to feed."

Trosper's Point had become the main headquarters for each hunt during the Running Moon. Since the near escape of the bronze man, Nate had purchased the very best of every possible surveillance equipment that money could buy, ranging from infrared body-heat sensory night vision cameras to hundreds of ultrasound motion detectors placed strategically so before the prey left one area, another detector had already picked him up. A prey was tracked from the moment it started on the hill to the time it was caught.

Tyrel walked up to the tent where the equipment was stored. Nate and Billy Ray were monitoring the screens. The prey was about a mile away from the starting line when Tyrel had released the pit bulls. There were six bulls bearing down on the prey.

"This won't take long. The prey is heading toward Blue Ridge. He'll be overtaken before he can get halfway up. Another disappointment. Just like you, Tyrel. Why don't you get us a *real* prey to run? You got garbage duty tonight. You understand?" Nate shouted.

"But it's not my turn. It's Billy Ray's," Tyrel claimed.

Billy Ray had moved behind Nate and was making teasing faces at Tyrel.

"Are you back talking me, Tyrel?"

"No, sir."

"I suggest you find us a worthy opponent or you will forever be on garbage duty. You have thirty days before the next full moon. Don't be another disappointment. Billy Ray, come over here and see this," Nate declared as he pointed to one of the radar screens.

The screen showed a single white dot, and then suddenly six red dots appeared at the bottom moving toward the white dot. Their formation looked like the first six pins in a bowling pin rack. Then they broke rank and circled the white dot and slowly closed the circle until it looked like one big red dot with a white in the middle. And then the white dot turned to red and disappeared.

Nate looked at his watch. "Fourteen minutes. You will do better next time, or you will be the one running."

Billy Ray winked teasingly at Tyrel.

Tyrel wanted to attack his brother at that moment, but he knew he could get even with Billy Ray in other ways. Billy Ray was Tyrel's deputy. Tyrel set Billy Ray's work schedule. *Two weeks of graveyard shift ought to do.* Tyrel smiled.

"Billy Ray, what's taken so long? I'm ready to go a-huntin'," Jake proclaimed as he walked up to the tent. He was wearing a camouflage shirt, a green Bass Pro hat, and a pair of faded blue overalls, which sported a set of holes in each knee. He had a SpongeBob backpack on alongside his wooden rubber band gun strapped to his shoulder. When he smiled, he exposed a gap between his teeth, a gap given to him by his favorite brother, Billy Ray.

"Let's go, Billy Ray," Jake said impatiently. "Com'on."

Jake looked like an oversized kid with his hands shoved down in his pockets. He had a big grin on his face like a young boy waiting eagerly to ride for the first time one of those rides at a small town carnival. He removed his hands and waved frantically for Billy Ray to hurry out of the tent.

Tyrel leaned toward Billy Ray and whispered in a small, still voice. "You mustn't keep your clone waiting."

Billy Ray fumed when he heard the words and stared angrily at Tyrel. He hated the fact that every run, he was forced to let Jake tag along.

"You three go find the downed prey. I'll stay here and man the post. Call Jim Bob and Skeeter and tell them that they won't be needed tonight. The celebration begins in one hour. Don't be late. Billy Ray, you get honors. Tyrel, I heard what you said about Jake. And you won't say it again," Nate commanded. He walked back to the radar screens.

"Yes, sir," Billy Ray replied.

"Yes, sir," Tyrel echoed with less enthusiasm.

"Goody," Jake chuckled as he bolted from the tent, skipping to Billy Ray's squad car. He tried to crawl into the back seat but his wooden gun kept getting caught on the top part of the car. He kept jerking back and forth, hitting his head on the entry way. "This stupid car keeps gettin' smaller, Billy Ray. You need a new car. I hate this car."

Jake removed his wooden gun and started hitting the top of the squad car. Billy Ray screamed for Jake to stop and then grabbed his gun and broke it in half over his knee. Jake exploded in tears.

"How am I goin' to shoot the prey now, Billy Ray? You broke my gun in 'alf!" Jake wailed.

"Shudup! You're not going to shoot anything. The prey's already dead!" Billy Ray yelled. "I'll make you another one. That's only the millionth one I've broken."

"Promise?" Jake blubbered as he sank into the back seat.

"Yeah, sure. Whatever."

"Look, Billy Ray, I can fit now. It's arright. I can fit now. I'm ready. Let's go," Jake said as he slammed the car door.

"I'm taking my car. My stomach won't take riding with the two of yous," Tyrel pointed out.

"Good idea, Tyrel. You're goin' to need your car for garbage duty," Billy Ray jeered.

Tyrel slammed his car door, pretending not to have heard Billy Ray's last comments. He sped out ahead of Billy Ray and arrived first at the scene of slaughter ten minutes later.

Tyrel got out of his car and went straight to the trunk and opened it. He removed a large black canvas bag. It was a body bag he had stolen from the county morgue. He put on a pair of elbow-length latex gloves. He looked around for the bulls, but they had fed quickly and were probably on their way back to the holding pens, he thought. He knew the remains would be scattered everywhere. The first part he found was a left arm. Not much meat left. Same for the two legs. The bulls had pretty much picked clean anything that was edible on the body. There were large teeth marks in each bone that was found. *Here's what's left of the torso. At least the body won't be too heavy for me to throw into the pit.*

Billy Ray drove by slowly with his window down. "Havin' fun yet?"

Tyrel had just found the head. A great idea to give Billy Ray a start had formulated in Tyrel's mind. He picked the bloody head up by the hair and threw it through the open window, landing in the lap of Billy Ray. "Here's your honors, Billy Ray."

But Tyrel didn't get the reaction he had hoped.

Billy Ray smiled and picked up his six inch hunting knife that had been lying on the seat beside him. He lifted the head and quickly removed the top half of the scalp. He held the head in his palm and then hooked shot it back to Tyrel. "You don't want to forget this."

Tyrel dropped the head into the bag and hissed, "I will get you back, my dear brother. Vengeance will be mine." Billy Ray laughed as he drove away.

"Can I have it?" Jake asked from the back seat.

"It's yours, little bro," Billy Ray replied as he tossed the scalp toward Jake's direction.

"Thank you. You're the best. But, Billy Ray, Tyrel sure was mad. You know how he gets when he's mad. I don't want to be anywhere around him when he's mad like this."

"Don't be scared. He'll calm down by tomorrow. You'll see. Everything will be okay," Billy Ray lied, knowing full well that he had opened up a can of sour worms.

The confusing thing for Billy Ray was he didn't know why he had challenged his brother to begin with. Maybe it was because he was tired of taking orders day in and day out. *It's time I step up and make some decisions on my own. I don't want to be my brother's shadow or my daddy's for that matter. And I'm tired of taking care of that idiot in the back seat. I'm not running a daycare. Let someone else look after him.*

"You're the best, Billy Ray. You're the best, the best," Jake repeated several times as he combed Ethan's scalp, which he had placed on top of a teddy bear he had pulled from his backpack.

Billy Ray watched his brother in the rearview mirror. Anger and hatred swelled up inside. Anger and hatred of himself. *I must not be weak like my brother Jake. I must be strong. Survival of the fittest. I must carry on for my daddy. There is no room for weakness. That's why Daddy makes me watch out for Jake because I'm the strongest in my family. I am the greatest. I will smooth things over with Tyrel at the celebration tonight.*

But Tyrel had other plans in mind.

School—Day One

Bryson showed up at a quarter till seven, hoping to beat Hitchcock, but she was already there. He parked his Jeep three spaces down from her Explorer although there wasn't another car in the parking lot. He didn't want to get too close. *A little childish*, he thought but suddenly shrugged it off.

When Bryson arrived at the principal's office, it was empty. The secretary didn't have to be at work until 7:45 a.m. Bryson knocked on the opened door.

"Hello. Is anyone here?"

"Yes. In my office."

Bryson walked around Ms. Betz's desk and entered Hitchcock's office. She was sitting at her computer typing a memo for the after-school staff meeting.

"You wanted to see me at seven a.m.?" Bryson asked matter-of-factly. He glanced at the wall clock—6:50 a.m.

"Yes. Have a seat," Hitchcock responded dryly, never looking up from her computer.

Bryson sat down.

"You're early," she stated more to herself than to him.

"Well …" Bryson was going to say something conjecturally but stopped. He wasn't going to let her spoil his day.

A few long moments passed before Ms. Hitchcock glanced up at Bryson. She was going to take her time. She was in charge and wanted to make sure he knew it. But those moments of control quickly faded. She couldn't help herself. Her eyes had gone from Bryson, back to the screen, back to Bryson. A double-look. *Is this the same man who Hoot Brown had hired more or less against my will? It can't be.*

Bryson Keahbone was wearing a pair of khaki slacks, a light-blue shirt (which made his eyes glow, she thought), a pastel tie, Doc Martens, and a tweed sports jacket. He had shaved, exposing a dimpled chin and high cheek bones. His jet-black hair was trimmed and tapered on the sides and back. He combed the longer hair on top straight back except for a few strains that fell across his forehead.

Piper felt a strong attraction toward Bryson. But the infatuation was very short lived. Her wall of protection had quickly come up like Sulu raising the force field around the USS Enterprise on Star Trek when the Klingons were about to attack. She rolled away from her computer and removed her glasses from her nose as she moved back to her desk.

"Mr. Keahbone, I'm glad to see you made it on time. You will be in room 35. Your lesson plan and record books are right here. I expect these to be updated weekly. There is a mandatory staff meeting after school today at three thirty sharp. Do you have any questions?" She handed Bryson two, thin green books.

"Not at this point."

"There is one more thing. Every new teacher on my staff, whether a veteran or entry year, must be evaluated by me at least three times a school year. I will not give you a notice. I will simply pop in and sit quietly in the back. This afternoon I will be conducting your first evaluation," Ms. Hitchcock informed.

"I haven't scheduled too much for today's lessons—rules, procedures, expectations, and simply getting acquainted with the students—you know, feeling out their interests."

"Perfect. I hope you enjoy your first day here," Hitchcock said, trying to sound sincere, but Bryson could tell she was anything but sincere.

"I have been looking forward to it," Bryson said as he stood up and walked toward the doorway. He half-turned. "By the way, thank you."

Piper looked puzzled. "For?"

"The warning about this afternoon's evaluation. Thanks again, Ms. Hitchcock. I'm sure this is going to be a most memorable day."

"Good day, Mr. Keahbone," Ms. Hitchcock fumed, trying really hard not to show any emotion. *I'm in control.*

The school day was pretty much uneventful up until lunch anyway. The other staff members were very helpful on the ins and outs of the teacher's duties and procedures. Bryson had spent most of the morning class periods going over the rules and classroom expectations, what genre would be covered in class, what would not be covered, and what the students might want to cover.

The lunch room was small. There were three rows of cafeteria tables with three double seats in each row. The students would eat according to their grade. The classes would rotate each week. The freshmen were scheduled to eat first this week. After they ate, they went outside to a common area for a short recess. Some played hacky sack, others chased each other around, some played catch with whatever was in season, but most of them just stood around and talked. The hot topic was the new English teacher, Bryson Keahbone. The word was out that he had already butted heads with Ms. Hitchcock. When the bell rang, Bryson would take them to their next class, which was his ninth grade literature class. They had five minutes to get to their lockers, get their stuff, and then get to class.

It was fifth hour. The other teachers had warned Bryson that this class period was the worst one out of all the other class periods. The students were wired after being outside on lunch recess. They told him he would be lucky if he got them settled down at all by the end of class.

This was also the class period that Ms. Hitchcock decided to do her evaluation. He had forgotten about the evaluation. She was already sitting in the back row with the evaluation form on her desk, writing down information about the classroom setting.

The tardy bell echoed down the empty hall.

Bryson walked through the door. He sat his briefcase on the seat part of a student's desk and went to the chalkboard. A young man reached forward to look in Bryson's bag. "I wouldn't do that pilgrim if I were you. There may be a rattlesnake itching to bite someone in there," Bryson declared using his John Wayne voice.

The class erupted in laughter as the young man hurriedly pulled his hand away from the briefcase and fell out of his desk onto the floor landing flat on his back. His face turned tomato red. He abruptly picked his stocky frame up off the floor. He was wearing camouflaged pants and a black tee shirt that had a large skull print with a pair of wings coming out each side where ears should have been located. The skull was wearing a big top hat with the ace of spades tucked inside the band. The words "Born Loser" were beneath the skull. He looked around and shouted, "Shudup!"

But the class just laughed louder. The young man lunged toward a boy sitting in the next row. "We'll see whose laughing tomorrow at recess."

"Okay, okay. That's enough. We've had enough fun at the expense of this young man. What is your name?"

The young man didn't answer. He stood up and moved angrily to the back and sat at the opposite end of the room from Ms. Hitchcock. His hands were balled in white fists.

"My name is Mr. Keahbone. This is Freshman English Comp. If you are in the wrong class, you have my permission to leave. No takers, then forever hold your peace. You're in for the long haul. Allow me to take roll then, we'll get started with our lesson."

Bryson pulled a green roll book from his briefcase.

"Alexander, Lori."

"Here."

"Atencio, Rocky."

"Yo."

"Atwood, Jeremy."

"Present."

He continued down the list.

"Mackey, Rick."

"Here."

"Monger, Rubin … Is Rubin Monger here?" Bryson paused.

That strange, uneasy feeling began to creep over Bryson when he heard the name Monger. It's the same restlessness he felt at Vicki's house a few days before. It was like he was reliving a dream he had or someone else had had, and he was now a living and breathing part of it.

What is with this name? Why is it so significant to me? Why?

The feeling quickly passed when a voice from the back blurted out, "It's Mr. Monger to you, Peebone." It was the young man who had fallen out of his chair.

Bryson smiled. He knew he was being tested by this young man. He had embarrassed him, and now Rubin was trying to save face. "Fair enough. But if I am to respect your name, then in turn you must respect my name, Mr. Monger."

Rubin Monger didn't reply. He just stared back at Bryson.

Bryson smiled and continued with roll call. After he had called the last name on the roll, he put the roll book back in the briefcase and walked around and sat on top of the teacher's desk. "Before I tell you about myself, let's talk about the rules and procedures of this classroom," Bryson charged as he pointed to a laminated poster with a list of the classroom rules located on a bulletin board behind the teacher's desk. Bryson briefly went through each rule and then asked if there were any questions. "Yeah. When's this class over I'm bored?" Rubin chuckled, but no one else laughed.

"Soon enough, Mr. Monger. I know this stuff is kind of boring, and I apologize, but it needs to be addressed. I want you to know what I expect from you, as well as what you can expect from me. One more thing, and then we'll move into our lesson. I have high expectations for you in this classroom. This classroom will not be a place where you come to listen to lengthy lectures that will bore you to tears, nor will I smother you in a mile-deep stack of worksheets. This classroom is a place we can be responsible for each other and a place to gain knowledge. The classroom is a place to become successful. You will dictate the direction this class will take. If you want to spend a lot of time studying Shakespeare, we will. If you want to do a lot of creative writing and poetry, I'm game for it also."

Several students moaned when the words "creative writing" and "poetry" were mentioned.

"Poetry is cool," a young man sitting in the front row closest to the window declared.

"Whatta geek. Poetry is for girls. You must be a girl, Landry," Rubin howled, this time the whole class laughed.

Bryson held up his hand for the class to settle down and then replied, "On the contrary, Mr. Monger. What this young man said is correct. Poetry is cool. What's your name?"

"Jared … Jared Landry."

"I agree wholeheartedly with you, Mr. Landry. Poetry is an awesome way to express one's personal feelings. Poetry is powerful. It's *emotionally charged writing*. You can say a whole lot of cool things by using a few words." Bryson glanced back at Ms. Hitchcock and caught her staring at him. "I am one who does not like to talk, but through poetry, I am given the opportunity to express myself."

Caught off guard, she quickly looked down at Bryson's evaluation form and pretended to study it. *Maybe I prejudged Mr. Keahbone—a little.*

Bryson walked to the chalkboard and wrote—

Life is not a destination.
Life is a journey.
As long as you continue the journey,
You will always be a success.

—French philosopher, Albert Camus

"Your journey begins today. Work hard and do your best in whatever task you are undertaking. I ask nothing short of your best. Any questions?"

"How much time now?" Rubin asked.

"Close—fifteen minutes," Bryson stated patiently. "Mr. Landry, we will be writing a lot of poetry in this class. Matter of fact, our first assignment today is for you to get pencil and paper out and write a list poem stating the top ten things that are most important in your life. It can be a person, a task, a place, a hobby, or your personal inspiration … whatever you want it to be. For example, I will read a few off my top ten list." Bryson pulled a sheet of paper from his briefcase and continued, "Number ten—be a lighthouse to my students, number nine—be the first to say 'hello,' number eight—go for a long run. I will read some more of mine if there is time at the end of class. You have ten minutes to complete your list, and then I will ask some of you to share. Any questions?"

Everyone started writing their top ten list, even Rubin Monger.

"At the top of your paper you will title your top ten—*Raison d'être*. It is French for *reason to be*. I want to know your *reason to be*."

Ms. Hitchcock was impressed. As bad as she hated to admit it, Mr. Keahbone was pretty good. All the students were dialed in and on task. Even Rubin Monger, every teacher's nightmare, was working. She had personally picked Rubin to be in Bryson's class. Her plan didn't work, but she liked the outcome just the same.

The students spent the next ten minutes working on their list. Some finished early and were sharing with other students. There was giggling in the back.

"Who would like to share first?"

No one raised their hand. Then there was some more giggling.

"Landry would. He's the poet who didn't know it," Rubin Monger announced.

"Jared?"

"Not really."

"Are you sure?"

But before Jared could answer, Rubin had the classroom chanting, "Ja-red, Ja-red, Ja-red."

Bryson grinned and raised his hand. The class fell silent. He hadn't noticed that Ms. Hitchcock had suddenly become very uncomfortable with the situation. Jared was looking down at his paper.

"You only share if you want to share. Nobody will ever be forced to read their writing unless they agree to read it."

"C'mon, chicken," Rubin taunted and then made a clucking noise. "I'm not scared. I'll read mine. Number ten—hunt, number nine—hunt, number eight—hunt, number seven—hunt, number six—hunt, number five—hunt, number four—hunt, number three—hunt, number two—hunt, and number uno— running moon. Yeow! That's what I'm talking about."

The students laughed.

"I like your enthusiasm. Let me guess what your *raison d'être* is ... hunting. But is there anything else that might be important to you?"

"There ain't nothing else better than the hunt," Rubin said, sounding very psychotic. His granddaddy would be proud.

"C'mon, Jared, read yours. It's cute," Sasha Jo said, a very attractive auburn-haired, brown-eyed girl who was sitting in a desk beside Jared.

After hesitating for a few moments, Jared stood up and read his list. "Number ten—be grateful for everything I have; number nine—refill the ice trays; number eight—have a firm handshake, number seven—look people in the eyes when talking to them, ... number two—give God the praise and glory for everything, and number one ..." Jared paused for he knew what was coming when he read the phrase. "My number one *raison d'être* is my mother."

The classroom erupted in laughter. Jared deflated himself in his seat.

Hitchcock eased out of her chair and then stopped. *I must not interfere. He must work out his own problems. I must not interfere.*

Bryson lifted his hands and waved them to indicate to the students that it was time for them to settle down.

"Momma's boy! Momma's boy!" Rubin chanted.

I must not interfere. Piper repeated several times. Tears were forming in her eyes. She couldn't let anyone see. She was very proud of her son but also very protective. Maybe too protective. Jared Landry was her son. Her only son. She let Jared keep his father's last name although he had absolutely nothing to do with Jared. Darin Landry had since remarried and now has two children with a different woman. The same woman who lost a few teeth when Piper caught her sleeping with her ex-husband.

Again Bryson lifted his hands for them to be quiet. This time, they began to settle down. Rubin had fallen out of his seat and had curled up in a ball laughing hysterically until tears were streaming down his face. "Wait until I tell the boys."

I must save him. I must—

"That's good stuff, Jared," Bryson pointed out. "It takes a big man who is in control of his feelings to write such a bold statement. Mothers are the greatest. None of us would be here without one. *Dang* good stuff. I'll be honest with you, I was about to read you my number one, but I don't know now. It pales in comparison to this."

Ms. Hitchcock had quickly wiped the tears away before anyone noticed. *Thank you, Bryson Keahbone.* She knew she wouldn't be able to say it to his face, not right now anyway.

"You have to read yours. Jared read his number one, you have to read yours," Sasha Jo coaxed, using the same charming voice she had used earlier on Jared. Then others chimed in with her.

"Okay, okay. But it's not going to be anything near as good as Jared's."

The class listened intently as Bryson read his number one. "My number one—'dare I eat a peach?'"

He saw the dumbfounded look on their faces. They didn't even know how to respond to the statement.

Bryson smirked and repeated it again, "Dare I eat a peach?"

The bell sounded, announcing the end of the class period.

"What does it mean? You have to tell us before we leave," Jeremy Atwood demanded.

"C'mon, Mr. Keahbone. What does it mean?" David Barker echoed.

"Nope. Extra credit. I want you to tell me what it means by tomorrow. Have a great day."

The students packed up their books and things and left the room. All except Jared. He took his time on purpose so he could talk to Bryson alone.

"Thank you."

"For what?" Bryson asked.

"Saving me from the lynch mob."

"I did no such thing. I just broaden their awareness of what an awesome number one you had written. We all have deep feelings for our mothers. It's a bonding issue from birth, I suppose. It's really hard for a lot of people to express these feelings. Even me."

"Thanks, anyway."

"You're welcome, anyway." Bryson winked.

Jared grinned and exited the classroom. He walked past the principal-mother without saying a word but did manage a quick smile as he went by. Bryson had been shoveling books and papers in his briefcase and didn't notice Principal Hitchcock standing by his desk.

"Hmmmmm."

"Sorry. I didn't see you standing there. I was kind of lost in thought."

"Your mannerism and lesson today were interesting. Unfortunately I was unable to complete your evaluation. Therefore I will be back tomorrow as well."

"Wonderful."

Lone Wolf

B ryson felt very tired on his drive home after school. His ankles were sore from standing all day. The feeling of tiredness was bittersweet. He enjoyed being in the classroom again. He loved working with students.

The road to his house was still in very poor driving condition. Hoot had talked to his good friend, the county commissioner, and he assured Bryson that the road to the cabin would be graded before the end of the month. The service also included trimming back the trees and getting the power lines serviced for use.

He arrived at the old iron gate about twenty-five minutes after he had left school. He climbed out of the Jeep and removed a pair of bolt cutters from the back. The rusty lock was no match for the three-foot-long bolt cutters. He swung the gates open and tied them against the fence on either side of the heavily overgrown road. He climbed back into his Jeep and drove down the middle of the valley. Something caught his eye by the big oak where Bryson's mother, Katherine Abigail Keahbone, was buried. He steered the Jeep in the general direction of the tree. The grass was very high and made driving very hazardous and slow.

There it is again. It's some kind of furry creature. I'm not sure what it is.

He pulled the Jeep up to the front of the broken-down cabin. Instead of climbing out of the Jeep, he stood up on the driver's seat for a better look at the creature. The sun had gone down behind the hills, casting long shadows in the shade of the trees. Whatever it was had disappeared in the high grass around the area of his mother's grave. He would have to get out. Cautiously he walked toward the big oak. He had pulled a tire tool from beneath the back seat and was ready to club anything that moved.

Bryson waded through the tall grass and walked up behind the big oak. He eased around the base of the tree with the tire tool raised high above his head. He was less than six feet away. He almost dropped the tire tool when he saw what was laying on his mother's grave.

It was a wolf.

Bryson remembered the first day he had arrived, only three days ago, having seen this strange flattened area on his mother's grave. The wolf had made the imprint. *Why?*

Bryson should have been frightened, but there was something in the eyes of this creature. A gentleness Bryson couldn't explain. An air of comfort surrounded him. There was familiarity in those eyes. *'Come find me,' my father had said a long time ago. But where?*

"Hello there, boy. What are you doing here?" Bryson placed the tire tool gently on the ground by the big oak tree. They stared into each other's eyes. The wolf had beautiful golden eyes and a light, blackish-gray coat. *What are you doing here? I don't believe wolves are common to this area anymore.*

The wolf stood up and circled around the big oak to the opposite side Bryson was standing. He stopped in front of the carved heart and scratched three times beneath it. Then he trotted off toward the north into the timberline located next to the pasture. Bryson watched curiously as the wolf disappeared into the woods. *Come find me.*

Bryson shook his head to clear his mind. *What does it mean?* He studied the carved heart paying close attention to the carved wolf figure. The wolf figure seemed to move and transform. The head was changing from a human back to a wolf, then back to a human form. There were three lines etched on the figure's back. *What does it mean?* He was becoming confused and frustrated at the same time. He shook his head again and rubbed his eyes. The figure quit changing. He wondered if the figure had been moving at all. *I just imagined the whole thing.* He halfheartedly tried to convince himself it was all mind play from being exhausted.

He walked back to the cabin, glancing over his shoulder a couple of times to see if the wolf was coming back. Nothing. He walked to the Jeep and pulled out a sleeping bag and a bag of clothes. He had been staying in a hotel in town for the last two nights. *This is my home. This is where I will stay.*

He had no electricity or running water, but he would make do. This was where he needed to be. There was a mountain stream out behind the cabin, and he could use his cell phone as an alarm clock. That was about all his cell phone was good for. He was in a dead zone for cell phone reception. Bryson didn't mind; he liked the solitude. He was no stranger to this type of living. He had spent the past two years wandering through Europe and living like a nomad off the land, taking what was offered and being thankful for it. Bryson had become very accustomed to being a nomad. A loner. *A lone wolf. Am I ready to jump back into society? Time will tell.*

The sun was setting low in the west. The shadows had taken over the countryside. Bryson had lit a lantern and was writing an outline of the next day's lessons. He closed the green book and turned down the light. He crawled into a red sleeping bag that he had spread across the broken wooden floor and turned over to look up at the ceiling with his arms crossed behind his head.

I wonder if my new friend has returned to spend the night. Probably not. Probably out hunting. Hunting what?

With his last thought, Bryson fell asleep. A very restless sleep.

Bryson's alarm sounded off at 5:30 a.m., but he had been awake a long time before that. He grabbed a bar of soap and towel and walked out to the stream. He stepped in the cold stream. The cool water took his breath away. *Wow!* He quickly bathed and brushed his teeth. He glanced up and saw the wolf staring at him from across the stream.

"Good morning, boy. I hope you slept better than I did."

The wolf tilted his head side to side in response.

Bryson reached up and tried to rub the soreness out of his neck. "I'm getting too old for this. I'm buying an air mattress to sleep on."

He picked up his shaving kit and toothbrush. "See you around. I have to go work now. I have a boss that's meaner than a porcupine and twice as prickly. She won't understand me hanging out with a wolf."

Bryson started for the cabin and then stopped abruptly. "Hey, if you get a chance, I notice some nice, big, fat juicy rats hanging around the house. Could you take care of them for me? I would really appreciate it."

The wolf turned and darted off.

"Okay, I see how it is. See if I invite you to dinner again," Bryson hollered jokingly across the stream.

Bryson hurried to the cabin, got dressed, and drove into town.

Bryson was about one mile from town when he heard a siren. He glanced in his rearview mirror and saw a sheriff 's car flashing its lights for him to pull over. He looked down at his speedometer. *I wasn't speeding. I wonder what this is all about?* He pulled onto the shoulder. He reached into his billfold and pulled out his license and insurance verification.

The police officer walked slowly up to Bryson's Jeep.

"License and verification, please."

Bryson handed them to the policeman. "May I ask what I was doing wrong, Officer?

The officer didn't reply. He studied the license and verification form.

"I'll be right back," the officer said as he retreated to his car.

The policeman remained in his car for well over thirty minutes. Bryson looked down at his watch. *What is taking so long? I'm going to be late and have to face the wrath of Queen Hitler.* Bryson scanned his mirrors.

The squad car's door opened. *Finally.*

"I apologize for the delay, Mr. Keahbone. You have an out-of-state license, and I needed to verify some information about you. I hope you understand. I pride myself on running a clean town here. I always do a thorough background check on everybody who moves to this area," the officer informed.

Bryson looked at the officer and couldn't help but think that this man looked like a human weasel.

"That's quite okay. I understand. Better to be safe than sorry," Bryson said as he thought about reaching out and grabbing his license and verification. *Not a good idea.*

Bryson for the first time read the officer's name tag. *T. Monger.*

"I apologize for my rudeness. My name is Tyrel Monger." He must have noticed Bryson looking at his name tag. "You have my son in your ninth grade English class, I believe. His name is Rubin Monger. Quite an afternoon yesterday, by the way, Ruby boy explained it."

Bryson did not respond immediately. He knew he was being baited by Tyrel Monger. "Quite a day."

Tyrel and Bryson stared at each other, sizing up one another for a possible future showdown. A showdown that was sure to come. A showdown that would no doubt have a tragic end for someone or something.

Tyrel handed Bryson his license and verification.

"Have a nice and pleasant day, Mr. Keahbone."

Bryson took the items from Sheriff Monger and placed them back in his billfold. "Thanks."

"Mr. Keahbone, I will be watching you."

"I'll be careful," Bryson uttered as he drove away from the shoulder of the highway.

Tyrel grinned wickedly, "Or you'll be dead."

Dare I Eat a Peach?

B ryson arrived at Talihina High School with not a moment to spare. Ms. Hitchcock was standing in the hall just a short distance from Bryson's classroom. She glanced at her watch.

"Good morning," Bryson said.

"Good morning."

Bryson walked past Hitchcock and stopped at the closed door of his classroom. He pulled his key out and placed it in the door lock.

Hitchcock walked up behind Bryson as he opened the door.

"Mr. Keahbone, may I have a moment of your time?"

"Sure," Bryson replied as he turned around. "Would you like to come in?"

"No, I'm good right here. I was unable to complete your evaluation yesterday. Therefore, I will need to come finish it today. Same time, same class period," Hitchcock stated.

"Marvelous."

The morning had gone by quickly. Bryson wondered if Ms. Hitchcock was going to back off. *She should have gotten well enough information for her evaluation yesterday. What is the real reason she's coming back?*

Lunch had just ended. Fifth hour was about to start. Maybe he would get his answer today.

Bryson walked through the doorway as the bell rung.

"Hello."

A few students replied. Bryson turned around, walked back out of the classroom, and then reentered. "Hello," Bryson announced with a lot more enthusiasm.

"Hello," the class exploded in unison. All except one— Rubin Monger.

"Much better."

Bryson smiled as he placed his briefcase behind his desk and grabbed a dry erase marker from a pencil holder on his desk. He walked to the dry erase board and wrote "Dare I eat a peach." He turned and glanced around the room sizing up the students as he tapped the marker on his left palm. He could tell by their expression that they had forgotten about the challenge he had given the day before. They were either looking down at their desk or out the window, avoiding eye contact, all except one.

"Did any overachievers find out what this phrase might mean?" Bryson asked, pausing a few seconds for a response that never came. "Jared Landry, did you dare to eat a peach?"

Jared started to reply when a loud voice from the back of the classroom yelled, "Jared is a cherry boy. He don't eat no peaches. He's an all-American cherry boy."

The class erupted with Rubin's words.

Jared turned around abruptly, jumping out of his desk. Rubin stood up as the two squared off.

"What are you going to do about it, cherry boy? Are you going to let Mr. Peebone rescue you again?" Rubin threatened as he charged up to Jared, shoving his palms into Jared's open chest.

Jared went flying back over his desk, spilling his notebook and English textbook to the floor, but surprisingly, Jared flipped over in an athletic move and landed on his feet, coiled, and ready for action. An action that never came—at least not right now.

Rubin froze in his tracks. Jared's agility had momentarily caught Rubin off guard. He wasn't expecting a super geek to be so agile.

Bryson started to say something, but Ms. Hitchcock intervened first. "Rubin Monger, report to my office immediately. We will not tolerate any form of bullying in our school."

Rubin turned his twisted face and mouthed something under his breath that Bryson was sure wasn't very pleasant. Then Rubin walked very slowly toward the door, never taking his psychotic eyes off Ms. Hitchcock. Piper stared back unyieldingly. Each year, Rubin was becoming more and more out of control, Piper thought. *He's going to go over the edge someday, and someone is going to get hurt or possibly killed by this troubled young man.*

Rubin didn't bother to shut the door after he exited the room. Bryson walked briskly to the door and stood in the doorway, watching Rubin walking down the hall punching lockers as he headed in the direction of the principal's office. Bryson grabbed the door handle closing it slowly on squeaky hinges.

"That's very annoying," Bryson stated matter-of-factly, and then paused, as he looked around the classroom at a lot of blank faces. "What?"

Bryson opened and swiveled the door again on its hinges making a high pitch noise.

"The door … it's very annoying. It needs some oil."

Most students smiled halfheartedly, and one girl even let out a slight giggle. Bryson tried to play off the whole episode with

Rubin as no big deal, but the students knew that Rubin wasn't going to let this end today, tomorrow, or ever.

Jared picked up his notebook and textbook, placing them loudly on the desk he had flipped over. He glanced around the room as he sat back down at his desk. Most of the faces were solemn except for Atwood's face. It said, "Boy howdy, are you ever going to die when Rubin gets hold of you."

Bryson was standing in front of the dry erase chalkboard. He underlined the phrase he had previously written on the board.

"Now where were we? Ah, yes. Dare I eat a peach? Mr. Landry was about to inform us about this phrase," a smiling Bryson instructed as he motioned toward Jared with the marker.

"I was? That's funny because I don't recall that taking place before all the excitement," Jared said as he caught a smiling Sasha Jo out of the corner of his eye. He dared a quick glance at Sasha Jo. *Yep, she is smiling and staring straight at me.*

Jared's stomach felt like he had a swarm of butterflies dancing around in figure eights. He was a very shy and reserved person. He did not like to draw attention to himself, especially since his mother was the principal. He didn't want anyone to think or believe that he was getting any special treatments because of his mother. He had a lot of high self-esteem in his schoolwork and was very intelligent. But when it came to talking to girls, his knees melted like butter.

Jared had totally forgotten about his run-in with Rubin five minutes before. He was now trying to figure out how to impress this girl, Sasha Jo, without making a total fool out of himself.

Sweat was caking up Jared's hands, and his tongue felt like it was twisting in knots as he again glanced over at Sasha Jo.

She smiled as she placed her elbows on her desk and both her fists under her chin.

Here goes nothing, Jared thought as he quickly stood up, knocking over his chair. "Sorry."

The class laughed. Even Piper, who had gone back to the desk she was sitting in prior to Rubin's outburst, chuckled at his clumsiness. *Just like his mother*, she thought.

"It's quite all right. Please proceed."

"Last night I was bored, so I googled that phrase on the board, 'dare I eat a peach'?' It's actually supposed to be a little different than how you wrote it. The correct phrase should have said, '*Do* I dare to eat a peach?' It threw me off for a little while, but I was able to figure it out."

"Awesome! You're exactly right. I changed it a little to fit what I was writing. Carry on, pilgrim," Bryson cheered, excited that one of his students actually took the time to research something on their own without him making it for a grade.

"The line comes from a poem written by some guy named T. S. Eliot. The poem is called 'The Love Song of J. Alfred Prufrock,' which makes absolutely no sense to me, because this poem is the opposite of a love poem," Jared declared as he again glanced toward a smiling Sasha Jo.

"Good. What do you mean opposite?"

"You would think the poem is a love poem, but it's not. It's about this old dude, probably your age, Mr. Keahbone, who really likes this woman, but he is afraid to ask her this question," Jared said as the class snickered at the comparison. Even Piper chuckled a little. "Sorry."

"No offense taken. What is the question?"

"I'm not sure. Probably to go out on a date or go steady. He's afraid she might say no, so he wouldn't dare to take a chance. He was so full of doubt that he didn't even know if he should eat a peach or at least something like that," Jared concluded, feeling very proud of himself because that was the most he had ever talked at one time in front of his classmates.

Piper was very proud of Jared also. Her son was growing up. Too fast for her liking. She had wondered what he was working on last night while he sat at the computer. Jared had simply said homework when Piper had asked.

She glanced up at the clock—five minutes before the bells. *I better slip out of here and go take care of Rubin Monger.* She knew too well that Tyrel would be in her office raising Cain for suspending Rubin, for it was never *his* fault. But she was in control and wasn't going to tolerate any form of bullying whether toward her son or any other student. She needed to make an example of the type of punishment that would be handed down to any violators.

She picked up Bryson's evaluation form and slipped it into a manila folder. She eased out of her desk and quietly exited the classroom unnoticed except for Bryson. She had rather stayed but knew her duty to deal with this discipline problem would only fester if she put it off.

"Excellent! Anything else?"

Jared shook his head.

"Thanks. You may be seated," Bryson offered as he walked and stood behind his podium. "Jared is right on. The phrase comes from the T. S. Eliot's poem, 'The Love Song of J. Alfred Prufrock.' The narrator, or old dude, as Jared put it, is afraid to ask this woman an overwhelming question. The question could possibly be simply to go out on a date with him. We never find out because Prufrock will not get out of his comfort zone, or the box, as I like to call it. He is afraid of the r-word."

"Irresistible, like me," Rocky Atencio blurted out.

"Bzzzzzt! Wrong answer, try again later."

"That begins with an *i.* What an igmo." Jeremy Atwood laughed.

"Who else?" Bryson asked, sounding like a game show host. "Anybody?"

"Rejection," Jared muttered.

"Correct! Why do you think he is so afraid of rejection?"

"Because being rejected stinks, not that I'm rejected a lot," Rocky claimed, trying to save face but didn't succeed.

"Yeah, right!" Jeremy jeered, this time the whole class erupted in laughter.

"You're right, Rocky. Rejection does stink. You will go through your entire life dealing with being rejected. Did you know that rejection is the number three most feared thing in the world behind snakes and public speaking? It has some of us so afraid that we will not take a chance at something we want to pursue in life. Thus, we are exactly like Prufrock and will not dare to eat a peach. Be bold and get out of your comfort zone, *the box.* If you don't, the fleeting moment will pass you by. '*Your moment of greatness will flicker.*'"

The bell rang sounding the end of the hour.

"Have a good day," Bryson announced, "and don't be afraid to eat a peach."

The class quickly deserted the room as Bryson was straightening up papers on his desk.

Jared was walking up to Bryson's desk when Sasha Jo stopped him. "Jared, will you walk me to my next class?"

Jared's jaw dropped open. He was mesmerized and caught totally off guard by the question. "Huh? A-a-a … well … I need to talk to Mr. Keahbone. I'll catch up with you later," he stammered.

Bryson's smile suddenly turned to a frown when he saw the dejected look on Sasha Jo's face. That must have been very hard for her to get out of her box and ask Jared to walk with her, thought Bryson.

Jared watched her walk out the door and wondered if he should have chased her down and walked with her.

"I hope it's important, because you may never get a chance with Sasha Jo again," Bryson informed. "What's up?"

Jared glanced at the door and then back at Bryson, "You bought the Old Kinsey Place out off of County Line Road?"

"Yes. I use to live there when I was a boy. I moved away when I was eleven years old. I wanted to come back to my native land. But the old place hadn't been lived in for a very long time. It's a wreck," Bryson admitted.

"I know. I heard the place was haunted, so I was wondering if you have seen any ghosts or werewolves. Old man Kinsey told Mr. Brown that there were werewolves roaming the countryside. And on every full moon, they would come to his cabin and terrorize him and his wife," Jared proclaimed.

"And you know this, how?"

"Well … it all happened before I was born, but I've heard lots of people talk about the *legend*," Jared informed.

"Usually legends are tales from a past long ago."

"Exactly! It all happened before I was born," Jared informed.

"Well, sorry to disappoint you. There was a full moon the other night—no werewolves …" Bryson paused when he thought of the wolf and then continued. "Just a lot of spider-filled cobwebs, broken boards, missing windows, and tons of dust."

Jared wrinkled up his nose in thought. "Sounds like you need some help. I'm pretty handy with a hammer and saw, and I work cheap … free."

Bryson started to politely refuse the kind offer.

"I won't be in the way. I only live about a mile away—by way the crow flies. I can work after football practice except on Fridays. If you're not too busy, maybe you can come watch us play. We make it to the state playoffs every year," Jared proclaimed proudly. "I can work all day on Saturdays. I'm really quite the handyman. I constantly have to fix things for my mom."

"I will definitely come watch you play." Bryson paused for a brief moment. "You may help me repair my cabin on two conditions. One, your parents must be okay with your helping me. Two, I insist on paying you a fair day's wage for a fair day's work."

"Deal," Jared hooted, sticking out his hand.

"And your schoolwork must come first."

"Always."

"And one more thing," Bryson added, extending his hand. "That will be four conditions. Before too long I will have to read a three-hundred-page carpenter's manual." Jared grinned as he was walking toward the door.

"Last thing—there will be no more Prufrock moments in my classroom." Bryson smiled.

Jared started to ask Bryson what he meant; then he remembered Sasha Jo asking him to walk her to her next class, and he sort of *chickened out*.

Jared smiled. "Yes, sir."

Meet Mr. and Mrs. Monger

It was five minutes before the dismissal bell was to sound. The last two periods had been abnormally quiet. *I guess the word about Rubin had gotten around pretty quick. I wonder what happened to Rubin. What punishment did Ms. Hitchcock hand down?*

Bryson glanced up at the clock.

"Remember to read pages 28–33 in your book. It is the short story 'The Monkey's Paw,' and be prepared to discuss the literary elements of this short story."

Some of the students moaned.

"But it's Friday, Mr. Keahbone. We're not suppose to have homework on Friday at this school," a small freckled-face kid with a long country drawl replied.

"I'll check my box for that memo, but until then *ya'll have to read that-there story, you hear?*" Bryson said, using his own country drawl.

Several giggles sounded around the room.

"Mr. Keahbone," Ms. Bretz's voice sounded from a speaker in the ceiling.

"Hello."

"Ms. Hitchcock would like for you to report to her office directly following the final bell."

Ooh! The students moaned again, this time sarcastically.

161

Bryson smiled playfully at the students, but inside he knew there would be no smiling at this meeting with Hitchcock and Rubin's parents.

"I'll be there."

The bell rang.

"Remember your assignment," Bryson hollered out to the students as they rushed toward the door. If they heard Bryson they never acknowledged they were listening.

Bryson put the last of some papers he needed to finish grading into his brown leather briefcase. He grabbed the case by the handle and walked out the door locking it behind him. His room was only two classrooms down from the office, but the walk was weighing heavily on his mind. Dealing with discipline problems and irate parents "whose children never do wrong" was the only drawback to teaching. Even grading papers was more tolerable.

I had the problem under control until Ms. Hitchcock butted in. She should have let me handle it. She should have been a silent observer, not the control freak she can be. Why does she always feel the need for complete control? Bryson wondered with his jaw and lips clinched tight.

"Howdy, Ms. Bretz," Bryson announced as he walked into the principal's office.

"Hi." Jody smiled halfheartedly. "Go in. She's expecting you."

Bryson nodded as he headed back to Ms. Hitchcock's office. He started running through his mind all things he was going to say to her—*mainly how big of a control freak she is.* He was going to let Hitchcock have it, no holds barred, guns ablazin', Butch Cassidy, and the Sundance Kid!

But that was not to be.

"Come in and shut the door, please," Ms. Hitchcock said. "Have a seat, please."

Whoa! Two pleases in the same day—that's more than I thought I would see in a lifetime!

Bryson was caught off guard but quickly gathered himself. He was about to give her not one piece but his entire mind. But to his surprise, he couldn't do it. He really wanted to tell her off, but instead, he remained speechless. *Why?* He didn't know.

"Mr. Keahbone, please accept my apology for my conduct in your classroom today. I was totally out of line. I went completely against everything I preach to my teachers about taking charge of their classrooms." Piper paused as if this was something that was hard for her to say. "I should have allowed you the opportunity to handle the discipline in your classroom. It's just … that … well …"

Ms. Bretz gently tapped on the office door as she opened it slowly. "Sorry to interrupt, but Mr. and Mrs. Monger are here."

"Give me a minute, Ms. Bretz."

Piper turned her attention back to Bryson and was about to finish her excuse. She wanted to explain how her motherly instinct had taken over. She was taking up for her son, but she thought that he had already figured that out.

But she was wrong. Bryson still hadn't a clue that Jared was her son. But that would soon change.

"I suspended Rubin for the rest of the nine-week grading period. You will need to make a folder and put his makeup work in it and bring it to the office. Rubin's family member will pick up the folder every Friday."

"Yes, I will do that," Bryson matter-of-factly stated.

Piper got up from her desk and walked to the door. She poked her head out the opening, "You may come in now."

Bryson stood up and moved to stand by the window, leaving two chairs empty in front of Ms. Hitchcock's desk.

Piper motioned for Mr. and Mrs. Monger to sit down.

Mrs. Monger came in first. She was a very petite and meek-looking woman wearing a gray cotton skirt and a white long-sleeved blouse, which was buttoned up to the top. Her brown-and-silver hair was pulled up in a bun, exposing a very pale face and dark sunken eyes. Her lips were like a thin, hueless line drawn beneath her nose. She never looked up. Her gaze seemed to be locked on a small black coin purse that she held tightly with two hands. She stopped just inside the doorway waiting for her husband to enter.

Bryson looked at her fervently. *Where have I seen her before? She looks very familiar.* Flashes from his past entered his mind, but he was unable to grasp them before they quickly vanished. *I can't remember. This is probably the first time we've met. I just don't remember.*

Tyrel stepped around and stood in front of his wife. He was wearing his sheriff 's tan-colored uniform. His Old Spice aftershave immediately filled the room. His hair was dark and greasy looking. He had a hat ring imprinted around his head. He had his hat in his left hand and right thumb hooked in his belt inches away from his nine-millimeter Beretta.

Uneasiness crept into Bryson's spine. Although Tyrel had an unusual smile on his weasel face, hatred filled his eyes. A hatred unlike anything Bryson had ever seen before. His black eyes were like port holes to a damned soul bent on destroying whatever lay in its path.

Bryson shuddered at the thought of what life must be like with Tyrel Monger. He pitied his wife and son.

"Sheriff Monger, this is Bryson Keahbone, our ninth grade English teacher," Ms. Hitchcock said.

"We met this morning."

Tyrel extended his hand toward Bryson.

Bryson stepped forward with an outstretched hand.

The two hands met like two gladiators in an arena. Tyrel tried to gain an advantage by squeezing very hard the first firm grip on Bryson's hand, but Bryson was ready and countered with his own firm grip. To each other's surprise, they were both very deliberate and strong. Bryson stared into Tyrel's soulless eyes. Bryson could smell Tyrel's foul breath, a mixture of coffee, cigarettes, and who knows what else. They defiantly held on until Ms. Hitchcock's voice sounded.

"And this is Elizabeth Monger, Tyrel's wife."

Bryson would not let go until he felt Tyrel ease his grip and then extended his hand toward Mrs. Monger.

"Nice to meet you," Bryson greeted.

Without looking up, Mrs. Monger slowly released her purse and shook Bryson's hand. Her white fingers were long icicles to the touch, like the frozen hand of the Queen of Narnia.

Mrs. Monger's touch had a more profound effect on Bryson than Tyrel's. *What is her story? Very odd. I've seen a lot of strange things and people overseas but none quite this bizarre.*

"Please have a seat," Ms. Hitchcock offered, extending her hand toward the two empty chairs.

Tyrel hesitated and then motioned for his wife to sit. He looked cautiously around, absorbing every detail of the room and then accompanied her, filling the empty chair beside her.

"I believe we know why we are all here," Ms. Hitchcock began as the Mongers remained motionless, like gargoyles on their chairs. "Rubin was involved in a bullying situation. This is his third bullying offense. In other words, strike three. Our school discipline policy states that if an offender performs a third offense, then he or she will be suspended for the rest of the nine weeks grading period. If there is less than five days left in the nine week grading period, then he or she will be suspended for the semester …"

Ms. Hitchcock paused and looked up from the discipline policy of the students' handbook.

To her surprise the Mongers never even twitched on their chairs. No emotion. No arguing. No "my son is being picked on and singled out." Nothing.

"Do you have any questions?"

"What exactly is Rubin's punishment goin' be?"

"He is on step four of his seven-step discipline plan, which is very bad for this time of the year—this being the second day of school. That's two major infractions per day. I have been way too lenient with Rubin. I've decided to suspend him for the remainder of the nine-week grading period," Ms. Hitchcock proclaimed.

Tyrel leaned forward as if to quickly jump up and say something in protest but stopped before anything came out of his mouth. He gathered his wits and eased back into his chair. "That seems a little harsh to me. According to Rubin, he never even threw a punch. Yet you're going to suspend him for almost nine weeks. It makes no sense to me, Ms. Hitchcock," Tyrel complained through gritted teeth, having a hard time keeping his voice under control.

"Rubin has been in some sort of trouble almost every class period since school began. My teachers have been very patient and indulgent to his misbehavior. It's got to stop. If this line of behavior continues, he will be expelled for the school year," Ms. Hitchcock warned.

"What happened to the other boy involved? What was his punishment?" Tyrel asked dryly.

Bryson leaned away from the window sill, unfolded his arms, and calmly stated, "The other young man in question does not need to be involved in this meeting. This is a situation about *your* son and *his* actions and consequences for those actions. The young man did nothing and is the victim, not Rubin."

Tyrel looked over his shoulder at Bryson. His jaw locked tight, causing his jaws muscles to protrude at the temples. He started to argue, but he knew it would do no good. There would be time for that later. *Rubin is an aggressive kid, and I am preparing him for the future.*

"He needs to be in school to get a proper education. I can't give him what he needs to learn at home," Tyrel lied, for in his mind he believed Rubin would be better off at home learning the hunt. That's the only thing important in this world. Tyrel knew that Rubin needed to stay in school and keep a low profile and not draw attention to himself or the family. *Three days in the sweat box should cure that.*

Tyrel grinned at the thought.

Bryson noticed and wondered what game Tyrel was playing.

"If Rubin hadn't left the campus, I probably would have given him five days of in-school suspension," Ms. Hitchcock continued.

"I've seen many criminals in my time act out in haste when a situation could have been avoided if they would have just stepped back and removed themselves from that particular situation. I have instilled that same concept in my son. Walk away before you do something you will regret."

"I agree to an extent, but I gave Rubin that opportunity by sending him to the office to cool down. You need to see it from my perspective. I am responsible for each and every student that sets foot on this campus from 7:30 a.m. to whenever the last student leaves to go home. I am responsible for the safety of Rubin, and I can't do that if he leaves the premises," Ms. Hitchcock asserted boldly.

Bryson was a quiet observer, leaning back upon the window sill with his legs crossed beneath him and arms folded against his chest. He thought about butting in but declined, because he knew Ms. Hitchcock didn't need his help. If anything, he would probably be in her way.

"Rubin can take care of himself."

"I have no doubts about that, but by law, I'm still responsible, as you well know," Ms. Hitchcock countered.

Tyrel started to retaliate but knew it wouldn't do any good. Rubin would take his punishment like a man. *But this was not the last Ms. Hitchcock would hear of this. She will take responsibility for her actions. Besides I need to talk to Mr. Keahbone alone before this gets out of hand.*

"Arright, if we are finished, me and my wife will be leaving here. I don't agree, but the law is the law. Elizabeth will pick up Rubin's work every Friday," Tyrel concluded as he got up and headed for the door, leaving his wife sitting in her chair.

Bryson opened and walked through the door holding it open for Tyrel to exit. He did not notice that Mrs. Monger had stayed in the office.

Tyrel stopped by Ms. Bretz's empty desk and turned toward Bryson, who was standing by the door with one hand on the door knob. "Mr. Keahbone, I'm going to believe whatever you tell me. Did Rubin really bully that kid the way she stated?" Tyrel charged, trying hard to sound very sincere.

"Yes, it happened just like she explained," Bryson paused, trying to find something positive to say about Rubin, but nothing came to mind.

"Very well." Tyrel turned as if leaving then abruptly stopped. "You just moved into the Old Kinsey Farm? How's that going?"

Bryson shrugged and nodded, wondering where this conversation was heading.

"My daddy tried to buy that old run-down place years ago after it was promised to us, but that Buchanan woman bought it out from under us. I would be deeply indebted to you if you would consider selling. I'll pay double what you paid for it. It has a lot of sentimental value to me and my family." Tyrel smiled.

Bryson smiled back. "Not interested."

Tyrel's grin abruptly turned to a scowl. "Maybe I didn't make myself clear. It's important to my family. The Mongers use to own it a long time ago, but my granddaddy lost it in a poker game. And we never had the opportunity until *now* to get it back. Will you reconsider?" Tyrel persisted.

"I'm sorry, Mr. Monger, but this property also holds sentimental value for me. I was born in that old cabin. My father loved that land. My mother died and is buried there. So no, Mr. Monger, I will not sell. I am here for the long haul. This is my home," Bryson proclaimed.

Tyrel's face remained stolid, and then his lips turned up into a virulent grin. "If you change your mind, I would like first shot at buying the land," Tyrel offered, but thought, *You will change your mind one way or another—I promise.*

"I won't, but thanks just the same," Bryson politely refused.

Elizabeth Monger did not get up from her chair when Tyrel got up to leave. Her gaze remained locked on her black coin purse. A few tears fell, landing on her purse and hands.

"Are you all right?" Ms. Hitchcock asked as she got up from behind her desk to offer a tissue to Mrs. Monger.

No reply.

"Everything okay?"

"No," Mrs. Monger whimpered, barely above an audible sound.

"Please talk with me," Piper sympathized as she closed her office door.

"I can't—I don't know … what to … say. I really try to … be a good wife … a good mother … but I'm no … good at it," Mrs. Monger murmured.

Piper put her hand consolingly on Mrs. Monger's shoulder. Elizabeth flinched, then relaxed. But just a little. Piper could feel the tension throughout her body. *Life must be a living hell for this woman*, Piper thought.

"I cook and clean. I do the all things a good wife is suppose to … I really try …"

"Yes, Elizabeth, I can see that you are a good mother and wife. Please don't beat yourself up. A person can only do their best in any relationship, but it's up to the others involved to do their part also," Piper sympathized.

"I do my best to raise Rubin where he will be a good student. I want him to get good grades and not be in trouble all the time," Elizabeth claimed, her crying had died away.

"That's all you can do. You can only point Rubin in the right direction, but he has to choose to follow the right path. I believe Rubin will mature into the young man you want him to be. Some young boys take longer than others," Piper assured, thinking about how she sometimes is too protective of her own son and maybe doesn't allow him to mature like he should.

"I sure hope you are right, Ms. Hitchcock," Elizabeth admitted, dabbing her nose with a tissue. "Thank you. I feel much better."

"Anytime," Piper replied as she reached for a sticky note pad and pen. "Here is my phone number. Call me, day or night. I will be there to help."

"Again, I can't thank you enough. You are a godsend," Elizabeth said as she grabbed the note and put it in her coin purse.

"You're welcome."

They embraced.

Mrs. Monger stood up and tossed the used tissue into a wastebasket by Piper's desk. She straightened up her dress and started toward the door with chin down and both hands holding onto her coin purse just above her waistline.

Piper smiled warmly and opened the door.

"Call me anytime you need someone to talk to," Piper whispered. Her heart went out to Elizabeth Monger. *How unhappy she must be. I know, I have felt this loneliness for way too long.*

Tyrel turned his attention from Bryson to his wife as she cleared the doorway.

"Ready?"

Mrs. Monger never looked up.

"Sleep on it. I will pay big," Tyrel avowed to Bryson, but this time he wasn't talking about with money.

The Mongers left without saying another word.

"That is a very strange couple," Bryson decided.

"Yes, they are rather odd," Piper agreed. "I really feel sorry for his wife. She is a very sad and lonely woman."

That was the first thing they have totally agreed upon.

Bryson turned toward Piper. "If I'm not needed, I have a busy weekend planned starting this evening."

Ms. Bretz and Piper shot Bryson a curious look.

"I'm repairing my house. The county finally repaired the roads to where a person can drive on them. The lumberyard delivered all the materials I need to refurbish my cabin. I'm getting tired of taking a cold shower every time it rains."

"Good luck," Ms. Bretz chimed.

"Thanks."

Destiny' Doorway

The small branches slapped across his face, like tiny bullwhips leaving bright red cuts. He veered away from the creek and began climbing a moderately steep hill. Although the full moon illuminated the landscape, the shadows were still thick under the canopy. The underbrush had thinned a little. Pine trees stood about sparsely allowing in more light. He grabbed small trees and vines to aid him in his climb. He was almost to the top.

No time to rest.

He heard snorting grunts down by the creek where he had come from.

They were looking for him.

They were close. Too close.

The top of the ridge was clear of underbrush and briars. Pine trees and oaks stood sporadically around him. Black and gray flashed around him as he picked up to a break-neck speed on the backside of the ridge's slope. His legs and lungs were a burning fire. Toward the bottom, small tree branches reached out with grasping hands trying to take hold of his arms and legs, slowing him for the closing stalkers.

Another creek appeared. He ran down the middle of the shallow water hoping to cover his scent and throw off his pursuers.

They were upon him. He could hear the small trees and branches breaking and being uprooted by the stalkers. He felt their breath on the back of his neck. It was hot and smelled of rotting decay.

The stream had widened and became very deep. He fell into the pool of water. Its coldness was refreshing, yet very numbing at the same time. He swam to the bank. He looked around as he started to climb out but abruptly stopped. He saw several pairs of red eyes surrounding him. The red eyes were like little laser beams pointing at him, tracking his every move. He tried to scream defiantly at the red eyes, but no words came out. His arms and legs wouldn't move. It felt like a hundred pairs of hands had taken hold of his entire body. He tried to fight back, but he was only sinking down, down, down into the black abyss until only his eyes remained atop the water's level. He coughed; water was filling his lungs. His lids twitched as his eyes rolled back. He tried again unsuccessfully to free himself from this watery grave.

Suddenly he caught a bright flash out of the corner of his eye. The hands loosened their deadly grip on his arms and legs. He lifted his head from the icy water. The red eyes scattered. *What was that light?* He eased toward the shore. He pulled himself on to the soft grass, panting hard to catch his breath. As he was coughing up water, he looked around for the red eyes. No red eyes. No more bright light. He stood and began to walk but abruptly stopped, dropping his hands to his knees. His legs felt like they were moving in quicksand. He couldn't run anymore. He would have to fight until he could fight no more.

But there was only silence.

The moonlight reflected off the calm, clear pool of black water. The peaceful tranquility was soothing, comforting. After hours, days, maybe years of running, being chased by demons, he felt peace. A restful peace. His legs, arms, and body were no longer tired. But more than that, his soul seemed to be at rest.

What is this place? Heaven? Had I died in my sleep?

Beneath a patch of moonlight, a man suddenly appeared across the pool of water. He wore a breechcloth with a sleeveless buckskin vest. His moccasins were knee-high with leather tassels on top. His hair was jet-black and braided in a single ponytail. A single feather hung off to one side from the top of his head. He had beaded bracelets from his wrist to mid-forearm. He walked toward the pool's edge. The moon was at the native man's back. It cast a shadow over his face, darkening his facial features. He stopped and stood at the water's edge. The reflection in the water was not that of a man but a wolf.

"Bryson, my son, come find me beneath the Moon When Wolves Cry."

Bryson stood erect from his slumped position. He recognized the man as the man turned toward the moon. It was his father.

Bryson tried to talk, but the words were momentarily lost. He reached out to touch his father, then lowered his hand, for the man was still on the other side of the pool.

"I don't understand, Father," Bryson finally responded as he looked up at the full moon.

The moon's craters had begun to move and then realigned in the image of a howling wolf fully enclosed inside the moon.

"Come find me beneath the Moon When Wolves Cry," Bryson's father repeated.

"Help me understand," Bryson pleaded.

The figure turned and walked away.

"No! Don't go! Help me!" Bryson demanded, but to no avail. Bryson's father disappeared in the shadows of the underbrush.

Bryson fell to his knees, burying his face into his hands. Anguish tormented Bryson's soul.

How many more times?

Bryson heard a loud noise that sounded like hundreds of bumblebees during a swarm. He raised his head. A bright light shined from the direction his father had departed. Bryson raised his left hand to block the light, but he couldn't make out anything. The buzzing became louder, then abruptly stopped.

Within the bright light, a silhouette of a woman appeared. She wore a long white silky gown with a white belt around her waist. Her hair fell in long curly locks. She moved forward with an elegant grace as if she were floating above the ground and not walking. She stopped by the water's edge.

Bryson couldn't make out her face. He squinted again, peering unsuccessfully under the shade of his hand.

"Who are you?" Bryson asked hesitantly.

She remained silent.

"Who are you? Where is my father?" Bryson asked as he stood to his feet.

"The answers you seek are right there in front of you. Seek the lady of the streets. She will guide you in the right direction," the lady in white revealed.

Sorrow suddenly overwhelmed Bryson. Although he couldn't see her face, he believed that he recognized the lady in white's voice. It was Becky's. *What does it mean?*

"Who are you?" Bryson asked again, not knowing if he really wanted to know the answer. He slowly walked with wobbly knees to the water's edge. "Are you Becky? Becky, is that you?" His voice trembled.

"Fear not, for the Lord has mapped out your steps. All you have to do is believe. Believe."

"The God I thought I knew left me alone and allowed all these bad things to happen. I did believe ... once," Bryson testified.

"There is a reason for anything under his realm. Things you cannot understand. If you continue to hold on to the past, you will never be able to move forward. As like as not when life spills through destiny's doorway, you must let it go by. You need only to believe," the lady in white said as her light slowly faded.

"No! Do not leave! I need you! I need you. I … need … you," Bryson said as the lady in white totally disappeared.

Clouds drifted in front of the moon, blanketing its light. The night became pitch black.

The red eyes suddenly reappeared. They were moving in. They had completely surrounded Bryson, but he didn't care. *Be done with it!*

They were upon him, creeping slowly, moving in a counterclockwise circle.

"Come on! I'm ready!"

They were only a few feet away, carefully stalking their prey.

The burning red eyes stopped, making a complete circle around Bryson.

He dropped his hands to his side. He wasn't going to fight.

They leaped into the air.

Welcomed Help

B ryson leaped up from his sleeping bag, grasping for air. Sweat covered his entire body. He quickly looked around the cabin. Nobody there. No red eyes. No lady in white. No father. He was alone.

He lay back down, looking at the hole in the ceiling. The quarter moon shone through the hole. His father's words came into his mind: *Come find me beneath the Moon When Wolves Cry.* He was becoming increasingly anxious. Not a night had gone by in the last two years that he had not had that same dream. He was no closer now to understanding the dream than he was two years ago. And now, the dream had changed. A lady in white had visited him in his dream.

Who was she? Was it Becky? What had she said?

He couldn't remember. The dream was very fuzzy. Frustration had consumed Bryson until he was about to explode. *What did she say? Why could I remember my father's words but not hers?*

He closed his eyes, trying to go back to sleep or at least remember her words. But the lady in white's words had faded from his memory. *Maybe she was never in my dream.*

Bryson pushed the light button on his watch. It was still two hours before dawn. He rubbed his eyes and remained in his sleeping bag. But he couldn't go back to sleep. He decided to get up and go to the stream behind the cabin where he had seen the wolf.

Bryson washed his face in the cold water. There was a rustling noise in the woods beyond the stream. He quickly looked up, but there was nothing to be seen but dark shadows. He was hoping to see the wolf. *Maybe the wolf knows the answers. The lady in white told me to seek someone. Who?* He remained frozen for a few minutes. Then he stood and walked back to the cabin. He crawled back into his sleeping bag, but he couldn't sleep, let alone dream.

Dawn was breaking in the eastern sky. He decided to get up. *A nice long run should clear my head.*

Bryson had taken back up his life's passion for running. He loved to go on long runs as a means of rationalizing his reality and returning his sanity. Every morning Bryson would run four to eight miles. The first few outings were rough; he had really gotten out of condition, but now he was beginning to feel like his old self again.

When Bryson got back from his six-mile run, he jumped in the stream to wash off. The cool water was refreshing, but he quickly rinsed off and climbed out onto shore, grabbing a nearby towel to dry himself. He had a lot of work to do on his cabin. He had the money to hire professional carpenters and get the place repaired in a short amount of time, but he was determined to do things himself. He didn't want to have to depend on anyone.

Bryson decided to repair the roof first. The house flooded every time it rained. After placing a ladder against the cabin, he carried up two bundles of shake shingles. There were several bare spots that needed to be filled in and covered up with shingles. It took Bryson about an hour and half to repair the roof.

"All right. I am officially dried in. I can now scratch off the roof repair from the list of a hundred and forty-three things to do." Bryson smiled as he hooked his hammer to his tool belt.

Bryson climbed down the ladder and was heading toward the porch when he saw someone walking up the road to his cabin.

It was Jared Landry. He was wearing a pair of blue overalls, white T-shirt, and work boots. He had a tool belt similar to Bryson's slung over his shoulder and a carpenter's hammer in his hand.

"Howdy."

"Good morning."

"What brings you to my neck of the woods?" Bryson asked.

"I've come to earn a man's wage for a man's work," Jared replied.

"Awesome. Do you know where I can find a good man?" Bryson laughed.

"Right here," Jared pointed out.

"I pay six bucks an hour."

"Deal."

"Plus meals."

"Deal. Where do we begin?"

"Next on my long list of things to do is the wiring. Rats have pretty much chewed up about everything they could get their teeth into. I need to rewire the whole cabin so I can get the electricity turned on. All I have for power is that little generator over there," Bryson stated, pointing at the 3000 watts Honda generator.

"Good thing the cabin is not very big," Jared declared.

"You're right. It shouldn't take long."

"Unless we're going to stay out here and talk about it," Jared mused.

"Okay, let's git'er done," Bryson ordered, mimicking Larry the Cable Guy.

The next few hours went by quickly. They rewired the whole cabin, which wasn't too difficult because the cabin was small and wide open. Jared's help proved to be most beneficial. He could easily fit in the small tight places in the loft. They stretched, ran the wire, and then tied all the loose ends together in the fuse box.

Next on the list, Bryson was going to inspect and replace bad plumbing when they ripped the flooring up. Almost all the wood flooring was rotten from the leaky roof. They started with the flooring in the back bathroom and worked their way to the front living room.

Bryson was impressed with Jared. He was an extremely hard worker.

Jared's parents have done a fine job instilling good work ethics. I will be sure to tell them when I meet them.

They had just finished ripping the floor in the bathroom and began working in the kitchen when Bryson asked, "Hey, Jared, are you ready for something to eat?"

Jared nodded. He hadn't realized how hungry he had become until Bryson mentioned food.

They set their tools down. Jared followed Bryson, who stopped at an old dusty dining table that had a red and white ice chest sitting on top. He opened the lid and grabbed out two blue Gatorades and tossed one to Jared.

"I have water, if you prefer?"

"No, this is perfect. Thank you."

"Have a seat. I stopped at that little deli in town and had them make me up a bunch of sandwiches. What do you prefer? I have roast beef, bologna, ham and cheese. I bought some peanut butter and jelly too. What's your flavor?"

"Roast beef is good."

"Nice choice," Bryson replied, tossing the sandwich to Jared. "I'll have me—bologna."

They took their lunch out to the front porch to eat. They sat quietly for a few minutes, enjoying the beautiful late-summer day. Autumn was officially only a week away. It would not be long before the leaves started to fall. Bryson was confident that he would have the cabin ready before winter, especially now he had such a wonderful helper.

"You make a good hand."

"Thank you. I like doing stuff like this. The bigger the job, the more I like it. How did you learn so much about building and wiring houses?"

"Back in Oregon where I grew up. I lived with my aunt and uncle. Uncle Art built houses for a living. He taught me everything I needed to know to build a house."

"Didn't you live here when you were a boy?" Jared asked. He had remembered his mom and Dr. Brown talking about it.

"Yes. Then I moved to Oregon to live with my mom's sister after my parents died."

"I'm sorry about your parents."

"Thank you. That was a long time ago. I don't remember too much." Bryson paused and then pointed with his right index finger. "My mom is buried over there under that big old oak. It was her favorite tree."

"It's beautiful. Is your dad buried there also?"

"No. His body was cremated for whatever reason. I'm not sure why," Bryson disclosed. He was usually reserved about his past, but he found it very easy to talk to Jared.

They both sat quietly for the remainder of their lunch. Bryson stared out over the meadow thinking about his childhood. He didn't remember a lot; it was very fragmented. The harder he tried to remember, the more he seemed to forget. He closed his eyes. Visions of last night's dream entered his mind. He remembered his father's every word, *Come find me beneath the Moon When Wolves Cry.* The lady in white suddenly appeared and spoke. This time the words were coming back to him. She spoke, *Seek the lady ... destiny's doorway ... believe.*

"Hey, Mr. Keahbone, this is no time for a nap. We've got to get that floor ripped out and replaced in that back room before dark," Jared announced sarcastically.

Bryson opened his eyes slowly. The lady in white vanished from his mind. He smiled halfheartedly at Jared.

"Yes'm, boss. You a loco slave driver."

"We're burning daylight. I need to earn my pay," Jared declare as he picked up his trash and headed back into the cabin.

"Comin', boss," Bryson mocked, picking up his tool belt and followed Jared into the cabin.

It was late evening. The mountains' shadows were beginning to blanket the flowery meadow. Bryson and Jared were very tired. They had finished the bathroom's floor and plumbing. The sink needed some small maintenance attention, but other than that, the bathroom was ready for use. Bryson was more than ready. He was tired of the cold baths every morning in the stream. All the plumbing in the house needed to be inspected and repaired before the water could be turned on. *Maybe a week or less,* Bryson thought.

"Let's call it a day. It's getting late," Bryson announced as he unbuckled his work belt from his waist.

Jared wiped the sweat from his brow with the back of his hand. "Sounds good."

"Come back anytime—as long as your parents don't mind. You are an excellent worker. I can always use your skills around here," Bryson said, pulling out a water bottle from the ice chest and tossing it to Jared.

"Thank you."

"I'll be working all day tomorrow, if you want to come back for some more punishment."

Jared thought for a few seconds and replied, "Tomorrow's Sunday. We have church. I'll have to come back on Monday after I do my chores at home when school gets out. Why don't you come visit our church? We have an awesome pastor and youth minister."

Bryson smiled hesitantly. He hadn't attended a church since Becky's funeral. "We'll see. But thanks for the invite."

Jared knew that Bryson's reply was probably a no. But it was good all the same. His youth minister, Joe, would be proud of him for getting out of his comfort zone and inviting someone to church.

"Cool. If you change your mind, it's First Baptist Church in town. Right by the post office. You can't miss it. See you later." Jared waved as he walked to the front door and stopped. "I don't want to get caught in these hills after dark."

"What? Come on, you're not afraid of the dark, are you?" Bryson teased.

"Nope. I just like to see where I'm going. A guy could easily fall off a cliff or into a cavern if he's not careful. Even with a flashlight, these hills can be so dark you can't see your hand in front of your face."

"Do you still think this place is haunted?"

"No, not now. Almost everybody thinks this place is haunted. Well, the kids do. My friend Jase Bode's grandpa would always hang out with Old Man Kinsey, who lived here before you. Well,

I mean after you. Anyway, down at the coffee shop, Old Man Kinsey would tell these crazy stories about werewolves and ghosts roaming the countryside. Everyone blew him off as crazy, so no one would ever come check out his stories. Jase and I used to sneak down here about once a month, but we never made it past that gate down at the end of the pasture. I was too scared."

"What changed your mind?"

"I don't know. I was worried before I showed up at the gate. I didn't know if I could pass through it. Then I wasn't afraid anymore. Pretty weird," Jared admitted. "It was like this place had a strange curse put on it, and then the curse was lifted. I can't explain it."

"You're right—pretty weird," Bryson agreed, remembering when he was in Europe, coming across a lot of strange occurrences during his journey that were unexplainable.

"See you later. Thanks for the water," Jared said.

"Wait. Here's your pay for the day," Bryson said, handing Jared three twenties. "Don't spend it all in the same place."

"Thanks, but I only worked eight hours. I earned forty-eight dollars, not sixty."

"Keep it. You've earned it."

"Thanks again."

"Let me give you a ride home. It will be completely dark in fifteen minutes."

"I'm good. I can be home faster if I take off across the hills. It will take me twice as long to ride in your Jeep," Jared informed.

"I don't want you to get in trouble."

"I won't."

"Have your parents call me if they have any questions. They'll have to call me at school. We're in a dead zone here; there's no service at all in these hills."

"I will," Jared indicated as he let the screen door slam shut. He jumped from the porch and jogged toward the gate.

Bryson stepped out onto the porch and watched Jared until he disappeared through the gate. *Good kid.*

He wasn't the only one watching. A pair of golden eyes watched from the dark underbrush near the stream.

Part Three
The Revelation

Earth, do not cover my blood; may my cry for help find no resting place. Even now my witness is in heaven.

—Job 16:18–19a (NIV)

Monger's Evil Plan

Tyrel drove up to the main house in his squad car and parked on the east side under a garage canopy. The house was a two-story frame structure with a porch that surrounded the entire house. The wood siding had never been painted and was now a dark weatherwood gray color. Black shudders bordered both sides of the windows that were covered inside with red curtains. A rock chimney extended from the foundation to the roof's peak. A small dusting of smoke filtered out the chimney's top.

Tyrel walked past the porch steps leading up to the front door and toward the back of the house.

Jake Monger was in the yard playing by himself. He had a pine cone and was tossing it in the air, trying to hit it with a broom handle.

Toss. Swing. Miss.

Jake had performed this ritual a thousand times and had yet to hit the cone. "Watch me, Tyrel, I'm getting pretty good at this," Jake said, tossing the cone up again. Swing. Miss. "Rat's rear! I'll get it next time."

"Ya, Jake, whatever. You do that," Tyrel said, leaving his brother in the yard alone.

Tyrel continued walking around the side of the house. He stopped dead in his tracks after glancing over at the sweat box where Rubin was imprisoned. Timer was sitting guard on the 4×4×4 metal shed. The sweat box looked like an outhouse that had been chopped in half. Rubin had been locked up in there since yesterday evening. He was to serve a three-day sentence.

Tyrel eased his way to the metal shed, glancing at Timer and then at the door. "Hey, boy. You still alive in there?"

No answer.

"You better answer me. You don't want me to come in there."

After a short pause. "I'm still in here."

"Good. I hope you learn something this time, boy. You needn't be drawin' attention to yourself or the family. You must keep a low profile. You'll be runnin' things around here someday. You gots to carry on the tradition. You understanding me, boy?"

"Yes, sir. I understand," Rubin begrudgingly stated. "When am I gettin' out of here? It smells like crap, and it's hot."

"Soon. Maybe tomorrow. We'll have to see how your attitude is gettin'."

Rubin cussed through the metal door.

Tyrel looked up at Timer, who hadn't moved throughout the whole verbal exchange with Rubin. Timer's red eyes burned through Tyrel until he could no longer look at Timer and had to turn away. As he stumbled away from the sweat box, he could feel Timer's red eyes draining his energy. He was under Timer's control. Timer had branded his soul. He couldn't break the spell. He glanced to the right to where the dog pens were located. Every pit bull was motionless and standing, staring at him, burning their red eyes through his soul.

Tyrel continued his zombielike walk toward the back door of the house. He dragged his legs up each step until finally he reached the top and swung the screen door open and entered the kitchen. Once inside the house and out of their vision, his head immediately cleared and energy came back.

Elizabeth was standing at the stove cooking meatloaf and fried potatoes. She glanced slightly toward Tyrel as he walked in.

"What'cha cookin'? I'm hungry enough to eat a mule." Tyrel didn't wait for a reply that never came as he hooked his hat and gun belt on a hat rack standing in the corner next to the dining room table.

The dining room table had been set for eight, but Elizabeth came in and picked up two plates—Billy Ray was on patrol and Rubin was in the sweat box. She placed the plates back in the cabinet.

Jake came in and set his stick and cone by the back door. "Is supper ready, Elizabeth? I'm a-starving. My stomach is hollerin', 'Feed me, Jake, feed me!'"

"In a minute. Go stand by your chair and wait for your daddy," Elizabeth ordered, pulling the hot buttered buns from the stove. *Just in time.*

"Goody."

Jim Bob and Skeeter were already standing by their chairs, waiting to be seated. No one ever had to yell at them twice to come eat a meal. They hadn't changed much in the last twenty years. Neither one had ever married or even had a woman. They both were pushing maximum density in their overalls, stretching the adjustments on their straps to the very end. Although they are identical twins over the years, it had become a lot easier to tell them apart. The scars from Tyrel's beating on Jim Bob's face had become more apparent and wrinkled with age.

The twins were itching to get their paws on some grub. They looked at each other at the food, then at each other, and then at the food. It had only been a few hours since their last meal, but it seemed like days to them.

Tyrel stood at the corner of the table. Elizabeth brought the last of the food and stood behind the chair directly in front of Tyrel.

Tyrel looked around to see if everyone was in their proper place behind their chairs. They were all accounted for and present, except for the two empty seats—one in the middle and one at the opposite end from Tyrel. He picked up a serving bell and rang it.

Everyone immediately looked down at the table.

There was a short pause; then a door from somewhere in the back of the house opened and slammed shut. They heard heavy footsteps moving down the hallway. The footsteps stopped. A grandfather clock had begun to chime—seven times it sounded through the quiet house. The footsteps began again.

Everyone's eyes at the table remained looking down. Tyrel wanted to look up. He abhorred the idea of this submissive behavior toward his daddy. *I should be head of this family. Daddy is too old.*

Nate entered the dining room.

No one moved. Especially Tyrel.

Nate smirked. *They're weak. All of you.* He walked up and stood behind the empty chair at the head of the dining table.

"Let us pray. Master of the Dawn, we come here to gather in your honor. Bless this food. Bless this family. Bless the time I have left with my family. Bless us with a quality runner for our next Running Moon. Master … I know you will provide a worthy opponent, my Master—until time is time. You may be seated."

They all sat in unison, but none ate. They were waiting on Nate.

Nate took his sweet time making sure everyone waited. It was his way of showing them who was in control. Nate was very deliberate in loading his plate with food while the others watched and waited. He forked a piece of meatloaf and lifted slowly toward his mouth. Once he clamped his mouth down on the fork, the table erupted in chaotic hands and elbows. It had become a free-for-all. The rest of the Mongers were grabbing and slinging as much food as they could get their hands on, except Elizabeth, who still had her hands in her lap patiently waiting for her moment to eat.

After the Mongers had pretty much inhaled their food, Elizabeth meekly dipped out a small portion for her plate. Jim Bob and Skeeter were leaning back in their chairs with their hands on their big bellies and a big smile on their face to match. Jake had finished eating and was playing with a pair of Hot Wheels cars around his empty plate. Even Tyrel with a toothpick in his mouth seemed momentarily content with his surroundings. Nothing like a good meal to put everything at ease.

Nate raised his hand like a sovereign king. "There are a few things we need to discuss before the next full moon. First, Rubin has got to get under control. He's worse than you ever thought about being when you were in school, Tyrel. You better put a short leash on that boy, or I will."

Tyrel did not say a word, but he knew that if Rubin didn't shape up pretty quick, Nate was going to reshape him and everyone else around here. No one made a sound—not even Jake, who had put away his cars into a front pocket. They were not allowed to speak until Nate had finished speaking his mind.

Nate continued after looking around the table. "Second, we do not have a prey at this time, but Master will provide. He always supplies our needs. We have fifteen days until the next Running Moon—*we will have a prey.* Finally, Tyrel, were you able to make an offer on our land that is occupied by Bryson Keahbone?"

"Yes, but he flat refused and told me he would never sell. I have an idea though. Why don't I just arrest him, bring him out here, and let the pits run him? Then we can just buy his land in probate court. He don't have nobody around here that will want that property. We get a prey and get our land back. We can kill two preys with one pit," Tyrel suggested, trying to sound clever.

"You stinkin' idiot," Nate wailed, standing on his feet and leaning forward on balled fists. "We tried that once, or don't you remember? Your impatience just about destroyed the whole family. I was close to getting that land, and you go and arrest Joseph Keahbone, that schoolteacher's father, and bring him here exposing our whole operation. What choice did I have but to run him?" Nate shuddered at the sound of that name. *Keahbone's legacy will end with Bryson, I will personally see to it.*

Nate glared at Tyrel. "Hoot Brown had every law enforcement agent in southeast Oklahoma lookin' for that Injun. Luckily we had that scumbag in the drunk tank that we threw on the railroad tracks. It took a lot of convincing to have the coroner pronounce that body to be Keahbone's. And then to get it cremated. Master was looking out for us. Bryson's mother also did us a favor by going into that coma and dying. We'll have to be careful this time around. We won't get a second chance. Tyrel, have you initiated phase one of our plan?"

Tyrel lifted his face and smiled slyly. He turned his head toward Elizabeth. "The seed of the plan has been planted and is ready to sprout forth. We should be good to go in two Running Moons."

"You better not fail."

"I will not fail. Seed has been planted and is ready to sprout, just waiting on your orders to proceed with phrase two," Tyrel repeated.

"When the time is right."

Elizabeth smiled ever so slightly.

Ishkitini

During the week, Jared arrived at Bryson's cabin every day around five o'clock and worked until almost dark. Bryson was very pleased with the progress they were making with the cabin's repairs. The plumbing had been replaced, and the floor had been resurfaced and needed to be stained. All broken windows and log cabin mortar on the inside and outside had been fixed. New doors were hung throughout the cabin, including the missing front door. A new furnace and air unit were wired and installed, waiting for the Rural Electric Coop electrician to inspect and turn the power on. Pretty much all that was left was hanging a few light fixtures, two ceiling fans, and staining the floor.

"Let's call it a night. Tomorrow's Friday. You have a game against Hartshorne, but I think we can finish this project by Saturday afternoon."

"I agree. We make a good team, Mr. Keahbone," Jared testified, admiring their work on the cabin.

"Yes, we do. Saturday we will celebrate. You like steak?

"Love it."

"Excellent. Are you sure you wouldn't like a ride home?"

"I told you, Mr. Keahbone, that would take too long. Besides, I need to stay in shape for football," Jared said, knowing someday he was going to have to tell Bryson who his momma was. *He'll find out soon enough, there's no hurry.*

Jared left after Bryson paid him.

From the porch Bryson watched after Jared until he had disappeared out the gate. *He should have enough daylight to make it home safely. I don't believe that the wolf will harm Jared. I could call Hoot just the same and have him bring his gun to scare off the wolf, not kill him, unless he tries something dangerous. It has probably moved on to better hunting grounds. I haven't seen it in a long time.*

Movement caught Bryson's eye by the stream. He stepped off the porch and walked to the creek. The stream was calm and had turned a dark blue beneath the fading light. He started to turn and head back to the cabin when from a huge creek elm he heard something.

Whoo! Hooo! Whoo!

Bryson looked up and saw a great horned owl perched majestically on a branch that extended out over the water. It was one of the most beautiful creatures he had ever seen.

Bryson suddenly remembered sitting on that decayed fallen log by the stream with his father the evening before he disappeared.

"*Ishkitini*, also known as the horned owl, is very important figure of your Choctaw heritage," Bryson's father, Joseph Keahbone, said.

Bryson didn't say a word. He was mesmerized by the beauty of the great owl as it proudly rested on the branch. The owl's plumage was a grayish brown color. Feathery ear tufts reached toward the sky. Facial discs captured each golden eye. Both the beak and talons were hooked and razor sharp, holding steadfast to the bough. *Awesome!*

"Ishkitini is the night messenger. Sometimes he carries the message of light. He will guide us through the dark valleys of the unknown and loneliness, helping us to embrace our fears. He sees what others cannot. The owl flies through the dark of night, unafraid of the shadow beings. The shadow beings are the evil things that take control of people and make them do bad things.

Ishkitini will aid us in our search for the light of a dark world when he must go away. He can be a good omen if that is his purpose," Joseph said.

"What is an omen?"

"An omen is a sign or happening believed to foretell a good or bad event," Joseph answered.

"How can you tell if it's going to be a good or bad omen?" Bryson asked.

"You don't know for sure, you just know Ishkitini is coming for someone."

"I'm confused."

"One must be aware of Ishkitini's presence. He is the messenger of light, but he is also the messenger of death. If Ishkitini is hooting, he is leading someone to the light, but if he screeches, death awaits in the darkness." Joseph paused and then held up three fingers. "*Ishkitini* serves three functions: First, it searches— seeking the soul of the person who is assigned by Chitokaka (the Great One). Second, it demands— pursuing relentless, waiting for the assigned moment. Third, it disciplines—following through with the fated moment."

Bryson looked up, studying closely the horned owl, soaking in all words his father had just informed him.

"Which messenger is he tonight?"

"I'm not sure. We must be patient, wait and listen for Ishkitini to tell us."

"I will listen, Father."

The great horned owl quickly spread its wings and leaned forward, lifting its body in a silent swoosh of its wings from the limb. He flew silently through the air and disappeared in the shadows.

"Father, I am listening."

When my time is time upon the final scene, come find me beneath the Moon When Wolves Cry.

Jared's Accident

B ryson got up a little before daybreak. He was feeling more excited about the direction of his life than he had in over two years.

He had put on his running clothes and walked out to the old oak tree to visit his mother's grave. Every day, before he would begin his day, he wanted to talk to his mother.

"Good morning, Mother. Another beautiful day. I dreamed about the lady in the light again. She keeps telling me something about finding someone. I don't have a clue what she's talking about. Her words always fade out before I can fully understand them." Bryson paused and looked over his shoulder at the cabin. "We're almost finished. The cabin looks almost as good as it did when you were living here, but not quite. It needs a woman's touch."

Bryson's smile faded as thoughts of Becky entered his mind. He had spoken to Becky several times about coming back here after the Olympics and maybe even making a summer home here. She was very excited about the opportunity. His heart had become overwhelmed with sorrow. He hadn't thought about Becky much this past week, but now, he couldn't shake these bitter feelings.

"Talk to you later, Mom. I need to go clear my head."

Bryson took off down the drive at a dead sprint but leveled his pace off by the time he had gotten to the gate. He tried to focus more on his running and less on Becky; then he turned his attention to the day's schedule to help occupy his mind.

It worked a little.

Bryson had stayed up most of the night staining the floor, so it would be dried by today. He had to sleep on the porch, but he didn't mind because the night was cool from a light northern breeze.

Bryson jogged all the way out to the highway before heading back to the cabin. It took him a little over an hour and forty minutes to make the thirteen-mile trip. His longest run since he had taken back up his running. In his prime running condition, this distance would take less than an hour. He could feel himself getting stronger, but he still was a long way from being in good running condition. *I will pay for the extra miles today, but it will be worth it.*

The stream was cool and refreshing to Bryson after the run.

Jared was going to be later than usual, probably midafternoon. He had told Bryson that he had a mega amount of chores to do before he could come to work on the cabin.

Apparently, Bryson figured, *Jared had been neglecting his chores at home because of all the time he had been working on the cabin. Good for his parents—I like them.*

Bryson finished rechecking the wiring on the new hot water heater. He picked up some old excess wiring and took it outside to a trash pile they had begun by the porch. He noticed Jared passing through the gate, but he was not alone. The wolf was following him, keeping to the shadows of the underbrush.

This is very odd. I need to talk to Hoot. I'm not going to say anything to the boy right now. I don't want to alarm him. It would be a good idea if I start taking him home in the evenings.

Jared waved.

Bryson waved back, keeping his eyes fixed on the wolf as he darted in and out of view. Until finally, the wolf disappeared altogether behind the huge oak where Bryson's mother was buried.

"Howdy. You didn't finish without me, did ya?"

"No way."

"Good. What's left?'

"I stained the floor last night, and it has dried enough to walk on. There were two ceiling fans to install, but I hung one this morning. I saved the other one for you," Bryson said after he saw the deflated look on Jared's face.

"Thanks. I want to earn my keep."

"You got it. The fan is all yours. I'm going to put this gas grill together. Then I am going to marinate a couple of juicy T-bone steaks. How's that sound?" Bryson asked.

"Perfect. Where's the fan?"

"It's in the living room. You can use the four-foot long bench stool or the eight-foot stepladder. The bench stool is safer, but the ladder might be easier. You decide. I'll be on the porch assembling the grill. Don't hesitate to holler for help."

"I'm good. Thanks. I should be able to manage. I put up all our fans at my house without any problems," Jared declared proudly.

"Good deal. You're on your own. But you know where to find me." Bryson winked at Jared. "Good luck."

Earlier Bryson had arranged all the parts and wiring in proper installation order for an easy assembly. All Jared had to do was attach the wires, mount the body to the base on the ceiling, and screw in the blades.

Jared put on his tool belt and walked inside. He looked at the mount. It was roughly ten feet off the floor. The bench stool would be too short for him, Jared thought. He grabbed and unfolded the stepladder. "This will work."

Two hours later, Jared was putting the finishing touches on the ceiling fan. He was very meticulous with his work. He would carefully read the directions, then look at the fan, and reread the directions before making his next move. He wanted everything to be perfect.

Bryson poked in his head from the front porch every now and then to check on his progress. Of course, Jared always said everything was going fine.

Bryson assembled the grill, but he decided not to start cooking until Jared had finished putting up the ceiling fan. That turned out to be a good choice.

Jared had only one blade left to screw in, but he was having trouble reaching the back screw on the blade bracket. He stepped up to the rung second from the top and twisted around to get in a better working position. Each time he tried to better his angle, a loud sigh escaped his mouth.

Bryson called through the screen door. "Need some help in there, Jared?"

"No, I'm …" Jared began but never finished.

Argh!

There was a loud crash.

Bryson jumped up and rushed toward the door, hoping Jared had dropped the ceiling fan and not flown off the ladder. When he rushed through the doorway, Jared was sitting on the floor holding his arm up against his chest.

"Are you okay?" Bryson knelt beside Jared. "Let me see your arm. Where are you injured?"

"My wrist. It hurts really bad. I think it's broken. My mother is going to kill me."

Bryson gently picked up his arm and examined Jared's wrist. "See if you can bend it a little—back and forth—like this." Bryson raised his wrist to show him how to bend it.

"I can't."

"Sure you can. Try for me."

Jared moved his wrist painfully up and down, and then he wiped away a tear. He was mad at himself for crying.

"Great job. We will need to put some ice on it. Now I have some good news and some bad news. Which would you like to hear first?"

Jared gave Bryson a puzzled look, and then he realized what he was asking. "Good news, I guess."

"The good news is through my very limited experiences with broken bones, I don't think it is broken, only a bad sprain."

"Great," Jared said sarcastically. "I can't wait for the bad news."

"No party tonight. We'll celebrate later. I need to drive you home and tell your parents what has happened."

Jared was extremely bummed out. He had looked forward all week to this day. *I'm so stupid.* Then he realized what was going to happen if Bryson took him home.

Bryson removed a plastic storage baggy and walked to the ice chest.

"Mr. Keahbone, that's okay. I feel fine. It's not hurting that much anymore. See," Jared lied, trying unsuccessfully to open and close his hand.

"Nice try," Bryson said as he filled the baggy up with ice. "Here, place this on your wrist for twenty minutes. I am giving you a ride home, and that's final."

Jared's eyes swelled again with tears. *I'm so stupid!*

Bryson must have noticed. "It's okay. Everything is going to be all right. It's not your fault. Accidents happen sometimes, regardless of how careful we try to be. Make sure you keep that ice on your wrist to keep the swelling down. Let me get the keys, and we'll head out of here."

Jared walked with Bryson out to the Jeep.

"It really does feel better," Jared said in a last ditch effort to avoid the unavoidable.

Bryson frowned and motioned to Jared to climb in the Jeep. He had to help Jared pull himself into the passenger seat.

Jared remained quiet during the ride except for the occasional offering of info on how to get to his house.

"Your parents will probably want to get it x-rayed as a precaution, but I really believe it is only a sprain," Bryson informed, lifting up the ice pack. "See. There is hardly any swelling, which is a good sign."

"It's not the swelling I'm worried about," Jared mumbled to himself.

After traveling several miles on a very winding road, Jared pointed at a dirt road beside a green mailbox. "That's my road."

Now I know why Jared wanted to walk home all those days. It's a long way around to his house. But today would not have been a good day to walk. Besides I am kind of anxious to meet his parents. I would like to inform them about how great a worker Jared has been for me.

Bryson slowed the Jeep and turned down the narrow road, which was lined heavily on both sides with black oaks. The sun was setting, making the road appear to be in a tunnel. It was a quarter mile up to the house from the main road. There was a small clearing to the right. On the opposite side of the clearing stood a large gray barn followed by a small rectangular rock house. It reminded Bryson of an old-fashioned bunkhouse. No vehicles were parked in the front of the long porch. He followed the road until it ended at the side of the house. There were two vehicles parked under a carport. One was a 1971 Ford pickup. The other was a red Ford Explorer.

Bryson recognized the red Explorer immediately. He looked over at Jared, who was staring down at his arm. If Jared could have crawled under his seat, he would have.

"Dude. Really?"

Jared raised his head to speak, but lowered it again, saying nothing.

"And you were going to tell me … when?"

"Sorry … I thought you knew," Jared lied.

Jared braced himself for the tongue lashing that he knew was coming, but to his surprise, Bryson just grinned and said …

Are You Gonna Kiss Me or…

"*Not!*" Jared jerked his head toward Bryson.

"What's with the confuzzled look on your face? You made a statement that I didn't agree with. So I said, 'Not.' It was popular in the day."

"Oh yeah? When was that, the sixties?" Jared chuckled, feeling a little more at ease.

"Ha-ha! A real funny guy with a busted chicken wing," Bryson laughed.

Jared tried not to laugh because it made his arm hurt, but he couldn't help it; he laughed anyway.

"Let me tell you what my great-grandfather, Jay Don Keahbone, the great philosopher, used to say, 'He who laughs last, laughs last.'"

"What? That doesn't make sense," Jared said, this time his side had begun to hurt from laughing.

"I know. But that's what he always told me," Bryson said. *Mission accomplished.* He wanted to ease Jared's mind from his worries. He wanted to let Jared know he wasn't mad. "We better get inside. I'm sure there will be a lot of explaining to do to your mom, and I'm very sure she's not going to be real happy either."

"I know. But technically I didn't lie to either one of you."

Bryson cocked a brow at Jared.

Jared lowered his head. "It was wrong. I should've been on the up and up with both of you. I guess I was afraid Mom wouldn't let me come over and help you. It just seemed like every time I saw you and Mom talking, one of you was always mad at the other."

Bryson couldn't argue. *It's true.*

"I'm really sorry."

"I forgive you. I actually understand more than you think, and I believe your mother will too."

"Thank you. Now I guess I need to go talk to Mom," Jared said.

They climbed out of the Jeep. Jared made it out without help. The pain had come back in his wrist.

They walked slowly up the steps to the porch. A radio on a small table was softly playing country music. Bryson felt tightness in his stomach as he knocked, and then he opened the door for Jared. Jared walked in first, and Bryson followed closely behind.

The front entry way opened to a large living area. The wooden floor was covered in part by a huge Santa Fe–style rug. The furniture was simple and plain—very homey and lived in. *I like it. Much better than her office.*

Bryson smelled food cooking in the kitchen. *It smells like spaghetti.*

Piper entered the living area from the kitchen. She was wearing jeans and a black tank top, which was partially covered by a red-checkered apron. Her black hair was pulled up in a ponytail.

This was the first time Bryson had ever seen Piper in civilian clothes.

Bryson's stomach turned again. He played it off as being hungry joined with the smell of food, but there was more to it than he was letting on.

She stopped in her tracks and was momentarily caught off guard. Then she figured it out. "You are the neighbor that Jared has been working for? He conveniently forgot to tell me that part. He does odd jobs for our neighbor, John Caraway, every summer and some weekends. I figured that was who Jared was working for."

"He has been helping me for a couple of weeks. I had no idea that he didn't tell you where he was. I just took it for granted that you knew," Bryson assumed. "To be honest with you, until now, I had not a clue Jared was your son."

"He's in your class. How did you not know he is my son?"

"He has a different last name for starters. And besides, nobody bothered to tell me," Bryson admitted, looking over at Jared, who had lowered his head. Bryson remembered what Jared had said about how every time he and and Piper would talk to each other, one or both always left upset.

"Mom, it was my fault. I'm sorry. I should have told you and Mr. Keahbone the truth. I really wanted to go help Mr. Keahbone fix up his cabin. You know how much I like to build and fix up things … but I was afraid you wouldn't let me go," Jared said.

"Why?"

Jared didn't answer.

"Tell her what you told me. By the way, you are right," Bryson confessed to Jared.

"Mom, every time I see you and Mr. Keahbone talking, you are always arguing with each other, and someone leaves mad."

Piper started to argue but realized he was right. She frowned and thought that if Jared noticed, then everybody else had noticed also. She glanced at Bryson, "Do we really argue that much?"

Bryson nodded, "I'm afraid so."

"We'll work on that. Agree, Mr. Keahbone?"

"Agreed."

Jared smiled and then grabbed his arm painfully, remembering his injured wrist.

"What happened? Are you okay?" Piper asked sympathetically. "I'm all right. It's just a little bruised. I fell off a ladder and landed on my wrist. It will be okay, Mom. I'm not a baby anymore."

Piper gently grabbed and inspected Jared's wrist. There was only slight swelling in the hand and wrist area. She shot Bryson a concerned look.

"I think it's just a sprain. We can take him to the ER in town, so they can x-ray it. But all they're going to do is wrap it in an Ace bandage and tell you to take him to your doctor on Monday. Your doctor will re-x-ray the wrist and proceed from there with either a hard cast or wrist support. Mind you, I'm no expert, but if it were me, I would wait at least until Monday."

Piper wanted to say, *Well, you're not me.* But she caught herself, remembering the words Jared had told them about how much they argue.

"Okay."

What? Bryson and Jared were both caught off-guard. *No argument.*

"We'll wait."

"Good. It's already feeling better. Mom, can Mr. Keahbone stay for dinner?" Jared asked through pleading eyes.

Piper hesitated.

Bryson decided to bail Piper out. "It's getting late. I probably should be getting back home."

What could it hurt?

"Mr. Keahbone, would you like to stay for dinner?"

"Well ... uhh ... sure. I'd love to."

"It's ready. Let me get the toast out of the oven, and we can eat."

Piper disappeared into the kitchen, stopping at the refrigerator. There was a small rectangular mirror on the door. She pulled the ponytail holder off and ran her fingers through her hair and then quickly wrapped her hair and pulled the holder up tight again. She brushed her face with her finger, smoothing out what little makeup she had put on. She was very thankful that she had even put some on. *I would have been way too scary for company. Why am I getting so worked up about this man? I don't need a relationship right now.*

"Awesome. Mr. Keahbone, my mom is a really good cook," Jared bragged as he led Bryson to the dining room table.

Piper quickly set out another plate setting on the table, followed by the noodles, meatball sauce, and slightly burnt toast. She wiped her hands off on her apron, more from sweat than anything else. *Why am I so nervous?*

"I believe we're ready. Sorry about the toast—a little overcooked."

Bryson remained standing until Piper had removed her apron and sat down at the table. She nodded at Jared. Jared asked for blessing over the food and their day.

"I'm starved."

"His hurt wing definitely hasn't affected his appetite."

"No, definitely not. He eats like a horse."

They all snickered.

The rest of dinner was surrounded with light conversation. Bryson still avoided most of the real personal questions, but he was beginning to feel at ease with Piper, making it a lot easier to talk and open up to her. She felt the same way.

After dinner, Jared started picking up their plates with his good hand to take them to the kitchen. "Mom, may I wash them after Mr. Keahbone leaves?"

"I tell you what," Piper smiled, "I'm putting you on the injured reserve list until your wing gets better. Leave them here on the table, and I will pinch-hit for you."

"Sweet!"

Bryson grinned at Piper. "You know baseball?"

"Why so shocked?"

"I don't know. You strike me as …" Bryson tried to pick his words carefully, "a person who is very busy with … work."

"Yes, I do work a lot, but believe it or not, I am an avid baseball fan. Watch it every chance I get, which is pretty much … never. We don't have cable or satellite, and the one channel we do get doesn't carry too many baseball games."

"At least you have electricity. I should have it turned on by Monday at the cabin."

"Yes, that's got to be a pain."

"No complaints."

Jared had returned to his chair and sat down. "Mom, the stories about the Kinsey Farm being haunted are not true. There are no ghosts or werewolves hanging around terrorizing whoever lives there."

"I never believed that they were true. The stories were invented to keep people from coming around the old place."

"Who invented the stories?" Jared asked.

"Old Man Kinsey invented tall tales to keep people away from his house. He was a crazy old man. When he came to town, which wasn't very often, he would tell wild stories about these demon dogs with bright red eyes that ran wild in the hills every full moon."

"Werewolves?" Jared wondered.

"No. There's no such thing."

"Did you ever meet Old Man Kinsey?" Bryson asked, becoming more interested in the story.

"No. This happened before I moved here. Hoot informed me about all the happenings in this small town. Of course, you know Hoot. He's friends with everybody he meets. I do remember Hoot saying that old man Kinsey always rambled on that these dogs were hellhounds."

Jared was sitting on the edge of his chair, trying to be polite by not interrupting, waiting patiently for a pause, so he could talk. But none came.

"What happened to Old Man Kinsey?"

"He lived at your place for a few years and then suffered a massive heart attack and died. The sheriff found him dead at the cabin. That's about all the details I know except for Vicki buying the place out from under the Mongers, who were not very happy."

"Tell me about it. Tyrel wasn't too thrilled when I turned down his offer to buy my land. He said he would pay double what I paid for it."

"The Mongers own almost all the land around us. I have a hundred eighty acres here. John next door has two hundred sixty. You have two hundred up in the valley. But other than that, they own pretty much this side of the county all the way out to the Ouachita National Park."

"Why do you think they want so much land?"

"Power. They like being in control. They have had their hands involved in just about everything around here for years except for the school. Hoot and Vicki help keep the education part in the hands of the people, but the Mongers do run the sheriff 's office and Leflore County Court House. Vicki is not a big fan of the Mongers. A long time ago, she noticed how the Mongers were buying up all the land and decided that she would do some buying of her own. Now she has almost as much land as the Mongers. Vicki leases almost all her land for different things. As far as I know, the Mongers don't let anyone near their land. It's really strange."

"Mom, look who you're talking about," Jared reported, proud that he finally got to speak. He was beginning to think that they had forgotten about him. Maybe they had.

"Be nice," Piper joked.

"Interesting, but weird."

Piper stood up and grabbed their tea glasses and headed toward the kitchen. She abruptly turned, catching Bryson staring at her. "Would you like some coffee?"

"Umm … s-s-sure … thank you," Bryson stammered, feeling a little embarrassed for being caught. *She is a very beautiful woman.* He started feeling very antsy. *It is probably past time for me to leave.* He stood up to tell her it was time for him to leave, but she escaped into the kitchen before he could speak. She returned a minute later with two blue coffee mugs.

"Thanks." Bryson sat back down.

Piper sat across the table from Bryson. She placed the two mugs down on the table. "Brewed it earlier. Sugar?"

Bryson waved his hand sideways. "No, thank you."

"Hoot told me that you used to be a marathon runner," Piper said.

Oh no. Here we go again. She's going to want to pry into my life— again. "Yes, awhile back I used to run a little bit," Bryson said, trying very hard to keep his cool. *Be patient here!*

"I can hardly run a mile let alone twenty-six miles. What made you want to become a long-distance runner?"

Harmless enough.

"That's a good question," Bryson indicated. "When I was growing up in Oregon, all I wanted to do was play baseball. I wanted to be a professional baseball player and play for the Yankees. My best friend, Johnny, and I were the only freshmen who made my high school varsity baseball team. We both played pitcher. I ended up pitching a lot of games. Do you know much about the conditioning of pitchers?"

"A little. I did play coed softball a few times." Piper grinned, not able to take her eyes off Bryson.

"Close … not really. Baseball pitchers have it harder than position players because their workouts consist of a lot of running to keep swelling and soreness out of their arms after they pitch. I was pitching a lot, therefore I ran *a lot*. My freshman year, we got beat out in districts, which was a day before the regional track meet. Our school's track coach always saw Johnny and me running after we pitched, whether it was after a game or practice, so he invited us to run the 3,200-meter race at the regional track meet. My baseball season was over for the year, and I had to run anyway, so we both figured it couldn't hurt. Besides we got to get out of school. So we both raced. I finished first, and Johnny finished second. We qualified for the state championship the next weekend. Johnny and I trained all that week and ran in the meet."

"How'd you do?" Jared asked, who had been a statue throughout the whole conversation between Bryson and his mom.

"Okay, I guess, for a rookie."

"What place?"

"Does it matter?"

"Yes. You should always do your best. That's what you told us."

"You're right. I did better than Johnny. He decided to do some extracurricular activities the night before."

"What are extracurricular activities?" Jared questioned.

"Partied with some not-so-good bad people."

"Oh, I see. So I guess you didn't do so well either."

"Although Johnny was one of my best friends, I refused to hang out with those bad people. I tried to get him away from them, but they always lured him back." Bryson paused, wondering where Johnny might be. "I ended up winning the state championship in record time. I decided that track was my best sport. I won the state championship three more times and eventually went to Oregon University on a full-ride scholarship for track. Although I've kept my glove handy all these years, hoping for a comeback, because I still love baseball very much. And that's the end of that," Bryson declared.

"That's a cool story."

"Thanks, Jared. You're pretty cool yourself."

"Not that cool," Jared said, grabbing hold of his wrist.

"You're cooler than you think. I should know, I'm a cool person expert," Bryson pointed out as he looked down at his watch— almost nine. *Where had the time gone?* He stood up and faced Piper. "I believe it's time for me to leave. It's getting late. Thank you for dinner. It was very good."

"Thank you. It was nice meeting *you*." Piper smiled.

"Yeah, I agree. It was nice." Bryson understood her meaning.

"Can I walk Mr. Keahbone out?" Jared asked.

"I need you to ice your wrist. I can tell it's bothering you again."

"Aw, Mom, I was going to walk Mr. Keahbone out." Jared sighed as he subconsciously grabbed his wrist and then quickly removed his hand.

"You can say your good-byes right now."

"Good night, Mr. Keahbone. Church tomorrow—don't forget."

"Night, Jared. We'll see. Hey, ice that wrist for twenty minutes before bedtime and take some Ibuprofen for the pain and swelling."

Jared gave a thumb up with his good hand and ducked out through the kitchen doorway.

Bryson and Piper walked out onto the porch, letting the screen door close gently behind them. They stepped to the edge of the porch and stopped. The outside house lights illuminated the porch but couldn't penetrate the surrounding darkness under the raven sky. Bryson eased down the slightly steep steps and then turned listening to a song that was playing on the radio. He grinned, "Great song, great group—Thompson Square."

When you smiled and said to me—Are you gonna kiss me or not?

Piper turned toward the radio and then back to Bryson. During the turn, she lost her footing and started to fall down the steps. Bryson stepped up and caught her before she fell. Their faces were only inches apart. They stared into each other's eyes.

Time was momentarily frozen.

The radio continued playing in the background.

Are you gonna kiss me or not?

Are we gonna do this or what?

Teardrop of an Angel

Their faces remained only inches apart.

Bryson eased forward.

Piper closed her eyes.

A bright light flashed in the ebony sky.

Bryson pulled back and looked up into the sky. Piper quickly opened her eyes and turned them upward.

A brightly lit falling star raced across the length of the sky before finally burning out at the edge of the stratosphere.

Bryson still had Piper in his arms, and then suddenly he felt a little awkward. He helped her regain her balance on the steps. He tried to speak. Nothing. All words had escaped him. He just looked into her eyes and smiled.

"Thank you. Nice catch," Piper said warmly, feeling a little embarrassed.

Bryson wanted to embrace and kiss her, but something was holding him back. He couldn't let go of this feeling. He wouldn't let go. "Thanks. I wasn't lying when I told you I wanted to be a baseball player," Bryson joked lightheartedly, but his insides were being wound up like a jack-in-a-box ready to spring out his belly button.

Piper laughed. Their eyes locked together.

Bryson longed to lean forward but was held back by the velvet chains of his past. He broke eye contact and looked toward the sky. "By the way, that was a teardrop of an angel."

"A what?"

"Teardrop of an angel is what some of the highlanders of Scotland call a falling star."

"Why is that?" Piper asked, unable to take her eyes off Bryson. *I could fall for this guy. But I shouldn't. Never date anyone you work with. Remember, it's your number one rule. Shoot—my number one rule lately is don't date anybody. But this guy is special—my intuition senses it.*

" When I was traveling in Scotland, I met an old highlander. He must have been a lonely old man. He saw me walking down a gravel road by his house carrying my backpack and bedroll. He insisted that I stay with him for he had no family to speak of. I'll never forget his name, Digger McGillycuddy. I believe he wanted to pass on all he knew before he died. He had a story for every event under the sun. He taught me all about his people, the clans of the highlands. I learned their customs. Their heritage. I really loved that old man," Bryson paused, remembering his long talks as they roamed the picturesque countryside.

"He explained the many purposes of life in ways I had never dreamed of. We were sitting on a couple of large stones by the ocean late one evening talking about life, when a bright falling star, similar to the one awhile ago, shot across the sky," Bryson said, this time he closed his eyes, visualizing the old man and the backdrop of his home against the ocean.

Bryson sat down on the top step and looked over at Piper, who was now sitting beside him.

"You probably have heard how rain is sometimes referred to as tears of joy or sorrow from an angel?"

"Yes. I have often thought that myself."

"Well, Digger believed that. He also told me that when you see a falling star, it was also a teardrop of an angel. But in a bad and sorrowful way. The highlanders believed that when there is an event in someone's life that was fated to be but does not come to be, then an angel will cry a tear that falls as fire across the sky," Bryson continued. His face suddenly turned on a frown as memories from his past raced through his head. *I should have been there.*

"That's very sad," Piper said, trying to read the emotions showing on Bryson's face. *His pain runs deep.* She wanted to reach up and touch his face and remove his sadness.

"The only hope for that fated person is to be there and catch the teardrop as it descends to earth …" Bryson tapered off. *I should have been there.*

There was a long silence.

Bryson looked away from Piper. A coldness suddenly consumed his heart. Memories of Becky filled his mind. *I should have been there! She should have never died! I should have caught the teardrop! I should have—*

"Are you okay?" Piper asked as she put a consoling hand on his arm.

Bryson glanced over at her hand. He stood up abruptly and stepped down to the ground and turned toward Piper, who had remained sitting on the top step. He somewhat gained his composure.

"Again, thank you for dinner. I am very sorry about Jared. I will pay for any and all medical expenses. Have a good night," Bryson said without emotion.

Piper was dumbfounded. *What just happened here? First, I thought there was a moment. Then BOOM! Mr. Freeze. I'm such an idiot. Capital i. Idiot!*

Bryson turned sharply and walked to his Jeep.

Piper was at a total loss for words. She sat and watched Bryson's taillights disappear behind the tree line.

I play the fool once more.

She stood up and knocked the dust from her jeans. She shook her head and stared into the darkness beyond the light for a short moment. She turned and walked inside, turning off the porch light as she shut the door.

A pair of red eyes watched silently, and then faded into the dark bushes.

Johnny Flake

Johnny Flake had been on the road a long time, living on the money his dad wired him or he hustled in the pool halls or on the streets. He was down to his last ten bucks. He didn't want to call his dad, who would give him a thirty-minute lecture about growing up and being responsible. Besides, he only had three minutes left on his Go Phone. He knew he was close to his destination.

"I need a ride in this godforsaken land. Will no one give me a ride?" Johnny yelled, listening to the echo in the Kiamichi Mountains. "My odds aren't good when you only see *three cars an hour!*"

Johnny had hitched a ride out of McAlester and was hoping to make it all the way to Talihina, but no such luck. His ride had turned off at Highway 82, twelve miles west of Talihina. He had been walking the last two miles. His bulky backpack was starting to take its toll on him. The sun was directly overhead, making the pavement very hot. His back and feet were burning with pain. He decided to stop and rest. He removed his pack and sat it down on the road's shoulder. He pulled out his Go Phone from a pocket on the strap of his backpack. He turned it on. *Great. No bars!* He turned it back off to save the battery and then placed it back in the strap pocket. He placed his pack beside a pole holding a speed limit sign and then leaned against it waiting for his ride to arrive.

Forty-five minutes had passed and only five cars had driven by, none offering to help a guy in need. Johnny picked up and shouldered his backpack. He figured he would get to town faster if he walked. He had been walking about a mile, most of it uphill, when he noticed a police car top the next hill about a mile ahead. He looked around for a possible place to hide because his track record with local yokels had not been very good.

Beep!

Johnny about jumped out of his pants. He turned around abruptly. An old Chevy Stepside had come to a skidding stop. The red paint had oxidized to a pink tone. The lifters were clicking and screaming for more oil. Smoke was bellowing out from beneath the truck, but Johnny didn't care about any of that. It was a ride! And if it would get him into town, that would be real *peachy*.

"You going to Talihina?" Johnny asked as he walked up to the window.

"Sure am. Chunk your junk in the back," a bearded old man said, who could probably pass for Santa at Christmastime if he traded his faded overalls for a bright red suit.

"Thank you," Johnny exclaimed as he threw his pack in the back and jumped into the front seat. He slumped down in the seat as the truck popped and jerked to a rolling start. The old man grabbed the shifter on the steering column and shifted to second, then third.

The police car had slowed down. Johnny tried not to look but couldn't help it. He glanced over at the black-and-white car. The officer driving was looking hard at Johnny when he drove by. Johnny thought how the policeman looked small behind the wheel and had a weasel-looking face. Johnny quickly looked over his shoulder as the patrol car drove by but didn't stop.

Johnny breathed a sigh of relief.

"What'cha goin' to Tali for?"

"See an old friend I haven't seen in two years."

"That's a long time. He a-know you comin'?" the old man asked, chewing on his chaw of tobacco like a cow grinding cud.

"No, it's a surprise. We have been best friends ever since we were kids. We grew up playing baseball and ran track together in college."

"Then how a-come you haven't talked with him in a while?"

"You sure are a nosey old coot."

"No need in gettin' rude, you young whipper-snapper," the old man mused. "I'm just prodded ya. I guess I could drop ya rat 'ere if you're ready?"

"No, that's okay. I'm good."

Johnny looked over at the old man as he was spitting out his chaw of tobacco. Most of it was running down the side of his truck. *I don't think it's going to hurt his paint job.*

"I'm fixin' to have me a cold one. Would you like to join me?" the old man asked as he wiped the tobacco stubble off his chin with the back of his hand. He reached into a small ice chest sitting on the floor of his truck.

"You betcha," Johnny proclaimed. "It's the best offer I have had all day."

He pulled out two Pearl beers, handing one to Johnny.

Not my favorite, but beggars can't be choosey.

"Thank you, kind sir," Johnny stated as he snapped the tab on the top and took a big swig. "Aah, that's pretty good stuff."

"Yessiree, Bob!"

Johnny glanced over at the old man, who had downed the first and was grabbing a second one from the cooler.

"Ready?"

"You betcha," Johnny sang out as he gulped down his first and then dropped the empty can behind the seat like he had seen the old man do.

"Talihina—2 miles," Johnny read the sign.

"Are there any good pool halls in town?"

"Yessiree, Bob. But sometimes they don't take too kindly to strangers."

"I'm a pretty friendly person. I won't cause any trouble."

"Listen, young fellow. Sometimes troubles hunts us out whether we're a-lookin' for it or not. You just needa be careful where ya go. I'd feel really bad if a somethin' happened to ya. You know what I mean?"

"You betcha. But nothing is going to happen. I have a really good knack of taking care of my hide. Now where did you say those pool halls are located?"

"There a-both sittin' on the east end of town right next to the railroad tracks out on Highway 1. But don't say I didn't warn ya," the old man said as they entered town.

"Thanks for the beer and the ride. You can let me off right here if that's okay with you," Johnny said, pulling the door handle up as the truck came to a rattling stop, one block shy of the signal light.

"Take care of yourself, youngster. Trouble lurks in the shadows in those kinds of establishments. Find your friend and beware those places," the old man cautioned.

"You betcha. Thanks again," Johnny said as he slammed the truck's rusty door.

The old man drove off, never looking back.

Johnny removed his blue do-rag from the top of his head. He ran his fingers through his long stringy strawberry-blond hair. He wiped his ruddy-colored face and freckled neck with the bandana before putting it away in his backpack. From a side pocket, he pulled a ball cap and put it on his head. The hat was a very faded, blue Boston Red Sox's cap with a heavy salty-sweat ring around the entire hat. He lifted up his hands and curled the inside of the bill with his thumbs.

Highway 1 was actually Second Street, which ran all the way through town. Johnny noticed a school crossing sign a few blocks up the street. He glanced at his watch—12:30 p.m. *School won't let out until at least 3:00. No use of me going there right now. I'm in serious need of something to do. And a little moola.*

Johnny reached into his front jean's pocket and removed a wrinkled-up ten dollar bill. His stomach suddenly rumbled. He looked over at the subway restaurant across the street. He really wanted to eat. It had been almost two days since his last good meal. He always rat-holed ten bucks because he knew he needed at least ten dollars to run his scam.

The old man told me to follow this road until I got to the edge of town. What can it hurt? I've been in worse predicaments than this one and always came out unscathed. Why would this town be any different?

He walked up Second Street until it reached the edge of town. Earlier, as he passed the school, he made a mental note of how long it took him to get to this point. *Twenty-two minutes. That gives me roughly an hour and a half to work my magic. It won't take longer than an hour.*

There were two bars at the edge of town—the Hilltop Saloon on the north side and Shooter's Bar and Grill on the south. The saloon was closed. Shooter's had a couple of cars and a large white Ford Dually, flat-bed truck, parked out front.

There she blows, Captain. Mighty fine weather we're having for a couple of pool games.

Johnny walked in and stood just inside the doorway, waiting for his eyes to adjust to the darkness before he moved in any further. After a few seconds, his vision cleared. He quickly scanned the room, taking into account the location of every door. One side door, a front door, and probably a door in the back. Two regulars, an older man and woman, were sitting at the bar nursing two draws, talking about how they need a new football coach. At the very back of the bar furthermost from the door, Johnny found what he was looking for—two rather large gentlemen playing pool on one of three old-fashioned pool tables that sat off to one side away from a small rectangular dance floor.

Johnny removed his backpack and sat it out of the way in a corner. He went up to the edge of the bar opposite the couple, who were staring curiously at Johnny. The two men playing pool had momentarily stopped to check out the stranger but then quickly proceeded with their game.

The bartender set down a glass he had been drying with a dish towel. "What can I do you for?"

"Can I have a draw and two dollars worth of quarters, please?" The bartender picked up the glass he had been drying and filled it up with beer, and then sat it on top of the bar top with the quarters. "That'll be a five spot."

Johnny handed him the ten dollars and got his change. He walked over to the pool table next to the two men playing pool. They had stopped their game to size up Johnny. Johnny ignored them as he clumsily kept trying to unsuccessfully rack the pool balls. When he finally got all the balls in the rack, he glanced over at the two men and asked, "Could you fellows help me out? Does this number eight ball go in the middle or number five? I never can remember."

The two men moved forward into the table's light. Johnny got his first good look at them. They were the biggest set of twins he had ever seen. At least he thought they were twins. One's face and nose were a little jacked up.

It was Jim Bob and Skeeter Monger. They were wearing blue overalls, white tee shirts, and work boots. The only difference in clothing was Jim Bob had a red Mack truck hat, and Skeeter had a blue. They turned to each other and smiled.

Jim Bob chuckled dryly. "The black one."

"Thank you," Johnny said as he walked over to a rack of pool cues. He picked out three and pretended to examine each one carefully. He turned back toward the twins. "How do you know which stick is any good?" He dropped one pool cue, and as he tried to retrieve it, the other two dropped to the tile floor.

The two men stepped around the pool table to the side nearest Johnny. "Why don't you come play with us? We can help you out with the ins and outs of playing pool. Now there may be some money involved here. Me and Skeet here only play for money. But don't you worry none, we're not no good," Jim Bob said as he turned and winked at Skeeter.

"Yep, that's right. We ain't no good," Skeeter agreed.

This is going to be like taking candy from two big old fat twin babies.

"Awesome. I'm not very good either. This ought to be fun," Johnny announced.

"Then you'll join us?" Jim Bob offered.

"You betcha. Can we practice a little first?" Johnny asked.

"Sure. Whatever trips your trigger."

They played on the table Johnny had racked earlier. Johnny shot the cue ball off the table four times in the first game. Jim Bob beat Johnny handedly the first game. Johnny made the next game a little more competitive with Skeeter by making two balls instead of zero.

"You're pretty good," Skeeter said.

"Thanks. I'm a fast learner."

"Yes, you are that. Like I was telling you earlier. We only play for money. Let's up the ante. How about we start off playing five dollars a game until we get warmed up?"

Johnny smiled. "You betcha."

"Rack 'em!"

Within an hour, Johnny had turned his life savings of five dollars into one hundred twenty dollars. The twins were out of money. They were too stupid to figure out that they were out-conned by a con man—a very good con man.

Or were they?

"Gentlemen. It's been *real*. It's been *fun*. It has been *real fun*. Beginner's luck. I have only played a few times. You guys are good coaches. I'm usually on the road all the time and never get a chance to play. Let alone win a few games."

"You did pretty good for a beginner. We'll be back tonight. We sure would like a chance to win our money back," Jim Bob said.

"We sure would. We have another brother that's pretty good too. We'll bring him. He has a lot more money than us," Skeeter informed.

"You betcha. I'll be back. I love this game. Besides you guys are awesome teachers, I might be able to get good at this game someday. Thanks again, fellows."

Jim Bob and Skeeter looked at each other and smiled. "Thanks."

"You betcha. See you around," Johnny said as he picked up his backpack and headed toward the door. He grabbed the doorknob and turned around. The twins were staring at him. Johnny waved. *Suckers!* The twins waved back as he walked out the door.

Jim Bob turned toward Skeeter and gave him a thumbs-up sign.

Skeeter grinned and returned the gesture, then made out like he was casting out a lure and reeling it in.

"Gotcha!"

Flake Reunion

J ohnny arrived at the school twenty-three minutes later. *Three fifteen p.m. Good. They're not out of school yet.*

Johnny scanned the teachers' parking lot looking for a familiar vehicle. *There!* He spotted Bryson's Jeep parked in the very back spot. He walked up and placed his backpack in the back seat. He unzipped a side pocket and pulled out an iPod to listen while he waited for Bryson to get out of school. He crawled into the front seat and adjusted the level of sound coming from his iPod. He pulled his hat down and closed his eyes. He thought about the day's events.

I think I'm going to really like it here. He moved his hand down to his left pocket, feeling the big wad of money he had just taken from the twins. *I know I'm going to like it here!*

Fifteen minutes later, the dismissal bell rang. Johnny lifted the hat off his nose to take a peek toward the front doors. Students were pouring out from all the doors, like they were trying to escape a rampant lion running wild in the halls.

Piper walked outside behind them to monitor any misbehavior.

Johnny saw her standing in the courtyard area and quickly pulled the iPod earphones out and sat up straight. "Wow! Hellooo, dolly!"

A mother passing nearby abruptly pulled her young daughter away from Johnny's general direction and then glared hard at

Johnny, but he didn't notice. His eyes were fixed on Piper, like a cheetah hiding in the high grass eyeing a grazing antelope.

Johnny glanced in the mirror above the visor. "Not too bad, if I say so myself." He leaped out of the Jeep and walked very quickly toward Piper.

Only a handful of students remained in the courtyard. Piper turned and began talking to a young girl.

Johnny was about fifty yards away from Piper when Bryson walked out the double doors.

Bryson's head was tilted down reading a guideline list from the local electric co-op.

Piper half-turned and glanced over at Bryson as he walked away, following him with her eyes.

Johnny stopped and smiled. *I'll be a spotted zebra—I believe someone is checking Mr. Keahbone out.*

Piper gathered herself and turned her attention back to the student. "That sounds wonderful. Come by my office tomorrow, and we'll talk some more."

The student's face twisted into a puzzled frown."A-a-a … sure."

"Thank you, Raylee," Piper said as she turned to follow Bryson. Piper wanted to talk to Bryson. There was something she needed to get off her chest, but the timing throughout the whole week was always wrong. Or she was simply avoiding the situation. Whatever the excuse, she needed to make a move before he left, so she took off after him. She wasn't about to let it simmer all weekend.

Bryson was still reading the guidelines as he traveled halfway across the courtyard. He stopped and turned the paper over to check for more information on the back. He suddenly noticed a pair of cowboy boots stepping up behind him. One boot had duct tape around the toe. He felt something being poked in his lower back.

"Go ahead, punk. Make my day."

Bryson grinned and abruptly turned around.

"Johnny!"

"The one and only."

Johnny opened up and held his hands out wide.

The two men clasped hands and then hugged.

Piper had stopped about ten feet away and curiously watched the two old friends reunite. She smiled warmly.

"What in the world are you doing here?"

"I've come to see you, my man."

"When … where did you come from?"

"Here. There. A little bit of everywhere."

"What? You haven't taken over your daddy's business yet?"

"Uhmm. No, not yet. You see, I—"

"You can tell me later. I need to get out to the cabin, so the electric company can turn my power on. I'm tired of living in the Dark Ages."

"That wouldn't happen if you paid your bill on time."

"Yeah, right. Very funny. You're one to be talking. Who was the one who would forget to pay the bills? You name it—the phone, electric, water. They were all being shut off—a different one each week."

"You forgot—cable."

"Yes, and that one too. Our money would somehow mysteriously end up down at O'Brien's pool hall."

"Oh … you knew about that?"

"Yes. Why do think your dad started sending me the bill money and not to you."

"Because you're responsible, and I'm not."

"Something like that."

Piper eased forward.

Bryson turned and saw Piper standing a few feet away. He stared at her and remembered how close they had gotten only a few days before, and now, they seemed light years apart.

"Hey, the stalker."

"What?" Piper and Bryson said in unison.

"Yeah, Kee, I saw her stalking you only a few minutes ago. Forgive my rudeness. My name is Johnny. Johnny … well, we will just leave it at Johnny for now. And your name is?" Johnny greeted as he extended his hand.

Piper grabbed his hand and tried to squeeze the feeling out of his fingers. "My name is Piper Hitchcock. And I wasn't stalking him. I was following him, trying to catch up to talk to him about a certain situation dealing with school. I wasn't stalking him," Piper repeated defensively. "I was trying to be polite and not interrupt your conversation."

"Johnny, this is my boss. Principal Hitchcock."

"She is a whole lot prettier than our principal back in high school."

"All right, Romeo. Back off and go wait by my Jeep or by your vehicle."

Johnny shrugged his shoulders to indicate that he had no vehicle.

"I should have known. Go wait by my Jeep. I will be there shortly," Bryson assumed, shaking his head.

"It was my most honorable pleasure to have met you, Piper."

"Likewise, I'm sure."

Johnny never moved, glancing back and forth from Piper to Bryson. The three stood quietly, forming a triangle. Piper and Bryson glared at Johnny, who suddenly looked down and began kicking around an empty gum wrapper.

Bryson cleared his throat.

"Oh, you guys want me to leave. Why didn't you say so? Piper, I hope I can see you again … soon."

Piper nodded, but said nothing until Johnny turned and started walking toward the Jeep. "Nice friend you have there."

"I know. He means well, but he can get on one's last nerve real quick."

"You think?" Piper uttered.

Bryson smiled. "I don't want to sound rude, but I need to get home to meet with the electric co-op. If I don't get the electric turned on today, I will have to wait until Monday. What's up? Jared okay?"

"Yes, everything is fine …"

"Go ahead, spit it out."

"I … I just want to thank you again for being nice to Jared. He really likes you and respects you."

"There's no need for all that. He's a great kid. I have really enjoyed having him around. He is an excellent worker. I look forward to having him help me finish my cabin. There's still quite a bit of petty work left to do."

"He would like that. You were right. The doctor said his wrist was only slightly sprained. Let him rest it for a few days before he comes back over to work. Besides it looks like you may have your hands full," Piper said, pointing over at Johnny, who was sitting in the Jeep bobbing his head up and down to his iPod music.

"Yes, I'm afraid so."

"Jared wanted me to remind you about church again on Sunday …"

"Okay. Yes, I promise I will try," Bryson assured, patiently waiting for Piper to finish.

There was a long and awkward silence.

"Again, thank you and … ," Piper began, looking down at the ground.

Bryson continued to grin. "What is it?"

Piper took a deep breath and looked up. "The other night … well, I hope I didn't send you the wrong message."

"About?"

"About … when I tripped … and fell … you caught me."

Bryson had a look of bewilderment on his face, then realized what she was talking about.

"Oh … no … No! It never entered my mind."

"Okay … good," Piper stammered, starting to feel a little embarrassed.

"Yes … it's all good."

"Good."

"Yes, good."

"Good."

"I believed we covered that," Bryson mused.

"Yes, we did. Well, have a *good* rest of the day."

"Thank you."

Piper quickly turned and walked away. *I'm such a blubbering moron.*

Bryson watched her walk away. *Hitchcock may be the weirdest girl I have ever met.*

About a block down from the high school parking lot sat a black-and-white patrol car idling in the shade of a large sycamore tree.

Tyrel rolled his toothpick back and forth between his teeth. His eyes were fixed on Bryson's Jeep. He raised a hand-held walkie-talkie and miked the radio. "Bob Cat, I have prey in sight. Location—teacher-man's vehicle—high school parking lot.

What a small world we live in. It's only a matter of time before Master delivers him to us. If he shows back up at Shooter's tonight, let me know, but I think it will be a day or so. He'll want to lay low. Besides we know exactly where he'll be if we need to go get him. Out."

"Copy. Out."

Tyrel grinned. "Yes, a small world indeed."

Flake—My Brother

B ryson climbed in under the rag top and playfully reached over and hit Johnny on the arm.

"Ouch! Dude, what was that for? Or do you treat all your long lost friends this way?"

"Who says you're my friend?"

Johnny's mouth had fallen open. "Come to think about it, you haven't called or talked to me in two years."

Bryson's smile curled into a frown. "I know. I haven't talked to anyone except Vick and Hoot."

"That's why I'm here—to catch up on old times."

"I moved here to put the old times behind me."

Johnny smiled, "Me too, bro. Me, too."

"Really, Johnny … what's up?"

"You know me. Same old song, same old dance. The only change is that the music keeps getting louder and the girls keep getting U-G-L-Y—you ain't got no alibi—'cuz you're ugly—I sure seem to attract them," Johnny swore, rolling his fists in circles like he was waving a pair of pompoms.

"Go figure."

Bryson hit Johnny in the arm again and shook his head. He turned the key, and the engine roared to life. Within a few seconds, Bryson had the Jeep in reverse and then popped the clutch shifting to first. In a blink of an eye, they were heading down Second Street.

"Easy, Earnhardt!"

Bryson grinned at Johnny. *It's good to see my old friend.*

Once on the highway, conversation was light between the old friends. The rushing wind around them made it hard to talk without yelling at each other. Johnny didn't mind. He had been contemplating over the past two years all the different things he would say to Bryson when he saw him again. But now, not one thing was coming to Johnny's mind. There would be plenty of time later to catch up. Or that's what they both thought.

There were only two days left until the next Running Moon, and eyes were keeping a careful watch on their next prey. Tyrel's patrol car kept a marginal distance behind Bryson's Jeep so as not to draw attention.

Bryson turned onto County Line Road and headed south. Tyrel drove slowly past the road and stopped on the shoulder watching the Jeep disappear into the woods. His lips twisted and twitched into an insidious grin. He pulled away from the shoulder and made a U-turn heading back to town.

Bryson and Johnny arrived at the rusty gate as the white rural electric truck was pulling away from the cabin. Bryson stopped the Jeep abruptly and leaned out toward the truck.

"Wait! I'm sorry I'm late. Do you still have time to turn the power on?"

The rural company electrician had a serious look on his face as he rolled down the driver's side window, hanging out one humongous arm with a barbed wire tattoo around his bicep. He barely fit his muscular frame behind the steering wheel of the company truck. "I'm not suppose to turn the power on without someone being here," the huge man said in a very deep and rough voice.

"I know. I'm ..."

The big man held up a big hand. "Hoot's a good friend, and he told me all about you. So the door was unlocked. I let myself in and did a quick inspection. By the way, your cabin looked like a professional had wired it—nice job."

"Thanks."

"I turned the power on. And now, you're good to go."

"Sweet. What do I owe you, George?" Bryson asked, after he noticed his name embroidered on his work shirt.

"Nothing. Just keep my daughter in line. You're her favorite teacher."

Bryson grinned. "Who's your daughter?"

"Sasha Jo."

"Yes, I will, but there's no worries there. She's an awesome student."

"Thanks, takes after her momma. Me, all brawn and no brains. See ya around," George said, lifting that huge hand in a wave.

"Again, thank you very much," Bryson hollered as the co-op truck eased away.

Bryson drove up and parked the Jeep in front of the cabin.

Johnny stepped out and looked around in awe. "This place is beautiful. Even more so than back home."

"I know. It's pretty amazing. You hungry?"

"Yes, starving!" Johnny exclaimed. He had forgotten until Bryson mentioned food. Now his stomach had suddenly turned into knots. "What do you have? Steak sounds good."

Bryson cocked a brow, saying, *Fat chance.*

"Here's your choices—ham, bologna, or PBJ."

"Ummm. That's a tough one. How about a ham sandwich? Do you have any cheese, lettuce, and tomato with real mayo?"

"What do think I'm running … a deli?"

"Hey, just asking," Johnny said, holding both hands up.

"You can have whatever's in there," Bryson said, pointing at the red and white ice chest. "We can head back into town in a little bit and buy some groceries."

"You betcha. Can we get a couple of rib eyes? I'm buying."

"You have money?"

"You betcha!" Johnny exclaimed as he reached down and touched the roll of money in his pocket.

Johnny opened the lid, reached into the ice chest, and pulled out everything he needed to fix a ham and cheese sandwich. After he completed his sandwich, he sat at the table and devoured it in five bites—one for each corner, and finally the middle in one big gulp. "I better have another," Johnny said, licking his fingers.

"I would ask how it tasted."

"Oooh … it's … very good," Johnny muttered through cheeks that looked like a chipmunk's.

"Slow down. You're going to make yourself sick. When was the last time you had eaten anything?"

Johnny took a long swig from a bottled water.

"Uh … just a couple of days. Wait, I did have a candy bar and half a Coke last night. You know me, I don't eat much, and I'm potty-trained."

Bryson, who had been standing the whole time, walked over to the table and sat down. He stared at Johnny.

"What? Why are you staring at me?" Johnny asked as he began removing everything from the ice chest to make another sandwich.

"What's up? What are you doing here?"

"What do you mean? I've come a long way to see my best friend. Is that a crime?"

"Johnny, you know what I mean. You father is one of the richest people in Oregon, and you're living in poverty. You look like you've lost twenty pounds since I last saw you. And you were skinny back then."

"Twenty-three to be exact."

"You're skin and bones."

Johnny finished making another sandwich and sat back down. He paused, taking a huge bite from his sandwich. "I don't know. My father wants me to be like him. I don't. I want to be me, the person I'm suppose to be. I'm no desk jockey. I'm a free bird … among other things."

"What do you want to be, Johnny? You can't run away from your dad all your life," Bryson declared.

"Says who?"

"Your dad wants only the best for you, like any good father would."

"He wants what's best for him, not me. I am an embarrassment to him," Johnny informed as he tossed over half of his unfinished sandwich into the trash can. He had suddenly lost his appetite. He had a sudden impulse to leave, move on.

"Hey, Johnny, I'm not trying to tell you how to run your life—"

Johnny glanced up from looking at the floor. "What then?"

"Ask yourself this: have I really tried to get along? Your dad has worked very hard for what he has, and he's told me several times that he wants you to take over."

"Yeah, when was that? You've been gone for two years. How would you know?" Johnny demanded as he stood up and walked toward the front door. He really wanted to bolt through the door and be gone.

Bryson paused.

Johnny stopped at the screen door and stared silently through teary eyes across the empty field. *I do want to make something of myself, but everything I do and touch winds up a complete and total failure. What's the use?*

Bryson got up from his chair and walked over to stand next to Johnny. He only wanted what was best for his friend. And the lifestyle Johnny was living right now was not it.

"You're right. I'm a hypocrite. I don't know anything except your dad was like a father to me, and you are my *brother*," Bryson proclaimed as he put his arm around Johnny's shoulder.

Johnny smiled, masking the tears that were about to fall. He wanted to explain to Bryson that Bryson was right, not him. *I am such a screw-up.*

"You are my only bro." Johnny laughed as the tension between the two friends faded away.

"My brother from another mother." Bryson chuckled, playfully pushing Johnny off to the side.

"Too bad I got all the looks."

"Yeah, whatever."

They laughed.

"Hey, I have completely forgotten about this evening. I have been invited to supper out at Vick's place. You can tag along with me. She's not going to care. Vick is always excited to see you."

"Great," Johnny said sarcastically.

"What?"

"That means old-sour-puss will be there."

"Who? Oh … Hoot. Yes, probably."

"Great," Johnny echoed.

"Hoot's harmless," Bryson defended. "Let's get cleaned up and head out. What do you say? It'll be fun. You wanted to catch up. Like old times."

"You betcha. Like old times," Johnny groaned.

Flake—A Surprise Guest

B ryson and Johnny pulled up in front of Vick's house. The sun had fallen behind the western ridge, casting a long shadow, chasing away the last bit of sunlight on the eastern ridge.

Bryson climbed out first and started up the porch steps when he noticed Johnny was still sitting in the Jeep.

"You coming or not?" Bryson asked over his shoulder.

"Yeah, yeah."

"Then come on. I smell good food."

"Go on. I'm right behind you."

Bryson turned and looked at Johnny, saying with his eyes, *I am not going in without you.*

Johnny let out a sigh before reluctantly climbing out of the Jeep.

"All right already."

Bryson opened the screen door and lightly tapped on the front door before opening it. Bryson stepped through the doorway with Johnny close behind.

"Hello," Bryson greeted.

"In the dining room," Vick called from the next room.

Bryson cocked Johnny a crooked grin as he shut the door behind him. Johnny sidestepped, trying to hide himself in the corner, wondering if this was a very good idea.

"I have brought a special guest. I hope you don't mind," Bryson said as he stepped from the foyer into the dining room.

Johnny remained in the foyer.

"Who have you brought?" Vick asked as she stood up from the table for a better look. Her stomach jumped and fluttered inside like it was full of hummingbirds. In her mind, she was hoping to see Piper.

Hoot was sitting in a brown leather recliner. He curiously glanced up from his newspaper. He was not in a very good mood and was not going to be the best of company right now.

Bryson turned toward the entry way and announced, "Here's Johnny!"

Johnny shyly stepped into the dining room. He had his hands tucked in his pockets. His shoulders were slightly shrugged. He was very apprehensive about this meeting.

"Johnny!" Vick roared as she ran toward Johnny, giving him a big bear hug before he could remove his hands from his pockets. The impact almost knocked them both to the wood floor.

"Thanks for the hug," Johnny joked. "You almost broke me in half."

Vick stepped back with her hands still on Johnny's shoulders, looking him up and down.

"Well, look at you. You're skin and bones," Vick declared.

"So I've been told," Johnny smirked.

"Hoot, it's Johnny."

Johnny looked over at Hoot.

"So it seems," Hoot said dryly, not sharing in the same enthusiasm that Vick had displayed. "*Flake.* Johnny *Flake.* It has been a long time. Pardon my rudeness if I don't get up."

Hoot raised the newspaper to hide behind.

What is Flake doing here? What a perfect ending to a perfectly bad day.

Johnny gave a quick wave and turned back to Vick.

"Never mind him, Johnny Lee. Hoot's not having a very good day. He received bad news today that the Oklahoma State Department of Education is cutting state funding by another five percent. He's worried that he may have to riff some of the teaching staff and support personnel, which are already understaffed. He's got a hard job," Vick sympathized, smiling warmly at Hoot.

Hoot mumbled something under his breath.

Bryson had also known that Hoot's position at the school carries a lot of weighted pressure. He also had known that Hoot was not very fond of Johnny either. Johnny was always getting himself into some kind of trouble. Hoot was afraid that some day, one of Johnny's schemes would entrap Bryson as well. Maybe he was right. Hoot was looking out for Bryson. He understood, but he had wished Hoot would at least treat Johnny with a little cordial hospitality. Bryson looked at Hoot buried behind his newspaper. *Probably not going to happen.*

"You guys come on in and sit down," Vick said as she dragged Johnny toward the dining room table. "Supper's ready. Just been waiting on Bryson to arrive."

"I hope it's not a bother," Johnny apologized.

"Not at all. I'm giving Hoot's portion to you if he doesn't get his nose out of that paper and get over here," Vick instructed as she set a new place setting on the table for Johnny.

"Thank you."

They all sat down waiting for Hoot to join them.

Vick cleared her throat.

"I'm coming, I'm coming," Hoot announced as he folded up the newspaper and tossed it back on the recliner. He again mumbled something under his breath before sitting down across from Johnny.

"Bryson, will you ask grace for the food," Vick asked.

Bryson hesitated.

"I would rather not. I don't pray anymore," Bryson informed. Vick smiled halfheartedly and then asked for the blessing over the food. She wanted to say something but knew in her heart that it would do no good right now. *When Bryson is ready, he will return.*

The small group ate in a cold silence until Hoot broke the ice.

"So, *Flake*, where are you working these days?"

"Well, I had this really good job," Johnny replied, trying really hard not to let Hoot intimidate him.

"Had a job?" Hoot wondered, who already knew the answer. Or so he thought.

"Had to quit … health reasons," Johnny informed.

"You have health problems?" Vick asked sincerely.

"Yeah … the people I worked with were sick of me," Johnny joked.

Bryson and Vick chuckled.

"Imagine that. Still haven't changed." Hoot said, glaring at Johnny. *What a waste of air.*

Johnny looked away from Hoot and thought that maybe the joke was not a very good idea to try to lighten the mood.

"Flake, what is the real reason you have graced us with your presence? Job hunting?" Hoot snorted.

"Umm. I was just passing through …" Johnny muttered, wishing he could have the words back.

"Passing through, huh?"

"Well, yes … I … just … came—"

"Did I ever tell you what happened in Italy that made me want to return home?" Bryson broke in, trying to save Johnny from Hoot, who apparently was not going to back off.

"No! You must tell!" Vick exclaimed.

Even Hoot turned his attention away from Johnny.

"As you know, I traveled here and there across Europe for two years before I came home. I would stay with old friends and made new friends. I mainly just traveled alone."

"Like a gypsy nomad? I can relate," Johnny testified.

"Yes, exactly. That is extremely funny you brought that up because that's what happened. I lived with a band of gypsies for a little while."

"Really! No way! You did?"

"Tell us more."

"Not much to tell really. I hung out with a group of Romanian gypsies called the Zlateri. They live in the northeast region of the Alps. During the summer, they lived up in the high country, and during winter, they migrated into the lowlands. They were gold panners, working the streams from the top to the bottom of the Alps.

"I stopped by a stream to cool off and refresh myself from a long climb through the mountains. There were four carts circled up with the horses tied off to the side. I didn't want to be an interloper, so I walked down a little ways before I stopped. I removed my heavy backpack and placed it by the stream. I was very tired and decided to stay there awhile. The grass was very soft and made for a good bed. I was leaning back on my backpack when out of nowhere a very, very, very old woman stood beside me. I never saw or heard her walk up. She was the oldest woman I had ever seen. Her face looked like one of those carved apple faces after it had set out a few days," Bryson said.

"Was she a gypsy?"

"Yes. She was a gypsy woman. A very old gypsy woman. Her skirt radiated with bright shades of green, blue, and yellow. Her shirt and scarf were a deepest purple, which made her eyes appear a dark violet hue."

"What was her name?" Vick asked impatiently.

Bryson shook his head and grinned.

"Have you not figured out why I don't tell very many stories around you?"

"Hush, it's your fault. You tell them too slow. You need to speed up, I am growing as old as that gypsy woman. Whatever her name is!" Vick claimed.

Johnny and Hoot chuckled.

"Her name was Tsura. She asked me if I would draw her a drink from the mountain stream and handed me a small wooden cup. I told her I would and took her cup and filled it with water. When I handed it to her, our hands touched as she went to remove the cup. She grabbed my hands over the cup and stared into my eyes. I will never forget the sadness in her eyes when she told me that she could feel my pain and how deep that it ran within my soul. She told me that the sadness would never leave unless I return to my place of birth."

"Oregon?"

"No. This is my birthplace. I stayed with the gypsies for two weeks. That old gypsy never left my side. It seemed like every waking moment, Tsura was urging me to return home. She carried around this small empty clay bowl. She would pull a small leather bag from around her neck and whisper something in Romanian and then open the bag and pour the contents in the clay bowl, circling and then making a crossing motion above it with her hand."

Vick remained tightlipped and refused to ask a question. But anyone could tell it was killing her.

"What was in the bag?" Johnny finally asked.

"Some weird looking roots, rocks, and bones from a small animal."

"Cool! I would have liked to have seen that."

"She would open her eyes and point at the contents and say, 'There it iz again. The zame thing every time. They never liezz. You must go home before the zignz zay no more,'" Bryson said, mimicking the gypsy woman's Romanian accent.

"Wow," Johnny mused. "Pretty cool."

"That's when I wrote you the letter, Vick. I had no idea I would ever get my family land back. I was ready to come home. That is how I came to be here. Thank you, my dear friends," Bryson choked.

Vick got up and hugged Bryson's neck.

"We are glad you're back," Hoot agreed, who had momentarily forgotten his financial problems. Hoot got up and hugged them both.

Johnny remained in his chair, watching the three embrace. He felt happiness for his friend, but he also felt jealousy and envy. He longed for that kind of relationship with someone—anyone, maybe even with his father. *Maybe I should call the old man and ask if I can come home. I like that idea. I think so.*

Vick waved Johnny over and hugged him.

Hoot reached out and shook Johnny's hand and apologized for being a butthead and continued to explain how the job sometimes made him become very irritable.

The rest of the evening was very quiet and pleasant. They laughed and told off on each other, recalling stories from their youth. Johnny tried on several occasions to tell them that he had made up his mind and that he was going home to mend his relationship with his father. But the timing was never quite right for him to divulge this information, at least that was what he kept telling himself.

Johnny helped Vick with the dishes after they had finished their supper. He would rather hide out in the kitchen than be the subject of Hoot's judgmental stares. Although Hoot apologized, Johnny knew that he didn't want him around.

Johnny had made up his mind. He was going to show Hoot, his father, the whole stinking world that he was a changed man and was ready to prove it.

Just not right then.

Tomorrow.

Hoot and Vick walked them to the front door.

"See you guys in the morning at church?" Vick asked through the screen door.

"Yes … yes. I can't speak for Johnny, but I will be there. I have been promising Jared that I would go. Now that all of you have ganged up on me, how can I refuse?"

"Awesome! Be careful." Vick and Hoot waved.

Johnny had gotten into the passenger's seat of the Jeep when Bryson stopped at the top step to look up at the nearly full moon.

My son, come find me beneath the Moon When Wolves Cry.

"What are you looking at?" Johnny asked, also looking up into the sky.

"I wish I knew."

Bryson Seeks Truth

T he sun was peeking over the eastern ridge. Bryson woke up in a pool of sweat. He pulled on his jeans and walked outside to cool off. The chilly fingers of the autumn air felt refreshing against his skin. He kept running the dream through his mind, over and over and over, trying with all his might to remember every detail.

He had no problem remembering his father's words, but the lady in the light was still fuzzy, fading in and out of his mind's eye. He closed his eyes. Her words were there in his mind. He could feel them floating around individually. He needed to connect them. *What are they? I can see them. Come together. Speak to me. I see you.*

He squinted harder, trying with all his being to concentrate on the words of the lady in the light.

"Believe. You need only to believe. Seek the lady of the streets. She will guide you to your path. Believe," the lady in the light said as the words faded to nothing.

Bryson quickly opened his eyes.

"Believe. Seek the lady of the streets," Bryson echoed.

He was running the words through his mind, trying to make sense of the dream, when a halogen light bulb beamed in his mind. His frown suddenly turned into a huge smile.

"Ms. Abbey! Ms. Abbey is the lady of the street!" Bryson exclaimed.

"Who … what?" Johnny mumbled from the living room couch. "What's … going on? Hey, you okay?"

Bryson rushed back into the cabin, running over to where Johnny had been sleeping.

"It's Ms. Abbey! Ms. Abbey is the lady of the streets," Bryson screamed as he pulled the blanket off of Johnny.

"Dude, I believe you. Whatever you say. Just let me have my covers back." Johnny yawned through half-opened eyes, reaching down for the blanket and then turning toward the couch. "Five more minutes."

"Come on. You have to get up. I need to run into town and see someone," Bryson urged as excitement was building inside him. This was the first time he had remembered the full dream, and he wasn't about to waste the opportunity.

"Go on without me. I don't want to go," Johnny snapped from beneath the covers.

"Come on. If you don't go with me, you will be stuck out here in the boonies all day by yourself. I don't know what time I will be back. Besides we have been invited to church," Bryson coaxed.

"I don't care too much about the church thing, but I definitely don't want to be stuck out here all day by myself in these hills," Johnny informed as he threw the blanket onto the back of the couch and sat up, dropping his feet to the wooden floor. Both of Johnny's big toes were sticking through a hole in each sock.

"Nice socks."

"You like that? They match my underwear," Johnny stated as he started to get up to show Bryson.

"Easy there. I will take your word on that one." Bryson laughed, waving his hand at Johnny not to get up. "If you want to make some coffee, the fixings are over there on the counter. I will shower first."

"Yes, dear."

Bryson was standing patiently on the porch sipping a cup of coffee as Johnny showered. He stared out over the yellow grass meditating on the words from his dream when suddenly, something caught his eye from the direction of the old oak where his mother was buried. He turned and looked hard at the area surrounding the tree.

Nothing.

Bryson took a sip of his coffee.

My mind is playing tricks on me. No, wait, there it is again.

The wolf stepped out from around the tree. He stood motionless.

"Hello, my old friend. I have not seen you in a while. I'm sorry I haven't paid much attention to you lately. It has been crazy busy around here these past two weeks or so," Bryson said as he took another sip from his mug.

The wolf disappeared behind the huge oak almost as quickly as it had appeared.

"Who you talking to?"

"Huh?"

"I heard you talking to someone."

"Oh, just thinking out loud."

"That's kind of dangerous, ain't it?"

Bryson shot Johnny a curious look.

"Thinking. That can be very dangerous for a man in your condition."

"Ha-ha!"

Bryson glanced back at the old oak, but the wolf was long gone. He didn't know why he didn't tell Johnny about the wolf. He just didn't.

"Ready?" Bryson asked as he climbed in the Jeep.

"Born ready," Johnny replied, throwing his backpack on the back seat.

They arrived in Talihina about fifteen minutes later. Traffic was light. Most people who were going to church were already at church. Bryson would just have to be late.

"I need to stop to talk to someone first. I hope you don't mind?" Bryson asked, slowing the Jeep to a crawl as he scanned the streets for Ms. Abbey.

"Don't mind me," Johnny answered as he pulled his iPod from his backpack and put on his earphones. He was in no hurry to get to church. It wasn't his thing. He attended a few times with Bryson before Becky's accident, but growing up, he never darkened a church's doorway. His parents were always too busy.

Bryson made a couple of passes through downtown, but there was no Ms. Abbey. He pulled over and stopped by the curb in front of Carla's Country Kitchen. The restaurant was closed and wouldn't open until after church. He looked down at his watch. *Five minutes before church starts. I better head to church. I made a promise.*

Johnny was busy scanning his albums and didn't take much notice to anything around him.

Bryson looked in his side mirror and then back down at his watch. He was about to leave when from behind, he heard an old familiar voice.

"Howdy, stranger."

It was the voice Bryson had been looking for. He was so ecstatic that he jumped out of Jeep and ran up to Ms. Abbey.

"Whoa! I see ya haven't changed much since the last time I saw ya, Mr. Bryson Keahbone. Rushin' around like the worlds comin' to an end. I'm a-guessin' that you found the school 'cuz you never came to bother me no more," Ms. Abbey asked as she sat down on a bench out front of the restaurant.

Bryson had a huge smile on his face.

Ms. Abbey was still wearing the same dirty-looking denim skirt and shirt. Her rusty-colored hair was tucked up in big-brimmed gardener's hat that had a light purple scarf tied around the crown.

Her face was tanned and leathery.

Bryson couldn't help but admire her crystal blue eyes. *They are so clear and alert. They remind me of my mother's caring eyes.*

"Who's this that ya got with ya?"

"That's Johnny."

Johnny's head was bopping up and down to the sound of techno music. He glanced over at Bryson and gave a quick wave, then proceeded to tap on the dash to the different rhythmic beats.

"Is he safe?"

"I think so," Bryson said. "He's a little weird."

"You don't say. I've seen some pretty strange creatures in my life, but this cat takes the bag," Ms. Abbey said, taking her laced-up boots off to empty out the rocks.

"Would you like to meet him?" Bryson offered.

"Maybe next time. What ya want with me? You only stop when ya wantin' somethin' from me. Well, what is it?"

Bryson started to argue but stopped. She was right. The only other time he had talked to her was when he needed directions.

"I'm sorry. You are right."

"Oh, stop. What can I help ya with? It's my pleasure."

Bryson hesitated. He didn't know where to begin? *She's going to think I'm crazy.*

"Today," Ms. Abbey snorted.

She really is going to think I'm crazy.

Bryson took a deep breath.

"I have been having this recurring dream. I mean I have it *every* night. It's the exact same dream. The only problem is that I cannot remember the details of the dream when I wake up. That is until this morning. I remember every detail of this dream."

"Tell me your dream."

Bryson wondered whether he should begin with the part about his father or the lady in the light. He decided to begin with the lady in the light.

"In my dream there is a very bright light with a lady standing in the middle of it. I can't see her face. She talks to me. She told me to seek the lady of the street. The lady of the street has some information for me. And, Ms. Abbey, I mean no offense here, but I believe that is you."

"None taken, young Bryson," Ms. Abbey said as she reached up and rubbed her chin, contemplating a possible answer.

Bryson patiently waited for her answer. He noticed that Johnny had reclined in his bucket seat and was tapping his legs along with the drums of some unheard song. He turned his attention back to Ms. Abbey. Her face was stolid. He started to apologize for bothering her. *I am crazy for even thinking that this is the woman that the lady in the light is talking about.*

"What is this lady of the street suppose to tell ya?"

"I don't know. That's why I am here."

Ms. Abbey motioned for Bryson to come sit down beside her. He walked over and eased onto the bench.

"I am the lady of the street," Ms. Abbey proclaimed.

Bryson's heart jumped in his chest and then immediately sank when he heard her words.

"But I cannot help ya, young'un."

Bryson was experiencing all those same harsh feelings of utter disappointment that had consumed his life. He slowly lowered his head until his chin touched his chest. He didn't know how many more times he could deal with these situations and still keep his sanity. Not many.

Ms. Abbey gently reached out and touched Bryson on the side of the face with the back of her hand. She smiled warmly. He looked into her deep blues eyes. He suddenly felt a calming sensation come across his entire being, a feeling he hadn't felt since he was a boy.

"I do not have the knowledge you seek, my dear boy, but I can put you on the path to the one who can help, but only if he chooses. He is a grumpy old cuss. He lives in the swamp lands east of town called Flagg Bottom. There is only one road in and one road out. Drive until you can drive no more. Then you must go on foot. Follow the path—there is only one path in and one path out. Do not leave the path, for there are many unspeakable things that live within the black depths of those murky waters. Unspeakable, nasty things, things that would like nothin' better than to gobble you up," Ms. Abbey warned.

Bryson had driven by Flagg Bottom Road several times. He knew where the road was located.

"Whom do I seek?"

"In the heart of the swamp is an old cuss by the name of Cherokee Billy. He is the most aggravating soul that ya will ever meet in ya life. Ya'll be lucky if ya can get anythin' worthwhile out of that vermin. I almost hate doin' that to ya, but if there are answers to your questions, he will know 'em," Ms. Abbey declared, shaking her head in doubt.

Bryson couldn't help but wonder if this was another dead end to his search for answers. He had no choice but to try.

"Thank you, Ms. Abbey. You are an awesome lady. You have been most helpful. Now what can I do for you?" Bryson asked.

"I want nothing but for ya to bring your hindside back out of that there swamp in one piece. I won't be able to live with myself if somethin' happened to ya. I've grown kinda fond of ya," Ms. Abbey barked.

"Thanks. I will do my best to take care of my hindside." Bryson grinned.

"One last thing, you must go alone and do *exactly* what Cherokee Billy tells ya … and believe."

Bryson touched her hands that were sitting in her lap. He wanted nothing more than to believe.

"Take care. You'll see me again," Bryson promised, standing up from the bench.

"Mr. Bryson Keahbone, we're all crazy in one form or another. Follow your heart and believe," Ms. Abbey assured, shooting him a wink.

"Yes, we are." Bryson chuckled as he turned and walked around to the driver's side of the Jeep and climbed in.

Johnny pulled out his earphones.

"That didn't take long," Johnny said as he rolled the wire around the iPod and stuffed it in his shirt pocket.

"What an interesting person."

"Who?"

"Ms. Abbey. The old lady on the bench."

"What old lady? I didn't see anybody," Johnny said, looking over at the bench.

"Don't jack with me. She was sitting right there on that bench," Bryson professed, pointing to the now empty bench. "She was *right* there."

"Dude, I never saw her. But I was jamming out and could've just missed her."

Bryson looked up and down the highway, but he didn't see the lady of the street. *Maybe I am going crazy?*

The Argument

Bryson and Johnny arrived at the Talihina First Baptist Church a few moments later. Bryson parked in the lot across from the yellow-bricked church building. They both sat in the Jeep debating silently within themselves whether to go in or not go in.

Bryson was fighting his own demons. That apprehensive feeling about returning to church had returned and was consuming his whole being. It had been two years since he last attended a church service. He needed inner strength. He had felt an inner peace when he visited the cabin and talked to his mother, but something was still turning and twisting his insides. He was becoming frustrated with his questions not being answered the way that he thought they should be answered. He did not like not being in control.

Bells from the church's steeple sounded out. Church was about to begin.

Bryson woke up out of his trance and turned toward Johnny, who sat like a statue in his seat.

Johnny was battling his own ghosts too. He wanted nothing more than to return home and talk it out with his father. He was afraid—afraid to fail. He was looking for encouragement. Any kind of nudge would work. He wanted to tell Bryson his plan. He was willing to make the sacrifice that would be needed to go work for his father. Hustling had been his life, and he knew that it was going to be extremely hard to quit. *I'm ready, I'm ready,* he kept repeating in his mind.

"Mr. Keahbone!" a voice sounded from across the street.

It was Jared.

Bryson waved over the steering wheel.

Jared was walking beside Piper. She was wearing an olive-green dress with a light green floral print. She gave a quick wave.

"See you inside!" Jared yelled.

Bryson nodded and gave a thumbs-up.

Johnny zoned back in from thinking about his father and the choice he wanted to make. That choice could wait a little longer, Johnny decided.

"Hey, the schoolmarm and her son," Johnny announced, looking over at Bryson.

"Her name is Piper Hitchcock, and her son's name is Jared," Bryson defended, breaking the silence.

"What's the scoop with you and the principal?" Johnny asked.

"What do you mean? What scoop?"

"You and her got something cookin'? I see the way she looks at you. I see the way you look at her."

"There's nothing there between us. No way! Not in a million years," Bryson said defensively. His smile faded a little. He all of a sudden felt weird. He didn't feel right talking about Piper like this, like he was talking behind her back.

"Bull crap!"

"She's my boss. Nothing more!" Bryson exclaimed, starting to feel a little perturbed.

"Yeah, whatever."

"Whatever."

"Dude … don't get mad at me. I'm just calling it like I see it."

"See what? You're making something out of nothing."

"Okay, dude, but don't you think it's about time to—?"

"Time for what?"

"You know … time to move on."

"Move on from what?"

Bryson's jaw was closed tightly, causing his temples to bulge. He didn't what to hear any advice from someone who was a flake and so named.

Johnny hesitated.

"Move on from what?" Bryson repeated, wanting Johnny to explain his meaning.

"Bryson, you have to put your past behind you. It has been two years. Becky's gone. You've got to let her go."

"What do you know about relationships? You don't even have a life!" Bryson exploded. "You run away from *all* responsibilities. When times get tough, you are out of here. No more Johnny. See you later. Vamoose. Later, dude. Sound familiar? And you're preaching to me! Why do you think I have been avoiding you these past two years?"

Johnny looked away from Bryson and stared out the side window. Tears were forming in his eyes. Bryson had never talked to him that way. He felt like his heart had been ripped from his chest. Johnny expected Hoot or his father to talk to him that way—but not Bryson, not his brother.

No sooner than the words had escaped his mouth that Bryson wanted to take them back, but he knew he couldn't no matter how hard he tried. *I should not have said those things to Johnny. He doesn't deserve it. Nobody does. But he made me so mad. Why?*

"You know what? You are so right. I am good for nothing. You, Hoot, and my father are absolutely right!"

"Look, Johnny, I'm—"

"No, save it. You're right. Believe it or not, I actually want to do what's right … but I keep screwing up," Johnny said as he lifted his finger to catch a single tear that streaked down his cheek. He didn't want Bryson to see him cry. He needed to leave. To remove himself from this situation. He looked down at the door handle.

Bryson started to speak, but Johnny held up his hand to stop him.

"Go into church. I'll be right behind you. I just want to sit here for a few minutes," Johnny said, still facing the side window.

Bryson wanted to argue but decided against it. He was still mad at Johnny. He thought it would be best if they both cooled down and then talked. *After church would be perfect. We'll go eat and work it out. I can never stay mad at Johnny, but he needs to know there are lines he shouldn't cross. We'll talk after church.*

Bryson pulled the handle and climbed out of the Jeep. He shut the door. As he held onto the handle, something inside Bryson was telling him to talk to Johnny right then. Johnny never looked away from the window. Bryson decided to wait. He turned and walked toward the yellow-bricked church building.

Bryson sighed under his breath, "We'll talk later when things cool down."

Johnny heard him walk away through the gravel parking lot. He turned around from the window and stared at his best friend through teary eyes. "Why am I such a screw-up? Everything I touch gets ruined. I am worthless … good for nothing," Johnny whined, feeling sorry for himself for being the only guest at his pity party.

Johnny debated with himself whether to go in or simply wait for Bryson to come out. *Religion and me just don't get along. Then again, do I get along with anyone or anything?* "I am good for nothing except …" *Hustling!*

Johnny reached down and touched the wad of money in his front pocket. *I doubt that the pool hall is open, but trying to see is better than sitting here moping and feeling sorry for myself. I can walk to the pool hall and be back before church is out. The pastor's probably long-winded anyway.* He grabbed his backpack from the backseat of the Jeep and opened the side door.

Johnny looked toward the church to see if Bryson would return.

No luck.

Two blocks east of the church on top of a hill, a patrol car was parked alongside a wooden stockade fence. Tyrel sat behind the steering wheel watching patiently, chanting a psychotic melody repeatedly:

"Come on, little prey, I know you want to play. Come on, little prey, I know you want to play."

Johnny climbed slowly out of the Jeep. He pounded a path in the dirt as he walked back and forth, running through his mind what his next move would be. He finally sat down on the front bumper, burying his face in his hands. *What do I do? Wait or go?* He stood up abruptly and looked sorrowfully at the church. He hesitated before grabbing his backpack. Shaking his head, he began walking north toward the pool hall.

"So the prey has emerged!"

Tyrel picked up the mike to his two-way radio, squeezing the button on the side. "Badger. Copy."

"Copy," Billy Ray answered.

"Go open up Shooter's. Prey's heading that way. Master has delivered again," Tyrel boasted as the excitement of the hunt began to boil in his veins. "Out."

Come on, little prey, I know you want to play. Come on, little prey, I know you want to play.

Tonight, the Running Moon.

The Sermon

B ryson eased through the front doors. A greeter handed him a bulletin and thanked him for being there. He walked in the auditorium just as the choir started to sing "I'll Fly Away." He scanned the pews for some familiar faces. Hoot and Vick were sitting up front, and Piper and Jared toward the middle, not that he would sit with her anyway. He slid into the back pew, trying not to attract any attention to himself. Besides, it would be easier for Johnny to find him when he came in.

Jared turned around and waved at Bryson.

Bryson smiled and waved back. *So much for not drawing attention to myself.*

Piper turned around and shot Bryson a quick smile.

Bryson smiled unconsciously. *She is gorgeous.* He couldn't take his eyes off Piper. *Maybe Johnny is right. Maybe it is time to shelve my past and move on. But I don't want to forget about Becky. Who says I have to?*

For the first time, Bryson was realizing that Johnny was right. He was developing feelings for Piper. No matter how hard he tried to suppress his feelings, they kept fighting harder and harder to get out.

The words of the lady in the light suddenly entered his mind. *If you hold on to the past, you will never be able to move forward. As like as not when life spills through destiny's doorway, you must let it go by. You need only to believe.*

Bryson blinked as if waking from a dreamlike state, and then the words vanished from his mind. He was now standing with the rest of the church. His knuckles were white from gripping tightly the pew in front of him. The congregation was singing their fourth hymn. Bryson didn't remember one song, let alone four of them. He looked at Piper, who was holding a hymn book and singing. He leaned over to pick up a hymn book from a rack located on the back of a pew in front of him; then the song ended, and everyone routinely sat down. Everyone except for Bryson, who was now the only one standing.

"All right, let's give a big hand for our next volunteer to lead our invitation song," a man standing at the pulpit joked.

Everyone started laughing and clapping.

Bryson looked at Piper and Jared, who were laughing hysterically. He felt himself turn ten shades of red before he sat down.

"I'm good, pastor. You don't want your flock to stampede out of here," Bryson said as he sat down slowly, wishing he could somehow slide on down and hide under the pew.

Again the crowd erupted in laughter.

"My name is Pastor Steve. Your name, I believe, is Bryson Keahbone. I've heard a lot of good things about you, young man." Pastor Steve was forty-four years old and had been preaching to youth groups and congregations for twenty-six years. He moved from Lubbock, Texas, to Talihina with his wife and family ten years this January. He enjoyed the mountain scenery compared to the flat lands around Lubbock, but he was still a die-hard Red Raiders fan to the bitter end.

"Glad to have you here today," Pastor Steve greeted as he stepped behind the podium. He wore dark blue slacks with a light blue long-sleeve collared shirt—no tie—it made him feel too restricted.

Bryson nodded and smiled.

Pastor Steve stared out over the audience for several seconds as if he were in deep thought about what he was about to preach. He took a deep breath.

"I had this big long, detailed sermon about the Good Samaritan prepared for you, and on the way to church this morning, the Lord God lay upon my heart to preach a totally different message. I am going to be brief and to the point."

"Amen," an elderly man in the back pew opposite Bryson crowed.

The congregation roared.

"I'm glad to see that one of us is fired up today." Pastor Steve laughed and then continued. "For whatever his purpose may be, God has in mind this message for you today, and I'm deeply obligated to preach about trials and why we must endure hard times."

Bryson sighed. *Boy, have I had my fair share of hard knocks.*

"A story comes to mind about a young man who died and went before the judgment seat of God. An angel standing outside the gate to the courtroom told the young man, 'Before God passes judgment on your soul, I should inform you that we've looked closely over your entire life, and to be perfectly honest, you really didn't do anything particularly bad or good. The committee is not really sure what to do with you. Can you tell us anything you did that can help us make a decision about your fate?'"

Pastor Steve stepped from behind the podium and continued, "The young man thought for a second and replied, 'Yes, once I was driving along on my way to work and came upon this kid who was being bullied by some gang members. So I pulled over, got out my Ping golf club, and went up to the leader of the gang. He was a huge, muscled-up dude with tattoos on his tattoos. He had this big ring pierced through his nose. Well, I quickly tore the ring out of his nose and told him he and his gang had better stop bullying the kid or they would have to deal with me!"

The congregation was silent.

"Now, the Committee of Angels was most impressed and asked, 'Excellent, when did all this occur?' ... About three minutes ago."

Pastor Steve's face turned from serious to a mischievous grin.

The church erupted in laughter.

Pastor Steve picked up his Bible and stepped to the edge of the stage, pausing momentarily before moving down the steps. He walked down the center aisle glancing out over the small group of 120 or so. He turned abruptly and headed toward the platform.

"Trials—what are they? Why do they happen? Trials are painful events in our life that are allowed by God to change our character and allow us to grow and rely on God. Everyone goes through many trials throughout their entire lives. There are several kinds of trials ranging from a flat tire to a nagging boss to a busybody neighbor."

Bryson glanced at Piper.

Piper tilted her head slightly toward Bryson, fighting the urge to look back at him.

"Sometimes these trials are small. Other times, they come in the form of the sudden loss of a loved one, whether in divorce or by imprisonment or even in death. Trials show no favoritism— they are simply allowed by God."

Becky's memories suddenly flood Bryson's mind. He thought of the happiness they shared and how they were inseparable. *How could God allow Becky's death? What purpose could it possibly serve?* This time, Bryson wasn't angry, but instead, he felt extreme sadness. He fought back the tears that were trying to fill his eyes. He wanted to understand. *Why, God? Why?*

"No matter how good we believe we have been, no matter how hard we try to do the right thing, bad things are going to happen. God *allows* bad things to happen. These bad things come in the form of trials. Sometimes we ask, 'Why?' We don't have a clue how God thinks."

Bryson stared blankly at Pastor Steve. He was in a perplexed state of mind. *What possible good could come out of the deaths of my parents and especially Becky's?*

"God is in control."

Pastor Steve paused to study the audience.

"Let me repeat myself. *God is in control!* No matter how hard we try or what we might think about a given situation in our lives, we are not in control—God is!" Pastor Steve proclaimed as he picked up his Bible and moved to the edge of the stage. He slowly raised his Bible.

"And there's more. Do you want to hear it?"

"Amens" and "Preach on, brother" sang throughout the congregation.

"God is in control and has a plan! Turn your Bibles to Jeremiah 29:11–14," Pastor Steve said, pausing to ruffling pages. "The Good Lord says in verse 11, '"For I know the plans I have for you," declares the Lord, "plans to prosper you and not to harm, plans to give you hope and a future."' Listen to me! Eyes up here! The Lord tells us he has a plan, a plan to prosper and not harm, a plan that gives us hope for a secure future. Who's in control?"

"God!"

"Amen! God has a plan for you. What is the plan? I don't have a clue. But you can find out. How? Let's read on. Verse 12 continues with God saying, '"Then you will call on Me and come and pray to Me, and I will listen to you. You will seek Me and find Me when you seek Me with all your heart. I will be found by you," declares the Lord.' Pray—that's how you learn of God's plan for you."

I prayed to God, and He didn't answer my prayer, Bryson recalled as thoughts of the hospital waiting room filled his head when Bryson and Hoot prayed for hours. Bryson looked down and clenched his fists. *What good came from that?*

"Some of you are thinking, 'I pray all the time, and God never answers my prayers,'" Pastor Steve declared, raising his free hand. "I've done it several times. Maybe one of you can relate. I know I can! I'm stepping on my own toes here!"

Bryson looked up, slowly unclenching his fists. He felt like the pastor was speaking to no one but him. There was a surreal calmness that seemingly crept over him.

"God always answers prayers in three ways—yes, no, wait! God's timing is always right on time. Our minds cannot fathom the depth of His wisdom. We must *believe* that God is in *control* and trust Him with all our heart."

I want to believe. I want to trust God. I want to have peace. I want to move on. I want to put the demons of my past behind me. It's so hard. I have so many questions I need answered.

"Joseph trusted God with all his heart. He had to endure many trials during his lifetime. Maybe you've heard of Joseph's story? It takes place in Genesis. His brothers were very jealous of Joseph, especially after Joseph told them they would bow down to him someday. They came up with this plan to sell Joseph into slavery to a caravan of merchants traveling to Egypt, and then they would tell their father, Jacob, that he had been killed by a wild animal. They even smeared the blood of a slain goat on his multicolored coat and said it was Joseph's blood."

"Little did the brothers know, that this plan was actually God's plan, not theirs. God took care of Joseph although he suffered through many trials, even imprisonment for something he didn't do. Yeah, Joseph was falsely accused of attempted rape by his master's wife. She wanted to have an affair, but Joseph knew it wasn't right in God's eyes.

"You might think that Joseph would start to become a little bitter by now—never happened. Through these trials, Joseph never blamed God, but instead, he embraced each situation and gave God the praise and glory. It turned out that there was a huge famine in the land. All the crops in Egypt and the surrounding countries were affected. But there was hope—God gave Joseph the ability to interpret dreams. Pharaoh had a dream about the famine prior to it happening. Joseph interpreted the dream and had the Pharaoh stockpile all the extra grain from the seven years of good crops because Joseph knew through the interpretation that there was about to be seven years of bad crops and famine.

"Most of the time, God had a special way he liked to speak to people. Does anyone here know how God chose to talk to people in the Bible?"

"Cell phones," a little girl in the front pew answered.

"Great answer, Jena. Close, but incorrect. Thanks for trying. Anyone else? Dreams. That's right. Dreams are what God likes to use to talk to His people."

Bryson thought of all the dreams he had every night. He wondered, *Are they from God? If so, what do they mean? I need answers.* Ms. Abbey's words entered his mind. *According to her the answers lie in the swamp with someone named Cherokee Billy.* He would try to find the swamp and the man after church.

"Thanks to God using Joseph, Egypt had plenty of grain to feed its people and still have some left over. God, not Pharaoh, made Joseph the right-hand man to Pharaoh, second in charge only behind the Pharaoh himself. Joseph's family was not doing so well back home. They were almost out of food. Jacob sent his sons to purchase grain from the Egyptians. They arrived several days later and were escorted to Joseph, their brother. Joseph was in charge of selling grain, so the brothers had to report to Joseph. They were brought before Joseph and bowed at his feet, thus fulfilling the dream he had had before they faked his death and sold him into slavery. Joseph recognized them, but they didn't recognize Joseph, and he kept secret his identity for several days. After awhile, Joseph finally revealed his true identity and forgave his brothers. Joseph had his entire family relocated to the best lands of Egypt called Goshen. Joseph told his brothers not to be worried or angry with themselves for what they did because everything worked out for the best because God had used him as part of God's plan."

Bryson glanced over at Piper. She must have felt him staring and chanced a quick peek his way. Their eyes met briefly. She abruptly turned and faced forward, feeling like a third grader with a huge crush on the new kid in school. Normally she would have been upset with herself for lack of control, but she wasn't. She glanced back again.

Bryson's eyes never left her. *What is God's plan for Piper? For me? For us?*

"David wrote in Psalms 139:16b, 'All my days were written in Your book and planned before a single one of them began.' As much as you try to predict and plan out your life, you never know when you're about to get a curve ball that will suddenly turn all your plans into a chaotic nightmare. It is most important when you are faced with life's trials that you trust and believe in God. God has ordained your paths and has provided you with the abilities to handle every challenge that life throws your way. God will show you a way out!"

Pastor Steve paused, raising his hands. "God is constantly showing you that you cannot trust yourself to find or follow the right road. When you are traveling on a clear road along the peak of a mountain, you are fine and feel invincible. But when you enter the dark valley, when you are weak and alone, you need someone to lean on. God wants you to lean on him, and not trust on yourself but to trust in Him thankfully."

God, I trust only in myself. I don't know what You want from me.

Bryson clenched his fists.

"God is telling you that you can overcome any trial that life throws at you, but you can't be passive. The time to act is now! Don't wait! But you can't do it on your own! You must rely on God! He wants you to seek out His wisdom. God's wisdom will answer all your questions. I will close by saying, God never leaves or turns His back on you. You turn your back to Him. God wants you to come back to him. Whatever trials fall across your path you need only to believe, trust in God, and seek God's wisdom. Be strong and courageous, and you will persevere!" the pastor concluded, slowly lowering his hands to side as if they were too heavy to keep raised.

"Be strong and courageous!" echoed throughout Bryson's soul.

Pastor Steve bowed his head, "Let's pray …"

Bryson bowed. The message had totally engulfed his entire being. He felt like the weight of the whole world was resting on his shoulders, crushing his existence into the ground.

I want to come back, God, but …

Flake Walks

Bryson walked through the double doors of the church building waiting outside for Hoot and Vick to exit. Perhaps anyone else for that matter that may come out first. He was shaking hands with women and men of the congregation when Jared burst through the doors and ran up to Bryson. He tried to slow down but lost his footing in the damp grass and landed right square on his buttocks. And to add salt to the wound, Sasha Jo happened to be walking by and saw the whole event, start to finish. She didn't laugh but instead had a concerned look on her face.

"Are you all right, Jared?" Sasha Jo asked, bending over as if to help him up.

"Yeah, yeah. I'm good. Nothing hurt but my pride," Jared moaned.

Sasha Jo stood up next to Jared with her hands crossed in front of her patiently waiting to see if he was all right.

"Thanks," Jared said as he stood up, brushing the grass from his jeans. He looked for the first time into her beautiful caramel-colored eyes. He wanted to say more, *anything*, but the words had vanished from his open mouth.

Jared and Sasha Jo remained standing in an awkward silence. Jared placed his hands in his pockets and looked around curiously for several seconds. Sasha Jo's face beamed like a ray of sunlight. He again tried to say something, but the harder he tried to speak, the heavier his tongue seemed to get.

Bryson chuckled as he watched the humorous scene. He thought about rescuing Jared, but he was too late.

"I hope you're okay. I will see you at school tomorrow, Jared. Bye, Mr. Keahbone," Sasha Jo said, smiling directly at Jared.

"Yeah … uh … thanks. Yes, I will … see you tomorrow," Jared stuttered, wanting real hard to kick himself in the butt for hesitating.

"See you tomorrow in class, Sasha Jo."

Bryson waved. Bryson and Jared watched Sasha Jo walk away.

"Nice job, Prufrock," Bryson jeered. "Dare I eat a peach?"

"I know. Right." Jared sighed, letting his shoulders droop as he exhaled. "I'm hopeless. Every time Sasha Jo comes around, I become this blubbering moron-idiot."

"It happens to the best of us," Bryson confessed, putting his hand on Jared's shoulders. "That's just one of many of life's lessons."

"Hello, I hope I'm not interrupting anything important?" Piper asked, walking up and stopping beside Jared.

"No. We're just … uh … talking," Bryson stammered, catching him off guard with her sudden arrival. "Now who's blubbering?"

Bryson winked at Jared, playing it off as if he did it on purpose. He didn't. He couldn't help it. His insides felt like Jell-O.

"I see what you mean." Jared laughed.

"Am I missing something here?" Piper's forehead wrinkled in a puzzled look.

"Sorry. It's nothing. We were talking about …"

Jared shook his head slightly, indicating that he didn't want his mother to know about his feelings for Sasha Jo. He had never had a girlfriend before and was afraid of what his mother might think. He didn't exactly know why he didn't want his mother to know. He just didn't—not yet anyway.

" … about how the etiquettes of speech will suddenly leave the most gifted speaker in the most bizarre situations," Bryson finished, cocking a brow at Jared, wanting to pat himself on the back in a rave of self-indulgence for coming up with such a quick and witty answer.

Piper wasn't buying it. She grinned at Jared, thinking there was probably a lot more to this story than they were letting on but thought it better not to ask. She had something on her mind. She paused and then suddenly turned toward Bryson.

"Would you like to have lunch with us today?" Piper uttered abruptly, blurting it out unexpectedly, wishing maybe that she should take it back. Or maybe not. She couldn't believe that had just come out of her mouth. *What was I thinking? Too late to take it back.*

"Yes, Mr. Keahbone, come eat lunch with us today! Mom's an excellent cook! Of course, you already know that," Jared exclaimed excitedly.

Bryson was momentarily taken back. Yes, he wanted to eat lunch with them, but before he could answer, they were interrupted.

"Bryson, I am so excited to see you here today," Vick sang out, wrapping her arms around him in a death grip.

"Thanks. It was my pleasure. I think," Bryson said playfully as Vick released her hold on him.

"Hello, Piper and Jared. I'm excited to see you too."

"Hi, Vick."

"Hello, Ms. Buchanan."

"Hey, don't forget about me," Hoot announced, stepping up to stand in the circle of friends.

Piper leaned in and hugged Hoot and Vick at the same time.

Pastor Steve came up after Hoot and extended his hand to Bryson.

"I'm glad you're here today. I hope I didn't embarrass you too much to where you won't come back and see us."

"No, not at all. Although I'm pretty sure you were stepping on my toes a little bit with your message today—it sure hit home—good preaching," Bryson complimented. "It's been awhile."

"Thank you. God has many ways to get his message out. God sent that one to me this morning on the way to church. I praise him every day, hoping he can use me. Take care. Hope to see you next Sunday. I have to run over here and see a man about a dog," Pastor Steve declared, giving a quick wave as he headed the opposite way he had just pointed.

They all had puzzled looks on their faces except Hoot. He just grinned and laughed.

"Ms. Webiener has been hitting up Pastor Steve for six weeks about singing a special duet with the good pastor on Sunday morning."

"So what's wrong with that? Let me guess—she can't sing a lick?"

"No, she sings just fine. It's the pastor who can't carry a tune in a bucket," Hoot roared.

They all laughed, and as the laughter began to die down, Pastor Steve came scampering by in speed-walk mode, followed by Ms. Webiener nipping on his tail. And the laughter broke out again.

Bryson looked over at Piper. Her face glowed from dimple to dimple. He liked this side of her. Very relaxed. He wanted to answer Piper's question. He thought it would be enjoyable to sit down and have lunch with Piper and Jared. He was about to tell Piper that he would love to when Hoot reminded Bryson something that he had totally forgotten.

"Where's Johnny?" Hoot asked dryly.

Bryson had forgotten all about the argument with Johnny.

"That's a good question. I'm not sure where Johnny is."

Bryson turned around, scanning the church yard. He glanced over at his empty Jeep, but Johnny was nowhere in sight. Bryson's feelings of regret and sadness returned. *I should never have said those things to Johnny. He may be right. I'm starting to see it.*

"I'm not sure. We had a little disagreement, and I guess he bolted."

"Imagine that."

"It wasn't totally his fault," Bryson defended.

"Never is," Hoot said sarcastically.

Bryson glared at Hoot. He wanted to tell Hoot that he needed to start backing off but decided not to; his mouth had already done enough damage for one day.

"He probably walked downtown to get something to eat. I need to go find him," Bryson said, glancing regretfully at Piper and Jared. Their smiles turned instantly to frowns.

"Thank you for the invite. I need to go find my friend, Johnny. May I have a rain check?"

"Sure. Another time would be fine," Piper pointed out disappointedly.

"Cool. I will see you tomorrow at school, Jared. Bye."

"See you later, Mr. Keahbone."

The small group waved to Bryson as he turned to walk toward his Jeep.

Johnny had waited until Bryson entered the church building before he got out of the Jeep. His first impulse was to go straight to the highway and thumb a ride out of there as fast as he could get away. But part of him wanted to stay and do the right thing and talk it out. He paced back and forth, contemplating his chosen dilemma. He sat down on the front bumper, burying his face in his hands. "I want to do the right thing. I want to. But …" Finally, he got up and reached in the back of the Jeep and pulled his backpack from the seat.

The sun was high overhead in the cloudless sky. Johnny looked up and squinted. He wanted to stay and hash it out with Bryson. He was ready to go back to his father and work things out. *Why did Bryson have to say those words? Why?* He stood still like his feet had taken root in the ground. He glanced at the church's doors, hoping Bryson would be coming out to talk with him.

No Bryson.

No talk.

"What's the use? I am worthless!" Johnny murmured disappointedly, finally giving up that Bryson would return.

Johnny pivoted and began walking toward the highway. He decided to walk toward the pool hall, knowing that it wouldn't be open on a Sunday. At least he could stretch his legs a little and then return and talk with Bryson. *That sounds like a good plan.*

Sometimes plans never work out like we want them to.

It took Johnny about thirty minutes to get to Shooters. He never noticed the patrol car mirroring his route one street over. He stepped onto the gravel parking lot. No cars were around. *Just like I thought—closed.* As he turned to leave, the side door of Shooters sprung open.

"Hey, where ya goin'? You up for some pool?"

Johnny spun back around.

Skeeter Monger filled up the whole doorway.

"Come on. Let's play a few games. My other brother will be here shortly. He's the one who has all the money."

Johnny smiled, "You betcha."

Bryson drove around town for twenty minutes, searching relentlessly for Johnny. Nothing. He was not at any convenience stores or restaurants. He was nowhere to be found. Bryson decided he would extend his search to the outskirts of town before he headed back to the cabin.

Bryson turned down Highway 1 and traveled east out of town. He slowed down to check out Hilltop Saloon and saw immediately that it was closed. He glanced across the street at Shooters. There were two patrol cars parked on the side of the metal building, but the place appeared to be closed also. Bryson pulled into the gravel drive and stopped but quickly thought that Johnny wouldn't be there if the police were around. Johnny liked to avoid authority.

Little did Bryson know, the police cars had just pulled up as Johnny was going inside.

Only moments before Bryson drove up.

Bryson shoved the shifter into first and spun out of the drive, heading east out of town.

Flagg Bottom Swamp

B ryson continued east on Highway 1. He doubted that Johnny had come out this far. He began looking for a good place to turn around when a sign appeared suddenly out of the waist-high Johnson grass. Bryson's heart began to race:

Flagg Bottom Road

He knew he was close to getting answers to his questions. He pulled down on the blinker handle, and then turned north, stopping abruptly after traveling a few blocks. He stared hard down the narrow asphalt road.

Where is Johnny?

He thought about sweeping back through town and checking out the hotels and then circling back later to find the swamp. He glanced suddenly at the backseat. That thought quickly changed. For the first time, he noticed that Johnny's backpack was missing. "Johnny has apparently moved on … again," Bryson assumed, not realizing Johnny's true fate.

As Bryson pondered his next move, Ms. Abbey's words came to his mind. *There is only one road in and one road out. Drive until you can drive no more. In the heart of the swamp is an old cuss by the name of Cherokee Billy. If there are answers to your question, he will know 'em.*

Bryson glanced in the rearview and then roared off down the road.

Flagg Bottom Road was very windy, ascending and descending almost with every turn, like a rollercoaster at an amusement park. Bryson's ears were stopped up due to the sudden gain in elevation. He yawned to clear them, and they both popped.

Pine trees walled in the road tightly across the top of a long ridge. A small clearing appeared on both sides of the road as it crested the mountain. Bryson pulled off the narrow road the best he could without disrupting traffic, not that there was any traffic to disrupt.

The view was breathtaking.

Bryson could see miles and miles of rolling green with patches of orange, red, and yellow. It looked like God had spread out this giant, beautifully speckled carpet over the entire region. Everything was so bright and vivid. The fall foliage was in the early stage of a full-blown epidemic of tantalizing oranges and lucid reds with splashes of yellow. Located at the base of the mountain was a bowl-shaped valley filled with dark bluish- green water.

"Flagg Bottom Lake. The swamp must be nearby."

Bryson savored the picturesque moment, enjoying the view and fresh air before finally moving on. He pulled from the shoulder and proceeded down the bumpy asphalt road, descending sharply into a dark tunnel of hickories and oaks, which have now replaced the towering pine trees. They were so tightly woven together that they appeared to be a single solid mass of branches and leaves, making visibility very limited. The thick overlay of trees made the day seem darker than a normal midday afternoon, like it was almost dusk.

Bryson felt like the road was cutting through a vast wilderness spiraling his vehicle down a giant funnel emptying into a greenish-black domain of nothingness. *I hope this is not some wild goose chase.*

He was beginning to wonder if this road had an end. How long had he been driving? Maybe twenty minutes. He didn't know anything except that his patience was wearing thin. The air suddenly became humid and smelled very musty. The road had leveled off and was now bordered on each side with a pool of black water. The trees were thinning and suddenly seemed to open up as the road abruptly stopped at a yellow-striped barricade at the end of a cul-de-sac.

A huge white rusty sign nailed to the yellow-and-black-striped barricade read:

BEWARE:
Snakes And
Quicksand
Are common to this area!

"Hmm … snakes and quicksand. Beware stepping on a snake only to fall into quicksand. Nice," Bryson scoffed as he parked the Jeep in front of the sign. He dropped the keys to the floor and climbed out.

The cul-de-sac was actually a small peninsula in the swamp. Huge bald cypress trees emerged out of the murky waters like soaring skyscrapers. Small tan cypress stumps protruded from dark waters, reminding Bryson of alien coneheads hiding just beneath the waterline exposing only the tops of their heads. He scanned the swamp further for some kind of path, but all he saw were a few thousand lily pads and roughly a million croaking frogs.

No path.

No boat. Just swamp.

There is no way I'm going to wade through this swamp. I don't even know if this Cherokee Billy dude is real.

Bryson walked along the shoreline, avoiding shrubs and saplings, to look for a possible hidden path. He wasn't going to give up easily—not without a fight.

There has to be a path. Ms. Abbey said there was a path. Where is it? I believe her.

A cool breeze passed by Bryson. He shuddered as the hair on his body stood up. He turned and saw a figure standing beside an old weeping willow, but he couldn't recognize who it was. Under the hanging branches of the willow, the silhouette appeared to loom on the water, raising slowly an arm in a gesture for Bryson to follow.

Bryson started to speak but remained silent, when he heard a small, still voice.

Come ... it is this way. You should choose.

Bryson stepped forward, momentarily losing his balance when he tripped on a sapling, causing his eyes to look down. After recovering his footing, he stood back up and looked toward the willow. Its long boughs were gently ebbing back and forth in the breeze, like they were underwater. He exhaled after holding a long breath. The figure under the willow was nothing more than a small cypress covered with long, gray strands of Spanish moss. There was a single branch that extended out from the trunk, which Bryson mistook for an arm.

"It sure looked like a person," Bryson attested, shaking his head slightly. "I believe it may be time to bug out."

Bryson had made up his mind to leave but abruptly stopped when he saw in the direction the figure supposedly had pointed—a narrow dirt path, no wider than a fallen tree, cutting through the middle of the swamp. The path was lined on both sides with beaver-gnawed logs and stumps, and musty decaying leaves.

"That was not there before. Or was it?"

He glanced around.

"I've come too far to quit now," Bryson determined as he climbed over the striped barricade.

As soon as Bryson stepped onto the dirt path, all the croaking frogs and chirping insects and birds ceased to make sound. He peered around curiously. The silence was a little unsettling, but he wasn't afraid. He felt like there was an invisible protective hedge surrounding his body, his mind, and even his soul. As creepy as this place appeared to be, he did not feel threatened.

The swamp had a special and unique beauty. Bryson marveled at the moss draperies hanging from the canopy of cypress trees. The water at the base of these trees was smooth as ebony glass casting formless shadows. Although the dark water rarely exceeded three feet, it appeared a bottomless pit, waiting patiently to entrap any lost souls.

The path wound around so that Bryson was confused in what direction he now walked. He looked at the location of moss on a nearby elm. His dad had taught him that moss always grew on the north side of trees because moss thrived better in shaded areas. Bryson quickly concluded that it didn't matter what direction he was going—there was only one way in and one way out.

A smoky mist suddenly appeared, hovering a few feet above the water. The vegetation of shrubberies and underbrush became thicker, hugging the edge of the path until it had almost disappeared. The land sloped up slightly. The fog lifted and vaporized as quickly as it had appeared. The path had opened up into a large clearing, forming an island in the middle of the swamp. The cypress trees were much taller, raising the canopy a good thirty feet from before. Vegetation had thinned out, and the green grass looked like velvet. Bryson gave a quick survey of the clearing looking for—*there!*

On the opposite end of the clearing was a small log cabin, a true log cabin—not a kit—made of cypress trees packed with swamp mud to seal the cracks between the logs. Prairie grass and pitch supplied the materials for a semiflat roof—no gables. A six- foot wooden awning extended off the front of the cabin serving as a covering for a porch. A single door stood in the middle of two windows. The cabin itself was very small, measuring sixteen feet by sixteen feet.

Bryson walked toward the cabin and noticed a huge pile of unsplit fire logs that were about forty feet from the cabin's front door. *Somebody's got some work to do.* Then it crossed his mind, *What kind of person secludes himself from the world like this person has done? I mean, I thought I was a recluse, but there is no comparison.*

Something was moving frantically around on the porch. Thick shrubs lining the porch obscured Bryson's view. Suddenly, there was a loud crash from the porch, and the largest raccoon Bryson had ever seen came bolting right toward him. It was nearly the size of a Labrador and had a piece of fish in its mouth. Bryson barely had enough time to dodge the furry missile.

"Come back here, you cursed coon!" a voice screamed from the side of the cabin. "Back in my heyday, I would have run you down and made a coon's hat out of you!"

Bryson watched the raccoon disappear into the underbrush, and then he turned back toward the cabin.

"Hello. My name is—" Bryson called out but never finished.

"Bryson Keahbone. What took you so long to get here? I was expectin' you over an hour ago. Gus's done ran off with our dinner," an old man declared, stepping from the shadows of the porch, holding a stainless steel frying pan.

Bryson was briefly caught off guard. *How did he know my name? How did he know I was coming? Who is he?*

The old man chuckled. "Pardon my uncouth manners. I am …"

Cherokee Billy

"Cherokee Billy Elihu Jones III. But you can call me Cherokee Billy," he said. He was a tall, slender black man whose voice was very raspy with a touch of gentle gruffness.

Cherokee Billy was a very old half-African American, half-Choctaw Indian. *Maybe older than dirt*, Bryson thought. A black derby covered his white nappy hair. A white beard sporadically covered a face carved deep with age. He grinned broadly, exposing ivory white teeth that glowed against his ebony-coal skin. He wore a faded white button-up collared cotton shirt. Suspenders held up dark pants that were tucked inside a pair of leather work boots. His legs were extremely bowlegged, and Bryson noticed that he walked with a slight limp. *Probably arthritis.*

"Howdy-do, young Bryson," Cherokee Billy said, extending his hand as he removed his derby with the other holding it to his chest.

Bryson saw for the first time Cherokee Billy's milky-white pupils. *He is blind!* He hesitated and then extended his hand slowly.

"It's arright. I don't bite."

"I'm sorry. It's … just that … I …" Bryson stammered, raising his voice a little after each pause.

"Easy does it, compadre. I'm blind—not deaf," Cherokee Billy pointed out as he turned and headed back to the porch.

293

He set the frying pan down on a table and picked up a ten-foot cane pole.

Bryson followed closely behind.

"I'll be right back. I have to go catch us some dinner, since Gus done run off with ours."

Bryson began to politely tell Cherokee Billy that he really wasn't very hungry.

"Nonsense. We gotta eat. You wait here. It won't take long," Cherokee Billy snapped, picking a small foam box full of night crawler worms as he began walking toward the swamp. He suddenly stopped and pointed at the cut wood pile. "If it ain't too much of a bother, would you mind splitting up the fire wood over there? You know, it's the pile you were admiring when you walked up. The splitter axe is sitting over there. I'll be back shortly."

Cherokee Billy smirked as he walked off.

Bryson was amazed and a little bewildered by how independent Cherokee Billy lived despite his supposed handicap. His limitations were not controlled by the environment in which he lived.

At the wood pile, Bryson picked up the heavy splitter axe, which was half sledge hammer and half axe. He rolled it around in his palms and then sat it back down. He looked around for a pair of gloves. No gloves. He turned up his hands and spit in the middle of his palms, rubbing his hands together vigorously until they heated up.

"Let's do this."

An hour later, Bryson was wiping the sweat from his brow as he put the finishing touch on the wood pile. He had stacked the split wood between two elms, which measured close to two ricks of cut wood. His shoulders and lower back were a little tight at first, but he worked through the soreness.

Bryson was putting his shirt on when Cherokee Billy came strolling up with an eight- and fourteen-pound channel cat on a stringer.

"I caught us some supper. Did you get the wood split up and stacked?"

"Yes, sir. But I'm really not—"

"Good deal. Now come with me," Cherokee Billy ordered, striding past Bryson without slowing down.

Bryson gave up. He knew it was no use trying to hurry this old man into answering his questions. Cherokee Billy was living on Cherokee Billy time. He would have to be patient. If Cherokee Billy had answers, then Bryson would have to wait.

Cherokee Billy stopped at the side of the cabin. He placed the catfish in a sink that was built in the middle of a wooden table. Bryson noticed the fish's mouths were moving, like they were trying to speak.

Cherokee Billy turned toward Bryson, handing him a filet knife, a gallon jug of water, and medium-sized bowl.

"You do know how to clean fish, don't ya?"

"Yes, I …"

"Good deal. I'll be back shortly. Throw the innards over there on the ground. Gus will come get 'em later. But be careful if the blasted coon shows up before you finish 'cause he'll steal ya *blind*." Cherokee Billy snickered as he disappeared into the cabin.

Bryson stared after the old man until he vanished, and then he picked up the knife and proceeded to clean the smaller of the two fish. It hadn't been but a few days since he had last cleaned a small-mouthed bass that he had caught in the stream behind his cabin. He could hear Cherokee Billy rummaging around the cabin as if he were looking for something but couldn't find it.

"Aha! There you be!" the old man clamored as sounds of numerous objects came falling and crashing to the cabin's wooden floor.

Cherokee Billy exited the cabin with a two-foot long cylinder wire cage and a pair of pliers.

"Hey! I like my cat skinned," Cherokee Billy informed, tossing the pliers in Bryson's general direction.

"My pleasure," Bryson replied sharply, snatching the tool from the air. His patience was beginning to wear a little thin. It would be dark in a few hours. Bryson was anxious to be heading home hopefully with answers about his dreams and a chance to talk to Johnny when he got there.

"I'll be back shortly, compadre," Cherokee Billy stated, holding up and shaking the wire crawfish trap. "Dessert's a-comin'."

"Hey, it's okay. You don't need to go to all this trouble on my account."

"No trouble. Be back shortly."

"So I've heard. I'll be right here … anxiously waiting your return," Bryson said sarcastically under his breath.

Cherokee Billy slipped back into the swamp again, ignoring Bryson's comment.

After Bryson finished cleaning the catfish, he poured fresh water over the eight fillets before putting them in the cooking bowl. He left the carcasses and innards piled up by a small oak, waiting for Gus to come scavenge the remains.

So far, no Gus.

Cherokee Billy entered the clearing carrying the crawfish trap by his side. The trap was loaded down with fifty or so bright red crawfish. He set the trap down by a circle of stones that were eight feet in diameter and stacked two feet high. It was a fire pit. Two iron rods extended up from inside the fire pit. A single rod with a hook in the middle ran across the top and attached to the other two, forming a square frame within the fire pit. He picked up a large black kettle and walked toward Bryson.

"Will you fill this up with fresh water and hang it over there on that hook above the fire pit?" Cherokee Billy asked, handing the kettle to Bryson.

Bryson grabbed the kettle and then bent over and picked up the container of fresh water he had used to clean the fish.

"There's more water on the porch if ya need it. Oh yeah, I just remembered—if you don't mind, would you start a fire over in the pit. The kindling and matches are right by the water on the porch, and you may need some firewood," Cherokee Billy added as he grabbed the bowl of fish from the table and walked toward the cabin.

"Thanks," Bryson uttered as he hung the kettle and poured in the water, filling it three-quarters of the way up. *That should be enough, I hope.*

Bryson retrieved the matches and kindling from the porch. He put the kindling in the middle of the pit beneath the kettle and stacked six logs in a teepee shape over the kindling before lighting the fire. Within seconds, the fire was dancing up and around the kettle.

Cherokee Billy came out of the cabin, carrying several lily pad leaves, shaved elm bark, inner cypress bark string, a jar of lemon balm, and the bowl of fillets. He knelt down and sat on a small stool by the fire pit. He sat the items on the ground. He quickly went to work. He picked up a fillet and covered it with the lemon balm. Next, he took the fillet and rolled it up in several lily pad leaves. To help hold the leaves in place, he wrapped river elm bark around the leaves. Then, he tied inner cypress bark string around the entire bundle.

Bryson watched curiously and marveled at the ease and fluency that Cherokee Billy had at performing, not only this task, but all the tasks he carried out.

Cherokee Billy placed the wrapped bundle on the ground and looked toward Bryson. "The rest are yours."

Bryson chuckled lightly. *Why am I not surprised?*

"When the fire dies down into the coals, dump the crawdaddies into the pot. And then sit those fillets at the edge of the coals. It won't be long before we's chowin' down. Any questions? I'll be back shortly," Cherokee Billy said, retreating toward the cabin before Bryson could even open his mouth.

"No … I guess not," Bryson barked out as Cherokee Billy was entering the cabin.

Again Bryson was beginning to doubt that he would get any of the answers that he sought here. The thought made him feel suddenly very heavyhearted. But he would make the best of the situation; he always did. He enjoyed the old man's company; it was just that he needed closure to his life—so many things he wanted answered or explained.

He glanced at the cabin, but the old man had yet to reappear. The fire had died down to hot glowing red coals. Bryson carefully placed the wrapped fillets around the outer edges of the coals. The water in the kettle was boiling. He dumped the squirming crawfish into the kettle. He felt sorry for the little critters, but on the other hand, he was thankful that he was on the opposite end of the food chain—at least for now.

Cherokee Billy returned carrying two black square stoneware plates and a plastic Walmart bag full of silverware and veggies. He set them down by Bryson. He picked out an onion, garlic, and some jalapenos.

"Cut these up in small pieces and drop 'em in the kettle while I'll season up the meat," Cherokee Billy ordered as he started shaking in salt, black pepper, and a little red cayenne.

Bryson pulled out a paring knife and quickly chopped up the veggies into small pieces, dropping them into the boiling water. The crawfish had turned to a deep red and were bouncing around in the bubbles. Bryson thought how good they looked to eat. Real good. His stomach grumbled and complained sullenly. He just realized that he hadn't eaten anything since before church.

"They'll be ready to eat in a few minutes," Cherokee Billy declared as he pulled two small metal cups from the plastic bag and filled them with water from the jug. He picked up a long stick by his stool and poked at the coals, causing the flames to briefly flare up.

Cherokee Billy grabbed from the plastic bag a pair of tongs and a wire mesh hand strainer customized for dipping out crawfish without getting burned. He set the hand strainer across his lap and leaned toward the fire with the tongs, digging around the coals for the fish.

"Grab ya a plate and let's eat. I know ya hungry. I could hear your stomach growling from the other end of the swamp like it was an angry honey badger fightin' a white-mouth moccasin."

Bryson picked up a plate, placing it under the fish just before Cherokee Billy dropped it. The inner bark string had burned off. Bryson used his fork to peel back the lily pad leaves and bark. The white meat was steaming and flaked apart as he touched it with his fork.

Gus must have smelled the tantalizing aroma of the fish and showed back up for another free meal. The raccoon sat a few feet from Cherokee Billy pawing at the air.

"Gus, ya goin' have to wait your turn. You furry vermin," Cherokee Billy said, and then he turned toward Bryson, bowing his head in prayer. "Yahweh, thank You, yet for another day I can walk this earth. Bless this food You have supplied, and we are about to eat. Above all, thank You for this young man. Bless his journey, guide his path, and give him the knowledge he seeks. Allow me to see what You need me to see. Guide, guard, and carry us in Your Spirit. Direct our paths as is Your will. Amen."

Bryson raised his head and took a bite of the fish. The meat seemed to melt against his tongue. *This may be the best fish I have ever eaten.*

"Mmm. It's very good."

"Wait until ya try these daddies."

Bryson was a little hesitant about the crawfish. Every time he had tried them in the past, they were always too fishy for his taste. But he didn't want to be a rude guest.

"Can hardly wait."

Cherokee Billy snatched up the hand strainer and dipped out six crawdads. He swung them toward Bryson and flipped over the hand strainer. Again Bryson just barely got his plate under the food before it spilled onto the ground. Then Cherokee Billy quickly dipped from the kettle a plateful of the shining red crustaceans for himself.

"Thanks."

"Make sure you eat all the good stuff. Don't be wastin' good food, you hear. First, you grab up the daddy and rip it in 'alf. Take the tail and place it up to your lips and suck the meat right out of the tail. Then the best part is when you take the head and place your mouth over the hole in the body and suck out the juicy brains until it's dry," Cherokee Billy instructed as he quickly downed three before Bryson started on one.

Bryson squirmed. In the past, he had only eaten the tail after he first peeled it. Never any crawfish brains. He looked at Cherokee Billy, who had crawfish meat all over his face but was enjoying himself way too much to care. *What's the worst that could happen?* Bryson abruptly ripped a crawfish in half and promptly put the body up to his lips. He hesitated and then sucked the succulent meat out of the head, throwing his head back like he was drinking from a shot glass. He expected a foul taste, but to his surprise, it was most excellent. It had a lemony-garlic taste to it. Bryson continued to feast on the crawdads and catfish until he could eat no more.

Cherokee Billy threw the leftovers to Gus, who had been patiently watching, waiting for his time to chow down. He instantly snatched them up and left to eat in private.

Cherokee Billy stood up and sat his plate on the stool. He unhooked the kettle and poured out the water onto the ground a few feet from the pit. He carried the empty kettle toward the porch, and then turned back toward Bryson.

"If you don't mind, will ya grab the eating tools and plates and clean them in the sink by the cabin? Thank you kindly. I'll be back shortly."

Bryson grudgingly gathered up the silverware and plates. He looked around the clearing. The underbrush was getting darker. The sun would be leaving the sky pretty soon. He could only imagine how dark this place would be without sunlight. He really didn't want to be in the swamp after nightfall. He was hoping for answers, but he really doubted he would get any tonight. He washed and dried the dinnerware, leaving the utensils in a wooden cup by the sink. He finished off the last of the water washing dishes and wasn't quite sure what to do with the empty plastic jug. *I'm sure he'll want to save this. I better take it inside.* He decided to take the empty jug into Cherokee Billy and tell him that it was time to head home. He was disappointed that this trip had ended in a dead end. He would have to find answers somewhere else. He smiled. *It was not a wasted trip. I'm glad I got the opportunity to meet Cherokee Billy.*

Bryson knocked lightly on the front door.

"Come in."

The door squeaked loudly as Bryson poked his head through the doorway. "I wasn't sure what I needed to do with this empty jug."

"Put it down by the others on the porch and get your tail end in here. I was beginnin' to wonder how long it takes a single individual to clean a few plates. Hurry on in! I'm a-waitin' on ya." Bryson placed the empty jug next to the full jugs, gently closing the door shut as he entered the cabin. He made a quick inspection of the cabin. It was very small but roomy enough for one man. The floor was made of straight cedar stripped of their bark and laid tightly nailed together. There was a small bunk by a fireplace at the far end. Cherokee Billy sat at a small round table with a book and kerosene lantern on it. The lantern was turned up high and illuminated the whole room.

"Have a seat," Cherokee Billy offered, motioning with his finger to an empty chair at the table.

Bryson walked over and pulled the chair slightly out. He regarded the book as he sat in the chair and wondered if it was written in braille. There was no title that he could see. *Probably a classic.*

"Now, Bryson Keahbone, my boy, what can I do for you?"

Bryson was slow to reply. He studied the old man's face. Cherokee Billy's pale eyes were fixed upon him with a determination unequal to anything Bryson had ever seen, like he was staring into Bryson's soul.

Bryson felt like every fiber of his existence was burning from within, a burning sensation that had been extinguished for a very long, long time. *Why now? What is going on?*

"Why have you come?"

Bryson was suddenly jolted from his trance by Cherokee Billy's words.

He paused briefly before beginning.

"I was told by Ms. Abbey that you could help me answer some questions about my past and possibly clear up the meaning of my recurring dreams."

Cherokee Billy's face was without emotion and apathetic.

He's not going to be able to help me.

"Ole Ms. Abbey ... you don't say," Cherokee Billy declared, whose face had curved into a tight-lipped grin. "Well, I'll be a jumping frog in a frying pan. Me and her go way back. Why didn't you say so in the first place? I thought you had done come all the way out here on your own to help me with my chores. I could have helped you out a long time ago," Cherokee Billy whooped, slapping the table with his hand.

Bryson lowered his head until his chin touched his chest. All he could do was smile. *You've got to be kidding me.* He raised his head deliberately. *Where do I begin?* That's just it. He had been waiting for this opportunity for a long time, and now, he didn't know where to begin. After pondering his predicament, he decided to start from the beginning—when he was a boy.

"I grew up here in Talihina as a boy. Something really bad happened to my father, and my mother lost her will to live. I can't remember much ... except for my dad coming to me in a dream the night he vanished. I have the same dream every night, and now there is more—a lady in a bright light has appeared. She indirectly pointed me in your direction. In my dream, my dad wears a wolf skin and tells me, 'When my time is time upon the final scene, come find me beneath the Moon When Wolves Cry.'"

Moon When Wolves Cry

"When my time is time upon the final scene, come find me beneath the Moon When Wolves Cry. Very interesting," Cherokee Billy repeated as he stood up and walked to the window by the front door. He stopped and separated the ragged curtains, staring out the window as if he were searching the swamp for some hidden answer. He opened the wood-framed window. The curtains swayed gently in the light breeze. He turned toward Bryson and gestured toward the open window. He dragged his old wrinkled hand across the sill gathering up dust on his fingertips, and then he blew the dust off his hand and through the open window.

"What do you see?"

Bryson studied the window and the area below and beyond. He didn't fully understand and said the first thing that came to his mind. "I see dust floating through a window and disappearing as if it never existed."

"Splendid guess. Time is like the dust that flew through this open window, returning to the ground where it began. You can never get back time. Yesterday is gone forever. This morning is gone forever. Three minutes ago is gone—forever. Time is time to act *now*, in that moment! Do not wait, or time will pass you by, and the window will close, never to open again," Cherokee Billy proclaimed as he closed the window.

Bryson pondered Cherokee Billy's words, and then they suddenly made sense to him. "There have been situations throughout my life where I had to make tough decisions regarding the path I should choose. By not acting or trying to run away from life's choices, I become like the meaningless dust returning to the unfulfilling earth of an empty world."

Cherokee Billy grinned through his pearly whites.

"I believe you may be on to something. But there's more. Come outside."

The two men walked through the front door. Cherokee Billy led Bryson back to the fire pit. The fire had died down into the white-ash coals, but Bryson could still feel the heat.

"Have a seat."

Bryson sat on one of the stools while Cherokee Billy picked up several small branches and twigs from the wood pile. He walked over and placed them next to the empty stool before finally sitting down. Cherokee Billy deposited the sticks on the coals. Both men watched silently as the sticks disappeared within a thick gray smoke.

Bryson broke the silence.

"I believe I understand the meaning of 'time is time,' but where is beneath the Moon When Wolves Cry?"

Cherokee Billy stared profoundly at Bryson.

"Tonight is the Harvest Moon. The next full moon is called the Moon When Wolves Cry," Cherokee Billy revealed, turning his gaze back to the smoky pit.

"Why is this moon called by that name?"

Cherokee Billy gazed into the blue sky.

There was a long silence before Cherokee Billy spoke.

"It was late fall,around this time,when the US government came up with this great plan to relocate our people—the Choctaws."

Bryson's brow wrinkled in bewilderment.

"I know you're thinking I must be a Cherokee Indian since my name is such. My father was a mighty funny man, but maybe not so clever. He thought it might help me get a wife from another tribe."

Bryson smiled. "How'd that work out for you?"

Cherokee Billy cocked Bryson a crooked grin and shrugged his shoulders, lifting up his palms slowly and then lowering them to his side.

Bryson thought he saw a tear swell up around Cherokee Billy's cloudy eyes as his grin faded to a scowl.

Bryson started to apologize but stopped.

"It was late fall, when the US government relocated our people, the Choctaws, forcing us from our homes in Mississippi to live here in Oklahoma. We had little food or shelter during the trip. We traveled upon the Trail of Tears, where thousands of our people lost their lives to starvation and the elements. The wolves followed, mourning the loss of our great people. Our people have a special bond with the wolf. Wolf is the symbol of strength and family. Moon is the symbol of guidance. This sacred full moon of autumn is called the Moon When Wolves Cry."

Cherokee Billy picked up a long, straight stick and began poking around in the pit, stirring up the coals. Bryson stared blankly at the billowing smoke, thinking about his parents.

"I knew your father. His Choctaw name was Tuchina Iyishke, which means Three Toes. Your daddy only had three toes on each foot."

Bryson looked up instantly. He remembered his father's strange feet.

"How did you know my father?"

Cherokee Billy remained quiet and then spoke softly.

"My son and your daddy were best friends. They ruled the swamp and these hills. They traveled every square foot of this county exploring the land, learning the disciplines of being a Native American. Never saw one without the other. That was ... until Little Billy got the fever."

"I'm sorry."

There was a solemn silence.

Cherokee Billy's jaw tightened. He took a deep breath and scratched his beard. He stared at the swamp, thinking of time past. "There is a war going on all around us. We just don't always see it goin' on."

"What war?"

"The war between light and darkness ... good versus evil. I see that demon runnin' around at night. Its name is *Na-lusa-chi-to*, which means soul-eater. It's a black, red-eyed beast resembling a dog with jaws so powerful that it could in a single bite rip out the heart of its victim."

Bryson wondered what he meant about seeing a beast. *What kind of beast could it be? How can he see it?*

"Has the beast been up here?"

"No. I'm guessin' the good Lord made my little island a safe haven. I hear him out there, but he never comes in."

Cherokee Billy paused, thinking about things from a different time.

"The beast cannot be killed unless you take away the only thing its existence depends upon—time."

Bryson studied Cherokee Billy's hardened face and wondered what connection he had with this so-called beast. *What about this beast? Is it real? Kill it by taking away ... time?* He looked around. The shadows of the underbrush were almost black. He figured there was about twenty minutes of daylight left, but in no way was he going to hurry Cherokee Billy along. He would stay as long as it took.

"That's not all I hear in these hills. For the past twenty years, I hear chanting throughout the swamp, echoing up and down these valleys. I hear the heartbroken song of a fallen warrior. It's the same words being sung over and over again: 'Mother Earth, do not cover my blood.'"

Bryson thought about his father. *Could it be my father?* He did not understand. He felt frustrated and overwhelmed like the weight of the whole world was resting on his shoulders.

"What does it mean?"

"A warrior, who has been slain violently, will not rest until his bones have been recovered and buried in their proper place and retribution—blood atoned for blood. If the warrior's bones are left unburied, he will roam the land as a shadow being usually in the form of a wolf."

Again images of Bryson's father entered his mind.

"The sheriff said my father was drinking and got run over by a train."

"And you believe that."

"No, not really. That's why I'm here. To seek the truth."

"Son, I don't have all the answers. I may not have any answers. I can only tell ya what I see with my ears, hands, nose, and mind—and that's not too far from being gone," Cherokee Billy snorted, stoking the coals until fire totally consumed the sticks he had placed earlier in the pit.

Cherokee Billy peered silently into the fire for a very long time before finally turning his emotionless demeanor toward Bryson. The fire reflected from his cloudy, unblinking eyes.

"Although I am old, blind, and full of days, I see the fire burning in you. Do you know the meaning of your name?"

"No, I do not."

"Bryson is the 'bright son'—child of the light. Keahbone means 'he rises and is stronger than the pit—salvation to the ones he loves.' God has called you. You need only to answer. Tonight is the Harvest Moon. Moon When Wolves Cry is next full moon. Time is time."

Bryson was trying to sort through all this information. His frustrations had returned.

"What does all this mean?"

"God will guide you on the right paths in ways you will not understand. Follow your heart."

Cherokee Billy stood up and extended his hand.

"You need to skedaddle. The dark is upon us."

"Thank you, Cherokee Billy, for everything. May I come see you again?" Bryson asked, grabbing and shaking his hand.

"God willing, young Bryson … God willing."

Bryson turned to walk away and then suddenly stopped when he heard Cherokee Billy's parting words.

"Do not let the fire go out. Be strong and courageous."

"I will do my best. Take care."

Bryson never looked back as he followed the same path that he had traveled earlier. He entered the cul-de-sac. He jumped over the barricade and climbed into his Jeep. He glanced up. Light had all but vanished. The trees were blocking most of the purple sky.

The landscape was completely blacked out, except for a pair of glowing red eyes that Bryson failed to detect. He groped around the floorboard for his keys. The red eyes moved furtively, circling along the edge of the underbrush. His fingers raked across the keys. He shoved the proper key into the ignition but didn't turn it over. Instead, he leaned back trying to absorb everything Cherokee Billy had told him, placing his hands behind his head.

The red eyes continued to stalk toward the Jeep until they were only a few feet away. The predator lowered to the ground as it prepared to leap from the shadows.

Bryson dropped his hands abruptly, cranking the engine and popping the clutch at almost the same time. He sped off down the road.

A black figure leaped over the yellow-striped barricade, landing on the cul-de-sac where Bryson had parked earlier. A low hideous growl sounded through huge yellow fangs that dripped viscous, milky saliva. Red eyes glared unblinkingly at the red tail lights that disappeared down the road.

Bryson followed the road as it ascended toward the clearing at the crest of the mountain. He pulled onto the grassy shoulder. The full moon was peeking over the eastern ridge, chasing far behind its brother, the sun, who had just hid itself beyond the western horizon.

"Harvest Moon is now. Moon When Wolves Cry is next full moon. That's thirty more days," Bryson moaned.

He climbed up on his seat to view the land, and again he was mesmerized by its beauty. Everything seemed to glow a deep purple under the red moon. He could see the roads cutting through the hills like ant trails, and the darker areas he recognized as valleys.

Pastor Steve's words came to his mind.

God is constantly showing you that you cannot trust yourself to find or follow the right road. When you are traveling on a clear road along the peak of a mountain, you are fine and you feel invincible. But when you enter the dark valley, when you are weak and alone, you need someone to lean on. God wants you to lean on him. Do not trust on yourself, but trust in him thankfully.

"I am so ready to climb out of the dark valley."

Flake on the Run

Johnny was lying on his side, trying feverishly to pull his bonded hands over his feet from behind his back. Just as he accomplished the task, the wooden door to the small shed swung open. Johnny stood up abruptly. He wanted to run at the huge man blocking the entire doorway but decided he would wait for a more opportune time to make his escape.

"Been havin' some fun, I see."

"Oh, you know it. What do you want with me?"

Nate Monger smiled. "You've been chosen."

"Lucky me. What's the prize?"

"Immortality."

"Oh yeah. What's the catch?"

"You are to participate in the Running Moon. You are to be hunted. I will give you an eleven-minute and a six-second head start, and then we will commence to huntin' your disrespectful sorry hide. If you make it alive to sunrise, you will be set free."

Right. That'll be the day.

"Piece of cake. You'll never see a runner better than me," Johnny boasted.

"We will see," Nate said as memories of the bronze man haunted his mind. He tried to discard them, but they would not go away. Then his face twisted into an insane grin as the thought of the hunt took control. He pulled the brown leather-bound book from under his arm and sat it on a small square work bench.

Johnny saw the nine-millimeter gun strapped to Nate's hip. It had been covered up by the book. On the other hip was a nine-inch bowie knife. He thought he would have a better chance going for the gun than the knife.

"You have been chosen. Time is time upon this scene. The Running Moon is climbing into the sky. You must sign the Book of the Running Moon," Nate ordered as he opened the book to the yellowy page marked by the black ribbon.

Johnny lunged for the gun, but swift as a mountain lion, Nate reached out and caught Johnny by the throat and lifted him into the air.

Johnny was kicking his feet widely several inches above the ground. He raised his bonded hands in an attempt to remove Nate's hand. Not happening. His world was slowly going black. The drop light above his head hanging from the rafters was fading in and out. Nate released his grip and dropped Johnny to the floor.

"Wrong move. Now sign, or next time, I will snap your pencil-neck."

Johnny, who was gasping for air, glared up at Nate and then stood to his feet and smiled. He wasn't going to let Nate get the best of him.

"A pen or some writing instrument would help."

"Raise your hands."

Nate retrieved a small tin cup from the table and removed his knife from its sheath. He grabbed the zip ties but didn't cut them. Instead, he made a small cut in Johnny's palm and let the blood drip down into the cup.

Johnny flinched but said nothing. He knew he couldn't overpower this man. He would have to wait for another opportunity to escape.

Nate removed a fountain pen from his shirt pocket and handed it to Johnny.

"Dip the pen into the cup and sign here," Nate ordered, pointing at the line beneath Ethan's name.

"You're going to regret this because I'm the best that's ever lived," Johnny bragged as he signed the book, dropping the pen beside his signature.

I wish Bryson was here. He would know how to get me out of this mess. I can do this. I don't need him. I can ...

Nate grabbed the pen and slung the excess blood onto the ground before placing it back into his shirt pocket. He blew on the signature to dry it. Then he closed the book, caressing its side with the front and back of his hand.

This is too freaky—I've got to find a way out of here.

Nate picked up the book and exited through the door.

"Time is time upon this final scene."

Johnny was about to bolt when Billy Ray and Tyrel walked through the door. They were dressed in their sheriff 's uniforms. They grabbed Johnny under each armpit and lifted him into the air.

"This is not the first time I've been picked up by the fuzz." Johnny half laughed, trying to mask his fear. "Hey, dudes, no hard feelings earlier. It was my lucky day. I usually don't shoot pool that well."

Johnny struggled to free himself from their grasp, but their hands were like vice grips around his arms.

"Yes, it's definitely your lucky day," Tyrel said as they ushered him out the door, making a beeline to the starting line, never letting Johnny's feet touch the ground.

At the starting line, two metal poles contained cut flares that had been sized down to last eleven minutes and six seconds. The twins were standing, one at each pole, grinning from ear to ear. They both raised a hand, rotating their fingers in a mock wave.

"Well, I'll be …Twiddle-dee and Twiddle-dum."

Billy Ray punched Johnny, sending blood into the air from Johnny's mouth.

Johnny's knees buckled. His captors picked him up and dragged him to the starting line. They tossed him to the ground. He remained on his hands and knees, spitting blood to the ground.

Low growls ranged out from the edge of the lighted area around the starting line. There were three crates covered with a large green tarp. The crates were rocking back and forth.

"What in the … ?" Johnny began but never finished when his jaw dropped open.

The crates stopped bouncing when Tyrel removed the tarp. Five pairs of glowing red eyes were fixed on Johnny. There was another pair that had just arrived and now watched from beyond the light. Johnny liked his situation less and less.

"What, no more smart comments?" Tyrel smirked as he pulled a radio from the clip on his belt.

Johnny wanted to say something, but nothing came to mind.

"Night Runner, you copy?"

"Copy."

"Runner at the line waiting your signal."

"Ten-four. Fire up the flares. I'm in position. Send Badger this way. Teddy Bear's already here. Let's get this show on the road. Out."

"But—" Tyrel accidentally muttered on the radio.

"But what!" Nate screamed.

"Nothing. I was talking to Bob Cat," Tyrel lied as his face twisted in bitter jealousy of his brother, Billy Ray.

"See ya, big brother, but I wouldn't wanna be ya."

Billy Ray winked at Tyrel.

"Yeah … see ya," Tyrel growled.

Billy Ray trotted off in the direction of Trosper's Point, where Nate had set up base camp. Jake was also there eagerly waiting for his favorite brother to show up to take him on the hunt.

Tyrel pulled his knife from its sheath as he watched Billy Ray disappear into the shadows. He mumbled something under his breath. He abruptly turned toward Johnny, who was now standing between the two metal poles. He reached out with the knife and cut the zip ties. Johnny rubbed his wrist where the zip ties had been cutting into his flesh. A white metal band remained on his wrist. Johnny looked at it curiously.

"Nice bracelet," Johnny commented callously.

"Yes, it's something for you to remember me by, sweetie," Skeeter indicated, puckering his lips in a mock kiss. Then, Jim Bob followed Skeeter's lead and began blowing kisses at Johnny.

"Light the flares!" Tyrel raged.

Jim Bob and Skeeter instantly pulled BIC lighters from their overalls. They flicked the small rollers with their thumbs and a flame appeared.

"Yes 'em, boss," the twins chimed in unison, raising the flames to the end of the flares.

"When the flares burn out, they will come for you," Tyrel informed, pointing at the beasts in the crates. "Running Moon is upon us. Try to give us some competition."

"You betcha," Johnny roared as he sprinted from the starting line, disappearing down the trail.

Johnny motored steadily across Blue Ridge. The path was clear and level, making maneuvering through the trees easy. The moonlight was very bright, illuminating the entire region. He felt good although he hadn't run in several months. All the time on the road had kept him in decent shape—that and the fact, he was jacked up on adrenaline. He thrived on competition. He kept his breathing steady and controlled.

They will not get me without a fight!

Johnny's mouth was parched. It had been eight hours since his last drink. He quickly decided that water would be extremely valuable right now. He needed to quench his thirst, but he thought that a stream might also help slow his pursuers down. *There will be no water on top of this ridge.* He slowed to a jog and glanced over the edges. *There will be water down there.*

Just then the song of the beast pierced the night.

I must leave this ridge. Now! He veered right and headed down the slope at a breakneck speed.

The hunt was on.

"We have the prey on radar. He's cruisin', but he is also taking the same path as the others. It's only a matter of time," Billy Ray announced, intensely studying the radar screens.

"Have you picked up the team?"

"Affirmative. Approximately three-fourths of a mile out. Wait …Timer just came on the radar. He's maybe a quarter mile above the ridge from the prey."

"I sure was hoping for a good hunt. I thought this cat would be different," Tyrel said disappointingly. He knew that if the prey wouldn't last much longer, he would be cleaning up the mess.

"I bet you were," Nate roared, who was sitting next to Billy Ray in a tent at base camp. "I bet you were. Head down to

Lightning Creek. Prey won't get much further than that. You've got the remains. Out."

Tyrel refused to reply. Instead, he turned toward the twins.

"Let's go. You two morons are coming with me."

They stared into Tyrel's crazed eyes. They weren't about to argue.

Johnny paused by a stream to get a quick drink. It had been around noon at the pool hall since his last drink of water. An hour had passed since the twins fired up the flares. The beasts were on the prowl. He could hear the screams of the beasts coming from the top of the hill he had just traveled. He figured he was about a mile ahead of them. He was anticipating being further, but the underbrush was very thick and hard to move through.

He felt refreshed.

Johnny took off running down the middle of the stream. The going was rough and slippery. He tripped and fell several times in the knee high water. The icy water took his breath away. In deeper areas, he dove and swam underwater for several feet. He knew he couldn't slow down. It was the only chance he had of gaining distance between him and the hunters.

He pressed on.

"Wait! Timer has stopped!"

Nate, Billy Ray, and Jake stared in disbelief at the radar screen. The white dot representing the prey was fading in and out. Nate reached out and tapped the screen vigorously with his index finger, but the image continued to fade and then reappear.

Nate turned toward Billy Ray with fury in his eyes.

"Did you and the twins scan the system and make sure it was working properly?"

"Yes, sir. With a fine tooth comb. Every inch of it, sir."

"Then, will you explain what is happening here on the screen!" Billy Ray didn't want to answer because he didn't know the answer.

"Answer me!"

"I can only guess, sir."

"What!"

"If the prey is below the ground level of the motion and heat sensors, then the prey may go undetected for a very short amount of time—only a few seconds. The prey has probably fallen in a pool of water. He should reappear quickly."

"And you were going to let me know about this glitch when?"

"A-a-a ..." Billy Ray stuttered.

Nate reared back and hit Billy Ray in the eye with his fist, knocking Billy Ray off his stool.

Jake, who had been a statue, jumped up and yelled at his daddy.

"What did ya do that for? Billy Ray ain't never done nothing to ya. It's not his fault this stupid machine ain't workin' right. You need to go buy a new one. And you need to quit hittin' my brudder."

Nate glared at Jake and doubled both his fists. He wanted nothing more than to pound Jake into mince meat for back talking. But something inside him made his fist relax. He turned back to the screen. The white dot had reappeared and remained constant. "Pick yourself up. We've got a hunt to finish. You have now replaced Tyrel on garbage duty. You better fix this glitch."

"Yes, sir," Billy Ray replied.

Jake went over and helped him up.

"Get off me! I don't need your help!"

"Sorry, Billy Ray."

Billy Ray waved Jake away.

"Let's finish this."

They were all back in their original places, staring at the screen.

"I see the prey, but where is Timer and the team?"

Johnny left the stream after it began to be barren and shallow. He ran along a game trail for a half mile and then decided to climb the mountain and travel the high road for a while. He was beginning to tire and needed a rest to catch his breath.

At the crest of the mountain, he stopped and straddled a fallen tree. He listened intently for any sound of his pursuers. Their angry wails seemed to be heading away from his position.

"This ain't that hard." Johnny smiled as he stooped over with his elbows on his knees. He chuckled again.

There was a sudden crash behind Johnny. He quickly stood up and turned toward the sound.

All he saw were red eyes.

Part Four
The Resolution

He draws near the Pit, and his life to the executioners. If there is an angel on his side, one mediator out of a thousand, to tell a person what is right for him and to be gracious to him and say, "Spare him from going down to the Pit, I have found a ransom."

—Job 33:22–24 (NIV)

Piper and Bryson

T he first major blue norther of autumn swept quickly through
the Kiamichi Mountains. The temperature dropped twenty-
five degrees in a matter of a few minutes, dipping down to the
mid-forties. A heavy drizzle from the black-blue clouds had
soaked the land.

Bryson stood on his porch sipping coffee. He was wearing
his green Oregon Track hoodie and sweat pants. The cool breeze
was rejuvenating and fresh. He took a deep breath. He debated
whether to get a run in or wait for the weather to break. He had
been running almost every morning since his return home. His
strength and endurance were coming back, along with his desire
to compete again.

He missed the competitive edge of racing.

Bryson sat down on a cedar bench and took another sip of
coffee. It had been two weeks since he last talked to Johnny. It
felt more like ages ago. He wished he could take back his words
or at least talk to Johnny and explain his feelings. He wanted to
tell Johnny that he was right. *A person cannot live in the past.*

Piper and Bryson were beginning to talk—not a friendly talk,
but the *talk.* He was letting his wall down, and she was falling
for him as well. Her number one rule for dating was never ever
date someone you work with—not anymore.

Bryson had gone over to Piper's house almost every day
for the last two weeks to hang out with Jared and Piper. They

watched a few DVD movies but mostly played games. Bryson was not in any way shocked when he discovered that Piper was a very competitive person—take no prisoners—during their game playing. Bryson and Jared would only look at each other and frown when she jumped up and down, hollering, "I am the champion of the world!" every time she would win a board or card game. What really stunk for Jared and Bryson was they rarely ever won, but when they did happen to win, they rubbed it in her face by jumping up and high-fiving each other, dancing and singing, 'Na-na-na-na, hey, hey, goodbye.' She took it pretty good—most of the time.

Bryson and Piper's favorite activity together was holding hands while taking long slow walks through the winding roads of the foothills. Their conversations were generally light and uncomplicated, but on occasions, they got serious, especially when talking about children and the effect the world had on them today compared to when they were younger. Other times, they didn't speak and were simply absorbed in each other's smile.

During beautiful autumn evenings, Bryson, Piper, and Jared spent a lot of time playing catch with a baseball. Bryson showed Jared how to throw a curve and circle changeup. Jared was hoping to make the varsity baseball team as a freshman. Bryson assured him he would have no problem making the team if he would work hard and command his off-speed pitches.

They also worked in the barn and on the house, getting them ready for the upcoming winter. They cut and stacked several ricks of firewood. Bryson remembered how sore his shoulders were from helping Cherokee Billy two weeks before. Jared continued to impress Bryson with his work ethic. He hoped that the Lord might someday bless him with the chance to have a son as awesome as Jared.

At the end of every night, Piper escorted Bryson to his Jeep. Piper always thanked Bryson for being kind to Jared and paying him attention because his father never did. Bryson would tell her to quit thanking him and that it was his pleasure to hang out with both of them. Although their feelings had grown strong toward each other, they had yet to make the total commitment by sealing the deal with the kiss. They wanted to kiss, but neither would yield the first move.

A smile formed on his face as he took another sip. He thought about his time with Piper and Jared. Then his smile faded a little. Despite the fact that the weather was damp and colorless, it was Saturday, and Bryson had hoped to spend his day off with Jared and Piper.

Piper had actually asked Bryson to come with her and Jared today, but he regretfully declined the invitation. They were going to an early morning funeral. Their neighbor, John Caraway, had died in his sleep from an apparent heart attack on Tuesday. Bryson had only talked to John a few times and didn't know him very well, but he thought he was a nice man, who looked to be in very good health.

Bryson wasn't ready to attend a funeral. Memories of Becky came to his mind. His eyes teared up when he visualized Becky in her coffin. He still missed her. He would always miss her. It was something that he was going to have to live with.

Bryson stared placidly across the yellow meadow from his porch. The meadow stretched out to the base of the mountains, whose tops were lost in the clouds. He took a sip of his cold coffee. He debated briefly whether to refill his cup or not. He decided to sit and enjoy the slow rain. It reminded him of his past life in Oregon.

His thoughts suddenly returned to Johnny.

He had called Johnny's father, Bill, the following Monday after Johnny had left the church. Bryson explained what had occurred and how he felt about the entire situation. Bill was sympathetic and wanted what was best for his son. He above all wanted Johnny to return home safely. Bill informed Bryson that he would let him know when Johnny called or showed. Bill reassured Bryson that Johnny was all right and would call when he ran out of money.

Bryson felt a little better after talking to Bill. He told Bill to call the school because cell phones were pretty much useless in this part of the country.

He stood up from the cedar bench and tossed the chilled coffee into the damp grass. He placed the cup on the arm rest. "Nice day for a run. I need to clear my mind."

Bryson pulled his hood over his head and leaped off the porch, cutting a trail through the pasture, running at a fast pace. He arrived quickly at the gate, and then disappeared down the road.

In the shadow of the fence line, the wolf followed close behind.

Bryson returned a little over an hour later. His original plan was to run five miles, but he felt so good that he ended up doubling the distance. He jogged up and jumped onto the porch, removing the wet hood from his head. His hair fell in damp strains across his forehead. He raked his fingers through his hair as he turned toward the open field.

The rain had stopped, but the temperature was still very cold. Bryson thought about removing his soaking wet hoodie but changed his mind when he thought of getting sick and not being able to work, but more importantly, not getting to spend time with Piper.

Bryson placed his running shoes by the front door before entering the cabin. He walked over to a wooden chest to look for his cowboy boots so he could haul up firewood to place on the porch to dry out. He was extremely upset with himself for not doing it sooner, but the weather had been so nice that the thought never crossed his mind. As he grabbed the boots, a nine- inch bowie knife in its sheath fell to the ground. He picked up the knife and looked out the window toward the huge oak tree where he had found the knife when he was a boy.

The wolf's statuesque form stood next to the tree staring back toward the cabin. His shiny fur coat was majestic and beautiful. His golden eyes glowed brightly against the gloomy setting.

Bryson glanced down at the knife. The initials "DM" was carved into the handle. *DM. What does DM stand for?* He searched every file of his memory bank, but nothing registered. He closed the lid and sat on the wooden chest, pulling his cowboy boots up over his sweat pants. He picked up the knife and glanced back out the window. The wolf had not moved. He headed out the front door.

The wolf suddenly vanished behind the tree. Bryson thought that he had left, but to his surprise, the wolf was sitting on the bare spot atop his mother's grave.

"Hello, my friend. It has been awhile. I thought maybe you had decided to move on," Bryson greeted as he absentmindedly shifted the knife from one hand to the other.

Without warning, the wolf suddenly stood up, never taking his golden eyes off the blade. A low, deep growl emanated from his throat.

"I'm sorry, boy. Forgive me. I would never hurt you. Let me put this away."

Bryson placed the knife in the front pocket of his hoodie.

The wolf lowered his head and walked around Bryson and stopped at the oak tree, pawing three times beneath the carved image.

Bryson studied the crudely carved heart and two sets of initials—*KK* and *BK.*

"It has to stand for Bryson Keahbone and Katherine Keahbone," Bryson stated as he reached into his hoodie pocket and touched the knife. "Who is DM?"

He glanced down at the wolf.

"Do you know who DM is?"

The wolf let out another long, deep growl.

"I wish I understood wolf. Better yet, I wish you could speak English."

Bryson turned back to the tree. He reached out and gently touched the carved figure of the dog or wolf. Its head appeared human. He ran his fingers along the three-grooves cut beneath the figure.

"Does this figure in the heart have something to do with you?"

The wolf tilted his head.

Bryson was beginning to feel a little ridiculous for trying to carry on a conversation with a wolf of all things.

"Do you ever cry when you see a full moon?" Bryson jested.

The wolf apparently didn't see any humor in Bryson's words. He turned and walked back to the grave, pawing the ground and grass beside the bare spot.

Bryson started to apologize because he felt that the wolf was trying to tell him something, but he wasn't taking it seriously. But before the words could come out, the wolf quickly looked alertly toward the gate at the end of the pasture. Bryson turned and looked in the same direction, but he couldn't see or hear anything. He watched and listened intently but could only hear the wind whistling through the trees. The wolf abruptly stood up and trotted away toward the stream. Bryson started to follow but promptly stopped when he heard a vehicle coming down the road.

Bryson's heart jumped in his chest.

A red Explorer passed through the gate.

It was Piper and Jared.

Bryson grinned. He glanced over his shoulder toward the wolf, but he was out of sight. He turned and began walking briskly back to the cabin. He just remembered that he invited Piper yesterday to stop by after the funeral if they weren't too busy.

The Explorer pulled up and parked in front of the cabin.

Piper rolled down her window as Bryson walked up.

"I hope we're not interrupting anything important?" Piper asked as her eyes scanned him from head to the tip of his cowboy boots.

"No. Not at all."

"I like your style."

"Huh," Bryson uttered, looking down at his green sweats tucked inside his cowboy boots. "You like that? I figured I would get dressed up for you guys."

Jared shot Bryson a thumbs up.

"Come on in."

Piper and Jared got out of the SUV and walked up to the cabin. Piper had never been to Bryson's cabin, but Jared had told her about all the work they had done to repair it. She was excited to finally see it, and she was even more excited to see Bryson. He was all she thought about the entire day.

Bryson stepped onto the porch and opened the door, waving them to come in. He closed the door behind them.

"I'm going to take a quick shower. Make yourself at home. Jared can show you around. I don't have a TV set, but there's a radio over there if you want some music." Bryson pointed at the counter in the kitchen.

"Thank you," Piper said as she looked around the cabin. *What a nice place.*

Bryson grabbed a towel from a cabinet and disappeared into the bathroom.

Piper and Jared settled on the couch after he gave his mother a quick tour of the small cabin. She undoubtedly was impressed with all the things that Bryson and Jared had accomplished here, and she was most impressed with Bryson and the way he handled himself. She had never met anyone like him. She had been hesitant about coming over to Bryson's cabin, but now she was glad she did. Jared had taken John's death very hard, and Bryson had helped ease his pain because of the relationship they were building.

Ten minutes later, Bryson emerged from the bathroom wearing holey jeans and a very wrinkled, red flannel shirt.

Piper smiled. "You are a fashion guru."

"I know, right? I have been saving this shirt for a very special occasion. I'm glad you get the privilege and honor to have shared it with me." Bryson laughed.

After the laughter died down, there was a brief silence. Bryson and Piper stared into each other's eyes. For a moment, they were the only two people alive.

"Hello. I'm still here," Jared interjected playfully.

Bryson broke eye contact first. "I'm sorry about the loss of your friend, Mr. Caraway."

"Thank you. He was a dear man and friend. The funeral was small and nice. John's family had all passed on. We were pretty much all he had." Piper sighed, dabbing her nose with a tissue.

"Again, I'm truly sorry."

"That's okay. He's in a better place."

"Did he have a heart attack?"

"They think so."

"He looked like he was in good health."

"I thought so too. I don't remember John ever being sick. Not once."

"You said earlier that John didn't have any family."

"Yes. They have all passed away. He had no children. His place will probably go up for sale. It's a beautiful ranch."

"Are you interested in buying it?'

"No way. I have more than I can handle right now."

"Yeah, I know. Me too."

"The Mongers will definitely be interested. They own everything this side of Talihina all the way out to County Line Road. Your place and mine are the only two ranches left on this road that they don't own."

"Do they ever use this road to get to their ranch?"

"No. They have their own private network of roads that goes into their place, and believe me, they are very protective of their property. They scared Jared half to death one day when he crossed the fence line to retrieve a turkey he had shot with his bow on our land."

"I was wondering because I believe that I have seen Tyrel Monger's wife driving an old Chevy truck down our road a few times. Especially earlier in the week."

"I don't know why Elizabeth would be out this way, except I believe she is probably trying to get away from her situation at home. I truly feel sorry for her. I wish I could help her."

Jared remained silent.

Piper looked around the room.

"I love your place," she complimented, trying to change the subject and lighten the mood.

"Thank you. I have to credit Jared for all his hard work."

"No, Mr. Keahbone, it was teamwork."

"Yes, we make a good team."

Bryson reached out with his fist and gave Jared a fist bump.

Piper turned away to hide her tears. Her son needed a father figure in his life, and she knew Bryson would make a great dad.

Piper was definitely falling for Bryson.

Kidnapped

The Mongers had gathered around the dining room table waiting for Nate to enter, so they could sit and eat their dinner. There were eight plate settings. Everyone except Tyrel was standing by their assigned seat. Rubin was digging a booger out of his nose with his pinkie. Jake watched closely, hoping to see how big it would be, so he could try and get one bigger.

Elizabeth had spent all afternoon preparing brisket and sliced potatoes with wild onions. She had placed all the food on the table.

The aroma was killing the twins. They could hardly control the impulse to dive in and start eating, but they knew that they would be eating crumbs for the next month if they broke their daddy's rules.

Jake was standing next to Billy Ray. He leaned forward. "I sure am hungry, Billy Ray. I bet Rubin's not. He ate a booger as big as his whole pinkie finger."

Rubin glared at Jake.

Jake looked away. Rubin had the same psychotic look in his eyes as his father, Tyrel. Jake was more afraid of Rubin than he was of Tyrel.

"Shudup, you moron! Or ya gonna get us all in trouble, and I ain't goin' back to the sweat box for some loser like you!"

"You got it, Rubin. I ain't sayin' another word. Not one word. No, not one."

Jake shut his mouth just as Billy Ray began to raise his hand.

Elizabeth brought in two pitchers of tea and sat them on each end of the table. She picked up a serving bell and rang it. The grandfather clock at the end of the hall immediately began to chime. Heavy footsteps moved in unison with the chiming clock.

Everyone looked down as Nate entered from the hallway. He stopped and scanned the room.

"Billy Ray, where is Tyrel?"

"I don't … know, sir. He was on patrol earlier today. I last saw him at lunch. After that … I'm not sure."

A car came roaring up outside. Nate walked to the window and peeked through the curtains.

It was Tyrel's patrol car.

Nate waited until Tyrel had entered the dining area and stood at his place. He studied each person before finally sitting down.

The family followed his lead by sitting, but did not eat.

"I hope you have a good excuse."

Tyrel felt like his father's eyes were burning a hole through him. He didn't want to look at his father, but if he didn't, Nate was going to go off on him for being a coward. He stared into Nate's good eye. Tyrel was afraid of nothing. But that other eye— the ghost eye—gave him the willies.

"I have bad news. Apparently Caraway had a will we didn't count on. He left his ranch to the Hitchcock woman," Tyrel informed as he braced himself for what was about to happen. He couldn't help himself. He stared down at the table.

"*Argh!*"

No one spoke.

No one moved. Not even blinked.

"You better be lying!" Nate screamed, as he jumped and slapped the pitcher of tea into the wall, shattering it into a thousand pieces.

Tyrel wanted to look up from the table, but kept his gaze down.

"I talked to Caraway's lawyer today at the courthouse. He told me that Caraway had the will drawn up this past summer. We should have got rid of him sooner."

"Does the Hitchcock woman know?"

"No, sir. The lawyer told me they have a meeting in the morning."

Nate's jaw locked tight. His veins were bulging at the temples. His lips were drawn thin and narrow.

"Daddy, it's goin' be okay. We just have to be patient … and wait. Remember the last time … with the Injun … we were impatient. I have a good prey … in the holding tank … at the jailhouse."

Nate was fuming with rage as the thought of Joseph Keahbone took over his mind. He was about to erupt like a bad radiator.

"Who died and put you in charge!" Nate hollered as he slapped Tyrel across the face. "You are not in charge! I will have my revenge! Nothing will stop me. Ya'll will do as I say. And if I say we put the full plan in motion, we put it in motion—*now*! There is one day before the next Running Moon. Master will provide our needs according to our deeds. We will move ahead. All the land from County Line Road to here will be ours!"

Tyrel wiped the blood from his lips with the back of his hand. He never hated anything more than his father at that moment. Everyone at the table stared at Tyrel, wondering what he would do next, but he just glared at his father. *Someday I will get my own revenge. Some day soon … very soon.*

"Yes, sir. Everything is in place. Waiting only for your command," Tyrel said grudgingly.

"Very well. We put the plan into action as soon as we finish eating. We need to have everything here ready to go by morning. That means some of you will have a late night ahead of you. One phone call tonight. Two phone calls tomorrow. Does everyone know their assignments?"

Everyone nodded in agreement.

Nate leaned forward and filled his plate with brisket and potatoes. He looked indignantly at all the people around the table. *You people are so pathetic.* He looked around again, flexing his will on them, before finally taking a bite.

The family immediately began filling their plates with food. All except Elizabeth. She got up and went to the wall where the pitcher had hit and shattered.

"No. Tyrel will clean that up after we eat."

Elizabeth bowed her head and sat back down. She put one small slice of brisket and one piece of potato on her plate.

After they all had devoured their food, Elizabeth removed their plates and cleaned the table. No one was dismissed from the table until Nate gave the word. Jake was squirming back and forth in his chair. Billy Ray reached up and squeezed the back of Jake's neck. He shrugged his shoulders and then settled down—a little.

Elizabeth came back in from the kitchen and sat down.

Nate stood up and leaned forward, placing his huge hands flat on the table.

"We have a lot of extra preparations tonight for the Running Moon. There must be a sense of urgency here. We will have to move fast. If our plans fall through due to your negligence, all of you will pay. Don't screw this up. Do you understand me?"

Nate nodded at Elizabeth. She stood up and left the room. Tyrel could hear her talking in the next room. She suddenly reappeared and sat down, lowering her chin to her chest.

"Tomorrow night, we will get back our land ... and I will get my revenge!" Nate laughed insanely.

The night air was cold and a little crisp. Bryson was sitting on the top step of the front porch at Piper's house. He stared up at the starry night. The moon was peeking through the tops of two pine trees. It was not quite full. *One more day and the moon will be full. It will be the Moon When Wolves Cry.* His father's words echoed in his mind. *Come find me, come find me.*

Piper gave him a start when she bent over to hand him a glass of tea.

"I'm sorry. I didn't mean to startle you."

"Oh, no. It's okay. I was … kind of … lost in thought."

Bryson grabbed the glass from Piper as she sat down beside him. He glanced back up at the moon. *One more day, I will have closure.* Some way, somehow, he was sure of it. He lifted the glass to his lips and took a drink.

"Thank you. This is very good."

"You're welcome. I apologize for taking so long … I just had a very strange phone call from a parent."

Bryson started to ask but decided not to. It was her job as principal to deal confidentially with all kinds of situations concerning the well-being of the school district's students. If she wanted to share details, he would gladly listen; if not, that was perfectly all right too.

Piper debated whether to tell him about the phone call or not. It made her sad to think about the abusive environment in which some people are forced to live against their will. She decided not to tell him. She wanted to keep the mood light and not depressing. She smiled at Bryson over the edge of her glass as she took a sip of tea. She wanted to kiss him. She longed to kiss him.

"What?" Bryson asked.

"Nothing"

"Are you sure?"

"Yep. Everything's hunky-dory."

"Oh, yeah. Hunky-dory, huh. Well, I think you're kind of … weird." Bryson grinned, wrinkling up his forehead at her statement.

"Thank you, I don't believe anyone has ever paid me that compliment before."

"Who says that's a compliment?"

Piper reached up and punched Bryson in the shoulder. "Ouch," Bryson exclaimed, grabbing his shoulder with his hand.

"You big sissy," Piper teased as she began poking and tickling his side.

"Okay … stop … tick …"

"Oh, so we are a little ticklish, are we?"

"Yes … hahaha … stop … okay … you … hahaha … win!"

Bryson was laughing hard. He rolled around on the porch, trying to keep Piper's hands off of him. They accidentally knocked a chair over. The front door suddenly flew open.

"What's going on out here? Can't a guy get a little peace and quiet so he can do his homework?"

Bryson and Piper were tied in a human knot. He had both of her wrists in his hands, and his legs had her pinned down to the porch in a leg-lock. When he heard Jared's voice, he quickly let go and sat up, feeling a little embarrassed. She removed her hair from her face and used her fingers as a comb.

"I was testing Mr. Keahbone's tickle meter. It's very high."

"Yes. Very high."

"Mine too. I hate when she does that to me," Jared moaned, retreating back through the front door.

"Hey, wait! Come here. You have something on your back," Piper claimed.

"Where?"

"Come here and I will get it for you."

Jared walked up to Piper, kneeling down with his back toward her. With catlike quickness, she grabbed him and began tickling his sides. Jared began to laugh and squirm like a worm on a hook.

"Hahaha! Okay, okay! Hahaha! Mom … I give … I give … hahaha!"

"Who's the greatest?"

"You … hahaha!"

"Who?"

"You … hahaha … are."

"I can't hear you."

"You!"

Piper let go and raised her hands, like she was Rocky Balboa. "I am the champion … of the world."

"Oh brother, not again." Jared sighed.

Bryson and Jared just looked at each other, and then they all busted out laughing.

Piper wiped a tear from her eye. She glanced down at her watch, realizing for the first time how late it had become.

"Wow. Time does fly when you're having fun. Go brush your teeth and hit the hay."

"Aw, Mom."

"It's a school night. You can stay up late tomorrow night. Although it's only Tuesday. Fall break begins on Wednesday. You will have a five-day vacation from school."

"Awesome, but—all right. Good night, Mr. Keahbone. Good night, Mom. I love you."

"Good night, Jared. I love you."

"See you tomorrow in class," Bryson said.

Jared gave a quick wave and then disappeared through the door.

Bryson got up and knocked the dust from his jeans. Piper stood up beside him. They looked into each other's eyes. Was this the moment? Would Bryson let go, yielding to a final closure?

"I better go," Bryson stated sadly, still looking into her bright eyes.

"Yes, it is kind of … late."

There was a long silence. Neither moved an inch. Finally, Piper grabbed Bryson's hand.

"I'll walk you to your Jeep."

"Thanks."

They walked slowly, swaying their arms slightly at their sides. Bryson hooked his index finger around her pinkie. There, in that moment, he felt no sense of urgency. Bryson wanted the night to last forever. He wanted to tell her how he felt. They stopped by his Jeep. He turned toward her and grabbed her other hand. Suddenly, Piper looked up, for a falling star blazed across the sky, crossing a path behind the moon. Their gaze remained fixed on the sky. He looked back at Piper. He really cared for this woman.

"Teardrop of an angel."

"You remembered."

"Yes, an angel's tear will fall as a fireball across the sky when something that was supposed to be does not come to be."

"But not all will be lost if the person involved will be at the right place and at the right moment in time to catch the falling star before it fades away. This is the only way to make sure destiny comes to be and is not lost … forever."

Bryson broke eye contact and loosened his grip on Piper's hands.

Tomorrow night will be good. I am falling for her. I will tell her.

But that chance may not come.

"It's late. I better go." He climbed into the Jeep. "Good night, Piper. I had a good time. Thank you. I will see you tomorrow," Bryson said as he gave Piper a quick look before driving off. Something inside his gut was screaming for him to stop and go back. But he finally decided, *Tomorrow. I will tell her tomorrow.*

Piper watched Bryson's Jeep until the taillights disappeared behind a line of trees. *I am falling completely in love with him.*

She walked back to the porch and slowly climbed the steps. She turned and smiled as she caught another glimpse of his lights. She couldn't wait to see him again at school. Then suddenly, her smile faded to a frown.

"Oh, drat! I forgot to tell him I have a meeting at 10:00 a.m. in the morning with John's attorney. Also, I have decided to go by and visit with Elizabeth at 9:00 a.m. She was so upset when she called earlier tonight. I must convince her to go to a woman's shelter in McAlester where she will be safe. I should have told Bryson, but everything will be good," Piper whispered dubiously as she turned and stepped through the front door.

Bryson arrived at school a little earlier than usual. He glanced at the passenger seat where his briefcase sat. He opened it and pulled out the bowie knife with the initials DM on the handle. He had brought the knife to ask Hoot if he had any idea whose it might be. He opened the glove box and shoved the knife inside, closing the door behind it. *I will ask later.*

He peered over at Piper's empty parking space. He chuckled when he thought of the first day they had met. *She wasn't very happy with me when I parked in her spot.*

He wanted to see Piper. He tossed and turned all night, thinking about the lost opportunity he had to share his feelings with Piper. The time he had spent with her was becoming very special to him. He didn't want to waste it.

I'm such a Prufrock!

When Piper didn't show up for work, he felt nervous and apprehensive. Something didn't feel right. The full moon was tonight. It was the Moon When Wolves Cry. Maybe that was what was eating him up. He should have been excited about finally getting some answers to questions about his past. But all he could think about was Piper and how stupid he was for trying to wall up his emotions.

He waited by the office until Jody arrived to unlock the door.

"Have you heard from Ms. Hitchcock today?" Bryson asked, trying not to sound too desperate.

"Yes. She called this morning and told me that the secretary of John Caraway's attorney had called and set up a last-minute meeting with her this morning. Ms. Hitchcock told me she and Jared would be in after lunch."

"Thanks."

This was the first time he wished he would have had landlines for telephone service. He hadn't used his cell phone in weeks. *She has no way of getting hold of me if there is an emergency. There is no emergency. I'm blowing this all out of proportion.* He kept repeating to himself. But his gut wasn't buying it.

Bryson left the office and went to his classroom. That bad feeling was really settling deep in the pit of his stomach. He couldn't explain why he felt that way. He just did.

The day seemed to last forever to Bryson, who was constantly looking at his watch or the clock on the wall. He tried to focus on his lessons and did the best he could to teach them, but in the end, he assigned silent reading from the textbook. Bad move. At least when he was teaching, the day passed a little more quickly.

Lunch time finally arrived.

Bryson poked his head inside the office for the fourteenth time. Jody just shook her head sideways, lifting her hands into the air. She mouthed, "Sorry." He left disappointed. He went to the lunch room and got a tray of food but didn't touch it. He had no appetite. He wanted to call Piper. He needed to know that she and Jared were all right.

The afternoon yielded the same results. No Piper. No Jared. He was almost in panic mode. It seemed to him that everything he had ever cared about in his life would end up hopelessly lost.

The final bell rang. The students were dismissed, bolting for the door like their hair was on fire.

Bryson stopped by the office—again.

"Nothing?"

"No. But she did call in a little after the last time you stepped in. She was coughing and hacking. I couldn't really understand her except that she told me Jared and she were very sick and wouldn't be back until Monday following fall break—"

"Is that it?"

"Well … it didn't sound like Ms. Hitchcock, but I couldn't really tell with her coughing between every word."

"Thanks. Have a good weekend."

"You too. I will."

Bryson walked out the front doors and headed straight toward his Jeep. He felt like he was carrying a pallet of bricks on his back. He decided to drive out to her house and make sure that she and Jared were fine. His eyes never left the ground until he got close to his Jeep. That's when he noticed a patrol car parked beside the playground.

It was Tyrel.

When Bryson arrived at his Jeep there was a note on the seat. His stomach knotted up. He glanced at the patrol car. He promptly picked up the letter and ripped open the envelope.

Come to my empire. Come alone! If you want to see the woman and boy alive again, then you had better come alone! If I see anyone with you, then they die. Believe me when I say, they will disappear forever! We have been watching you. We are watching you now. Come be a part of immortality! Don't be late. You have until dusk!

Bryson glared at the patrol car. His fear turned to hatred. He took off at a slow trot toward the patrol car. He crumpled the note in his right fist.

Tyrel rolled down the window.

"Look what we have here. Mr. Teacherman! What can I do for ya?" Tyrel grinned.

Bryson was about to explode. He didn't care about himself— only Piper and Jared.

"Where are they!"

"Where is who?"

"You know what I'm talking about! If you harm one hair on their head,—I'm coming for you," Bryson growled, pointing his index finger at Tyrel.

"I believe you are threatening a peace officer. I can arrest you for that. Thirty days minimal. Then what would become of your little girlfriend and her bratty son?"

"God willing, I will hunt you down to the ground. I will not stop until one of us is dead."

"God don't have no will in this. It's you against us. Don't be late. You have until dusk. Remember, we will be watching you. You talk to anyone, they die, disappear forever."

Tyrel took his index and middle finger of his right hand, placing one over each eye and then pointed his two fingers at Bryson. "I'll be watching you."

Tyrel drove off slowly, taunting Bryson as he passed by.

Bryson threw the wadded letter, bouncing it off the back window. The letter landed a few inches from his feet, but he never noticed it. He ran back and jumped in his Jeep but didn't immediately drive off. A million thoughts were screaming out of control in his head. He had to get dialed in. His number one objective was how to rescue Piper and Jared. He immediately thought of calling Hoot and Vick but changed his mind. He wasn't taking any chances. He would have to do this *alone.*

Or did he?

Bryson Must Choose One

Bryson blasted out of the parking lot and headed west out of town. He turned south on County Line Road. He decided to check out Piper's house first and see if they were there. He was hoping and praying in his mind that they were fine, and everything was just some strange dream.

He kept checking his rearview mirror to see if anyone was following. So far, no one that he could tell.

It took about ten minutes to get to Piper's house. Bryson breathed a brief sigh of relief, when he saw her Explorer parked in front of the house. He parked next to her car and jammed the parking brake to the floor. He jumped out and ran toward the front door, leaping onto the porch in two giant strides. He started to knock, but didn't because the door was partially open. He poked in his head and cautiously scanned the living room.

"Hello, Piper. Jared. Anybody home?"

He listened for a response but none came.

"Piper. Jared. It's me, Bryson.

Dead silence.

Bryson quickly ran throughout the house, entering every room. No one was there. He glanced sporadically around the dining room, almost in a panic. He saw a folded letter marked with "BK" on the table. He instantly opened the letter, and in block letters, it read, "Hurry. You have until dusk. Come alone or they die!"

He dropped the letter on the table and bolted through the door, leaving it swaying noiselessly on its hinges. In a flash, he was off the porch and in his Jeep. He grabbed hold of the steering wheel in a double-fisted death grip. *What am I going to do?* He took a deep breath.

"I need a plan. But what? I have no idea."

He looked at his watch. He had two hours before dusk. Not much time. He shifted into first gear and started for the Mongers' ranch. He would have to improvise when the time came.

Again, the thought of calling Hoot entered his mind, but he quickly dismissed it. He wasn't taking any chances.

I can do this!

Twenty minutes later, Bryson arrived at the eight-foot tall fence that surrounded the gray, two-story framed house. The Monger mansion. He parked the Jeep to the side of the gate. His eyes swept the yard and house, looking for anyone or anything. No one was in the yard or on the porch. He couldn't tell if anyone was looking out of the black windows.

Now what?

He didn't own a gun, not that he would have brought one if he did. A gunfight with the sheriff 's department didn't sound like much fun, but he would do whatever it took to save Piper and Jared from these psychopaths. Then he remembered the knife in the glove box, though he was thinking more in terms of a tool than a weapon. He quickly snatched the knife and put it in his left sock, pulling his pant's leg down over the knife.

The shadows of the tree were beginning to get darker. The temperature was already beginning to fall in the valley. It was going to be a chilly night. Bryson wished he would have worn his hoodie instead of his long-sleeve collared shirt. He crawled out of the Jeep and began walking slowly toward the house, carefully studying the yard and house. He stopped and rolled up his sleeves.

A door to the house opened, but Bryson couldn't see anyone through the screen door.

"That's far enough," a deep voice ordered from behind the screen. "Lift your shirt and turn around slowly."

Bryson did as the voice commanded.

Nate walked through the door and continued down the steps of the porch. Bryson had only seen Nate once before, and that was from a distance. He was surprised when he saw how massively Nate was built.

Nate stopped a few feet from Bryson.

"So you're the schoolteacher that's causing us all this trouble. You don't look like much."

"Where are they?"

"In due time … in due … time."

Tyrel and Billy Ray came around opposite corners of the house. They pointed their rifles straight at Bryson.

Bryson glared at Tyrel. "I am coming for you first."

"Eew,Tyrel. It looks like you have a fan club." Billy Ray laughed.

"Easy does it, schoolmarm. We can all be friends here."

"If I'm your friend, I sure would hate to see how you treat your enemies."

"We feed them to the pits." Nate smiled, pointing to the pens diagonal to the house.

Bryson hadn't noticed them until now.

The pit bulls were staring at Bryson. Not one moved or made a sound. They knew Bryson was their next prey. They were sizing him up.

A black pit suddenly appeared on the top of the pens. It was Timer. He stood poised as a statue. His eyes burned a fiery red.

The hunt was near. A feeding frenzy was upon them heavy in the air. They sensed that this was going to be a very special hunt like no other.

"That is Timer. You will make your acquaintance with him and his brothers very soon. But first there are some formalities we need to address.

"Billy Ray, do you have the zip ties?"

'Yes, sir. Hands and feet?"

"Just hands. He's not going anywhere."

Billy Ray handed his rifle to Tyrel, who kept his own rifle pointed at Bryson. Billy Ray pulled two zip ties and a white metal band from his vest and tied Bryson's wrists together. The ties dug deep into his flesh, but Bryson showed no emotion. Billy Ray popped the zip ties with his finger to test their tightness.

"Good to go."

Bryson was thankful that they didn't tie his ankles because they would have surely discovered the knife.

"What have you done with Piper and Jared?"

"They are fine … for now. Take him to the shed."

Bryson started to resist but knew it wouldn't do any good. He would go peacefully and wait for the right time to make his move.

Tyrel and Billy Ray grabbed Bryson by the elbows and escorted him to the shed. Tyrel was disappointed because he thought Bryson would put up more of a fight and not be such a coward. Billy Ray opened the door. Tyrel pushed Bryson through the doorway. Bryson tripped and fell to the ground. Billy Ray slammed and locked the door with a heavy metal chain and padlock.

Bryson quickly inspected the small shed. There wasn't much in the shed except a small table, a few fiddleback spiders, and a drop light. He squinted and wrinkled his forehead, the smell of urine and excrement was very strong.

Billy Ray, Tyrel, and Nate were talking about twenty feet from the shed. Bryson leaned against the side closest to the three men but couldn't hear what they were saying.

A few minutes later, Billy Ray returned and unlocked the shed. Bryson moved back to the opposite corner away from the door.

"Let's go."

"Where?"

"If ya need to know, I will tell ya. You don't need to know, so shuddup!"

Bryson walked through the door.

"Stop here. Turn around."

Billy Ray pulled a black hood from his backpack. Tyrel and Nate stood idly watching as Billy Ray unfolded the hood that was soon to be made into a blindfold. He placed the hood over Bryson's head. It fell down to the middle of his chest. Bryson was totally blind.

They led him to a four-door truck. Billy Ray opened the door and shoved Bryson into the backseat. He tried to use all his senses to determine where he was going and how long it took to get there. He counted in his head. The truck felt like it was going about fifteen to twenty miles per hour. The road was rough and zigzagged as it descended into a valley. When the truck finally came to a stop Bryson had counted to five hundred forty-five, which he figured—roughly a little over nine minutes. *Probably traveled a mile, maybe a mile and a quarter.*

The door opened, and Bryson was dragged out onto his feet. Tyrel removed the hood. They had taken Bryson to Trosper's Point, which was home base camp for the run.

Bryson quickly studied the surroundings, absorbing as much information as he could before they put the hood back on. Base camp was three canvas army tents—two small modular huts and a large command post. The wall flaps were pulled up and tied to the top of each tent. One modular tent covered the main generator and its backup, six five-gallon tanks full of gasoline, and several small wooden boxes, possibly some kind of ammo, but Bryson wasn't sure. The second modular tent, opposite the first tent, covered a table and two chairs. On the table were rolled and unrolled maps of the area. The third tent was larger and in the middle of the other two. It was Nate's command post where he kept all the surveillance system equipment, which contained a computerized radar system and GPS tracker that linked together hundreds of ultrasonic motion detectors and heat sensors.

Bryson stood bewildered. *How are they intelligent enough to use this sophisticated equipment. There's no way.* But what Bryson didn't know was that Billy Ray was an expert in setting up and operating this type of equipment during the Gulf War.

Nate walked into his command post and stopped by the radar screens. There were four screens in all. One for each quadrant. He motioned for Tyrel and Billy Ray to bring Bryson around to the front to view the screens. Nate pointed at the two screens in the middle. They each had one white dot in the center.

"That is the boy," Nate said, pointing with his right hand at the screen.

"Where is Piper?"

"There," Nate pointed out with his left hand at the other screen. "So what am I going to have to do to win their freedom? This has to be some kind of game."

"Right you are. You have been chosen to participate in the Running Moon. A chance for immortality."

"What if I don't want to live forever?"

"Then I will kill you right where you stand, and the woman and boy will also die. If you choose to run, then you will have the opportunity to save … one."

"One?"

"Yes. You will have to choose only one. The one you do not choose will die, but the one you do choose will live, provided you can stay alive until dawn."

"So you are going to be hunting me with those dogs back at your house, and I have to survive until dawn, then you will let me go?"

"No questions asked."

"You'll let me just walk right out of here?"

"It will be your word against mine."

Right. Dead men don't talk.

"What if I save both of them?"

"You won't. You will be lucky to make it past midnight. No one has ever beaten us in the hunt."

The last statement caused Nate's stomach to cringe when he thought of Bryson's father. *I will make you suffer for your father's deeds.*

"At dusk, I will give you an eleven-minute and six-second head start. Then we will hunt you down until you are dead. If you die, the woman and boy will be executed on the spot. You have been chosen."

So you've told me.

Bryson stared down at the two white dots. He must not let them down. He examined the tents again. The wheels were beginning to turn in his head.

Billy Ray walked up behind Bryson and pulled the hood back over his head. They led him back to the truck and drove off.

Bryson tried to pay close attention to all details. They were traveling a little faster, but this time the road was zigzagging uphill. He counted again, checking if they used the same route. He counted almost the same number. *Most definitely the same route. Probably only one road to their command post. It can't be more than a mile down in a valley. What direction? Not sure. I need to knock out that command center if I am going to have a chance. But how?*

Billy Ray dragged Bryson from the truck and placed him in the shed, removing the hood after he was inside. Billy Ray locked the door.

Tyrel leaned against the door. "See ya around, Shakespeare."

Both men laughed as they walked back to the main house.

Bryson watched Billy Ray and Tyrel through the cracks of the wooden planks. They disappeared into the house. Bryson's eyes caught movement on the outside of the shed, opposite where he was sitting. He walked over and stood by the door, trying to get a better look at the person standing outside the shed.

"Hello. Who's out there?"

No answer.

Then Bryson saw a man wearing overalls and a SpongeBob backpack.

"Hey, there. What's your name?"

"Jake Monger. I live here. What's your name?"

"Bryson Keahbone. Hey, Jake, you want to do me a favor?"

"I dunno. Maybe."

"Can you unlock this door?"

"Oh, no. Billy Ray will get mad."

"No, he won't."

"Yes, he will!"

Bryson knew he wouldn't be able to argue with Jake, and he also knew he didn't have much time. He looked down at his watch. Dusk was less than twenty minutes away.

"I will owe you a favor if you help me."

Jake wrinkled up his brow in thought.

"Can I see your feet?"

"What?"

"Can I look at your feet?" Jake repeated eagerly.

"Why?"

"I want to see if they're like your daddy's feet."

"What!"

"Do you have only three toes on each foot like your daddy?" Bryson was briefly stunned. *How would he know my father had only three toes? Unless ...* He had to think fast.

"I tell you what, Jake. You get this lock off this door, and I will show you my feet. Deal?"

"Deal! I'll be right back!" Jake exclaimed as he turned and trotted off toward the house.

It was almost dusk.

Bryson watched the house, but Jake never returned. He abruptly turned when from behind the shed a woman's voice spoke.

"He's not coming back. He's probably already forgotten what he's looking for. Besides I have it here," Elizabeth smiled coldly as she held the key to the padlock between her fingers.

"Mrs. Monger—" Bryson began but stopped when he saw pure evil across her face. The dark circles around her eyes were almost black against her pale-dead skin. Her lips were also painted black. She wore a black dress that fell in layers of fine linen. She looked like she was decorated in a Halloween costume.

"Yes, you almost remembered me the other day in Hitchcock's office. I saw it in your eyes, but you weren't quite sure. Maybe I can jog your memory a little."

Bryson stared at Elizabeth, but still nothing came to his mind. She pulled a small vial from a pocket in her dress and held it up in the air.

"You saw this once before. I had accidentally left it on the nightstand. Do you remember?"

Bryson studied the small container but didn't recognize it at first; then horror consumed his soul. He remembered the vial. Images of it came to his mind. It had been sitting on a nightstand at his cabin when he was a boy. The same nightstand that was next to his mother's bed. He had been holding his mother's hand when Elizabeth came quickly and snatched up the vial before anyone saw it.

"You were my mother's nurse when she got sick after my father disappeared. You were always at my mother's side. I thought you were helping my mother."

"Yes, she was such a dear woman too."

Bryson was ready to crash through the wood siding and kill this woman. He backed slowly away from the door. He was about to charge forward with all his might but suddenly changed his mind when he heard the chain and lock rattling against the door. Rage was beginning to take over. He reached down for the knife. *I must gain control.* He began lifting his pant leg. *I must gain control. I have to be disciplined for Piper and Jared.* He let his pant leg slide down. *Not yet.*

Elizabeth retreated and disappeared into the tree line.

Nate swung open the door and stopped in the doorway. He held a brown leather-bound book in his left hand. It was the *Book of the Running Moon.*

Bryson stood up and glared at Nate.

Nate glared back, but Bryson was not intimidated by the ghost eye.

Bryson stood his ground. He was prepared to go down fighting. Nate saw the same fight in Joseph Keahbone's eyes twenty years earlier on the very same night. *Finally, a worthy opponent.*

"You have been chosen. Time is time upon this scene."

Bryson immediately thought of his father's words. *Come find me when time is time upon the final scene beneath the Moon When Wolves Cry.*

"You have been chosen. The Running Moon is climbing into the sky. You must sign the Book of the Running Moon." He placed the large book on the small table and opened to the yellow page marked with a black ribbon. He walked to Bryson and raised his tied hands. He removed his knife from its sheath and made a small cut in Bryson's palm. He never flinched and maintained constant eye contact with Nate. Nate placed the tin cup beneath the cut to catch the blood.

Nate was impressed. He longed for this night. His hunting juices were on fire and boiling in his veins. He could hardly wait. He wanted to hunt *now*. He calmed his excitement a little. *First things first.* He removed a pen from his shirt pocket and handed it to Bryson. He pointed at the cup with blood and the book on the table.

"Sign!"

Bryson dipped the pen in the blood and walked over to the book, but instead of signing, he slammed the book shut. Before Nate could blink an eye Bryson had spun around and threw the pen toward Nate. It stuck in the wood three inches from Nate's good eye.

Nate calmly grabbed the pen from the wall and held it out to Bryson.

"Sign!"

"I will not!"

"Sign, or you die!" Nate ordered as he pulled his nine millimeter pistol from its holster.

"You need me to run. You have to have a runner for your game."

"I will kill you and run one of my own."

"No, you won't."

"Yes, I will!"

Nate raised the gun and pulled the trigger without hesitation. *Bang!*

Tyrel and Rubin had just arrived at their ambush station three hundred yards above Jared's location west of Trosper's Point, when they heard the shot echo through the valley.

"No way! That's daddy's gun," Tyrel screamed.

He was furious. This was the first run in years where he didn't have to be stuck with his daddy. He could do some real hunting. And now his father had ruined it for everyone—especially for Tyrel.

"Who cares? Let me go down there and kill Jared," Rubin said, pulling a six-inch knife from the sheath on his belt.

Tyrel looked at Rubin and smiled, "In due time, Ruby, in due time. Let us both be patient. Put away your knife. I'll call Daddy."

"Yes, sir."

Tyrel raised the radio to his mouth.

"Night Runner. You copy?"

Silence.

"Night Runner. You copy?"

"Night Runner. Roger."

"What happened? We heard a shot."

Billy Ray and Jake were already in position above where Piper was tied to an iron post east of Trosper's Point. They waited to ambush anyone who might try to rescue Piper. If the prey died, Billy Ray had orders to kill Piper.

Billy Ray and Jake looked at each other when they heard the shot.

"Who fired that shot?" Jake asked.

"That's Daddy's gun, but I don't know what he's shooting at."

"You reckon Daddy shot the prey? I sure did want to see his feet. He promised me he would show me. Do you think the prey has weird feet like his daddy's feet?"

"I dunno. Now, shudup!"

Jake pouted up and crossed his arms against his chest.

Billy Ray ignored him as he unclipped his radio from his belt. He was about to call Nate when he heard Tyrel's voice come through the radio.

"Night Runner. You copy?"

"Night Runner. Roger."

"What happened? We heard a shot!"

"Prey's being contrary. Situation under control. Is everyone in position with your red bands on?"

"Ten-four," Tyrel replied.

"Roger wilco," Billy Ray answered.

"Bobcat and Skeet?"

"We are ready, sir."

"Black Widow, are you at base camp yet?"

"Just arrived," Elizabeth confirmed.

"Bravo. In five minutes, dusk will be here, and I will set fire to the flares, but only if the prey is alive. Out."

Nate placed the radio back on the clip of his belt. He walked to Bryson's body to pick him up by the arm.

Bryson rolled over and looked up at Nate. He had lost his balance and fell down. His ears were ringing severely from the gunshot.

"This is your last chance. Sign!" Nate ordered as he pointed the pistol at Bryson's head.

"I will only sign if I lose. You hunt me down to where I cannot flee anymore, then I will sign your book. You need me. Dusk is here. Time is time, remember. You have never had a runner like me who will give you a hunt like no other … not even my father," Bryson hissed as he bowed his head breaking eye contact with Nate. *I pray I am making the right choice.*

Nate stepped back and studied Bryson. He smiled and picked up the book. *So he knows. Good!*

"Let's go!"

Bryson Runs

Bryson and Nate stood at the starting line between the two metal poles with flares mounted on top. Bryson stared down the dark path that disappeared in the black wood. He wondered how many victims had participated in the Running Moon. Low growls took his attention away from the path. He glanced at three wooden crates holding five pit bulls.

A stocky brindled pit was pacing back and forth. It stopped and started gnawing on the iron barred door, and then suddenly stopped and stared at Bryson. The other four followed suit.

Timer slowly stepped from the shadows and was now standing in front of the crates, watching and waiting patiently, like a vulture sitting at the top of a tree watching and waiting for his dinner to die.

There were four more large crates with a green tarp over each. They contained the rest of the team of hungry pit bulls, which were called into action when Nate ordered the floodgates to be opened. The crates were rocking and bouncing as the pits thirsted for the blood of their next prey.

Timer turned toward the tarped crates and barked. The crates immediately became still. Not a sound came from beneath the tarps. Timer twisted back and glared through cold, spiritless red eyes at Bryson.

"They are wanting a piece of you. But none more than Timer."

"Marvelous. I can hardly wait."

"Do you want your hands untied?"

"Does it really matter what I want? You're going to do what you want."

"This is true."

Bryson silently raised his bonded hands. "Thanks."

Nate quickly removed his knife and cut the zip ties. The zip ties fell to the ground, exposing a white metal band. Bryson rubbed the band and examined it, but his attention was suddenly drawn away when Nate spoke.

"You betcha," Nate replied as he placed his knife back in its sheath.

Bryson was caught a little off guard, not by Nate's quickness but by the words he had just spoken. Only one person he knew ever said those two words together.

Nate must have noticed it too.

"What did you say?"

"You betcha," Nate repeated, smiling from ear to ear. "It's a little phrase I have picked up lately. You like it?"

Bryson narrowed his eyes at Nate. *No way. There's no way. Johnny was not here. He didn't run. I don't believe it.* He tried to convince himself, but it wasn't working. He was slowly losing control. The unemotional wax mask he had been wearing was slowly melting under the heated pressure of suddenly realizing this family of evil beings had singlehandedly wiped out almost everyone that he had ever loved, except Becky. Then he remembered that her car wreck was caused by a large black dog. He turned and looked at Timer, who appeared to smile through imposing yellow fangs. He closed his eyes tightly. Bryson's world was spiraling out of control. He felt very lightheaded. He began doubting he could save Piper and Jared. *I have to gain control. For them.* He opened his eyes and lifted his head. He looked at Timer and then, Nate. A smile came across Bryson's face.

"Are we going to do this or what?"

"Time is time—"

"Upon this final scene," Bryson finished.

Nate stepped back a few feet to gain his composure, staring at Bryson. "Enough talk!" Nate hollered; then he pulled his radio from his belt and asked if everyone was in position. Each one answered confirming their readiness for the hunt. Nate gathered himself and licked his salty lips. He had waited for this moment a very long time—twenty years to be exact. He removed a lighter from his pants pocket and lit each flare.

Bryson poised himself for the run and then unexpectedly relaxed when he heard an owl screech, which echoed throughout the valley. He remembered what his father had taught him about the great owl, *Ishkitini. First, it searched.* He stared down the worn path as it disappeared beyond the reach of the light. He suddenly felt more confident. *I must find my own path.* He didn't say a word as he took off running at a fast sprint.

Nate watched until Bryson vanished into the darkness.

"Prey has been set free. We have ourselves a Running Moon."

The full moon had climbed above the trees. Bryson barreled down the path for three minutes before stopping. He looked up at the moon—Moon When Wolves Cry. He knelt down and pulled the knife from his sock. He glanced over and noticed a heat sensor mounted in the fork of a tree. He jogged over and placed his knife in his waist band. He quickly scanned the ground for—there, a three-foot-long stick. He picked it up and swung it like a bat at the wireless sensor. He knocked it from its mount, shattering it into a hundred pieces. *Maybe I can take these out one by one.* Then he caught a glimpse of several more heat and motion sensors scattered throughout the trees. *Not happening. I will have to take out the command post. But how? I don't even know where it is located. I will have to worry about that when the time comes. Right now I need to put some distance between myself and the beasts. They will be coming soon.*

Bryson looked down the path. *They will be expecting me to travel along this path. It will be heavily watched. But which way do I go?* He twirled around, second-guessing which direction to take.

Without warning from the shadows, the wolf appeared upon the path. His golden eyes were bright and alert. Bryson recoiled and then breathed easy.

"Hey, fancy meeting you here. How about a little help? Which way do you suggest I travel?"

The wolf spun around on his hind legs. He left the path and ran down the side of a steep hill, circling back toward the house. Bryson followed as closely as he could, but running through the woods was a lot easier for a wolf than for a man. The underbrush was becoming thicker. Briar and thorn bushes were ripping and tearing like razor-blades at his clothing. He picked up the pace when he reached a small clearing. The wolf was moving fast. Bryson was having a difficult time keeping up until finally the wolf disappeared altogether.

Bryson stopped at the edge of a small clearing. He was at the base of the mountain he had just descended. He could hear water trickling over small rocks. He realized that he was very thirsty. He walked over to the stream and knelt down to get a drink from a pool of water. He scooped up several handfuls of water, and then splashed some on his face. As he opened his eyes, he noticed in the pool a reflection of a man. He grabbed his knife and quickly looked up, but all he saw was the wolf standing across from him. He glanced back into the pool, but the reflection was gone. The wolf had turned and trotted off.

Bryson jumped up and followed. He didn't have time to try and figure it out.

Nate pulled his radio from his belt and miked it.

"Black Widow. You copy?"

"Copy, Night Runner."

"Do you have prey in sight?"

"Yes, sir. He's traveling along the same path as the others," Elizabeth answered as she sat viewing the four radar screens at Nate's base camp.

"Seriously. I thought he would put up a tougher fight. Three minutes until I release death. Doesn't look like we're having much fun tonight."

"Wait, sir. He has stopped. He's heading down the ridge and circling back beneath the house. Running straight for Lightning Creek Springs. He'll be there in one minute. Copy?"

"Roger. Are you sure?"

"Definitely, sir."

Nate paused.

Why would the prey go that way? A runner has never gone that way before. Except one.

"You see anything else on the screen with the runner?"

"No, sir. Like what?"

"Nothing. Keep me posted," Nate said as a feeling of uneasiness began to settle over him.

He walked over to the crates. The flares had almost burned down. He debated opening them early but changed his mind.

He's not weak. He wasn't going to give in to his fears. He looked over at Timer, who stood indifferently outside the pens. He had made the mistake of trying to make Timer stay in the crates before every run. Big mistake. That was how he got the ghost eye.

Bryson followed Lightning Creek until it emptied into a pool of clear water. He stopped and looked around. No wolf. He thought about going around but figured that if he swam across, he might throw the dogs off his scent for a little while, buying him some valuable time. He dove in. The water was very cold. He knew he would cramp up if he stayed in too long and possibly develop hypothermia. He swam as fast as he could to the other side but didn't get out. He studied the surroundings. There were sensors everywhere. *The sensors will have a hard time detecting me in the water because I am below their level of scanning, but I can't stay in the water. The beasts will eventually find me along with the hunters. I have to find a place below ground. But where?*

"Night Runner. You copy?"

"This is Night Runner. What is it?"

"Prey has disappeared off the radar at Lightning Creek Springs."

"What! Are you sure! Billy Ray did you service all the equipment before this run?"

"Yes, sir. I even added more sensors to the field."

"Then would you care to explain?"

"He will reappear. He's probably in the water. There's no way of monitoring movement in the water unless we revamp the whole system."

"And why am I just now finding out about it!"

Billy Ray did not respond.

"Black Widow, let me know the second he reappears. Badger, I will deal with you later."

"I will notify you when he reappears on screen," Elizabeth acknowledged as she moved the mouse around, making adjustments to the tracking system and trying to pinpoint Bryson's exact location.

Tyrel had been listening from his hidden post with a huge smile on his face. Finally, someone besides him was getting a butt chewing. He even gave Rubin a thumbs up.

Rubin couldn't care less. All he wanted to do was instill as much pain as he could upon Jared, and he never took his eyes off the target.

"Night Runner?"

"It better be good."

"It is, sir. I have the prey back on the screen. The bracelet's tracking device needed a little tender loving care," Elizabeth smirked.

"Excellent," Nate screamed, just as the flares burned out. He ran and opened the doors to the pens. Timer had already bolted down the hill.

The team of five was right behind.

The rest of the pits under the green tarps were in a frenzy so extreme that they were punching holes with their heads through the wooden sides of the crates. One pit had his head stuck and was bleeding profusely from a wooden stake that had lodged in its neck just below the jaw bone.

"The hunt is on!" Nate laughed insanely.

Bryson climbed out of the water. The cool air chilled him to the bone. *A fire would be nice.* He knew he could never build a fire although it wouldn't take much if he could ever find a secure place. He took his shirt and pants off and wrung out the water. He cut the legs off at the knees and kept the bottom part of his pants for later use. He looked around, as he redressed. No wolf. He decided to follow the creek.

He jogged carefully, staying in the knee deep water, trying to avoid the many big rocks so he wouldn't sprain or break his ankle. Any such accident and they were all dead. The going was very slow and hideous. He had been running along the creek for half a mile. He stopped briefly and listened. He could barely hear the beasts howling from the top of the mountain. He glanced down at his watch. It had been almost an hour since Nate lit the flares. *That gives me roughly eleven hours to stay alive. Oh, boy! It's going to be a long night!* He could hear distant growls. The beasts were on the move and closing fast. *A really long night.*

He knew he couldn't fight them all at once. He needed to separate them if he could, but he didn't have a clue how.

The wolf appeared from around a large cottonwood. He barked and took off in a direction perpendicular to the creek.

Bryson followed.

The beasts arrived fifteen minutes after Bryson had departed at the large pool of water on Lightning Creek. They were in their stalk formation with Timer in the lead, followed by two, and three in the back. They stopped at the edge of the water. Timer bent over and sniffed the ground and then raised his head and sniffed the air. The rest of the beasts did the same.

Timer barked, and the beasts took off at a dead sprint. Three went left and two ran off to the right of the pool of water. Timer watched as they disappeared into the dark wood. Then he abruptly turned and went in the opposite direction he had sent the other beasts.

Nate arrived at base camp and sat beside Elizabeth in front of the radar screens. She never looked up. She didn't have time. She was too busy adjusting the calibrations of the sensors to where the tracking system could determine if the signal being detected was human and not an animal.

"How's it goin'?"

"Good now. I constantly have to readjust the calibrations with the sensory system, so we're not tracking a deer or even a rabbit. The sensors are extremely sensitive to body heat and movement."

"Why has this not been a problem before tonight?"

"Because the prey was always caught within the hour. Last Running Moon, we were exposed a little, but I believe we have everything under our complete control now."

"Well done. What about the bracelet?"

"I've worked out the kinks. The bracelet is working perfectly.

"Here is the prey. He's moving northwest away from Lightning Creek," Elizabeth pointed.

"Where's the team?"

"Here. About fifteen minutes behind the prey. They have separated at the watershed pond. Timer has retreated and is moving in position to cut off the prey on the opposite ridge above Cooper's Canyon near the pit," Elizabeth said, pointing at the five small red dots and one larger red dot that was in the shape of an hourglass, but it suddenly faded from the screen.

"He's heading for Cooper's Canyon … just like his father," Nate announced as he picked up the radio. "Bob Cat, you copy?"

"Copy, Night Runner."

"Do you have the crates on the truck?"

"10-4!"

Nate smiled. Everything was working like clockwork. He was almost proud of his family. Almost.

"Open floodgates. Take team to east end of Cooper's Canyon. Stand ready at Taylor Falls. You will let the team down there when we have confirmation he is in the canyon."

"Roger. Team is loaded. We are on our way," Jim Bob answered.

Nate and Elizabeth followed Bryson's white dot on the radar screen. It would disappear and then suddenly reappear after a few seconds. Elizabeth was swiftly punching keys on the keyboard and moving around the mouse to make the necessary adjustments as the prey entered a different quadrant.

"He's making his way toward the woman. Good choice," Nate grinned as he looked over at Elizabeth.

She pretended not to notice as she reached down with her free hand to feel for the gun strapped to her thigh.

Nate pointed at the screen. The red dots appeared to be heading away from Bryson's location.

"Where are they going? The prey is the other way!"

"It's rough terrain above Taylor Falls. They will have to go around, sir."

"Where's Timer?"

"I don't know, sir. He's probably chewed off his tracking device, like he always does," Elizabeth said matter-of-factly.

Nate shook his head and leaned back in his chair, analyzing all four screens. The monitors with Piper and Jared displayed their white dots in the middle of the screen, and two sets of two red dots located at a short distance away from their position. The red dots were Tyrel and Rubin overlooking Jared, and Billy Ray and Jake were watching Piper. Then he noticed a large number of red dots appearing next to the words "Taylor Falls/Cooper's Canyon" on top of the screen.

"Night Runner. We are in position at Taylor Falls. Waiting your orders."

"Excellent. Stand by. Prey is above your position, heading your way on the other side of the falls."

"Do we shoot the prey if we see him?" Jim Bob asked eagerly, but the excitement quickly ended when he heard his daddy's thundering voice.

"That's an absolute negative. We are playing this one out. I want the prey to suffer. Copy?"

"Copy, sir. Out."

Nate dropped the radio to the table.

"Prey has stopped at the edge of Taylor Falls."

Nate smiled wickedly.

"He's resting. The team will be on him shortly."

Bryson followed the creek as it cut through the edge of the mountain. It was getting wider and deeper until it had developed into a small river. He had been crisscrossing the creek to try and hide his scent, but now he had to choose a side. Luckily, he chose the side opposite Jim Bob and Skeeter.

Bryson kept moving at a breakneck pace. His lungs and legs were a burning fire of tissue. He needed to take a break to let his breathing catch up and to ease some of the fatigue that was settling in his muscular legs.

He slowed to a trot before coming to a complete stop. He looked around and listened for the beasts. Then he heard a sound. A very faint sound. It was like water bubbling and running over rocks. He took off running toward the sound. It was becoming louder until it was no longer bubbling but roaring and thundering over a rock bed.

The sound was a waterfall—Taylor Falls. The large stream fell into Cooper's Canyon, cutting a path through the middle until it ran out the west end.

Bryson stopped at the edge. He decided to take a quick break. He sat on a rock, watching the mist float up from the base of the falls. He was contemplating his next move when he looked down at the white metal bracelet. He turned it over and spun it around his wrist. *How could I be so stupid? This is a tracking device.*

Bryson took out his knife and gently prodded the metal clip on the bracelet. He wanted to be careful not to damage it. He had a plan. After a couple of minutes of poking and prying the clip snapped open and fell to the ground. He quickly picked it up and examined the bracelet. *Good. It's not damaged.*

He looked around on the ground, moving dead leaves and small branches. *There.* He found what he was seeking. From the leaves, he pulled a four-feet-long log, which was about ten inches in diameter. There was a hollow indention where a woodpecker had been pecking years before. *Perfect.* He stuffed the bracelet into the hole and pulled from his back pocket one of the remains of his cut pant leg. He quickly cut four long strips and began tying and covering the bracelet to the log, so it wouldn't fall out.

He picked up the log and threw it into the stream. In a matter of seconds, the log was moving down the stream.

Bryson watched the log disappear over the edge of the falls.

Deadly Trap

"Open the floodgates! Prey is in the canyon!"

Jim Bob and Skeeter did not have to be told twice. They were the perfect working duo. They were out of the truck and lowering the first crate in just a few minutes. They knew they would have to hurry because they generally didn't make the drop here. It would take longer because it was a lot higher than their normal drop so they would need more time.

One crate came resting to the ground thirty feet from the pool at the base of the falls. Jim Bob was signaling Skeeter to hoist him back up. When Jim Bob arrived at the top edge, he stepped onto the flat bed. Skeeter quickly grabbed the hook and attached it to number two and lowered it into the canyon.

Bryson sat on a rock watching the pool of water below. He wanted to make sure the log cleared the rocks at the base of the falls. There on the calm surface he saw the log pass through the reflection of moonlight on the water. He breathed a sigh of relief. *That should throw them off for a while.*

"Yippee!" Jim Bob yelled, stepping off the ledge onto the crate as it descended into the canyon.

Skeeter was dancing around like he had won the lottery too. They were both in a great mood because this was the first time in years that they got to open the floodgates.

But their celebration would be short-lived.

Bryson saw Jim Bob riding a large box down into the canyon for a second time. Bryson missed the first trip, but when Jim Bob yelled, it caught Bryson's attention.

They must be lowering the crates full of pit bulls that I saw at the starting line. They think I'm down in the canyon.

Bryson had a plan. A dangerous plan, but he had no choice. Time was running out. He knew he would have to swim across the stream and fight through the strong current. If he waited too long, they would get all the crates lowered and leave. He needed the element of surprise on his side.

He dove in and began swimming to the other side. The current was a lot stronger than he anticipated. It was zapping all his strength. He could see the other side, but the current was drawing him toward the edge of the falls faster than he was making it to the shore. He began to feel a little panicky. He started swimming harder, trying with all his might to fight through the current. He finally swam into a small cove where the current was not as strong. He pulled himself to the grassy shore and collapsed on the ground. He didn't know how long the swim lasted, but he did know he had to get going.

Jim Bob unhooked number three and gave Skeeter a quick thumb up. He placed his foot in a loop above the hook. Skeeter pushed the green button, and instantly, Jim Bob was heading back up to the truck. He looked out over the canyon. He wondered if the prey was hiding or running away. Wherever the prey was located, Jim Bob figured he was close.

Closer than he ever imagined.

Bryson was easing through the pine trees, careful not to make any noise. He could hear the winch's gears grinding, as it reeled in the metal cable. He crept forward until he was at the tree line beside the road.

The twins had backed the truck to the edge of the canyon. The twelve-foot gin poles extended out over the canyon's edge. It was a forty-five-foot sheer drop down to the canyon floor. They finished hooking up number four. Skeeter pushed in the green button, lifting the last crate into the air.

"Let's get this puppy to the ground and suck us down a few brewskies."

"Sounds good, bro!" Jim Bob exclaimed as he stepped onto the top of the last crate.

Bryson eased away from the tree line. He squatted down and walked across the road. He stopped in front of the white Ford, placing his back to the grill. He peeked around the driver's side fender. Skeeter had the control panel in his hand, pushing a red button as he glanced over the edge.

Jim Bob was over halfway to the bottom.

Bryson would have to act fast. He jumped out from behind the truck. Skeeter had his back toward Bryson. Bryson stayed low as he inched toward Skeeter.

Nate's voice came on the radio.

"Bobcat. Jackrabbit. Do you copy?"

Skeeter turned around just in time to see Bryson stand up. He pulled his .38 special from a hip holster and fired three times.

Nate and Elizabeth were watching the screen where Bryson's dot had stopped to rest at the top of Taylor Falls. Nate was about to order Jim Bob and Skeeter to drop the crates at the top of the falls but quickly changed his mind when the white dot suddenly disappeared and then reappeared several feet away—indicating that the prey was now in the canyon.

"Open the floodgates! Prey is in the canyon!"

They followed the white dot as it slowly zigzagged through the middle of Cooper's Canyon. In the lower corner of the screen a mass of red dots were gathering at the base of the falls.

"It won't be long now. It looks like the twins have one more crate to lower," Nate smirked, who was enjoying life right now.

But that was about to change.

Another white dot appeared on the screen. It was slowly moving toward the twin's location.

"What's that dot?"

"Not sure. It came from the water. It's probably a coon or beaver," Elizabeth answered as she frantically tried adjusting the calibrations.

"What is it?"

"I'm trying to determine that, sir. Give me a second. It's …"

"Bobcat. Jackrabbit. You copy!"

Bang! Bang! Bang!

Bryson jumped back and dove in front of the truck as bullets ricocheted off the fender and bumper. He rolled onto his stomach, watching Skeeter's feet.

Skeeter stood very still. He had the gun cocked and pointed at the front of the truck. He grabbed the gun with both hands, trying to hold it steady, but his nerves were causing the gun to shake in his hands. Skeeter could hear Jim Bob screaming for him to lower the crate all the way to the ground. Skeeter had dropped the controller, landing a few feet out of his reach. He was hesitant to pick it up because he didn't want to take his eyes off the front of the truck.

Jim Bob screamed again.

"Just a second, bro. I have me a prey. I'm fixin' to put on ice," Skeeter declared as he slowly inched his way toward the front of the truck. He craned his neck so he could see the front of the truck. No prey.

Bryson pulled out his knife and crawled along the opposite side of the truck from Skeeter. Skeeter stopped and pulled a flashlight from his belt. He knelt down to look under the truck. Bryson climbed quietly onto the flat bed. Skeeter was on his knees sweeping the beam of light beneath the truck. Again no prey. Skeeter determined that the prey had run off when he shot at him. Wrong guess. When Skeeter stood back up, Bryson leaped off the flat bed truck, kicking Skeeter squarely in the middle of the chest. Skeeter went flying back toward the edge of the canyon but gained control of his balance before he fell.

Bryson was lying on his back and quickly jumped to his feet. He glanced around. There was nowhere to take cover.

Skeeter smiled and raised the gun, but suddenly the earth beneath his feet gave way—softened from the recent Oklahoma rains. Skeeter's three-hundred-pound mass of humanity was more than the edge could hold. His eyes grew as big as grapefruits as he plummeted to his death.

Bryson walked and stopped at the edge. He peered cautiously into the canyon. Jim Bob was screaming and cussing at Bryson from the top of crate four. Bryson left the edge and opened the driver's side door. He scanned the inside of the truck for some kind of weapon, but there wasn't one. In a cup holder, he saw a BIC lighter. He put it in his pocket. Then he placed the gear shifter in neutral and released the emergency brake. The truck didn't move. He slammed the door and looked at the tires. They were scotched under the back tires with large rubber blocks. He removed the scotches, but the truck still didn't move. He ran around to the front and began pushing the truck toward the edge.

His feet dug into the soft dirt as he pushed with all his might. Finally, it began rolling slowly toward the edge.

Jim Bob's screams began to intensify as he realized what was about to happen.

The truck rolled off the edge and exploded into a huge fireball on impact at the base of the falls.

Bryson went back to the edge. Smoke was billowing up in a mushroom cloud from the fire below. He looked for movement, but everything was still. He stared into the fire. He had never killed another human being until today. He pitied their souls. *This did not have to happen.* He tried to make sense of the last few minutes. *Why?*

The Pit

I t was shortly after midnight.

Bryson had taken to the high ground to cover a greater distance. His muscles were gassed, running only on his will to survive and the survival of Piper and Jared. He could hear the beasts running parallel to him in the valley below.

It wouldn't be long until they met up to finish the hunt. He needed rest.

But where?

Bryson stopped and looked around. He heard the grunting growls of the relentless monsters nearby, echoing up and down the valley. They were closing the gap. There was a sudden rustling of leaves behind Bryson. He turned toward the ruckus. The brindle beast appeared on the road and was rushing straight for Bryson. He pulled out the knife from its sheath and tried to stab the demon, but he was too late. The monster's jaws clapped down on Bryson's left arm but didn't lock. Bryson ducked and use the creature's momentum against him, sending the stocky projectile flying into the underbrush.

Bryson looked down at the wound on his arm. It was bleeding, but the damage was minimal.

The crazed beast came tearing back from the bushes. It stopped and then slowly walked toward Bryson. Low, hideous growls sang from its throat.

Bryson lowered his center of gravity, preparing for the attack. He knew the demon would not quit coming until it was dead. Or until Bryson was dead.

The malignant beast charged and leapt into the air. Bryson fell to the ground and brought his knife straight up. The creature landed on the ground and ran ten more feet before stopping. It stood there, frozen. Then suddenly its entrails fell to the ground, followed by the beast's body. Bryson had cut the monster from the breast to tail.

Bryson crawled on his hands and knees to the loathsome beast. Its heart was still faintly beating. It looked at Bryson and tried to get up. Bryson quickly brought the knife down, lodging deep into the beast's heart. He removed the knife and collapsed to the ground. He glanced over and noticed the red collar around its neck. *It's a tracking device.* He cut off the collar and held it in his hand.

Angry howls were coming from all directions.

Bryson looked for a possible escape route. He was tired. He would have to fight it out. *How many? Four or five were left.* He was overwhelmed with doubt. He knew he couldn't win, but he had to try. His energy was all but gone. As he was standing up, he spotted a hole in the side of a cliff about fifty yards away.

It's a cave.

Bryson stumbled and ran toward the cave. He could hear the foul creatures coming. They were on the road he had been running when he was attacked by the hell hound. Ten feet away. He tripped and fell.

Timer and the four demons arrived at the fallen beast at the same time. They all turned sniffing the air in different directions. Timer turned toward the cave just as Bryson disappeared into the darkness. He sniffed the ground and then rose up and barked some orders. The four beasts scattered in different directions.

Timer slowly walked toward the cave as his nose stayed close to the ground. Its red eyes scanned ahead.

Bryson saw Timer stalking his way toward the entrance of the cave. He stepped back. He noticed that the cave sloped steeply away from the entrance. He retreated slowly until he came to an edge. He dared not use his light on his watch or the lighter for fear that Timer would locate his position. He went down to his knees and cautiously moved along the edge, searching for a crevice to hide in. As he inched along, the floor continued to move and shift under his weight like he was crawling on sand. He burrowed his way down to hide. The smell was almost more than Bryson could stand. His eyes and throat were burning from the smell of what Bryson thought had to be a million rotten eggs that were covered in excrement and urine. The more he moved around, the more the smell intensified. It gagged him to the point he was fighting hard not to throw up.

Timer entered the cave and walked to the edge above where Bryson was hiding. His laser eyes cut through the dark. Bryson covered his mouth to control his gag reflex. Timer stood for several seconds, searching the darkness for Bryson. Then he turned and exited the cave to resume the hunt.

Ten minutes later, Bryson decided that Timer had left the cave and was a safe distance away for him to shine a light. He pulled the lighter from his pocket and lit it. He wanted to check out his refuge.

To his horror—he had found the pit.

Nate and Elizabeth were expressing their own horror as they stared at the baseball size red dot on the screen beside the label "Taylor Falls."

When the shock passed, Nate grabbed his radio and screamed, "Jim Bob! Skeeter! What happened?"

No response.

"Jim Bob! Answer me!"

Nothing.

"Night Runner. Do you want me to investigate?" Billy Ray voiced through the radio.

Nate did not answer. He was still mesmerized by the image on the screen.

"Repeat. Do you want me to investigate?"

Nate popped back to reality. He watched Bryson's white dot move across the screen followed closely by one red dot and surrounded by four more dots.

"Negative, Badger. Hold your position ... for now. Prey is surrounded by the team. Let's see how this plays out. Then you can investigate."

"What about the insurance chips on the stakes? Do we cash them in?" Tyrel radioed, referring to Piper and Jared.

"Wait until we have confirmation of the kill!"

"Copy. Out."

Nate pointed at the large red dot.

"Any way of identifying what that is?"

"Negative," Elizabeth replied.

Nate turned his attention disappointedly back to Bryson's dot. The white dot and red dot had become so close that they almost looked connected. The four remaining red dots were only a short distance away.

"One of the team is engaged with the prey. This shouldn't take long," Nate said, trying to convince himself that all would end well. "See. There. The prey is down! The prey is down! We have won!"

Bryson's white dot faded and then turned red.

Nate smiled at Elizabeth, but she didn't smile back.

"What's wrong, Elizabeth?"

"Sir, not to sound negative, but we need confirmation."

Nate's smile faded.

"Badger. Copy."

"Copy, sir."

"Go investigate. We need confirmation. Leave Teddy Bear. Repeat, Teddy Bear stays. And remind him to stay! Location is approximately fifty yards northeast of the pit. Radio me when you find downed prey. Out."

"Roger. Out."

Nate stared at the screen.

"See, Elizabeth. The team is feeding. They all have a piece of the prey and have taken it off to feed. Look, one has even gone to the pit to eat. You know they won't eat together because a fight will always break out."

Elizabeth stared at the screen and didn't reply.

The lone red dot that went to the pit was Bryson. The dead beast's collar was blocking his signal. The remaining red dots were the beasts scattering in all directions looking for the prey.

Except Timer—he had no dot.

Carry Me Away

Bryson released the button on the lighter. He was in shock and mortified by the carnage he had just witnessed. But the worst was yet to come. He closed his eyes and tried to calm himself with a deep breath, but the smell was horrendous. He opened his eyes and lit the lighter again, lifting it into the air for him to get a broader view of the cave.

He was laying in a sea of skeletal remains. Some were mere bones, but several still had sticky, fleshy meat hanging raggedly on gnawed bones. He accidentally dropped the lighter. He groped around, running his fingers over bones and oozing flesh. He remembered his watch had a light. He fingered the correct button and a dull light appeared. He spotted the lighter in an eye socket of a skull. He grabbed and lit it. He lifted it above his head, but the light didn't reach the ceiling. He shined it over the edge where he stood, but again the same results. He tried not to look down at the remains, but something caught his eye.

There was a head with strawberry-blond hair. It faced away from Bryson. He crawled over the bones until he was almost on the face side. The light went out. He held his breath and flicked it again. Bryson gasped for breath when the light exposed Johnny's face. Johnny's eyes were open and glazed over with a milky film.

This time Bryson couldn't hold it back. He spewed out everything that was in his stomach. He turned away. He couldn't go on. Tears filled his eyes until they overflowed to his cheeks. He began crawling desperately back toward the cave's entrance. *I can't do this anymore. Why? He didn't deserve this!*

He scrambled out of the bones and lay face down on the dirt. *Why did this happen? Why, God?*

Bryson didn't move. Fear was taking over—not fear of the beasts or Mongers, but fear of failing, the fear of letting down the people who depend on him. He didn't want to let Piper and Jared down, like he felt he did with Becky and his parents, especially his mom. *Can I do this?*

Remember the fire. His father's words came into his mind, reminding him of a time, not long before his father's death, when he was a young boy. A time before all this hate had touched his family.

Bryson was sitting with his father on the porch of their cabin. The sun was setting behind the blue-tinged mountains. Bryson looked up with a stern frown.

"How old do you have to be before you become a man?"

"How old are you?" Joseph Keahbone asked.

"I am twelve years old."

Joseph rubbed his chin.

"It's not how old you are that determines if you're a man or not. It is what you have inside you that matters."

"What's inside me? I don't understand."

"You are going to experience many difficult times and situations in your life that will terrify and hurt you both mentally and physically. You must kindle the fire inside and face life's adversities."

"How do I get this fire?"

"Come with me."

Joseph led Bryson into the woods. They walked together but did not talk. Joseph stopped by a huge hickory stump. He motioned for Bryson to sit down and pulled a red bandana from his back pocket. He took the bandana and tied it around Bryson's eyes as a blindfold.

"You must sit on this stump the entire night and not remove the blindfold until you feel the heat of the sun upon your face. You cannot cry out for help. If your fears become too much, remove your blindfold and return to the cabin. Good night, my son."

Bryson was overwhelmed with fear. He wanted to cry out right then, but he didn't want to let down his father. He knew he had to be brave.

"Good night, Father."

Bryson sat calmly on the stump. The wind began to howl through the trees. He heard many noises throughout the night. Some of the sounds he recognized, but most he did not know. Those are the ones that terrified him the most. His imagination tried to take over, but he remained steadfast, conquering his fears, never removing the blindfold. He knew he had to be strong if he was to become a man.

Finally, the sun rose above the land. Bryson removed his blindfold. To his surprise, his father was sitting beside him on the stump. Joseph had been there all night, protecting Bryson from any harm.

"You were here all night?"

"Yes. I never left your side."

"I thought I was alone."

"You are never *alone*."

Joseph smiled, placing a firm hand on Bryson's shoulder.

"I am your earthly father, but I will not always be with you. But I know someone who will."

"Who?"

"God, your Heavenly Father. Just because you don't see Him with you on the stump or in the field or at school doesn't mean He's not there to protect you."

"Does God give me the fire?"

"Yes. When bad things come your way, all you have to do is ask for the fire."

The memories faded away. Bryson remained face down. He didn't move an inch. Images from his entire life were racing through his mind. Two images kept coming up and staying longer than others—images of Piper and Jared.

Bryson slowly brought up his knees and pushed up with his hands. Long drool and tears fell to the ground. He teetered back and forth. The cave was spinning. Then Cherokee Billy's words came to his mind. *You are the bright son, who rises and is stronger than the pit, salvation to the ones you love. God will guide you on the right path. Follow your heart. Do not let the fire go out. Be strong and courageous.*

"I ... must be ... strong ... and courageous ... for Piper and Jared."

He stayed on his knees and lowered his face to his hands. Pastor Steve's words echoed in the cave—*God is in control and has a plan. God says, " You will call on Me, and come and pray to Me, I will listen to you."*

"My Heavenly Father, I lift up this prayer to You."

God, I trust in You and seek Your wisdom. Lift me up from this shifting sand. Cup me in Your nail-pierced hands. Carry me away, carry me away. Carry me away. Lord, rekindle the fire that had once burned bright inside me. Give me strength and courage. In Jesus's name I pray. Amen.

Bryson opened his eyes and stood up. His body and muscles ached and were exhausted and sore. But his spirit now had the fire.

He walked to the entrance of the cave and stopped. He looked up at the moon.

"It is time!"

The owl screeched. Second, it demanded.

Showdown

B illy Ray was looking down on the burning remains of the crates and truck at the base of Taylor Falls. Fires were sporadically burning around the crushed truck. Most of the crates had burned down to ashes.

"Night Runner. Copy?"

"Are you at Taylor Falls?"

"Yes, sir. It's not good. Truck is down in the canyon. Everything has been burned up. No team … no twins."

"Come again. Repeat!"

Radio silence.

"Everything appears to be … lost."

"Go up to the pit and find what's left of the prey."

"Copy, sir. I will report when I get to the pit. Out."

"Hurry!"

Billy Ray clipped the radio to his belt and jogged off toward the pit. Anger and hatred began to take over and control his inner being. He hungered to kill anything in his path. He was almost at a dead run.

He needed to be fed.

Jake Monger had become bored playing with the hot wheel cars in the dirt. He picked them up and placed them in his

SpongeBob backpack. He looked down the trail wondering when Billy Ray was going to return. He stood up and grabbed his wooden toy gun.

"I'm tired of waitin'. I'm goin' to talk to that girl. She is really nice and purty."

He headed down the path to where Piper was tied to a metal pole. He was humming the theme song to his favorite show, *SpongeBob SquarePants.*

Piper heard heavy footsteps through the leaves. She twisted her neck to see who it was. She hoped it was Bryson but was disappointed when Jake appeared on the trail.

Jake walked over and stopped in front of Piper.

"Hi, there. I'm Jake Monger."

"Hello. I'm Piper." She tried to force a smile.

"I'm helping my favorite brother hunt."

"That's nice. What are you hunting?"

Piper was trying to keep cool and be polite at the same time.

"A man."

"Have you caught him yet?"

"I dunno. That's where Billy Ray went to look, but he wouldn't take me with him. That's not right," Jake whined.

"You're right. That wasn't very nice. But do you think it's right to hunt people?"

Jake looked around. He shoved his hands deep into his pockets.

"I dunno. My daddy says it's right. And my brothers says it's right."

"What do you think?"

Jake didn't answer. No one had ever asked him what he thought before. No one had ever been nice to him either. Except Piper.

"I remember you, Piper. You helped me in the grocery store once when I accidentally knocked over a stack of cans. You helped me picked them up."

"I remember, Jake. That was a long time ago," Piper recalled, running the event through her mind.

"You are the nicest person in the world. I don't think you should be tied up."

Piper relaxed a little, but then she tensed back up when Jake spoke again.

"But I don't know. Billy Ray is going to get real mad if I cut you free."

"Yes, he probably will. But do you want to do what is right?"

Jake again looked to the sky in deep thought. For some reason unknown, the bronze man, Joseph Keahbone, came to his mind.

"Once, there was this brown man who had three toes on each foot. He could outrun everybody, even the dogs. They couldn't catch him, and he won. He lasted until sunrise. He won. I told Billy Ray that. And I tried to keep him from shooting that man. And you know what he did? He knocked this tooth right out of my head. Luckily I found it. I even got a nickel for it from the tooth fairy," Jake said, pressing his remaining teeth together to show Piper his gap.

"You did what was right. What do you think is the right thing to do here?" Piper asked, wondering if that was Bryson's father Jake was referring to.

Jake looked down at the ground. He quietly removed his backpack. In the side pocket, he removed a small pocket knife. He opened it up and walked behind Piper. He knelt down and cut the zip ties.

Piper quickly stood up and hugged Jake.

"Thank you, Jake. That was the right thing to do."

Jake smiled. His face was red from embarrassment. He had never been hugged before.

"Will you help me again?"

"S-s-sure." Jake grinned. He was eager to please.

"Do you know where the young boy is that came with me? His name is Jared."

"I sure do." Jake smiled, but his smile suddenly turned to a frown. "But that's where Tyrel and Rubin are. They have him tied up, like you were. Right over that hill."

"Will you show me?"

Jake shook his head.

"I'm too scared. Tyrel will hurt me and you."

"Please," Piper pleaded, trying really hard to keep her emotions in check. She could tell that Jake had a good heart. He just needed a chance to use it. She reached out and hugged him again. "It's all right, Jake. I understand. You need to take care of yourself. Again, thank you."

Piper turned to leave.

"Not that way. I know a better way. A way they won't see us. We'll have to two-time it. That's what my brother calls it when we need to hurry."

Jake took off running.

Piper followed close behind.

Bryson stood at the entrance of the pit. His eyes searched the patches of moonlight for any sign of the beasts or hunters. There was a small cluster of young pines nearby. He walked over and immediately cut two pines down to six feet spears. He stripped the small branches and sharpened the end to a needle point. He stood, placing the knife in his waist band. He touched his pocket, feeling for the beast's tracking device. Bryson was hoping it would give off a signal of a beast and not a prey.

"Which way is the command post?" Bryson mouthed under his breath.

The wolf suddenly appeared from the dark underbrush.

Bryson smiled.

The wolf trotted southwest, heading in the direction of the command post. They traveled along the ridge for about a half mile when the wolf darted abruptly from the path. Bryson stopped. He sensed something was wrong. Very wrong. He swirled and lifted a spear to throw but froze.

Billy Ray had stepped from behind a large pine. He had his sniper rifle strapped across his back, but his Colt .45 was aimed point blank at Bryson's chest.

Bryson lowered the spear. He didn't speak. His face remained stoic. There was zero emotion from Bryson.

"So you ain't dead after all, breed. Not yet, anyway. You're as slippery as a greased hog in a pig-catchin' contest. Even more so than your daddy. He sure could run. Too bad you and his fate are goin' be the same." Billy Ray laughed as he extended the barrel of the gun toward Bryson.

Bryson's face never changed. If he was listening—and he was—his face never showed it. He saw movement out of the corner of his eye. He dropped one spear.

Billy Ray cocked the hammer on the gun as he kept the sights aimed at Bryson's heart.

"Your daddy and his freaky feet sure could motor through the woods. Unfortunately for him, he couldn't outrun a bullet."

Bryson dropped the other spear and his knife.

Billy Ray stepped and leaned forward to get a better look at the knife. He lowered the gun. He recognized his brother's knife.

"You see, I know this for a fact because I'm the one who put a bullet in his stinkin' carcass. Now I'm goin' to do you for Dewey."

Just as he raised the gun, the wolf came charging from the woods hitting Billy Ray in the chest, knocking him to the ground. The gun went flying in the opposite direction, falling over the edge of a small cliff. Billy Ray lay on the ground with his legs and arms squirming about. The wolf was on top of Billy Ray ripping and tearing his throat to pieces.

Bryson could hear gurgling sounds coming from Billy Ray as he fought helplessly against the wolf. Almost as quickly as it began, Billy Ray's body went limp. He was dead. The wolf climbed off the lifeless body. Billy Ray's eyes were fixed in a horrific stare.

Bryson picked up his knife and spears. He walked over to Billy Ray's body. He saw the pistol go over the edge, but Billy Ray had a rifle. He rolled Billy Ray over, but to Bryson's misfortune, the rifle was broken. The stock had bent the bolt action at the end of the barrel. He released Billy Ray, who rolled over to his back. He noticed the red tracking device on Billy Ray's wrist. He walked over and stomped it with his heel, breaking the red eye that operated the device.

"Most unfortunate for you."

The wolf darted off. Bryson picked up Billy Ray's radio from his belt and followed the wolf down the side of a hill.

Command Post

Nate and Elizabeth studied the screen, tracking Billy Ray as he made his way from Taylor Falls to the pit. Billy Ray's red dot was coming upon one of the beast's red dots. According to the screen, they were only a few feet apart.

They both stared without talking until Nate finally broke the silence.

"Billy Ray must have found the body. One of the team must still be feasting."

They watched the screen as the two red dots became one.

"Elizabeth, what just happened?"

"I'm not sure."

She began hitting buttons and scrolling through different calibrations with the computer's mouse.

"What happened to Billy Ray's tracking device. That's the beast's signal! Right?" asked Nate, but he already knew the answer.

"Billy Ray's signal is lost."

"Well, find it!"

"I'm trying!"

"Try harder!"

Nate was losing self-control. He was on the brink of the threshold of insanity and reality.

Elizabeth reached down to pull her gun from her leg holster but stopped.

"Okay, settle down here. Everything's all right," Nate said to himself, trying to regain his self-control. He took a deep breath. "Badger, you copy?"

Nothing.

"Badger. You copy?"

Still nada.

"Night Runner. This is Coyote. Should I go investigate?"

"Negative. If I don't get some kind of answer from Badger pretty quick, you are to kill the insurance chips. Repeat! Cash in the chips!"

"Copy. We are more than ready. Out."

Nate placed the radio on his belt, and then sat down beside Elizabeth.

Bryson arrived at the command center. He could see Nate and Elizabeth sitting in front of the screens. He had heard every word Nate said to Tyrel. He knew he didn't have much time. He would have to take Nate down before he signaled Tyrel to kill Piper and Jared. He moved around behind their position so he could see the screens over their shoulders. He started to step forward toward the edge of the tent when the wolf growled lightly. Bryson stopped his foot in midstep directly above an iron ankle trap. He slowly brought his foot back and placed it on the ground. He scanned the grass and leaves. There were ankle and knee traps everywhere around the perimeter of the tent except for the main entrance. He would have to retreat, but not until he found the location of Piper and Jared. He could almost see the screens clearly. He needed to move about five more feet to his right.

There, he could see perfectly.

Piper and Jared's white dots were close but not together. Two red dots were located a short distance from Piper and Jared, moving in their direction. *They're not far from here.* Bryson glanced at another screen. Four red dots were not far from his location. *The beasts are close. Where's Timer?*

Nate jumped up and screamed. "How did she get loose? Her dot is moving toward the boy! Jake! That idiot!"

"Sir, we have another problem. That red dot we thought was a team member is now right outside our tent."

"What!" Nate yelled as he jumped up and spun around. His face was twisted and warped in madness.

Bryson grabbed one of the spears and crouched down in the underbrush.

"Come and get me, breed! Your Injun' daddy couldn't stop me. Nor can you. Come on, breed! I'm waitin'!" Nate laughed hysterically as he pulled his gun from its holster and began shooting in Bryson's general direction until he had emptied the gun's clip. He reached in his belt and retrieved another clip.

Bryson peered around the oak he had used as a shield. He saw Nate preparing to reload. He stood up and threw a spear at the plastic gas cans, but it glanced off and disappeared into the woods. He quickly grabbed the other spear and hurled it at the middle can. Bull's eye—a direct hit. Gas was gushing everywhere.

Nate caught a glimpse of Bryson when he released the second spear. He pointed the pistol at Bryson, showering his area with bullets. Bryson dove behind the oak. One ricocheted off the oak's trunk two inches above Bryson's head.

Bryson cut two long strips from his shirt and wrapped them with dry grass on a two feet long stick. He didn't know how well the cloth would burn, but right now, it was all he had.

The bullets stopped flying, as Nate reloaded for the third time. This was Bryson's chance. He pulled the lighter from his pant pocket and flicked the roller. Only sparks. He flicked again. Then, finally a flame. In a matter of seconds, the stick had transformed into a torch. He peeked around the tree.

Nate saw the torch and immediately removed the radio from his belt. "Condition, *code red*! Kill them! Kill them!"

Bryson jumped from behind the tree and threw the torch at the pierced gasoline can.

Elizabeth had been watching from her chair. She dove to the ground beneath the tables, out of Bryson's sight.

Nate raised his pistol, just as the cans of gasoline exploded into a fiery mushroom cloud. The force of the explosion knocked Bryson flat on his back. He rolled over and pulled himself up.

The whole command center was engulfed in flames. Nate looked like the Michelin Man on fire. He was spinning around and running in all directions, until finally, he reached the perimeter where all the iron traps were set. He stepped on the first trap, breaking his ankle. He stumbled, stepping on another trap with his free foot. Both ankles were trapped. He lost his balance and fell to his knees. A large iron trap closed angrily on his left knee. He was screaming in double agony as the fire melted his flesh from his broken body. He tried to break free, but instead he fell face first into a huge bear trap that crushed his skull, like a sledge hammer striking a big melon.

Nate was dead.

Bryson scanned the tent for Elizabeth, but he didn't see her. He figured she was burned up in the explosion. He couldn't worry about her right now. Nate had given the order to kill Piper and Jared. He had to save them.

Bryson looked into the sky. The purple night was beginning to lighten in the east.

"Thank you, Lord. Do not let me fail. Continue to stoke my fire."

Bryson picked up his knife and took off running toward Piper and Jared's location.

Time Out for Timer

The moon hung low in the western sky. Dawn was rushing away the darkness. The shadows were slowly fading from the underbrush.

Jake led Piper down a trail that twisted along the side of a mountain until they entered a clearing at its base.

Jared's hands were tied behind his back to a steel pole in the middle of the grassy valley.

Piper ran forward and embraced her son.

"Are you all right?" Piper sobbed.

"Yes. How did you get away?"

"A friend cut me loose," Piper informed, turning toward Jake, who ran up panting.

Jake smiled and turned red again. He had never been called a friend by anyone before.

"Jake, will you cut Jared free?"

"Yes 'em, I will. Anything for my new friends," Jake declared as he removed his knife from his backpack.

"Thank you, Jake."

Jake cut Jared's zip ties. Jake stood up and looked around. He thought he heard someone coming.

"Mom, we've got to get out of here. I know Rubin and Tyrel are close by," Jared said as he stood up beside Jake.

"Yessiree, we gots to go. Jared is right."

"Have you seen Mr. Keahbone, Mom?"

"No … I haven't."

Jake lowered his head.

"Jake, have you seen Mr. Keahbone?"

"No … but I heard Billy Ray say … he was dead."

Piper and Jared stared at each other. They didn't want to believe it.

Their eyes teared up. Piper grabbed and hugged Jared. Jared buried his face into her shirt.

"We gotta go."

Piper reluctantly pulled away from Jared.

"We better go."

Jared nodded.

But they may have been too late. Something or someone was tearing through the woods, like a run away rhino. The small group braced themselves for the worst that was sure to come. Jared stepped in front of his mother.

It was Bryson.

Piper and Jared ran forward and grabbed Bryson. They were ecstatic.

"We thought you were dead," Piper cried as she increased her grip.

"No, not yet, but this family keeps trying. Where's Tyrel?"

"I don't know."

"We have to go. Now!"

Bryson looked over at Jake with concern. Jake had his hands in his pockets and was smiling ear to ear.

"It's good. All good. He saved us. He's a friend," Piper instructed as she gently placed her hand on Jake's arm.

Bryson extended his hand to Jake. Jake shook hands with Bryson.

"Thank you, friend."

Jake dropped his head and grinned childishly. "You're welcome."

Bryson turned back to Piper and Jared. A heavy burden was lifted from his shoulders, but he knew that they were not out of harm's way yet.

There were still four beasts plus the demon-dog, Timer, and Tyrel and Rubin. He looked around for the wolf, who had led him to Piper and Jared, but he was gone.

"We need to leave now. We'll head south, putting as much distance between ourselves and this nightmare."

But as they turned to leave, a very familiar whiney voice yelled out.

"Well, well, well, look what we have here. A Shakespeare family reunion."

They all turned around and stared in disbelief at Tyrel and Rubin.

"Daddy, let me do him. Let me cut him. Cut him deep!"

"Shudup, Rubin. You'll get your chance."

"You're not goin' to hurt my friends," Jake defended as he stepped forward extending his pocket knife toward Tyrel.

"I should have done this a long time ago," Tyrel declared, pulling a pistol from his side holster. He aimed it and shot Jake without hesitation.

Jake hit the ground with a dull thud. Piper ran to help Jake. The chest wound was bleeding profusely. She applied pressure over the small hole. Jake moaned and then passed out.

"You murderer!"

"Thank you. That's a very nice compliment."

Bryson stepped toward Tyrel. "You are a flesh-monger, a fool, and a coward."

"Easy does it, Shakespeare. I'm going to enjoy killing you real slow."

"Let me go first, Daddy. Let me cut Jared."

"Patience. You will get your turn."

Suddenly, from the tree line, Timer and the four beasts appeared. They had the small group surrounded. They were in their kill mode. Timer stood beside Tyrel.

"The troops have finally arrived, now that I've done all the work myself," Tyrel puffed up as he peered around. "Timer, you guys are sitting this one out. Go on back home, you hear. Go on!"

Tyrel taunted Timer by waving his pistol at the beast.

Timer turned toward Tyrel. He growled. His red eyes pierced Tyrel's soul.

"No! Timer! No—"

In a split second Timer leapt through the air and ripped Tyrel's head from his body in a single snap of his jaws. Blood erupted from the top of the neck, and then the body flopped to the ground. Timer still had the head in his jaws.

They all watched in horror. Piper wondered if this was real. Timer dropped the head, and it rolled away four feet. Rubin squealed like a little girl and ran off through the woods.

Timer barked.

The four beasts immediately chased after Rubin. Within seconds, Rubin squealed louder this time, and then they heard nothing but the gnashing of teeth.

Timer looked defiantly at the group. Jared had walked over to Piper to see if he could help with Jake. Bryson removed his knife from its sheath. Timer flinched and turned sideways. He recognized the knife. His red eyes blazed brighter than ever on the knife's initials—DM. It was the same knife that stabbed him twenty years earlier, drawing his precious blood.

Timer growled as he slowly approached Bryson. Bryson held out the knife and squatted into a defensive stance. He was going to let Timer come to him and then counterattack. Timer charged, leaping through the air. Bryson sidestepped, letting Timer fly by. Timer landed and circled around Bryson, sizing up the prey, looking for some kind of weakness.

Bryson prayed in his mind for strength and courage.

Timer suddenly attacked; this time, Bryson sidestepped in the opposite direction, catching Timer off guard. He buried the knife deep into Timer's furry side.

Yelp!

Timer ran a few feet and collapsed.

Bryson remained on his hands and knees. *It's over. Finally over.* Then he remembered the four beasts. He crawled over to Timer and pulled out his knife.

The four beasts returned to the clearing when they heard Timer's yelp. They were lined in a row, standing shoulder to shoulder. The sun had climbed just above the eastern ridge. Bryson noticed for the first time the different and peculiar colors of each beast. One was white; another a reddish brown; another was black like Timer; and the last was a pale grayish green. They stood like statues at the outer edge of the clearing.

Bryson stood up to face them.

"Wait, Mr. Keahbone, I'll help you," Jared offered as he looked around for some kind of weapon.

"No, Jared. I've got this. You protect your mother."

As Bryson stared at the four beasts, there came a sudden growl from behind him. He spun around abruptly.

It was Timer!

Timer charged ahead, hitting Bryson in the chest, like a battering ram. The impact sent Bryson one way and the knife another.

Bryson lay on the ground. He couldn't move. The breath had been knocked out of his lungs. He tried to push himself up as he gasped for air.

Slowly. Deliberately. Timer began to circle its prey.

Bryson looked around frantically for the knife. He spotted it ten feet away. He watched Timer. Saliva was hanging in long sticky streams from blood-stained fangs. His red eyes beamed at Bryson.

It was now or never.

Bryson gathered himself together. *Wait ... wait ... now!* He leaped for the knife, snatching it in a single swift motion, as he rolled away.

Timer rushed forward but missed.

Bryson rolled again and stopped, just in time to see Timer leaping through the air. Bryson elevated the knife in a lightning-quick thrust, stabbing Timer on the white hourglass on the beast's chest. The knife lodged deep in the white patch, but instead of blood coming out, a white sandy grain fell to the ground.

Timer let out an ear-piercing scream, then staggered off several feet and collapsed to the ground. Bryson walked over and knelt down by Timer. He was about to remove the knife and cut Timer's head off but changed his mind when the beast's red eyes faded to black. Bryson knew then that Timer was dead.

Bryson stood up and turned to look at the four beasts with the knife in his hand. *Only four more. It could be worse.* They watched impassively. He glanced over his shoulder at Piper, who was helping Jake. She had stabilized the bleeding, but Jake still was in need of serious medical attention.

The white beast turned and vanished in the underbrush followed by the remaining three.

Bryson lowered the knife and collapsed to his knees.

"Are they gone?" Piper wondered as she held onto Jake.

"Yes. They are gone," Bryson answered, staring at the evergreen where the four beasts had disappeared behind.

"We have to get Jake to the hospital. He's hurt pretty bad."

Bryson scanned the land for a vehicle, but there was none in sight. Then he thought he heard a motor vehicle roaring down a road. He pivoted and listened again.

"I hear a motor. Maybe there is a highway or road nearby." The motor was getting closer. Then Bryson heard several sirens blaring. Coming down a road near the edge of the clearing were several emergency vehicles, ranging from a highway patrol cruiser to a fire truck to an ambulance. Leading the way was a four-door black suburban from Oklahoma State Bureau of Investigation.

Riding shotgun of the OSBI vehicle was Hoot Brown.

Hoot had brought the cavalry.

The owl screeched. Third—it disciplined.

Fall of the House of Monger

It was midmorning. The sun was burning bright in the sky. After Bryson had finished giving his statement to the agent, he walked up to Hoot, who was talking to Vick and a highway patrolman. The patrolman walked off as Bryson approached. Hoot reached out and grabbed Bryson, followed by Vick.

"Thank you, guys. But, Hoot, how did you know? I never called you."

Hoot smiled.

"It was easy. I followed the paper trail."

Bryson's face wrinkled in bewilderment.

"I saw you and Tyrel from my office window get into an argument. You threw a wadded up piece of paper at his patrol car. After you left, I walked out and picked up that paper and read it. I made a few calls to some buddies at OSBI, but they really needed more evidence. I went out to Piper's house and found the second letter. I wanted to go out to the Monger's house immediately after I read the note, but Detective Burnside talked me into waiting for the troops so they could organize a search and seizure operation. It was the right choice. It took some time, but they finally showed up."

"How's Jake?"

"The paramedics said he's going to be okay but sore. The bullet went clean through, missing all vital organs."

"Did you find all the Mongers?"

"All but Elizabeth."

"Did you search the command post?"

"Yes, but it has a lot of traps around the debris, so the search is slow."

Bryson looked over at Piper and Jared.

"How are Piper and Jared doing?" Bryson asked Vick.

"Holding up quite well considering. She is a strong woman, and Jared ... such a brave young man," Vick sobbed, dabbing her nose with a tissue.

Bryson stared at Piper as she spoke with a female OSBI agent. Jared was listening to the details of his mom's version of what happened the night before. She paused while Jared talked. She glanced over at Bryson. She wanted to hug him, cry on his shoulder, to get lost in his arms, and to finally kiss him.

Bryson was lost in her gaze. Hoot and Vick were talking to him, but he wasn't listening. He wanted to go to her, to comfort her. He could see the pain on her face, in her soft blue eyes. Piper smiled. He excused himself from Hoot and Vick and began walking toward Piper. He stopped unexpectedly. Something was pulling at him to go in a different direction. Piper's smile turned to a frown.

Come find me, my son. Come find me.

Bryson looked around as if his father was standing next to him, but there was nobody around. Then Bryson spotted the wolf at the edge of the clearing where the four beasts were earlier. The wolf turned and trotted off.

Come find me.

Bryson looked at Piper twice and then the wolf. He ran by Hoot and told him he would explain later. Right now, he had to go.

"Believe in me," Bryson mouthed the words to Piper as he took off running toward where the wolf had left the clearing.

Piper stared at Bryson as he ran away. Tears filled her eyes and flowed down her cheeks. She loved Bryson with all her heart, but she didn't know if he would ever love her the same way. Her heart ached like it had never ached before. She looked at Jared. *At least I still have Jared.*

Jared came up and hugged his mother.

The wolf led Bryson into Cooper's Canyon. They came into the west end and then traveled along the cliff 's southern face. The wolf finally came to a stop. It was the same place where Billy Ray had shot Joseph Keahbone, and he fell and landed in the canyon. The wolf walked over to the underbrush and pawed the ground.

Bryson slowly followed. In his heart, he knew what he was about to find, but he didn't know if he was ready. He moved aside the branches of a dogwood. There in the dirt, slightly covered with leaves were the skeletal remains of Joseph Keahbone. Bryson knew instantly that this was his father because of the shape of his feet—Tuchina Iyishke, Three Toes. He collapsed to his knees and planted his face on the ground. His feelings were in a sense bittersweet because now he could have closure. Bryson prayed and thanked God for his strength and courage and for answering his questions about his family.

Bryson rose to his knees. Cherokee Billy's words came to his mind. *Mother earth do not cover my blood. When a warrior has been slain violently, he will not rest until his bones have been recovered. If the warrior's bones are left unburied, he will roam the land as a shadow being usually in the form of a ...*

He looked at the wolf, who had pawed the ground until he had dug a small hole.

"I understand."

Bryson gathered up the bones and headed back to his cabin, cradling the bones in his arms and shirt.

Two hours later, Bryson arrived at the huge oak outside his cabin. He gently placed his father's bones beside his mother's grave. He ran to the cabin and retrieved a shovel.

It was almost dark when Bryson shoveled the last spade of dirt onto his father's grave.

"Rest in peace, Father. Rest in peace, Mother. I love you both." A single tear fell from both eyes. He looked up. The wolf was standing at the edge of the pool of water. Bryson smiled contentedly as he noticed two reflections on the water. One appeared to be his father; the other was his mother. Then the wolf turned and trotted off. A ripple danced across the water. The image was gone. Ishkitini, who had been perched on a branch above the water, lifted silently with a single thrust of its wings and followed the wolf until they both disappeared into the foliage.

Bryson lay on his father's grave and fell into a deep sleep from exhaustion, the kind of deep sleep that followed the utter exhaustion of your body, mind, and soul.

Had I but a Chance

Piper had a restless night of sleep. She slept less than an hour. She got off the recliner and dressed in sweats. She thought about taking a walk to clear her mind. She went into the kitchen and poured a cup of coffee. As she returned to the living room, she stopped and stared at Jared, who finally fell asleep in the early hours of the morning. They talked a lot last night about what had happened with the Mongers, but they mostly talked about Bryson. Neither one could figure out why he didn't come by or at least call.

Piper smiled and thanked the Lord for their safety. She ran her fingers through his hair. He moaned and turned onto his side but stayed asleep. She walked out onto the porch and sat down on the steps, where she and Bryson had had several long conversations. The morning temperature was a little crisp. She took a sip and felt the warm coffee going down. Thoughts of Bryson faded in and out of her mind.

The air was quiet and still. She watched a single leaf fall endlessly until it became one with the other leaves on the ground. She took another sip of coffee and debated whether to go back in and try to sleep or take a walk. She stood up to go back inside but stopped when she heard a vehicle driving down the road. Her heart fluttered when the thought of Bryson driving up came to her mind. But her excitement quickly turned to disappointment when she didn't see his Jeep coming up the road.

"It must be the mail truck, although it's kind of early. Maybe Jenny started her route backwards today. I remember her saying she likes switching up her routines so they won't become too monotonous … me too."

She placed her coffee cup down on the railing and decided to walk to the mailbox at the end of her drive. "It will be better than sitting in the house trying to sleep when I'm not sleepy." As she walked along the gravel road, her thoughts focused on Bryson, wondering if she would ever get together with him. She loved him, but it was clear to her that he didn't share the same feelings.

When she arrived at the end of her road, she glanced at her mailbox. She couldn't remember the last time she checked it or why it really mattered. *There's nothing in there.* But something was drawing her to the mailbox. She walked over and pulled down the front door. To her surprise, there was an unsealed envelope with the capital letter *P* written on the front.

She opened it slowly. Her hands were trembling. She pulled the letter out carefully like it was tissue paper.

Teardrop of an Angel

Had I but a chance
To catch a falling star,
Descending from heaven
As a teardrop of an angel

Would I reach out
And touch the radiance
That surrounds
Her essence?

Dare I the chance
As I am lost
In the splendor
Of her beauty

Could I but gently
Caress her cheek
As though it were
A rose covered with morning frost?

Or let my fingers softly comb
Through her long dark hair
As it dances away
Within the rushing wind?

Or surrender my spirit
As her bright eyes
Capture and hold me charmed
To a life of destiny's wonder?

If time shall not slow
Will the fleeting moment pass me by?
For I see the moment of her brightness fade
As she slowly turns to fly away.

If never I have the chance
Again to catch a falling star
I know I have been touched
By the essence of heaven

Through the teardrop of an angel.

B—

Tears filled her eyes, falling onto the paper, causing the ink to smear. Her gaze remained fixed on the poem. She read it again. Her eyes remained locked and hanging on every word, not wanting to remove her eyes for fear that these words were not real and would disappear.

Finally, she looked up slowly. Her hands were trembling. She heard a dull pop. Again—*pop!*

Pop!

Piper turned toward the sound.

Bryson was leaning against his Jeep, throwing a baseball into his glove.

"I'm here to catch a teardrop of an angel."

Piper bolted toward Bryson, falling into his arms.

Bryson moaned a little as his achy muscles reminded him of all the pain that led him to this place—both physically and emotionally.

"Sorry."

They embraced and stared into each other's eyes. Tears began flooding down her face. He gently wiped them away with the back of his hand.

"I have always prided myself on my self-control. I believed that I was in control of everything … but in reality, I controlled nothing. God is in control," Piper sobbed, never taking her eyes off Bryson.

"The whole time I have been here, I have been running away from you, but God kept putting you back in my path for me to catch … if you fall. I see that now." Bryson smiled, pulling her tight against his chest.

Finally.

The kiss.

Epilogue

Dust mites danced in the sunlight as it angled through the ragged curtains covering a smoky glass window. The yellow beam came to rest in a rectangular shape on the dirty wooden plank floor of a broken-down shack deep in the Louisiana swamp. A mouse ran from the shadows and stopped at the edge of the light. It eased around the edge of the light, careful not to touch the shiny area for fear of being instantly turned into a furry blaze, or so it seemed.

The mouse scampered away, disappearing beneath an old twenty-five inch console television set. The channel was set on a local station. Deep in the swamp, the rabbit ears with aluminum tips only picked up one station. There was no DirecTV or Dish satellite reception this far out in the Bayou wilderness, not that the receivers couldn't get service, no satellite installer would dare venture this far out into the black swamp.

At least, no human being in their right mind.

The evening news was on, but the volume was turned down. The Sonic dudes suddenly appeared, arguing about shakes or getting beat up by some fourteen years olds—*a bunch of 'em.*

The room was silent, a vast void of nothingness leaking from the floor and walls. Then rhythmical creaks of a wooden rocking chair swaying back and forth began to fill the small room. The mouse poked its head out from beneath the TV set, watching cautiously as black-soled shoes go from flat to tippy-toed back to flat, disappearing beneath a dark gray dress with each sway of the chair.

The rocking abruptly stopped. The mouse scurried for the hole in the wall behind the set. The feet flattened on the floor as the woman rocking leaned forward.

A pretty female news reporter for ESPN was standing in the middle of the screen talking to the camera. She was wearing a blue suit and a silky, pearl-colored blouse. She raised her free hand to remove her wavy blonde hair from her face, and then waved for someone to come stand beside her.

A man walked up and reluctantly turned toward the camera. The pretty woman playfully swirled the man around to face the camera. His black hair fell in long strands along the oval of a well-defined face that was partially covered by a groomed beard.

A very light audible grunt came from the person sitting in the rocking chair. A small, scarred hand retrieved a remote from an end table next to the rocker. The slightly bent finger pressed down to increase the volume.

"Hi, I am MiKaylyn Jordan reporting live from Bourbon Street, New Orleans. We have with us today Bryson Keahbone, runner extraordinaire."

"Hello, Ms. Jordan. I don't know about all that."

"Oh, call me MiKaylyn,"she announced, leaning uncomfortably close with the microphone extended toward Bryson's face.

Bryson smiled. "Hello, MiKaylyn. It's good to be here." He was trying to be friendly, but he really wished she would back off a little.

"So, is the rumor true—and I do love rumors—you are coming out of retirement to race again, beginning with this year's Rock 'n' Roll Mardi Gras Marathon?" MiKaylyn asked, turning the mic toward Bryson.

"It is true. I will be traveling with the Rock 'n' Roll Marathon series. I am trying to prepare myself physically and mentally for the Olympic Trials in six months. I will run here in New Orleans in three days and then move on to Dallas next month and finish in Portland the following month."

"Why did you pick New Orleans as your first race back?"

"That's a good question. The course is relatively flat and fast and very beautiful. I have to be careful. Sometimes, I find myself slowing down through the French Quarter section of the race course. Plus, the field of runners will be very competitive. I would like to see where I stand. There will be a lot of good runners racing on Sunday."

"A lot of people are saying you are *way* past your prime. You are simply too old for this young man's sport and should probably take up recreational jogging or coed softball," MiKaylyn said, baiting Bryson to argue her point.

Bryson grinned, "They may be right. It's been awhile."

"When was the last time you ran in a race?"

Bryson hesitated. He thought deeply about his answer. He wanted to say a little over a year and a half ago, when he was racing not only for his life but Piper and Jared's also.

"Well over three years ago. The last Olympic Trials before the London Olympics," Bryson replied, lowering his head, feeling uncomfortable about the question and his answer.

MiKaylyn felt like the interview was beginning to drag and decided to change directions. She glanced down at her notepad.

"So I hear you have been recently married?"

Bryson raised his head and beamed a crooked smile. He looked past the newswoman, staring into the crowd. He spotted the most important person in his life. His grin turned to a broad beaming smile. He couldn't take his eyes off her.

"I married the most amazing woman in the world," Bryson declared; then he waved for his new wife to come stand beside him. "This is Piper."

"Hi," Piper greeted, waving shyly toward the camera as she came to rest beside Bryson.

"*No!*" The voice was barely audible and gurgled as if the word was cascading over jagged vocal cords. The scarred hand dropped the remote to the wooden floor. Two AA batteries went flying from the back of the remote as the cover broke in half. The scarred hands grabbed the armrest of the rocking chair tightly and then released.

There was mumbling in the back corner of the shack. A human figure was curled in fetal position, rocking frantically back and forth. The murmurs were getting louder, repeating psychotically, "I will cut him, cut him deep. I will cut him, cut him deep."

"It is all right, my son," the voice was calm and clear. The grunts from the corner had faded to a light whimper. The scarred hands were now resting in the lap of the woman in the rocking chair as she began to rock slow and steady. The woman had regained her composure as she watched patiently the remainder of the interview.

"Piper, how do you like New Orleans?" MiKaylyn asked, but she was looking at Bryson.

"It's awesome. I can't wait to—"

"That's nice," MiKaylyn interrupted, pushing her way passed Piper to stand next to Bryson.

Piper's lips pressed together and stiffened as she backed up. She wanted to say, *Excuse me!* but she just smirked instead, visualizing herself grabbing MiKaylyn's bouffant hair and swinging her around until the lights went out in this town. *Oh my, am I an Okie redneck or what?* She returned to stand next to Vicki Buchanan and Hoot Brown.

Jared and a large man in overalls wearing a SpongeBob backpack walked up and stopped. The large man put his big hand on Jared's shoulder and smiled as he put a huge helping of cotton candy in his mouth with his other hand.

"That was very rude," Vick declared.

"It's okay." Piper smiled as the WWE vision came back into her mind. *It would be fun. Really fun.*

The camera scanned back to the interview.

"Now where were we? Aw, yes. The public would like to know about what else has been happening in your life. You have kind of dropped off the face of the earth for the past three years. A few months back, you had a run-in with this maniac, hillbilly family. Do you feel this occurrence will affect your racing? Or make it better? I heard they were hunting you?"

"It was over a year and half ago," Bryson corrected. The smile faded from his face. He looked over at Piper. She tried to give an encouraging smile. They had talked about how reporters were going to ask those questions concerning their encounter with the Mongers. She mouthed the words, *I love you!*

The rocking chair eased forward and stopped. The black-soled shoes were flat on the floor. The woman turned her left ear, which wasn't as scarred as her right, toward the television to better hear Bryson's answer. The grunts from the back corner had silenced. Even the dark walls appeared to wait in an eerie anticipation.

MiKaylyn started to retrieve the mic and conclude the interview when Bryson finished his answer.

"I don't fully understand what God has planned for me, but he is in control—not me. The events that happen in my life are because God has a reason for them."

"That may be true, Bryson. Thank you for your time," MiKaylyn interrupted, not wanting to give air to a Christian sermon. She turned toward the camera as it zoomed in. "This has been MiKaylyn Jordan reporting live from Bourbon Street here in New Orleans."

The woman in the wooden rocker stood up and turned the TV off and then walked to the window. She raised both scarred hands and separated the curtains. She stared out over the murky swamp. Her right hand slowly removed a brightly colored scarf, exposing a bald, disfigured head.

"Bryson, in two days, there will be a Bayou Moon. Then we will see who's in control."

She smiled through where lips should have been.

Chapter 1—*Bayou Moon—*
Island of the Shadow Beings

About the Author

B rett Hayes is currently teaching creative writing and English 2 and coaching middle and high school athletics. He is married and has four sons. He lives in southeastern Oklahoma, where he enjoys fishing and chasing his kids all over the country to watch them play whatever sport is in season, sometimes two or three at the same time. He enjoys writing and reading as a means of winding down after a long full day of activities, whether on the field, classroom, or gym.

Reading Group Guide
Discussions Questions

1. Which characters or events in this novel can you relate to? How has your life been similar? How did you cope with these life-changing experiences? What motivates you to either act or avoid the situation? Give examples.

2. There are many symbolisms used in the novel—some are direct and some indirect. What are some of the symbolisms you have noticed within the story? When the clock in the Mongers' house chimes seven times it is a tribute to Poe's *Masque of the Red Death?* How does the symbol of *Seven Deadly Sins* compare to the whole Mongers' family?

3. Consider the symbolism of the healing Bryson and Jared experienced as they worked on Bryson's cabin. Have you ever experienced a healing time like this, or known someone who has? Describe the process. Do you think a "healing" project is more typically a male or female experience? Or both? Why or why not?

4. Compare and contrast the wolf who helped Bryson with the hell hounds that hunted him. Who do think the wolf may have been symbolic for? How is the wolf symbol used in Native American cultures?

5. There are at least four major themes covered in this novel. One major theme is *'Why does God allow bad things to happen to good people?'* Bryson struggles with this issue throughout three-forth of this novel. What happened to

Bryson to change him? What can you tell someone who is struggling with the same issues? What scriptures might be helpful? Refer to Pastor Steve's sermon in the novel and scriptures from James 1:2-5.

6. Another theme is *'People are not in control—God is in control.'* Bryson and Piper both thought they were in control of their lives but in truth they were spiraling out of control. What events in the story changed them? How did they change? Read the scriptures from Psalm 139:16 and Jeremiah 29:11-14. How would you talk to someone who might be like Piper and Bryson before they changed in the novel?

7. The final two major themes are *'Good vs evil, Reason for living vs Life without meaning'* and *'Our timing is not always God's timing.' Time* is used as theme throughout the novel. Compare and contrast how Nate Monger and Joseph Keahbone talked of *'when my time is time upon the final scene.'* What does time mean to each person? Explain. What does *time* mean to you? Do you feel you have a lot of *time* on your hands?

8. How was Timer killed? Why was *time* important to him? How was he symbolic to the story? Who did he represent?

9. How do you think the setting became a character in the story? Does carefully naming the trees and descriptive language of the setting help the reader to better visualize the environment within the story? Explain.

10. Who is the *wolf*, the *lady in the light*, *Cherokee Billy* and *Ms. Abbey* in relationship to Bryson's past? How did they aid Bryson during his life's journey? Was Ms. Abbey real—no one ever saw her but Bryson, or was Johnny too busy messing with his IPod to notice? How about the wolf, Cherokee Billy,

or the lady in the light, were they real? Do you have anyone guiding or inspiring you, living or dead? Explain.

11. Johnny and Bryson get into a verbal fight. Johnny believed he was trying to help Bryson by telling him it was time to move on and leave the past in the past. But Bryson lashed out at Johnny, telling him he had no right to tell Bryson how to run his life because Johnny's life was worthless. Did Bryson regret saying those words to Johnny? How should have Bryson handled the situation? Have you ever lashed out at someone speaking before you thoroughly thought out what you should have said? Explain how you felt and how you could have handled it differently.

12. How did you feel about Bryson's apology to his mother for having twenty years of bad feelings for his mother for losing her will to live after his father died? How did you feel when you found out the truth about his mother's death? Have you ever lost someone and didn't get a chance to tell them something important before they died? Maybe they died in a car wreck or had a heart attack? How did you feel? How would you feel?

13. Flashbacks are used throughout the novel—like a short story within the story. Some examples are the *Irish Shotgun Wedding*, the Scottish tale—*Teardrop of an Angel*, the *slingshot at the mourning dove*, *Ishkitini*—the owl, to name a few. Which was your favorite? Explain.

14. *Ishkitini*—the owl serves three functions in some Native American cultures. In Chapter 22, Bryson had a dream in which his father explained the three symbolic functions of the owl. First, it searched; second, it demanded; and third, it disciplined. What does it mean to Bryson? How can this meaning be compared to our lives? Explain.

15. Pastor Steve and Cherokee Billy both tell Bryson, 'be strong and courageous.' Why must Bryson be strong and courageous? How can we be strong and courageous during life's trials. How can we help other people to be strong and courageous? What scriptures can we read? Start with Joshua 1:9.

16. If *The Running Moon* was to be made into a movie what songs might be a good fit within the story? I like Kings of Leon's *Use Somebody* when Bryson and Piper are beginning to fall in love in Chapter 38. Or maybe at the very end when Bryson and Piper are trying to seal the deal with a kiss— Gloriana's *Kissed You.* I like also like Third Days' *Mountain of God* when Bryson is searching not only for his cabin but an inward peace at the beginning of Chapter 6. What are some other songs?